Praise for *The Third to Die*

“A lean thriller with a strong and damaged protagonist as compelling as Lisbeth Salander.”

—*Kirkus Reviews*

“Fans of Jeff Abbott and Karin Slaughter will find this crime novel hard to put down.”

—*Publishers Weekly*

“Brennan’s broadest and most expansive novel yet, as much Catherine Coulter as David Baldacci, with just enough of Thomas Harris thrown in for good measure. A stellar and stunning success.”

—*Providence Journal*

“The first in Brennan’s new series...and fans will look forward to the next installment.”

—*Booklist*

“You’ll be turning the pages as fast as you can, rooting for Matt and Kara and the FBI team. The best part? *The Third to Die* is the first thriller in Brennan’s amazing new series.”

—Catherine Coulter, #1 *New York Times* bestselling author of *Deadlock*

“Riveting, terrifyin
ratchets up the te
is classic crime fic f
the thriller.”

—J.T. Ellison, or
art

“An edge of the seat, can’t-put-it-down thrill ride.”

—Marcia Clark, author of *Snap Judgment*

ALLISON BRENNAN

THE THIRD TO DIE

ISBN-13: 978-0-7783-8835-7

The Third to Die

First published in 2020. This edition published in 2021.

This edition published by arrangement with Harlequin Books S.A.

For questions and comments about the quality of this book, please contact us at CustomerService@Harlequin.com.

Mira
22 Adelaide St. West, 40th Floor
Toronto, Ontario M5H 4E3, Canada
www.Harlequin.com

Printed in U.S.A.

This book is for Dan Conaway, agent extraordinaire,
who loved this story from the beginning.
Third time's the charm.

THE THIRD TO DIE

1

Wednesday, March 3
Liberty Lake, Washington
12:09 a.m.

Warm blood covered him.

His arms, up to his elbows, were slick with it. His clothing splattered with it. The knife—the blade that had taken his retribution—hung in his gloved hand by his side.

It was good. Very good.

He was almost done.

The killer stared at the blackness in front of him, his mind as silent and dark as the night. The water lapped gently at the banks of the lake. A faint *swish swish swish* as it rolled up and back, up and back, in the lightest of breezes.

He breathed in cold air; he exhaled steam.

Calm. Focused.

As the sounds and chill penetrated his subconscious, he moved into action. Staying here with the body would be foolish, even in the middle of the night.

He placed the knife carefully on a waist-high boulder, then removed his clothes. Jacket. Sweater. Undershirt. He stuffed them into a plastic bag. Took off his shoes. Socks. Pants. Boxers. Added them to the bag. He stood naked except for his gloves.

He tied the top of the plastic, then picked up the knife again and stabbed the bag multiple times. With strength that belied his lean frame, he threw the knife into the water. He couldn't see where it fell; he barely heard the plunk.

Then he placed the bag in the lake and pushed it under, holding it beneath the surface to let the frigid water seep in. When the bag was saturated, he pulled it out and spun himself around as if he were throwing a shot put. He let go and the bag flew, hitting the water with a loud *splash*.

Even if the police found it—which he doubted they would—the water would destroy any evidence. He'd bought the clothes and shoes, even his underwear, at a discount store in another city, at another time. He'd never worn them before tonight.

Though he didn't want DNA evidence in the system, it didn't scare him if the police found something. He didn't have a record. He'd killed before, many times, and not one person had spoken to him. He was smart—smarter than the cops, and certainly smarter than the victims he'd carefully selected.

Still, he must be cautious. Meticulous. Being smart meant that he couldn't assume anything. What did his old man use to say?

Assume makes an ass out of you and me...

The killer scowled. He wasn't doing any of this

for his old man, though his father would get the retribution he deserved. He was doing this for *himself.* His *own* retribution. He was *this close* to finishing the elaborate plan he'd conceived years ago. He could scarcely wait until six days from now, March 9, when his revenge would be complete.

He was saving the guiltiest of them for last.

Still, he hoped his old man would be pleased. Hadn't he done what his father was too weak to do? Righted the many wrongs that had been done to them. How many times had the old man said these people should suffer? How many times had his father told him these people were fools?

"The system is fucked! It's us versus them, kid. They think they know it all. They think they have all the answers. They take everything I have and leave me with shit."

Yet his father just let it happen and did nothing about it! *Nothing!* Because he was weak. He was weak and pathetic and cruel.

Breathe. Focus. All in good time.

All in good time.

The killer took another, smaller plastic bag from his backpack. He removed his wet gloves, put them inside, added a good-sized rock, tied the bag, then threw it into the lake.

Still naked, he shivered in the cold, still air. He wasn't done.

Do it quick.

He walked into the lake, the water colder than ice. Still, he took several steps forward, his feet sinking into the rough muck at the bottom. When his knees were submersed, he did a shallow dive. His chest scraped a rock, but he was too numb to feel pain. He broke through the surface with a loud scream. He couldn't breathe; he couldn't think. His heart pounded in his chest, aching from the icy water.

But he was alive. He was *fucking alive!*

He went under once more, rubbed his hands briskly over his arms and face in case any blood remained. He would take a hot shower when he returned home, use soap and a towel to remove anything the lake left behind. But for now, this would do.

Twenty seconds in the water was almost too long. He bolted out, coughed, his body shaking so hard he could scarcely think. But he had planned everything well and operated on autopilot.

He pulled a towel from his backpack and dried off as best he could. Stepped into new sweatpants, sweatshirt, and shoes. Pulled on a new pair of gloves. There might be blood on the ATV, but it wasn't his blood, so he wasn't concerned.

He took a moment to stare back at the dark, still lake. Then he took one final look at the body splayed faceup. He felt nothing, because she was nothing. Unimportant. Simply a small pawn in a much bigger game. A pawn easily sacrificed.

He hoped his old man would be proud of his work, but he would probably just criticize his son's process. He'd complain about how he did the job, then open another bottle of booze.

He hoped his father was burning in hell.

He jumped on the ATV and rode into the night.

2

Liberty Lake
7:30 a.m.

Los Angeles Police Detective Kara Quinn was technically on vacation. Technically, because she was being paid. She hadn't come up here to Liberty Lake willingly. But the only reason she hadn't thrown a complete fit with her boss was because she had been wanting to check in on her grandmother anyway. Emily Dorsey had been sick over Christmas and unable to visit Kara in Santa Monica as she'd done every year since Kara moved from Liberty Lake to California. So the mandatory vacation—otherwise known as paid administrative leave—was a good excuse to come up to Washington and visit.

But that didn't mean Kara was going to sleep in or watch television half the day.

She didn't relax well; she needed something to do. Anything.

The cold morning air burned in her lungs as she ran along the familiar eight-mile Liberty Lake

Trail. She'd already run the loop her second day here, worked out at a gym in nearby Spokane the next day, and was taking the trail again this morning. She much preferred to exercise outdoors than in a gym, no matter how cold it was.

A February storm a few weeks earlier had left behind two feet of snow that was now a slushy mess. While there would likely be at least one more good snowfall before spring officially arrived, right now Kara took advantage of the unseasonably warm weather—if anyone could call the expected fifty-eight degree high *warm.* She was surprised that she didn't hate the cold as much as she thought she would after living in LA for the last twelve years. In fact, she found it refreshing. Of course, anything was better than ten degrees in the middle of January, as it had been when she left this place for good at the age of eighteen with a GED in her pocket and the hope of being a cop in her heart.

Eight miles was a good run for Kara. Longer than the five miles she regularly trekked. She liked to push herself. If she didn't challenge herself, who would?

She stopped at the four-mile marker, drank half her water bottle, and stretched. The morning sun glistened off the water, refreshing and calming. When she first arrived on the trail, a low layer of thin fog had covered the ground, but as the sun rose, the fog evaporated. She almost wished it hadn't—she loved running in the mist, where she couldn't see the rest of the world around her, where she felt like she was wrapped in a damp blanket, the only person on the planet. She'd commented about that feeling once to a long-ago boyfriend, and he said he thought it would get lonely. She just smiled and let him think he was right, but truth be told, she liked solitude.

People, mostly, sucked.

The fog would return. March in the Pacific Northwest? Oh yeah. She'd see rain and fog and more snow before she left—if her boss held her to the two weeks he'd ordered her to take. She'd already been laying the groundwork for an early return, but she couldn't ask her sergeant for at least a week. That gave her three more days here to suck up her punishment before plotting her return. Maybe she could sneak back early to LA and grab a case before Lex even knew she was in town. He probably expected as much, so what would be the harm?

It's administrative leave, Kara, not a vacation. You lost it with a suspect.

Lex's voice bounced in her head. She wished she could make it shut up.

The snow that had built up along the banks was nearly melted, except in the shadows the sun couldn't touch. No one else was running this early. Liberty Lake was a tourist town during the summer when the population more than doubled, but in March? Only the local yokels. One of the benefits of living in the middle of effing nowhere was that she didn't have to see anyone if she didn't want to. She loved Los Angeles, but she didn't like all the hordes of people. Fortunately everyone in LA tended to ignore everyone else. She took comfort in that—unlike going to high school in Liberty Lake where everyone knew everyone else's business.

She wasn't naturally a people person, though she could be if she had to. She could be anyone she needed to be. That was her job.

Her grandma wanted her to move back to Liberty Lake permanently. If Kara was going to do anything for anyone, it would be for Em.

"Spokane isn't far. They need detectives in Spokane. The nice policeman who didn't arrest you when you vandalized that car in high school? Remember him? His mom—Bridget, I think. Yes, Bridget Maddox. She's always asking about you, says her son talks about you from time to time."

Such was the life here—where no one forgot anything. She'd slashed the tires and dented up the car of a bastard who'd drugged and raped Kara's one real friend. People forgot about *that*, because, you know, no fucking *proof* of rape. But no one forgot what she did to the rapist's damn car.

Of course Kara remembered Brian Maddox. He'd been a cop in Liberty Lake at the time. He'd stopped her from doing something more stupid than vandalism, taught her more about right and wrong, crime and punishment, than her parents ever had. He hadn't wanted her to drop out of high school, but when she was eighteen, she had had enough. She got her GED, and he then suggested she test for the police academy.

"I'm transferring to Spokane. More opportunities. They could use a cop like you. You have great

instincts, Kara, especially for a kid. The sky's the limit with a little training and experience."

It was because of Maddox that she became a cop, that she hadn't followed in her parents' criminal footsteps. She'd been so angry as a teenager—angry at everyone, including herself. Mostly, she recognized now, her anger stemmed from feeling she had no control over her life. That the luck of the draw or a cosmic joke had given her two of the craziest, stupidest parents who had ever procreated.

No way she'd move back now to this seven-thousand-person town after living more than a decade in a city of millions where she cherished her anonymity. It wasn't like Liberty Lake—or even the larger neighboring Spokane—was really home to her; she hadn't had a *real* home growing up, not until her mother dumped her at her grandmother's house when Kara was fifteen.

"Just for a few months, baby, until we get back on our feet."

Right. Kara knew it was a lie the minute her mother opened her mouth. As if her mother—or any of her asshole boyfriends she ran with when she wasn't with Kara's father—could actually do anything productive with their lives. Now the only time Kara heard from either of her parents was when one of them needed something—money, a place to crash, bail. *Losers*. Both of them. Every time one of them walked into her life, shit happened. She had enough shit in her job, which she actually *liked,* that she had no desire to deal with anyone else's shit.

But for all intents and purposes, Washington's

Liberty Lake was Kara's hometown. She loved her grandma Em in all her weirdness. At least Em had given her a home base. Still, as soon as her boss cleared her, Kara was going back to LA. The longer she was away from her job, the more nervous and jittery she got.

What did that say about her? She was an undercover cop—all she did was play the part of anyone except herself. She preferred it. Who was she anyway? She'd much rather be another person and forget the two who'd spawned her.

Kara started to run again, but the break had tired her out more than rejuvenated her. All those damn memories that coming home had stirred up. She should go back to the gym and beat on one of the dummies. That always brightened her mood.

She was only a few minutes past the marker when she saw deep tire impressions in the mud off the path heading toward the lake. Riding ATVs was a blast—she'd loved it as a teenager. But why go toward the lake? It was usually too rocky and thick with vegetation to maneuver effectively.

Something bright in the direction of the tire treads caught her eye. Neon? Maybe the ATV driver lost control and crashed.

Her cop instincts took over before she consciously thought about it. She stopped, assessed her surroundings. No one was around. The ATV tracks had come from the left of the trail, over the path, and then down toward the lake.

"Hey! Is anyone down there? Anyone hurt?"

Her voice echoed, but there was no answer.

She walked parallel to the tracks, hands free where she could grab her gun if needed.

Yeah, she was weird—she ran with a gun in a fanny pack. Better safe than dead was her motto. It was probably nothing, but *something* was down by the lake, and neon was a favorite color of bikers and hikers, especially in rural areas where you didn't want to get mistaken for a deer during hunting season.

She hadn't heard anything but nature's sounds since she arrived at the lake for her run—no trucks or ATVs or snowmobiles, so these tracks were likely more than an hour old. But they were relatively fresh, the peaks of the melting snow still sharp. That told her the sun hadn't hit the tracks, so they were made after sunset last night.

The tracks led almost directly to what Kara had thought was a neon vest. But as she got closer she realized it was much smaller—a bright pink stethoscope. A stethoscope that was wrapped around the neck of a dead woman dressed in green scrubs.

The woman lay faceup, eyes open and glassy, on the rocky ground near the water's edge. Her stomach had been flayed, and blood soaked into the damp earth beneath her. Her face was so pale, so young, so lifeless, that Kara hesitated. A shiver ran through her body before she locked down her emotions and focused on the crime scene. She realized she'd drawn her gun. She hadn't consciously remembered, but seeing a dead body did that to a cop—muscle memory took over. Murder victim equals murderer; he might still be around.

She stood silently and assessed the surroundings. Making sure the killer wasn't somewhere, watching her. She heard nothing except birds happily chirping even as this woman lay dead. Everything else was still. Not even a breeze to rustle the leaves or stir the water. More blood was on the ground to her right, opposite the ATV tracks. How did she come to notice it? How had she picked up on its subtlety?

It's your instinct. You're a cop.

But she was more than a cop. She was also a con artist. And being a con artist meant you had to read every person, every situation, every landscape perfectly.

She looked back at the dead woman. From the visible injuries, blood, and lack of bruising around the neck, she was likely exsanguinated. A nurse, by the look of her clothing, as if the stethoscope wasn't the giveaway. Probably too young to be a doctor.

Too young to be dead.

Kara walked back the way she'd come, retracing her footprints to avoid further contamination of the crime scene, until she reached a spot on the trail where she had a cell signal. She called 911.

"This is LAPD Detective Kara Quinn. I'm about a quarter mile past the four-mile marker on Liberty Lake Trail. I have a DB, adult white female. You'll want to call in Spokane's crime scene unit. She's been murdered, and it ain't pretty."

3

Washington DC
4:30 p.m.

FBI Special Agent in Charge Mathias Costa hated sitting at a desk and itched to get out in the field, but he had a team to fill. He'd been stuck in the DC headquarters since the New Year, when the new Mobile Response Team was officially approved and budgeted, and he and his boss, Assistant Director Tony Greer, could start interviewing agents and requesting transfers.

The MRT was Tony Greer's brainchild, but Matt immediately understood the value of the unit when Tony tapped him to run it. Many areas of the country were underserved by law enforcement, either because of limited forensic capabilities or lack of trained investigators. Several FBI jurisdictions covered hundreds of thousands of square miles—two field offices covered three states each.

Besides himself, the only full-time hire who'd already started working for the team was Ryder Kim, the team analyst. The kid was smart, fast, and didn't seem to have the animosity toward bureaucracy that Matt had. Ryder knocked on Matt's open door.

"Assistant Director Greer needs you in his office immediately, sir."

"Thanks."

Ryder's only problem was formality. Matt had plucked him right out of Quantico. The kid had served three years in the military out of high school, studied criminal justice at SUNY Albany on the GI bill, then spent fourteen weeks in the advanced analyst program at the FBI Academy. He was fucking brilliant, and Matt enjoyed grabbing him out from under three other offices who'd wanted him.

Matt took the stairs up two flights to Tony's much nicer digs—which included not one but *three* windows. His secretary motioned him to go right in.

"The Triple Killer is back," Tony said.

Serial killer. Contrary to popular television, there weren't many out there. Depending on which report or analysis you read, the figure was anywhere from fifty to two thousand. Matt leaned toward the smaller number, but there was compelling evidence that hundreds were operating completely under the radar.

"The sicko who murders three random victims—including two cops—three days apart, every three years?"

"That's him. And each of his cycles have started on the third of March."

"That's today. We were looped in fast."

"At the beginning of this year, the Behavioral Analysis Unit sent out a memo reminding all law enforcement agencies what to look for in a Triple Killer crime scene." Tony handed Matt a slip of paper. "From a Detective Andy Knolls—the *only* detective in Liberty Lake, Washington."

"Never heard of the place."

"Town of seven thousand outside of Spokane—which itself is not a major metro center. Served by a small Resident Agency under our Seattle field office."

"Why are you telling me this?"

"It's your first MRT case, Matt. I have you and Ryder booked on the last flight out to Spokane tonight—you're gaining three hours, so you should be able to hit the ground running in the morning. I asked Ryder to print out the complete case files on the previous murders, but they are bare bones—two different states, bodies found at various stages of decomp. But we did a preliminary profile on the case three years ago." Tony paused, and Matt knew what was coming next. "Catherine wrote it."

Dr. Catherine Jones was arguably the most brilliant profiler the FBI had currently working for them. She was one of Matt's closest friends—at least, she had been until last summer. Still, there was no one else Matt would rather have working with him on a complex case like the Triple Killer.

"That's terrific," he said.

"She's not coming back, Matt. You know that," Tony said.

"For this case she will."

"She's been on leave for eight months."

"Six months of that was a suspension, which was

bullshit, and you know it." Matt glanced at his watch. It was five-ten. "I'll get her back. What time does the plane leave?"

"Nine-forty. Brief layover in Chicago."

"I'll pack a bag and stop at her condo on my way to Reagan. I can bring her onto my team, right? That hasn't changed, has it?"

"Of course not, but she doesn't want the position. I talked to her twice in the last month, and she is not budging."

"She will."

Tony continued as if Matt hadn't spoken. "Catherine recommended a new profiler, a Dean Callahan. He has solid references—before Quantico he worked in—"

Matt cut him off. "I want Catherine."

Tony threw his hands in the air. "Good luck."

"She wrote the profile on the Triple Killer—she'll want to be involved. You and I both know that."

Tony nodded his agreement. "So you're going to guilt her into it?"

"If that's what it takes." Matt had known Catherine since their time in the academy. They'd become good friends over the years, to the point that he'd been an usher in her wedding and had become best friends with her husband. Matt understood her better than she knew herself, and he wasn't going to let her sit this case out. Not when she'd written the original profile.

"I suppose if anyone can convince her, it's you—but tread carefully. Catherine has been through hell and back. I don't have to tell you that."

No, he certainly didn't. Matt opened the door to leave, then turned and said, "If this guy kills three people every three years, how much time do we have?"

"Six days total."

"Six?"

"Two and a half to his next strike. He'll attempt to kill again on March 6 and then again on March 9 if his pattern holds."

"So we have less than three days to stop him."

"Good luck with that—based on his profile, he has his second victim—and likely his third—already selected. He stalks them, knows their habits, when to grab them without anyone seeing. Seven dead and no witnesses, no DNA, no suspects. Once you're out there, you'll have less than forty-eight hours before another body drops."

"I'm not willing to accept that we're going to lose someone else," Matt said. "Like you said, we have forty-eight hours and more information about him now than we did in the last two killing sprees. The local cops are already on it, plus we have my new team."

Tony shrugged. "Read the files. We have shit on this guy, even with the murder today. An MO and a rough profile. You're going to have to make some fast hiring decisions. Right now, besides Ryder, you've only approved Michael Harris out of Detroit—I'll expedite his transfer. And we have Jim Esteban from Dallas ready to come on board."

"The cop who ran the Dallas crime lab?" Esteban was both a sworn officer and a crime scene investigator—many jurisdictions required at least one member of their forensics team to be a law enforcement officer.

Tony nodded. "He might see something in the forensic reports that others have missed. I'll have Ryder send him everything we have before he leaves, and Esteban can get started before he gets to Spokane."

"Good."

"What's up with the candidates I put on your desk this morning?" Tony asked.

Matt sat back down, realizing he couldn't avoid this conversation. "No, no, and absolutely not."

"We need this team staffed, Matt. I don't like sending you out West with only three people besides yourself—two of whom aren't going to be there for more than twenty-four hours."

"I'm not bringing in just anyone."

"I thought the kid out of Sacramento would be a good fit."

"Can we talk about this after we stop the Triple Killer?"

Tony sighed and rubbed his eyes. "I have a few more files to go through—I'll send them through Ryder after I vet them."

Matt stood again. "I'll call you after I talk to Catherine."

"If she'll let you in."

"I'll break down her damn door if she doesn't."

4

Georgetown, Washington DC
8:10 p.m.

The doorbell chime made her jump.

Catherine reddened, embarrassed that the sound of a visitor made her heart race. She knew who it was. She'd been avoiding Matt's calls for the last two hours, but Matt was stubborn, and he would never take her silence in the way it was intended.

Which was: *Leave me the hell alone.*

She was even more irritated because she lived in a secure building, and no one could come here without her buzzing them in through the main doors. No one, that is, except Mathias Costa because they had once been friends and her husband, Chris, had given him a key to the condo years ago. When Matt came to the city, he would stay here because they had an extra room. And until she'd separated from Chris, the condo was rarely used.

Now he was abusing their friendship. What did she expect of him? Respect? Understanding? Common decency?

This was *Mathias Costa.* He thought he was a demigod and the world revolved around him.

Angry, she walked through the living room and foyer and opened the front door before he used his key to come in.

He already had it in hand.

A charming smile crossed his face. "Hello, Catherine."

She sighed and let him enter. She shut the door behind him and was surprised that, when she turned around, he pulled her into a hug.

"Don't," she said, stiff.

He squeezed her before dropping his arms. His dark eyes followed her as she walked into her gourmet kitchen. She straightened her spine, felt her bones creak. She had been inactive for far too long. She hadn't left her condo in two days, even to go to the community exercise room.

Catherine poured herself a second glass of wine. She didn't offer one to Matt, even though her manners almost compelled her to. Instead, she put the bottle down and walked to the living room.

Matt helped himself to a glass. Of course he did. He drank his wine as he walked around her half-packed living room.

"You're not moving," he said.

"The condo is on the market."

"That may be the case, but in this market you would have sold it in a day—and you listed it two months ago. You don't want to move, hence a half-packed house."

"Don't psychoanalyze me, Matt."

He sat in the chair across from her and put his glass on a coaster. Matt had always been able to get under her skin, like an annoying little brother. Just the way he was looking at her made her… What? *Nervous?* Hardly. Angry, more like it. Frustrated that he wouldn't leave her alone. Nostalgic for a time when life wasn't so complicated and painful.

He said, "The Triple Killer is back."

"I got your messages. And Tony's."

"I need you."

"I resigned."

"And your boss put you on a sabbatical."

"Formality. I'm going into private practice."

"You'll die on the vine."

"This job has cost me my marriage. My family. Or do you not care about anything or anyone but yourself?"

She said it to make him angry, and she saw a flash of his Cuban temper. But he controlled it. Matt had become much better at controlling his temper as he aged.

"Catherine," he said softly. "Chris loves you. Lizzy loves you."

"Stop." She was not going to talk about her family with Matt.

"Dammit, Catherine, you brought it up! Chris is my best friend—we both know you think you need to be punished and that's why you left him. He's giving you time and space, even though I told him not to."

She hated that Chris had talked about their relationship with Matt. She probably shouldn't blame him—he needed someone to vent to. And probably better to Matt than Chris's sister—who had never liked Catherine—or a colleague. *Still.* It bothered her on multiple levels.

"Stay out of my life, Matt. You just don't get it. I'm *broken.* I can't do the job anymore. I don't *want* to do the job anymore."

"That's bullshit, Catherine. You're the single best profiler the FBI has. You're the one who has these skills, this awesome and terrifying ability to get into the heads of killers. Yeah, it sucks, it hurts, but you've saved people. That's all you've ever wanted to do. Help the helpless and put the bad guys behind bars."

She hated that Matt knew her so well. It's why she had been avoiding him for so long. Without him in her ear, she had almost convinced herself that she could walk away from this work without regrets. Yet he was right. And he knew he was right. Her job was more than a job. The dark side of humanity had called out to her since she was young. But at what cost?

"I don't know," she said, choosing her words carefully, "if I can find a way to save my marriage if I go back."

"You moved out—you're not doing shit to save your marriage now."

"That's not fair."

"You're the one who walked out on Chris and Lizzy. You could have let Chris help you grieve. Instead, you pushed everyone away after Beth's murder."

"It was more than that, and you damn well know it, Mathias," Catherine snapped.

His voice softened. "I know. I'm the only one who knows."

And that was the crux of her problem. Only *he* knew she had lied to the FBI, lied to her husband, lied under oath—and Matt had backed her up. He had never wavered. How did he do that? How could he put everything that happened with Beth—with her killer—behind him so easily when the guilt ate at Catherine?

That's why she had to leave Chris—because she couldn't live under the same roof with the man she loved when she had lied to him. She loved her daughter, but she didn't have it in her to be a good mother. The last thing she wanted to do was bring the darkness of humanity—the evil Catherine worked with every day—into her daughter's life. Beth's death had brought it all too close to home.

"Catherine, if you leave the FBI now, because of your sister's murder, it will haunt you forever. Stop another killer. Get justice for other victims. It's what we do—it's what we are so good at."

"I really wish you would respect my decision," she said.

She'd had eight months to brace herself against any argument to lure her back into the darkness, and she stood firm now, even though he was right.

He made no move to leave. He looked at his watch, and she suspected he was on a tight time schedule. For some reason that irritated her. He expected to be able to change her mind with just one conversation sandwiched in between headquarters and the airport? He stared at her as if he saw right through her.

"Catherine, just this one."

That angered her even more. It was his tone—as if he knew if she took *just this one case* that she'd be back for good.

"What can I say to you?" she said. "You think I blame myself for Beth's death? I do—and I blame *you.* I was a fool to believe for a minute that you had changed, that you could care about anyone but yourself. I thought because my sister was beautiful and funny and smart that you would love her like I did, but you're incapable. You broke her heart, Matt—and I should have warned her. Leopards don't change their spots, do they?"

Matt mumbled under his breath in Spanish, which he often did when angry or thinking. *"Eres imposible. No sabes cuándo parar."*

She was impossible? *She* didn't know how to stop?

He rose from the chair, fists clenched. She almost wanted him to hit her. The physical pain might numb the ache inside her that would never fade.

He was angry, yes, but she saw his pain, too, as clear as day. She'd spoken to hurt him, because he had burst through her carefully built wall. Her words had cut deep. She wished she could take them back. Matt had once been her only true friend. Everyone loved Chris, because he was that kind of guy. She and Chris had friends because of him, not her. She didn't know how to communicate with people in any depth. She didn't want to. Everything seemed so...fake, superficial. Almost unreal, as if she were watching every interaction from above.

Matt understood her, they'd trained together, they'd worked cases together, and best, Chris respected their friendship. It had been Chris's idea to ask Matt to be their daughter Elizabeth's godfather. And now Matt and Chris were still close and she was on the periphery again. As she had been her entire life. Trapped by her own personality, by her isolation. Watching the world turn without her.

"You wrote the profile on the Triple Killer, Catherine. I need you on this case. I will be sending you an update when I get to Spokane, as soon as I get something from the locals. I'll send you the autopsy report, victimology, photos."

She didn't say anything.

"I want you as part of this team for many reasons. First, you're the best. Second, I don't believe you can put your successful career aside and go into private practice to help people quit smoking or forgive their parents for being cold bastards. But mostly, because I know you want to be home with Chris and Lizzy. But you can't be there all the time—it's as if the good in your life is too good and you have to immerse yourself in the dark in order to enjoy the light. This job will give you exactly what you need."

Matt walked to the door, but he didn't leave.

Please go, Matt.

But she just stared at his back, because she knew he was right. And she was sorry she'd hurt him.

"You don't even have to come out to the West Coast, Catherine," he said quietly, "but I need you.

The victims need you. This killer isn't going to stop. He's going to kill again, and if you don't help me stop him, he's going to get away with it." Matt turned and looked at her. The anger was gone, and all that remained was sorrow.

Apologize, Catherine. Tell him you didn't mean it.

She sensed he wanted to say something more, and she found herself wanting to know what it was—because this was one of those rare moments that she couldn't predict what someone was thinking. What someone was going to say.

Matt didn't say anything.

Instead, he walked out.

And just like that, Catherine realized she may have lost her only real friend in the entire world.

Isn't that what you wanted?

Maybe in that moment, but not anymore.

Catherine felt lost, torn over her career, her marriage, her friendships.

But the one thing she wasn't confused about was her vocation.

She knew she could get into the mind of the Triple Killer and find out what made him tick. And if she did so, she would be able to give Matt what he needed to stop a brutal killer.

And maybe, just maybe, she could prevent another family from suffering like she suffered.

5

Thursday, March 4
Liberty Lake
7:45 a.m.

Matt stared down at the lake near the spot where the victim met her violent end. She had been identified as Victoria Manners, a nurse from Spokane.

It was a cold but clear morning—exactly as it had been the day before. According to the Liberty Lake detective in charge of the murder investigation—and the only detective in their small police department—he'd called for the Spokane crime scene investigators to collect and process evidence. They had transported the body to the Spokane morgue, and Matt planned to view the autopsy and talk to their ME at nine this morning.

But he wanted to walk the crime scene first, to give himself some grounding and a place to start. At least, to start on this case—he was already well versed in the previous victims of this serial killer. He'd read those files on the plane flying out here last night, including Catherine's preliminary profile.

There was no doubt in his mind that Catherine would be working the case; he'd pushed their argument out of his head. He'd deal with Catherine's guilt later; for now he had a killer to stop.

He looked around the area, getting a sense of how it might have appeared at night. Dark—there had been minimal moonlight on March 3. Why had the killer picked this spot? Not just Liberty Lake—though that might be as important to the killer as Portland and Missoula were in the first two sets of murders—but why had he picked *this exact spot* to kill Victoria Manners? Convenience? Privacy? Did it hold a special meaning for him?

Matt took a few pictures on his cell phone, even though Detective Knolls was putting together a complete file for him. Just being here, in the middle of the woods next to a gorgeous lake—hell, just being *outdoors*—made Matt happier than he'd been since he'd been forced into that tiny office at DC headquarters. He thrived in the field. And this case—if his new team could identify and arrest the killer—would give the MRT major points among their detractors at HQ who thought the creation of such a team was a waste of resources. Matt needed a win—but he needed a solid win, fast.

Victoria Manners was the seventh known victim of the Triple Killer, though it wasn't until after the fifth victim three years ago—almost to the day—that law enforcement had made the connection. Then the bastard gutted an off-duty cop and slipped away. Disappeared for three years.

Because of the pattern, the FBI had sent a warning in advance to all law enforcement agencies to be on the lookout for any victim who might have been similarly mutilated on or around March 3 of this year.

Although they were unable to prevent her murder, they were extremely lucky that Victoria Manners's body was discovered so quickly. But it was experience, skill, and a competent local police department—not luck—that landed Matt Costa here just twenty-four hours after the body was found. Because of that, they had a real chance to catch the killer before he took his next victim. But because his victims *appeared* to be selected randomly and within a small window of time, Matt knew his team was on a very tight clock.

The tracks that the killer had left when he—and they assumed it was a "he" because of Catherine's profile—drove an ATV from the wide running path to the water's edge were still partly visible in the slush. There'd been no fresh snow recently, and while the mountaintops were still pristine and white, most of the town was dealing with remnants of the last storm. According to the local authorities, they'd been able to take good impressions of the tire treads. Matt already asked them to ship the impressions to the FBI lab if they didn't have the capability to process them quickly. Once his mobile crime unit was fully staffed and operational, they wouldn't have to rely on local labs or the national lab for results. Until then he would use any facility at his disposal.

Matt continued to take his own pictures, starting from where the tracks deviated from the trail.

He couldn't yet see from here the exact place where Manners's body had been found—it was downslope about fifty feet. What had the witness seen from here that caused her to investigate?

He walked downhill parallel to the tracks until he reached where they'd stopped. Obviously the body was gone. The crime scene investigators had collected samples of soil and other potential trace evidence, but they hadn't found anything obviously connected to the killer. According to Detective Knolls, Manners was registered with a temp agency that specialized in health care staffing. She was in the middle of the third week of a six-week nursing assignment in the trauma ward of a Spokane hospital. Her shift ended at 8:00 p.m. on Tuesday, March 2. She'd clocked out at 8:09 p.m. No one reported her missing. She was 28, single, no known boyfriend. Her hospital ID was in the pocket of her scrubs, which was how they'd identified her, though Knolls also said they'd confirmed the ID through her prints.

Manners had never made it home that night—at least, her car wasn't at the small duplex she rented downtown, near Gonzaga University. Her car also wasn't at the hospital, and Detective Knolls had issued a BOLO for the vehicle.

If they were dealing with the same serial killer, even if they found the car, it would most likely yield no evidence. He was a wily bastard, smart and sick, who had never been seen with any of his previous victims. Four women, three men. Three under thirty-five, four over thirty-five. Caucasian woman, a stay-at-home-mother of three. Caucasian woman, a high school vice principal. A Japanese-American cop. Those three were killed in Portland, Oregon. But the cop was off duty and the killer may not have known he was a cop.

Catherine thought he knew; she'd said as much in her preliminary report. But did it mean something?

The next three didn't fit a pattern, either—other than the last victim was a cop. An Asian nurse. A black college professor. A Caucasian cop. They were killed in Missoula, Montana.

And Victoria Manners, Caucasian female nurse, the first—and hopefully the only—victim in Liberty Lake, Washington. Three different cities now, with no obvious link among any of the victims.

Matt needed more coffee and a good two hours to process the details from the crime scene and reread Catherine's report carefully.

A sound distracted Matt. He gazed back up toward the trail. Since a jogger had discovered the body, he wouldn't be surprised if he encountered one or more this morning on the path. He could barely see the trail from his vantage point. Still, he didn't see anyone.

He walked slowly back up the slope. The last thing he wanted to deal with was the press. If a photographer was out here trying to document the crime scene for some lurid report, Matt would go ballistic. Internally, at least. He was exceptionally good at controlling his temper. He'd learned the hard way.

Matt sensed he was being watched. Killers, on occasion, returned to the scene of the crime.

He had his hand on the butt of his Glock.

When he reached the top of the slope, he saw a petite blonde in black skintight jogging pants with a bright green stripe down the side and a matching Dri-Fit jacket. She wore a fanny pack and was drinking water from a neoprene bottle. She looked right at him. He adjusted his hand so she didn't see his gun. No use scaring the locals, though this was the West and rural communities generally had their fair share of gun owners.

"Hope I didn't startle you," Matt said. She was the first person he'd seen on the trail.

"You didn't. Andy said he'd called in the feds, figured you'd all be sniffing around, so I thought I would check out the situation."

"You on the job?" Local police, he figured. Most civilians didn't call FBI agents "the feds."

"Kara Quinn, LAPD."

Quinn. That was the name of the witness. She looked barely old enough to drink. Rookie cop stumbles across his DB?

"Matt Costa, SAC of the Mobile Response Team."

She raised an eyebrow. "Special Agent in Charge? In the field? Never seen that before. Every ASAC and SAC I've met is a dick. Boys and girls both."

He didn't know how to respond to that. "LA as in Los Angeles?"

"Yep."

"You're a long way from home."

"Cliché."

"Vacation?"

"Of sorts."

Why wasn't she giving him straight answers? "You found the body."

"I did."

He glanced at his watch. He still had an hour before the autopsy; he could spare another fifteen minutes before heading back to his car.

"I planned to talk to you after the autopsy. But since you're here—" odd, he thought, but didn't ask her about it "—could you walk me through it?"

"I stopped back there—" she gestured down the trail "—to stretch at the four-mile marker. Started off again, and when I rounded the corner saw the ATV tracks going off toward the lake. At first I didn't think much about it, but when I glanced down the slope I saw something odd—a hint of color. Neon."

"And then?"

"I followed the tracks. The neon was the pink stethoscope around the victim's neck. It was clear she'd been murdered—cut open, bled out there."

"You could tell that with a look?"

"There was a fucking lot of blood."

"You didn't touch anything?"

"It was obvious she was long dead, I figured four to twelve hours. I didn't need to check for her vitals." She was assessing him, and there was a slight shift in her posture and demeanor. So subtle that if he wasn't a trained interrogator, he wouldn't have caught it.

"Based on the visual evidence," Quinn said, "it appeared that the killer brought the victim to this location. No sign of a struggle or attempt to escape—the environment at the time was undisturbed, unlike now that the crime techs and police have gone over it. She was likely unconscious or drugged to the point of compliance. He laid her down, head toward the lake—Why? A ritual? Convenience?—and then sliced her from sternum to navel."

Quinn's tone had definitely shifted, from borderline playful to no-nonsense cop.

"How could you possibly know that?"

"Did you look at the crime scene photos?"

He'd glanced at them, but he hadn't analyzed them. "Briefly."

"It might not be obvious unless you enhance them," she said, "but based on the killer's footprints—not so much *prints* as *impressions* because the ground is rocky underneath the slush—he stood over her body, one foot on either side of her thighs. He's right-handed—he sliced down, pulled the knife out, and stood above her. There was a significant pool of blood on the right side, where it likely dripped from the knife as he watched her die. Well, that was my sense when I saw it. I could be wrong."

She spoke as if she knew she wasn't wrong.

"Then, whether because the victim wasn't completely dead or he had a compulsive need or was in a rage, he cut her from left to right three or four more times—there was significant blood spatter on the leaves and foliage to the right of the body. He didn't specifically gut his victim—didn't take out the organs, unless something's missing when they autopsy her—but he certainly enjoyed the mess he made." She paused a moment, then added, "He wasn't in a rage. A rage would be multiple stab wounds, not a few slashes. At least, that's my educated guess."

She pointed north. "The killer left a different way than he came—he rode along the lake as far as he could until the terrain forced him back up to the trail. I told Andy—Detective Knolls. He's the only detective in Liberty Lake, by the way. Good cop if you like your t's crossed and your i's dotted, if you want to find a thief robbing vacation houses on the lake or locate a serial rapist. But not so much a homicide cop. Anyway, I told him the killer cleaned up in the lake. I can't prove it, just my gut. And the evidence supports it. The killer walked about fifteen feet from the body—away from her, but where he could still see her. There were many footprints between where the ATV was parked and the edge of the lake. Both with shoes and barefoot. Andy said the water was too cold for a dip, but I think that's part of the ritual. Were the other bodies found near water?"

"No." He hesitated, then decided to share a bit with this cop. Because she was more astute than most rookies he'd worked with, and definitely better than the average witness. "This is the fourth victim out of seven who was found outdoors. Only one of the previous victims was found near water—next to the Columbia River, in Portland."

"I'm surprised I didn't hear about these murders."

"Missoula was three years ago this month, Portland six years ago."

She looked up, as if thinking, then nodded. "I was deep cover."

"You're an undercover cop?"

"Detective."

"Detective?"

"Am I not speaking clearly?"

"Sorry."

She smiled, but didn't answer his unspoken questions—how long had she been a cop, what kind of undercover work, did she have homicide training. If she was a detective, she had to be older than he initially thought. She knew he wanted those answers. Was she going to make him ask?

He didn't. He'd find out on his own.

"Maybe not a ritual, but a convenience," Quinn said. "Seven victims?"

"That we know about."

"You think there's more?"

"I'm not ruling it out."

"When did the feds get involved?"

He hesitated. This was the kind of information they kept in-house, though Quinn was a cop. Even if she was on vacation.

Quinn said, "Do you want to see my badge?"

He almost said yes, then didn't. There was nothing he was telling her that couldn't be found through other channels. "Three years ago—but the killer's been on a hiatus, of sorts. Now that he's active again, we're using every resource at our disposal to stop him."

"Any suspects?"

"Not yet—we haven't had an eyewitness or any forensic information that matches anything in our database."

"Smart killers are rare, but they're out there."

He wasn't confident that her tone referred to killers—or cops. Then she smiled at him.

"If you need anything else from me, call. I'm sure Andy gave you my contact info."

Matt nodded, trying to think of more questions because Kara Quinn was different—and he couldn't put his finger on why. But he simply watched as she jogged off at a quick pace.

Then he pulled out his cell phone as he walked back down to the lake. "Ryder, it's Matt Costa."

"Yes, sir."

"Don't call me *sir*."

"Sorry, sir."

Matt rolled his eyes, feeling like he was in a damn movie. He liked Ryder a lot—they'd been the only two people officially working on the MRT unit until now—but the kid couldn't seem to drop the formalities, no matter what Matt said or did. Matt supposed he couldn't undo three years in the military in only a few months.

"I need everything you can find on the witness who found Manners. Detective Kara Quinn, Los Angeles PD, here on vacation. Confirm her identity, background, training, how long she's been a cop, what she did before, the name of her superior officer. If he'll talk, talk to him. Find out where she's staying locally, if she has family here, the whole nine yards."

"I'm on it, sir. Special Agent Harris will be arriving at sixteen hundred hours, and Jim Esteban is flying in tonight from Dallas."

That was fast—Matt didn't think he'd have Michael or Jim until tomorrow.

"And the mobile crime lab?"

"AD Greer is working on it, but it likely won't be ready for at least a week."

If they didn't solve this case in the next week, they wouldn't need the mobile lab.

"I'll play nice with the locals and see if we can have access to their lab if we need it, to save time instead of shipping everything to Quantico. I'm still at the lake but heading to the morgue in Spokane in a few."

Matt ended the call, wondering how the hell they were going to logistically manage an MRT crime lab. It wasn't an issue for this case because they didn't have the lab yet, but even if they had people rotating while driving 24 hours a day, it would take a minimum of three full days and nights to drive one cross-country. Once in full operation the MRT wouldn't be able to wait days for the decked-out RV. Tony had said if the MRT program was successful, his goal was to have two fully equipped RVs, one on each coast. But what about snow? Storms? This was the one part of the program Matt didn't think Tony had fully thought through.

In concept the MRT was terrific. One of the reasons it would be an asset was that most rural communities didn't have extensive forensic capabilities, and having an FBI mobile lab available and prepared to process evidence would be a huge benefit. But practically? Matt didn't see it working.

He supposed they could load the RV up on a military transport plane. For now, he didn't have to worry about it.

Matt glanced at his watch. It was a straight shot

west on I-90 from Liberty Lake to Spokane, about twenty minutes, so he had a bit more time to look around. He walked fifteen feet along the edge of the lake. It was clear to him that Quinn was right—the killer spent some time here. The rocks were pressed into the damp soil, there were footprints, though nothing clear enough to get an impression, and several plants that had been flattened.

Why?

To wash his hands?

Change his clothes?

Dispose of the weapon?

He stared out at the lake, at the thin layer of fog over the surface that didn't reach the shore. He squatted and dipped his hand in the water.

Damn, that was fucking cold.

He jotted down a few notes—Manners was killed at the edge of the lake, but the water didn't touch her body. Quinn had spotted the neon stethoscope from fifty feet—not impossible, because it was a bright pink beacon in a sea of brown and green. And she was a cop, so it was reasonable that she might investigate out of sheer curiosity.

The ATV had been parked five feet to the left of the body. That was evident because of deeper ruts from when the killer started up the vehicle and drove off. Ten feet from the ATV, right on the edge of the lake, is where he may have cleaned up.

Matt followed the ATV tracks fifty feet north, along the water's edge. Then they turned and went back up to the trail. Why had the killer not returned the way he came? Had he disposed of something in the lake? Was someone else in the vicinity he didn't want to come in contact with?

He started back up the slope toward his car and called Ryder for the second time that morning. It took several rings before he answered. "Sorry, sir, I was speaking with—"

"No need to explain. Call Jessica Torino—she's the SSA in charge of the Spokane Resident Agency. First, explain our unit and what we're doing in her jurisdiction. Apologize that I didn't call her myself, that I'm with the locals or whatever sounds good. If she pushes back, call her boss in Seattle." He hadn't had time between last night and this morning to smooth over jurisdictional issues, even though it was on his list of things to do. Tony had made it very clear that he needed to befriend the locals—including regional FBI offices—to help with the MRT image. He hoped Torino wouldn't cause a problem. This killer wasn't going to wait around for pleasantries, and neither was Matt. "Find out if they have an underwater search and rescue or recovery unit. If not, find out who they use and whether they're good. I need divers at the lake. I'll send you the area I want searched."

"Looking for a body or evidence?"

"Evidence," Matt said.

"Agent Harris is certified for underwater search, rescue and recovery."

Matt knew that; he'd forgotten the fact. Michael was a former Navy SEAL and had many skills that were useful to the FBI.

"We'll still need equipment and support."

"On it, sir."

"Don't—" But Ryder had already hung up.

6

Spokane, Washington
9:05 a.m.

Detective Andy Knolls was taller than Matt by a good three inches—and Matt wasn't a short guy. Knolls was also reed thin with a long face and pale blue eyes. He walked with a slight hunch as if he hadn't been comfortable with his height growing up.

"Good to put a face with a voice," Knolls said, and extended his hand when Matt met him outside the morgue.

"I just came from the crime scene," Matt said. "The witness showed up. Kara Quinn."

Knolls smiled widely. "Ain't she something? Eyes like a hawk."

"I gather you know her?"

"Not really. I mean, Liberty Lake is a small town. I know Emily Dorsey—her grandmother. Met Kara a few times back when she was a teenager and living with Emily. I was a rookie. She's a cop now, down in Los Angeles."

"You didn't tell me that our witness was a cop."

"I guess I didn't. Sorry." He didn't sound sorry or worried.

"I found blood on a rock near the crime scene—where the killer stopped and may have washed up."

"You know how cold that water is, Agent Costa?"

"Call me Matt."

"It's barely above freezing, Matt. Most winters it freezes over, though we don't let people skate on it. It's deep, the ice is thin. The guy would have to be crazy to jump in that."

Jump in the lake? "I didn't say he went for a swim. I said he cleaned up."

"Kara seemed to think he jumped. You should talk to the head of Spokane's forensic investigations, Miles Jordan. Anything like this, Spokane comes in to assist. Jordan thoroughly processed the crime scene. Kara talked to him, pointed out a few things. Don't know that he appreciated her help, but I did. Couldn't have asked for a better witness."

Matt was still skeptical. He didn't know Quinn or her background, and that she was involved with the investigation—before he even got here—made him both curious and suspicious.

A woman in scrubs pushed open a swinging door. "You can come in and suit up, Officers."

They used the small staff room in the morgue to pull on disposable gowns, booties, gloves, and hats. "We don't usually have law enforcement witness our autopsies," she said. "We record every homicide or suspicious death."

"Good," Matt said, "but I'd like to get a sense of what happened to the victim."

The woman eyed him as if he'd never investigated a homicide. "Dr. Reynolds will provide a full report, and we video every exam," she repeated. "Your presence isn't necessary."

"It helps me, from a profiling stance, better understand the crime when I observe. I'll stay out of your way."

She gave him a skeptical look, then led them inside the autopsy room.

Dr. Reynolds didn't seem to have the same animosity at being observed as his pathologist. He laid out his lab rules, and then said, "The last cop I had in here puked. I do not tolerate puking in my lab. You will leave before you contaminate my space, understood?"

"No puking. Got it," Matt said.

The victim, Victoria Manners, had been prepped. Now that her body was naked and clean, it was clear that the killer had cut her body sternum to navel, then sliced it three times across the midsection, giving it the appearance of having been gutted. It seemed ritualistic. Kara Quinn had been right.

Three times across the midsection. Three is important to him. March 3. Three victims, three days apart. Three years to cool off and start again. Three.

The wounds were so deep that no one could have survived even the first cut.

While observing autopsies wasn't routine for FBI agents, Matt had done his share over the years, sitting in on a couple dozen, starting with two during his training at Quantico. He wasn't concerned about his reaction, though Knolls looked a little green.

"No puking, Knolls," Matt whispered.

"You don't mind if I sit this out?"

"Not at all. Can you inspect her personal effects, see if there's anything the CSI missed? And arrange a meet with Jordan. I have some questions."

Knolls nodded, then left the room. Matt caught the disapproving eye of the pathologist and winked. She frowned and turned back to the doctor.

The pathologist started the recording. "Nancy Waring, senior pathologist with the Spokane County Medical Examiners Office, assisting Chief Medical Examiner Douglas Reynolds during the autopsy of Victoria Manners, twenty-eight." For the record, she detailed how Manners had been identified. She glanced at Matt. "Also present is FBI Agent Mathias Costa."

Matt said, "Special Agent in Charge. Just to clarify. You can call me Matt."

He'd told Tony he didn't want or need the promotion—Quinn was right about one thing, once agents moved up the ranks, they often turned into dicks. But having the promotion was vital to establish a chain of command, and it gave him authority in most investigations—including seniority over local FBI staff.

Since he didn't particularly like Nancy Waring or her bureaucratic attitude, establishing a bit of *authority* right from the gate seemed both appropriate and fun.

Dr. Reynolds worked swiftly and methodically on the autopsy of Manners, both the external and internal examinations, while also asking Matt questions. "You're not from the Spokane office. Seattle?" The

Spokane Resident Agency was under the larger Seattle district office umbrella.

"No, Doc. I'm with the FBI Mobile Response Team."

"Never heard of it. Is it like the Evidence Response Team? They have one out of Seattle. I've worked with them a few times over the years."

"Similar, yes. The ERT has advanced training in evidence collection and processing. But they're limited in scope and only work in their local jurisdictions. The MRT was established to assist in special circumstances—like this case—specifically in small, rural communities underserved by local and state law enforcement. Our team—which, to be honest, is still being built—has a broader jurisdiction, and consists of experts in every facet of criminal investigations. We're not limited to forensics, but handle the full investigation." At least that was the goal once the team was fully staffed.

"Spokane is hardly rural."

"The body was found in Liberty Lake," Matt said. "And we believe the Manners murder connects with several other homicides over the past six years in two other states."

"Serial killer," Reynolds said bluntly.

Matt didn't comment. Instead, he let the Chief Medical Examiner do his job.

Spokane might be a large city by Washington standards, but its Resident Agency had a large geographic jurisdiction and bare-bones staff. Matt hadn't even had time to meet with the Spokane Supervisory Special Agent, Jessica Torino. In a perfect world, he would have gone through her office first to minimize stepping on too many toes, but this case was time sensitive. He hoped Ryder had reached her and she was cooperative.

The ME repeated his findings for the tape. Manners died of massive blood loss as a result of four deep knife wounds. "It's my opinion, Agent Costa, that the first cut was fatal. The knife went so deep it punctured the posterior of her stomach. Then he sliced down, through her other organs. It takes some strength, and there doesn't appear to be any hesitation marks—though with the extreme damage to the body, they may not be obvious."

"And the other three cuts?"

"Not as deep, but they would have certainly been fatal as well. Every organ was compromised in some way."

"The killer right-or left-handed?"

"The victim was on her back during the attack. The cuts on her right side—or the killer's left side, since he had to be facing her—are deeper, then become more shallow as the knife reaches the opposite side and exits the body. As if he stabbed the knife into her, then sliced through at an upward angle. I would be confident in stating that the killer is right-handed."

Along with 90 percent of the population. But Quinn was right again.

"Was she drugged?"

"There are no defensive wounds, and I've sent blood and tissue samples to our lab. It'll take a couple of days to process."

This was where the MRT crime lab would come in handy. They could process evidence far quicker because they would only be working on one case at a time. Jim Esteban would be here tonight and Matt was going to have him sweet-talk the crime lab into access and quicker results.

"What about a blow to the head? Any other external injuries?"

"No excessive bruising, no blunt force trauma. There were bindings on her wrists and ankles—but she didn't struggle against them, so that suggests she was tied up while unconscious."

Matt would work with CSI on expediting the reports, but he was almost positive she had been drugged. But how? She hadn't fought back. He also wanted any trace evidence from the restraints.

"Sexual assault?" Matt asked.

"No," the ME said. "A small blessing."

Hardly a blessing when Victoria Manners was still dead.

"If I send you the autopsy files of six other victims we believe are the work of the same killer, would you be able to review them and give your expert opinion as to whether they are the same, different, or indeterminate?"

"I would."

"You'll have them before the end of today." He quickly sent Ryder a message to expedite delivering the reports to Reynolds.

If this was the same killer—and Matt was 99 percent positive it was—then he would kill someone else on Saturday. Less than thirty-nine hours from now. Man, woman, black, white, didn't matter—it was random.

Appeared random, he told himself. Because to the killer, Matt was certain there was a reason he chose each victim. The dates were important to him—perhaps the only thing that was important—but it stood to reason he chose his victims as carefully as the dates of their murders. Just because they couldn't see the connection didn't mean there wasn't one.

"Is it possible to give us specs on the weapon?" Matt asked.

"I need to do some research on that. The blade was at least four inches and double-edged. That's all I can determine without taking additional measurements and running them through the computer."

"Fair enough." All the other victims were killed with a double-sided blade.

"I did notice something else," Reynolds said.

Matt stepped forward. Victoria's body was still open; Reynolds would sew her up and store her until her family claimed the remains. Anger hit Matt, as it often did when he saw an innocent victim. But he swallowed it. He was the calm one, the reasoned, methodical cop. It's why he did his job so damn well.

Didn't mean he wasn't pissed off.

Reynolds said, "One of her shoes was missing when she was brought in, and according to the CSI report, it wasn't at the crime scene. I don't know if the killer takes souvenirs, or he tossed it in the lake, or what."

"No souvenirs, to our knowledge." Which was interesting in and of itself. Most serial killers took *something* from their victims. Most—not all. Shrinks had different theories about souvenir collection, but Matt thought that when *this* particular killer was done, he was done. Victim dead, didn't give them a second thought. Didn't need to relive the moment months later. Maybe that's one reason he was so methodical in his timeline—he didn't need an object to remember his crimes.

"She was wearing a special brand of support panty hose that many nurses wear while on duty—the hose on her right foot was cut."

"On purpose?"

"I don't believe so. It seems that it was snagged on something sharp. The bottom of her foot has a small cut on it at the point where the hose was snagged."

"That's good, Doc."

"I swabbed her foot for particulates, which I also sent to the lab. There appeared to be a color to it, possibly paint, but to the naked eye I couldn't state with certainty."

"So, theoretically, she could have lost her shoe during the attack or in the vehicle the suspect transported her in." Which may have even been her own car because they hadn't located it yet. "Cut her foot at some point, but on something that was painted, which wouldn't be in the middle of the woods."

"It's a theory, at any rate."

Definitely something to mull over. But the key thing was that if they found a suspect, they had something specific to look for on his property. Matching trace evidence could make the difference for the prosecution.

Reynolds said, "You didn't ask about the stethoscope."

"I didn't think she was strangled. Was she?"

"No. The stethoscope was wrapped around her neck after she was already dead. I sent it to the lab—I don't think it was hers."

Now *that* was interesting. "Why?"

"It was new. I don't think it's been used much, if at all. There was still some plastic around a portion of the tubing. Plus, we found a second stethoscope—a used one—in the pocket of her scrubs.

More than a little interesting, but Matt didn't know what to make of it. "Thanks."

"Did the other victims have stethoscopes around their necks?"

"No."

What did it mean? Matt had no idea. It seemed random, but it may have meant something to the killer.

Or he could be simply fucking with them. Leaving something with one victim, taking something from another, cleaning up—he had a plan and executed it, yet tweaked a few small details. But never the manner of death. At least, he hadn't if they had identified all his victims.

He cut them down the middle, then sliced them another three times for good measure.

Or three times because that was his lucky number. Three victims spaced three days apart every three years—starting, always, on the third day of the third month.

Matt had his work cut out for him, and he didn't even have his full team in place.

Matt thanked Reynolds and Waring for their time, stepped out into the hall and emailed Catherine all the information he had at that point, including confirming that the MO held: they were looking for the Triple Killer. He then texted Ryder to send Catherine the Liberty Lake case files with photos. She hadn't confirmed that she would assist, but Matt knew she would. She just needed the push. Seeing the crime scene, looking at the victim, would be that push.

Matt had sympathy, but it was wearing thin. If Catherine hadn't been a friend—if her husband wasn't as close to him as his own brother—he wouldn't have even had sympathy to begin with. What did that say about him?

He closed his eyes, took a deep breath, and focused on the case and what needed to be done. It was daunting.

Maybe he would ask LAPD Detective Kara Quinn for an assist. If he could get over this uneasy feeling that he shouldn't trust her.

7

Spokane
11:15 a.m.

Detective Andy Knolls introduced Matt to the head of the Spokane CSI unit, Miles Jordan. As soon as the thirty-five-year-old expert opened his mouth, Matt realized Jordan had been born a crotchety old man.

"First LAPD, now the feds from DC? What the hell, Andy?" Jordan said. He acted more high-strung than angry.

"Detective Quinn found the body. Los Angeles isn't involved in your investigation."

"Detective Quinn wants my fucking job," Jordan grumbled. "'Did you look in the lake?' she asks. 'Did you collect a sample of this blood?' she asks. Do I look like a fucking idiot?"

It was a rhetorical question, but Andy responded. "She doesn't know you, Miles. You know how people are down in Cali. All rushing around and rude. If there was evidence at the crime scene, you got it."

"Don't I know it," Jordan said. "I think I might have something for you, Andy."

"I knew you would."

Andy was an odd duck. He had the *aw, shucks* small town cop shtick down, but Matt suspected he was a lot smarter than he acted. One kiss-ass comment and Miles Jordan had calmed down.

Matt decided to let Andy run with it—Andy knew what Matt needed, and Jordan seemed to respond better to him than to an outsider.

Jordan tapped on a computer keyboard. The large monitor came to life. He typed as fast as he talked and crime scene photos popped up on the screen, one after the other. Matt wanted to look more carefully at them, but Jordan *click click clicked* them away until he stopped at one of the clearing where Kara Quinn thought the killer had cleaned up. He zoomed in.

"I suppose because that Los Angeles cop is originally from Liberty Lake she's not as stupid as I'd normally think," Jordan said. "These are deep footprints on the edge of the lake, fifteen feet from the body. The water eroded them some, and they're gone by now, but if you look carefully you can see the curvature of a foot. It's clear they were made coming *out* of the lake. If you're just going to wash your hands, you'd face the lake, right? But coming *out*?"

"He waded in," Matt said.

Jordan shot him a dirty look. "No brainer, Mulder." This wasn't the first time Matt—or dozens of other feds—had been called Mulder after the popular '90s television show, but the joke had worn thin years ago. "And he was barefoot. But there's not enough detail in the mud to get an actual print. The area is too rocky."

"That's good," Andy said. "What else?"

"So I processed the blood on the rock and it was definitely the victim's blood—I don't have a DNA match yet, but all the major points match and we'll get it confirmed at the state lab."

Matt cleared his throat. "If you can't process the evidence in-house, send it to Quantico, not the state lab. This is our case."

Jordan glared at him, then turned to Andy. "You okay with this, Andy? With the feds?"

"Like I told you this morning, it's a federal case. They have more resources than we do, and they have more bodies."

"And you put me in the middle of this?"

"I don't understand," Andy said. "In the middle of what?"

"Your boss called my boss and my boss called me and reamed me for not telling him the feds were jerking us around." Jordan glanced at Matt. "His words, not mine."

Andy said, "When?"

"Last night. I was having dinner with my sister, and you know how she *hates* when I answer my cell phone at the table, but when the chief of police calls—it was fucked. He's pissed, and my sister is pissed."

Matt asked Andy, "Do we have a problem, Detective?"

"I didn't think so—I'll straighten it out."

Matt was skeptical. It seemed Andy wanted the

help, but maybe the political types in charge were going to be an issue. Andy was a detective, not the chief of police.

Matt's phone was vibrating; it was Ryder, and he sent the call to voice mail.

Jordan said, "You know, our lab is one of the best in the West. I can handle most everything you need here."

"We can prioritize the evidence," Matt said. He didn't want to deal with jurisdictional bullshit when the timing of this killer was so tight. "If your lab can put this case to the top, you run with it. If not, we'll take it." Jordan still looked skeptical. "Andy is a major part of my investigation," he added. "He'll be working *with* me." One reason Tony asked Matt to head the MRT unit was because he generally worked well with local cops. Tech guys? Politicians? Not so much.

Andy nodded. "Matt's been up-front from the beginning."

Matt was relieved Andy was backing him up on this; it could mean the difference between total cooperation or complete shut out. He hoped he had the same success with the chief of police.

"Victoria Manners is the seventh known victim of this killer and we have evidence from previous crime scenes," Matt said. "Two of the victims were cops. That means another cop may be in danger here." He glanced at Andy. "We're going to have to alert law enforcement in particular. The two cops killed were both off-duty and out of uniform, but my instincts tell me they were specifically targeted *because* they were law enforcement. We don't know *why* yet. And I'll tell you something few people know—if we don't find something soon, he'll kill again in less than forty-eight hours on Saturday, March 6. He hasn't deviated from his timeline yet."

"Sick prick," Jordan mumbled.

Matt asked, "Were you able to get prints from the rock?"

He shook his head. "The surface isn't conducive for prints. We didn't find anything, even on the stethoscope. In fact, there were no prints on the stethoscope at all. He had to have worn gloves." Jordan glanced smugly from Andy to Matt. "I should point out something else, because neither of you saw it."

Qué asno superior típico. Juega bien, Mathias.

Asshole. Matt told himself to play nice, but it would be hard if Jordan played games.

"Show me," Matt said and put on his most diplomatic smile.

Jordan zoomed in on one of the photos near the edge of the lake. "My educated opinion is that when the killer came *out* of the lake—he would have been freezing by the way—the lake temperature was thirty-nine degrees at 9:30 a.m. when I began to process the crime scene. I think he was in sort of a shock and fell down. Here—knee marks. Here—hands." Jordan pointed to the impressions in the soil.

"That's good," Matt said.

Jordan was pleased with himself. "I did some calculations to see if I could determine height, but because of variations in average bone length, I can give you a rough estimate. He's between five foot ten and six foot two—which is about 90 percent of the male population. And he wears between a size eleven and size twelve shoe. I would edge closer to size twelve, but again, because of the erosion from the water, it's more difficult to give an exact number."

Matt decided to give Jordan a bone. "I can confirm that he wears a size twelve shoe. We have very little physical evidence at any of the previous crime scenes, but there were clear footprints left at two different crime scenes, both of which were outdoors."

Jordan was again pleased with himself. Sometimes, tech guys were the easiest to make happy, even though they frustrated Matt. Acknowledge their intelligence and skills, and they became your best friend.

"My forensic expert will be here late today. Would you object to him stopping by and chatting with you tomorrow?"

Jordan frowned. It was clear his lab was his domain. But he shrugged. "If I have time, I'll debrief him. But I have to get it cleared with the chief. He'll have my ass if I give you feds access to anything without his A-okay."

"Understood." Matt glanced at Andy. "And we should nip any problems in the bud real quick, Detective."

Andy agreed.

Matt hoped Andy dealt with any of the interjurisdictional bullshit that came up. Matt hated playing politics.

To Jordan, Matt said, "I appreciate your cooperation. Please make a full set of your findings, including photos and tox screens, for my guy Dr. Jim Esteban. He's retired from Dallas PD, where he was the chief criminologist for their lab for the past ten years."

Andy said, "Thanks for your help, Miles. Good work here."

"Yeah. I better get back to it." Then he turned his back on them. "Just cover my butt with the chief, okay?" he called after them.

"You got it," Andy said.

Matt and Andy left the lab and walked down the long hallway that connected the forensics building with the police department. Andy nodded to a cop who passed.

"Miles is a smart guy, just prickly," Andy explained.

"Not my problem. Jim's problem. Delegation has never been an issue for me. I just wish I had my full team here now. What's going on with your boss?"

"My apologies—I should have insisted you meet with him this morning when you arrived. We don't get much violent crime in Liberty Lake."

"What'd you tell him?"

"Unfortunately, he was out of the area yesterday. I immediately called about the homicide—but he didn't know I had contacted your office until I sent a copy of my report. In hindsight, I should have asked you to contact him directly."

"Does he want to be involved?"

"Not really—"

"Spill it," Matt said when Andy's voice trailed off. "We don't have time for this shit."

Andy cleared his throat. "He wants to be a part of every decision. Well, between you and me," he said lowering his voice, "the chief wants credit for everything, but doesn't really know what to do. He was elected Liberty Lake Chief of Police, but he wasn't a cop. Everyone knows him."

"I get it," Matt said. "Let's get a meeting together ASAP, okay? I can't dick around with this shit, but I don't want to cause any delays in processing evidence. If I have to take over the entire case, I will, but I'd rather work with you—and I'll tell him that if I have to."

"He won't like threats, Matt." Andy looked squeamish as he opened the door into the main police building. "Maybe the more-flies-with-honey approach?"

Before Matt could comment, a high-ranking cop hailed them as they stepped inside.

"Andy, have a minute?"

"Of course, Chief."

Matt assessed him. He was a short, physically fit cop in his midforties with laugh lines around his eyes.

He glanced at Matt, then said to Andy, "Miles treating you well?"

"Very. Deputy Chief Brian Maddox, this is Special Agent in Charge Matt Costa. The FBI sent him and his team out from DC when they determined we may have ourselves a serial killer. A new mobile resource unit for rural communities."

"Sounds like an interesting operation," Maddox said.

"We hope it'll be a valuable tool for local law enforcement," Matt said.

Brian Maddox shook Matt's hand. "I was a cop in Liberty Lake for the first twelve years of my career. Trained Andy here. Moved to SPD ten years ago last month."

"Left us for the big city," Andy said with a grin.

"Left for the money," Brian countered. "Not much room for advancement in a small police department with one detective and a chief for life."

"Not much happens at the lake, until now."

"Just so you know," Brian said to both of them, "our resources are your resources. I'm assuming if the feds are here, there's something serious going on."

"Yes, sir," Matt said. "Seventh known victim of a killer who has killed in three states. He kills three random victims every three years."

"The Triple Killer? I read a federal briefing about him. That's our victim at the lake?"

"Yes, sir," Matt said.

"Call me Brian—or Maddox, I'll answer to both. Do Dunn and Packard know?"

"Yes," Andy said. "I put it in my report last evening. I may have stirred the pot a bit by not talking to either of them directly. I don't want Jordan to get in trouble for working with us. We need him."

"Shit," Brian mumbled. "I got your back, Andy, and I'll take care of it, okay?"

"Thank you," Matt said, relieved.

Brian asked, "How much time do we have before we expect another body to drop?"

"Less than forty-eight hours," Matt said. "His pattern has been to kill on the 3rd, 6th, and 9th of March. The first victims in both previous cycles were killed the morning of March 3, and the third victims in the evening of March 9. Twice he's grabbed a victim before midnight the day before but waits until after midnight to kill them. It's the date that seems to matter to him more than the time of day."

Brian said, "Matt, Andy, I need to get any information you have to my officers. I know this is going down in Liberty Lake, but the Spokane Valley isn't that big. I live in Liberty Lake myself, several of my cops do, and I'll do whatever I can to help, starting with taking point with the two chiefs." He glanced at his watch. "Swing shift comes in at three-thirty, out at four—I'd like you to come back in a few hours and give us a briefing. I'll keep the day shift over for a spell. You may have to deal with some local political shit, but ultimately, we have a good department. I don't see Packard pulling some interagency crap, provided he gets a photo op."

"I'll be here, Brian," Matt said. "I appreciate your help."

"We all want the same thing—to find out who killed that nurse."

Brian Maddox nodded at them, then turned and left.

"I screwed up," Andy said.

"Trust me, the feds rarely act this fast. I'll take the heat, I'm used to it. Brian's a good guy?"

"The best. He was born and raised in Newman Lake, a tiny spot just north of Liberty. We went to the same high school—fifteen years apart. His wife is from Liberty and they still live there, on a spread east of the lake. He trained me my first year on the force, before he transferred to Spokane. That was more than ten years ago. If anyone can keep the politics to a minimum, it's Brian."

"Do you ever want to move up and out?" Andy was in his early thirties. Liberty Lake was a small town—like Brian said, not much room for advancement.

"My family is here. My fiancée's family is here. I'm the oldest of four, she's the oldest of six. I don't need a fast-paced life, and I wouldn't care if Victoria Manners is the last murder I ever investigate. And besides, Chief Dunn is sixty-one. He retires in three years. I can wait that long for the title and pay raise."

"I'll meet you back here at three-thirty for the briefing?" Matt said. His phone kept vibrating, reminding him that he had to return Ryder's call.

Andy nodded. "I'm going to the hospital to follow up on the security tapes and talk to Manners' supervisor, then go to her employment agency and her apartment. I'll send you a report when I'm done."

"Appreciate it," Matt said.

Matt slipped into the driver's seat of his rental sedan before calling Ryder back. "Sorry, I'm still in Spokane, just leaving the police station now."

Ryder got to the point. "Assistant Director Greer

is trying to reach you. Says he got an irate call from the Spokane Police Chief, Jeffrey Packard. Says that you're using his resources without requesting assistance."

"I'll call Tony."

"I talked to Jessica Torino, the Spokane SSA, like you asked. She's not being helpful. It might help for you to stop in."

"Not being helpful how?"

"I did exactly what you said—explained the MRT unit to her, what our commission is, gave her the background on the case, and asked about search and rescue. She asked why her office is being excluded from the investigation. I told her they weren't, but she seems to think they're on supersecret probation or something."

"A joke? You made a joke, Ryder." Though Torino's attitude irritated Matt, he couldn't help but laugh out loud. Maybe Ryder had a sense of humor after all.

"It didn't make sense to me, but I may have not understood what she was saying." There was a touch of humor in his tone.

"I'll head over there and read her into the program. And what about search and rescue?"

"I learned from another source that the Spokane County Sheriff's department is the one with the search and rescue team for underwater recovery. I didn't know if you wanted me to reach out to them directly or not."

Why was Matt not surprised that after less than twenty-four hours Ryder had already developed local sources? The kid was amazing. "Yes, do it. Tell them we're looking for evidence and where. I can meet them out at the lake in—" He looked at his watch. He'd be cutting it close to get back to Spokane for the briefing. "Ninety minutes?"

"Sir, I don't know that they'll be able to get their dive team together that fast. Can I suggest that I ask for access to their equipment and Agent Harris can handle the heavy lifting here? It would minimize bringing into the investigation yet another jurisdiction."

Matt sighed. "You're right—find out what you can and set it up at their earliest convenience, but as soon as possible. We can use Liberty Lake PD for assistance, or the Sheriff's—whatever works here. The Spokane crime lab as well. If there's evidence in the lake, we need it."

"You think he dumped the weapon in the lake?"

"I don't know—but we have reason to believe he uses a new weapon each time. A common, double-sided, four-inch blade. We've recovered two identical knives available to purchase in a multitude of sporting goods stores. Maybe this one is different. Maybe not. But if the weapon is there, I want it."

"Yes, sir."

"You sent the information to Dr. Jones?" he asked Ryder.

"Yes. She hasn't responded yet."

"Did she read the email?"

He heard clicking in the background. "Yes."

"She'll respond when she has something," Matt said confidently. "When's Harris getting in?"

"He lands at sixteen hundred this afternoon."

"Bring him up to speed, including the dive in the morning. I'll be briefing the Spokane PD this afternoon and will head back to the hotel when I'm done in Spokane. What, if anything, did you learn about the witness, Kara Quinn?"

Ryder didn't get much more than confirmation that Quinn was a detective with LAPD Special Operations, but he'd put in a call to her direct supervisor and would let Matt know when he heard back.

"Run her name by our people down there, too. If there are no flags, I might want to tag her. We're shorthanded."

He hung up. At this rate, he'd use anyone and everyone the next two days if it would stop the Triple Killer before he took his next victim on Saturday.

Matt looked at his GPS and realized that the Spokane FBI office was only a few minutes south of police headquarters, which gave him just enough time to call Tony while he drove.

"Greer," he answered.

"It's Costa."

"And here I thought you were the one who knew how to make friends and influence people."

Matt wasn't going to take shit from his boss about the waves he was making. "Twenty-four hours ago I was going through files of agents to staff this team, and now I have to pussyfoot around and play politics with my own fucking office?"

"Explain."

"The SSA of Spokane's Resident Agency gave Ryder an earful—thinks we're swooping in because her office is under investigation or on probation or some such nonsense."

"I smoothed things over with the main Seattle field office, learned that even if Spokane wanted the case, they don't have the resources. Torino's staff is spread thin with other investigations. Plus, I implied that you have experience with this case."

"You lied," Matt said flatly.

"You have more information and experience than anyone else."

Matt almost laughed. *Twenty-four hours more experience counts?* But he was still too irritated to find much humor. "Tony—we're going to have to figure this out before the next time, I don't want to be battling the locals *and* our own damn people."

"You're right. I should have reached out to Seattle initially. But if you can appease Torino, it would go a long way."

"I'm on my way."

"I know you'll fix it—you always do, Matt."

Didn't mean he enjoyed it, especially when he would rather have been at the Sheriff's office pushing them to drag the lake.

"Shifting gears," Matt continued, "if I can't get the Sheriff's department help with dragging the lake tomorrow, what's my budget to bring in a civilian crew or rent equipment?"

"Loaded question."

"I need an answer."

"We have some discretionary money in the MRT budget. You and Ryder can authorize spending up to a certain amount—I believe five thousand, but Ryder will know. Over that, call me."

Matt said to Tony, "Tell me about the chief of police. He called you?"

"What an ass."

"And you're supposed to be the diplomat."

"Ultimately, it comes down to money. I told him to send me a bill. That seemed to appease him."

Of course. Money made the world go 'round.

"If Chief Packard gives you any shit, take it—to a point. He's all bark, no bite. But if he interferes with you getting the job done, shut him down. We're fucking paying for the privilege of catching this killer, and he's going to get at least half the credit simply for staying out of our way, so he can sit on his ass for all I care if he doesn't want to do the work."

"Understood. Thanks, Tony."

"And Matt?"

"There's more?"

"You've been on the ground there for less than eighteen hours and we already have more than we had at the beginning of any of the other investigations. Keep it up—and catch this bastard."

Matt ended the call as he pulled into the Spokane FBI parking lot and shut off his engine. There were fifty-six regional FBI offices, and each regional office had one or more resident agency, depending on both population and geographic size of the district. The Seattle field office had nine, including this one in Spokane. But RAs were sparsely staffed, anywhere from two to a dozen agents.

Matt went into the Spokane FBI office and

smoothed things over, using a little bit of honey and a little bit of authority. By the end of their conversation, SSA Torino agreed to assist in whatever capacity he needed.

Maybe he was born to be a diplomat after all.

8

Washington DC
5:45 p.m. ET

Catherine Jones closed the doors of her office, effectively shutting out the seven crime scenes she'd laid out.

She'd told Matt *no*, she had quit the FBI, but he hadn't believed her, and he was right. As soon as he walked out of her condo, she pulled out the case files she kept at the condo, simply to prepare them for another profiler in her office—except she was immediately drawn back into the case.

The Triple Killer was *hers*.

She'd spent the day reacquainting herself with each case—every forensic detail, every commonality and difference, each victim—but she needed a break. Eight hours of violence, even on paper, got under her skin. It was supposed to—because that's how she got into the heads of psychopaths—but she was also professional and had learned to take a breather.

She opened a bottle of sauvignon blanc, poured

a glass, and added an ice cube. She didn't care that it wasn't the proper way to drink wine. Her mother would look at her with mild disdain, her disapproving glance reminding Catherine that she was both ill-mannered and ill-suited for society.

She took her drink to her balcony overlooking Rock Creek Park and tried to push aside the darkness she'd exposed when she opened the Triple Killer files. She'd told herself that she wouldn't let the killer get into her head, but of course that was impossible. They all ended up inside, and this particular killer had been in her head for three years, ever since the case files were dropped on her desk. She'd been the one to connect the Portland murders to the Missoula murders. By then, the killer was long gone, but the case still needed to be solved; the victims still needed justice.

One more case, Matt had said. It would always be one more case calling to her, one more case to be solved. But the killers wouldn't stop. Psychopaths were born and bred, created from both nature and nurture. They would keep coming, and nothing she did could deter them from their destructive path.

She might make another mistake. She might miss an important detail. And then where would she be? Washing more innocent blood off her hands?

Except.

The Triple Killer was hers.

She'd hated then that she'd only been able to write a partial profile. Partial because there was far too much she didn't know. Partial because local law enforcement hadn't thought a serial killer was at work and she'd had to restructure each crime scene under a different lens, looking for patterns as proof—and differences as key pieces of evidence. Back then, she'd barely read and absorbed all the information before he took his sixth victim, then disappeared for another three years.

Until now.

She brought her wineglass to her lips and realized it was empty. It was too cold to stay out here anyway, no matter how lovely the view.

You barely noticed the park lights. You weren't looking at the skyline. You were thinking about murder, violence, and why. What triggered the Triple Killer and who will he target now?

Catherine closed her French doors and poured a second glass of wine over the half-melted ice cube. Who was she fooling?

"Don't lie to yourself, Catherine," she said out loud. "Above all, don't lie to yourself."

She'd wanted the case from the minute Matt told her the Triple Killer was back. She'd opened Matt's emails as soon as she received them. She reopened the files and read the case reports and worked her way back into the mind of this methodical butcher. And though her condo was half-filled with boxes, all she'd really done was pack up clothes she hadn't worn in years, extra linens, and some of her books. She'd given a couple boxes of popular fiction to the local senior center, not because she regularly donated to them but because the center was located between her condo and her favorite coffee shop. They'd had a sign in the window asking for donations of books, games, magazines. It was, she thought, a sign for her to purge.

But she hadn't touched her office. She hadn't packed one file. Maybe, in the back of her mind, she knew that something or someone would draw her back in. That another killer would claim her time, her attention.

It was after six. She should think about dinner. Getting a good night's sleep and looking at the cases fresh in the morning. But they beckoned her.

Help us.

She could practically hear the victims begging for justice.

Help me, Cat. Help me.

A faint moan escaped her chest as if she could hear her sister desperately calling out for her. She hadn't been able to save Beth; she *could* save the next victim of the Triple Killer.

She opened the doors of her office and strode over to the wall where she'd had a custom white-board installed. Floor to ceiling. She'd stuck up the crime scene photos. Written dates, names, personal information of the victims. On her large desk she'd spread out the actual police and autopsy reports.

Catherine was old school. While nearly everything she had was available in the FBI database, she liked having a physical copy. Things looked different in print; she could move pages around, analyze them singularly or as a group, turn and twist photos.

From the very beginning, when Catherine got this case three years ago, the random nature of the victims seemed incongruous with the pattern of his kills. Killers rarely deviated from a victim profile, yet the Triple Killer had—and that was a stumbling block. It made this case more complicated, but more intriguing. Catherine was certain that there *was* a pattern to his victims—she just needed to figure it out.

From her previous analysis, she was certain of only two facts:

First, the serial killer was a male between the ages of twenty-five and forty. Second, he was highly intelligent, though likely held a job beneath his capabilities; his job probably used his intelligence but didn't require teamwork. He could interact with people without leaving any real impression, which suggested he was articulate and pleasant enough looking but didn't stand out. Neither too fat nor too thin, too short nor too tall.

Catherine disliked the word *normal* because there was no true *normal.* To her, *normal* simply meant a person who flew under the radar, who didn't register as good or bad, kind or cruel, attractive or unattractive.

What stood out to her was that the Triple Killer was meticulous in his execution, yet unnecessarily brutal. He didn't so much torture his victims as most were unconscious when he killed them. He didn't sexually assault them. Yet the way he sliced them open, then sliced them across—it was methodical, ritualistic. All the autopsies concluded that in each case, the first vertical cut would have been fatal. Why did he use a knife? Was there a level of comfort to him, of control? Did he want to feel their blood on his skin, smell their death, watch the life drain from their eyes? Or was the knife out of habit? A means to an end? Nothing more than a tool?

She didn't think so. If only a tool, he would have changed his approach, choosing more effective knives or using any weapon at his disposal. The same type of knife was used in each murder, suggesting it *was* an important symbol to the killer and he would be hard-pressed to deviate. Yet he never used the same knife twice—at least that was her opinion, based on the fact that two of the knives had been recovered near the crime scenes. She suspected he'd disposed of every murder weapon. It wasn't the *actual* knife that he was attached to. It was the size, shape or brand. A reminder of something—or someone.

"That helps," she muttered to herself. "Why? Why *that* knife? Why slash the victims? What are you doing? Who are you seeing as they die in front of you, by your hand?"

The organization, the planning, the pattern—all suggested a specific motive, beyond convenience, for choosing his victims. This was her biggest obstacle now: how did the Triple Killer decide whom to kill? How did each, in his sick mind, satisfy his pattern? It wasn't wholly unusual for a serial killer to mix victim races *or* ages, sometimes out of opportunity and impulsivity, but it was highly uncommon to mix races *and* ages *and* genders. That suggested a more random approach... Yet some of the victims did have things in common, even if none of them knew each other, as far as each investigation had been able to uncover. But two nurses? One Asian, one Caucasian. Two off-duty cops? The first Japanese, the second Caucasian. And, she supposed, the vice principal in Portland (Caucasian) and the college professor in Missoula (Black) could be considered working in the same field—they were both, in a sense, educators. But he deviated on race *and* gender *and* age. Rare. Very rare.

Maybe drawing any conclusions from the few similar elements was a stretch. Nursing and education and law enforcement are common professions. Could the killer have an issue with authority? She almost laughed out loud at the thought. Of course the majority of serial murderers had serious problems with authority—it was usually an authority figure who first identified the future killer's psychopathic tendencies—a parent, a teacher, a cop. Or an authority figure who abused the killer in his youth.

Perhaps his parents were in one or more of those professions. Perhaps his mother was a nurse, his father a cop. His mother a teacher, his father a doctor. Maybe. Maybe…

There was something here, but she couldn't quite grasp it.

She needed more background on all the victims. That had been a problem from the start—these victims all appeared to be average people leading average lives with no apparent connection to one another. But each had to hold a particular significance for the killer. The more Catherine thought about it, the more convinced she became that he *specifically* chose these victims.

Don't judge a book by its cover.

Cliché, but it was cliché for a reason. The circumstances *appeared* random. Indoors, outdoors. Two in their own homes, but most in places they didn't frequent. It was too early to know if Victoria Manners was connected to Liberty Lake—or if the killer purposely chose that location for another reason. She lived and worked in Spokane. Why kill her and leave the body in Liberty Lake?

Catherine flipped through her notes, thinking she might see something relevant, but she was wrong. One of the first victims lived in a Portland suburb, but was killed within the Portland city limits, on the banks of the Columbia River. Two of the Missoula victims lived outside of the city limits but worked within the city—and their bodies were found within the city.

Did the killer want the victims to die within the particular city limits for a reason, or was it a mere matter of convenience?

Federal law enforcement was pulled in too late to stop the murder of the sixth victim, a cop. And because the killer disappeared for three years, the case had grown cold, each individual jurisdiction trying to follow leads that dried up quickly. The FBI had kept the case active longer, had ultimately connected the first victim Anne Banks with the others because of the slash marks on her chest—but still, more dead ends. As new cases piled high, this case went to the bottom of the stack.

Until now.

She stared at the information in front of her. The

names of the victims. Their photos. Their jobs. It bothered her that the third victim and the sixth victim were both off-duty cops. That had to mean something. In Catherine's work, coincidences were rare.

So did the killer choose his victims based on their profession? Was that his pattern? Possible, but then the first victim, Anne Banks, was an outlier. She wasn't a nurse; she was a stay-at-home mother. The only one of the seven who didn't have outside employment. And the only one with young children. Was this first victim personal? Did the killer know her? Did she have any connection to medicine or education in her background? Nothing indicated this in her file. If she had a connection to law enforcement, that would have come out during the investigation. Still, Catherine made a note to confirm.

Three years ago, Catherine's focus had been on putting together the profile, but it was incomplete, and she blamed herself—as well as local law enforcement that hadn't wanted federal involvement and hadn't provided her with all the information she needed to better understand this killer and his methodology. Yet, she couldn't blame others. Her workload had been heavy, there was little forensic evidence, and not everyone involved in the investigation believed that the Portland murders were connected to the Missoula murders.

Matt was right once again—being on the ground working a case was far more effective than sitting behind a desk.

Yet, they had been focused then on connecting the victims, and they'd gone back five years to try and figure out if one or more of the victims had known each other. They hadn't found a connection.

She sent Matt a quick email.

Matt,
We need more background on Anne Banks, the first victim. What did she do before she had kids, before her marriage? Where is she from originally? Could she have been a former teacher? Nurse? Cop? She's the outlier. We need to find out why.
Catherine

The first crime scene and the first victim's background always yielded more clues over time—things that might have been overlooked the first time through, things noticed with the benefit of hindsight, that might connect that victim to the subsequent victims.

The only other obvious pattern besides the method of death was the killer's obsession with the number *three.* While three was important, Catherine believed that it was the date—March 3—that had personal significance for the killer.

That was Catherine's original focus when she first caught the case—the date and the number *three*. She'd looked at every possible religious motivation—like the Holy Trinity, for example. She looked at the number not only in the Bible, but in other religions, too, and in triangles and triangulation theories. They had mapped out the victims' houses and where they were last seen and where their bodies were found, to see if there was another pattern to emerge when putting three points together—nothing. They looked into the date itself—March 3—and any significance for any of the victims. None were born on March 3. Of those married, none were married on March 3. Of those who had children, none had children born on March 3. No major life events or tragedies occurred on March 3 for the victims that might tie them together or create a pattern.

Catherine knew the number and date were important to the killer, but *why*. Something must have happened to the killer on March 3—3/3—that led to his obsession with the number three.

Until she figured out how and why the Triple Killer targeted his victims, they'd never solve this case, that is unless he was caught red-handed, which would be unlikely considering how well he planned. She had initially suspected he'd moved from Portland to Missoula primarily because they were different states and it would take the police longer to connect the murders, giving him time to execute his plan then disappear. And because the FBI had been called in so late, that is exactly what happened. Now, Liberty Lake. A very small town near a small city in yet a third state. Were the locations important to him? Did he pick them for a specific reason?

There wasn't one witness who had come forward who had seen anyone or anything suspicious near where any of the victims had been kidnapped. Matt's new information that the killer had cleaned up in the freezing water, disposing of his knife and the clothing, told Catherine that the murderer did the same thing at the previous crime scenes—he was careful to destroy evidence.

She had to look at not only each case individually, but at all the cases together in different ways. Because a pattern was there—maybe not one she could see yet, beyond the number three—but a pattern that made sense to the killer. She just had to find it, crack it. She had to think like he did, and she would find him.

9

Spokane
3:30 p.m. PT

He itched to kill, but he couldn't. He had to wait until Saturday. Had to be patient. He just *had* to. Or he would ruin the plan.

He was antsy, so stayed inside all day and worked. Routine computer programming was the perfect ritual to keep him from thinking too much about his upcoming plans. He worked remotely, could work from anywhere. He only had to visit the main office once a month for staff meetings, and the occasional project meeting—the last was in February, and he had two weeks before the next.

Because he was so good—so damn *smart*—he could do his work in a fraction of the time his employer believed it could be done. He was paid for a full-time job, but could work an hour or two a day and get the job finished on time—and better than anyone else.

The small, nondescript house he had rented in Spokane had been perfect for the past month. He could work here, hide here, plan here… It was centrally located, making it easy to track his prey. Best, it was near the college, so no one thought twice about someone they didn't know in the neighborhood.

But when he was done with his work, the walls felt closer, the lights darker, the carpet dingier. He remembered why he was here. To finish what he started. He was so very close…

So close.

But he'd planned it methodically to minimize the risk of being caught. If he rushed, he'd make a mistake. He would not go to prison like his father. He would not be in a cage like an animal. Feral, miserable, trapped.

You haven't made a mistake yet; you won't make a mistake now.

His fists clenched and unclenched. He stared at his hands, willed them to stop. They did. Of course they did—he was in control.

Complete control.

He knew why he was upset—the nurse's body had been found faster than he'd expected. He thought it would take a day or two, which is why he picked the edge of the lake where it might be harder to see because of the density of the trees. But some jogger had found the body only hours after he had struck, according to news reports—news that he devoured like the butterscotch candies he and his aunt loved.

He missed the sweet, tingling anticipation he felt waiting for the police to find the body. He savored the information, gloated at his brilliance. He watched the police from afar—via the internet, through the news, through press conferences—to learn whether there was a witness, if they found evidence, if he had made a mistake. And now that was gone. They'd found the body and he had to be extra careful before his next kill.

So far he'd been perfect. No mistakes. No flaws. The police never even made the connection between his victims in Portland. Then it took them too long in Missoula before suggesting there *might* be a "serial murderer." Only one television newscast and two newspaper articles reported on it, then nothing. He waited. Searched archives. They found nothing because he'd left nothing. The case turned cold, and he breathed easier.

Then he picked up his plan. To track his target and know when and where to come in for the kill.

He was smart. Careful. Masterful.

His precision calmed him down. Reassured him enough that he stayed put. He wouldn't leave early; he didn't need to kill early. He could wait. He had taught himself patience.

Still, he went to his toolbox. Slipped on gloves and retrieved one of his many knives.

He sat back down at the kitchen table and balanced the knife on the back of his hand. Three fingers. Two fingers. One finger. It teetered, then slowed, then stopped. It was a perfect knife. Simple, inexpensive, but balanced and sharp.

His father tossed the knife in the air. It spun around and he caught the wood grip midair. He smiled at his son.

"Will you teach me to do that, Dad?"

"You shouldn't be playing with knives, sweetheart," his mother said from the kitchen, where she was baking cookies. "They're not toys. They're tools with a purpose."

Tools with a purpose.

He tossed the knife in the air and caught it, just like his father had done so many times when he was a child. When his father was sober, he could catch it perfectly each and every time.

When he was drunk, he failed. His father had the scars to prove it.

Rage filled his veins, memories of the past, the light and the dark, the good and the very, very bad. He tossed the knife in the air, caught it. Over and over, until his calm returned. Until he could breathe easier.

He would stick to the plan. The plan, the pattern, had never failed him. It wouldn't fail him now.

He couldn't risk leaving the house to track his next pawn. He'd followed that victim regularly since February 1, but he'd been researching him for far longer. The victim had no planned vacations until June. No girlfriend. The only standing activity was Sunday brunch with his family.

He would be dead long before brunch.

The killer could scarcely wait. After this death, he had only one more. The most important, most deserving victim on his list.

He needed to finish the cycle, and feel the warm, guilty blood coating his hands. To watch the bastard's life end. Then justice would be done.

10

Liberty Lake
3:45 p.m.

Kara answered her cell phone and said, "You told me I was persona non grata for two weeks, and yet you call after only four days? I miss you, too."

"I told you to take a vacation. A real vacation. It was an order, Kara. And now I hear you're a witness to murder? Can't you just take a break for once?"

He was angry—as if she'd hunted down a dead body for fun and games.

"You make it sound as if *I* killed someone."

"Dammit, Kara, this was meant as a compromise. You take two weeks with your grandmother, and I don't send you back to the department shrink."

She bristled, but kept her voice light and airy. "Lex, do you know how many murders are committed in Liberty Lake, Washington? Less than one a decade. It's a sleepy little town outside Spokane. I wasn't looking for trouble. I was running and found a body. Should I have jogged on by? Ignored her?"

"Don't be a bitch."

"I was being sarcastic. But I'll take *bitch*, if you prefer."

Lex sighed. "I don't know what to do with you."

"Do nothing. I promise, I won't be back to work until March 15."

"The feds are calling about you. Checking your credentials, verifying your identity."

"Well, *yeah.* I'm a witness, I'd expect them to follow up." Was she supposed to lie about being a cop? Like *that* would have gone over well with the feds.

"I had the feeling that they're digging around more than they should. I called them back before they started making a stink. The kid I talked to—something Kim—he said they're part of an FBI mobile response team, whatever the hell that means, and are tracking a serial killer. Not only are you a witness, but a serial killer? *Really?* Why can't you binge watch *Breaking Bad* or *The Wire* to get your fix of violence?"

"I'm not looking for trouble."

He actually laughed at her. "I've known you since the academy, sweetheart. You make it very easy for trouble to find you."

Now she was pissed. "Look, *Sergeant*, I'm taking the time off you ordered me to take, and if the feds want my help, they'll ask. If they don't, they won't. I'm not going to listen to you bitch and complain about what I'm doing or not doing on my fucking vacation. I'm the best fucking detective on your squad, and you *fucking* damn well know it."

"Kara—"

"Are you going to *order* me to steer clear of the

investigation? To sit on my ass watching Walter White run circles around cops and criminals alike? Or maybe I'll binge watch *SpongeBob* and *really* let my mind and body go to shit."

"You just don't listen."

"I listen, Lex."

"You need time to process what happened on your last assignment. I would not be a friend or a boss if I didn't recognize that that case got to you."

"They *all* get to me because I deal with the scum of the earth. But we shut down the sweatshop, and I'm not losing any sleep over shooting anyone. It was justified, you *know* it, and I already spoke to Internal Affairs *and* a shrink *and* was cleared. This two weeks is bullshit, but I've taken it, haven't I?"

"Kara—"

She didn't want to continue this conversation; she didn't want to take a lecture from her boss. *Right.* Her boss. She almost snorted. Technically Lex was her boss, but they'd also been friends for years. She trusted him, as much as she trusted anyone, but one of the problems was that he knew almost everything about her. He could push and pull her strings to make her explode or do anything he wanted. "What are you telling the feds?"

"I can't tell them much of anything because most of your cases are sealed, but I had to give them something because they kept calling, and the last thing I need is someone from our local FBI office waltzing in asking about you. You didn't make any friends with the feds down here."

"Because they're all tight-ass bastards who have no idea what the real world is like."

Lex had originally recruited her into Special Operations right out of the police academy for reasons she didn't fully understand; she'd been working undercover on and off—mostly on—for nearly twelve years. He only forced her to take a vacation now because she'd lost her informant, and, yeah, it had gotten to her. Finding Sunny's body? Knowing she'd been tortured and murdered? Yeah, it had fucked with her head. She'd roughed up a suspect and killed another—justified—it was the cost of doing business catching scumbags no other cop could touch.

She didn't need a break. She needed to get even. And Lex took that from her.

"You know I have your back, Kara. Just tread carefully."

"It wouldn't be an issue if you'd just let me come back."

"I can't. Not until the fifteenth."

"You mean you won't."

He sighed. "You're impossible."

"Do you have a case for me? I can start research. Come up with a background, a cover. Give me something to do while I'm twiddling my thumbs up here."

"Kara—when you return you're going into the pool."

"Hell, no."

"It's not my call. It comes from on high."

"That's fucked."

"It won't be forever."

"How long? Weeks? Months?"

"I don't know."

"Goodbye." She ended the call before she really did something that would get her in trouble, and resisted the urge to throw her phone across the room.

She was the best undercover detective they had, but they were putting her in the detective pool because *why*? She was effective? *No*. Because of goddamn office politics.

She walked downstairs and found her grandmother Em in the kitchen making soup.

Emily Dorsey had a greenhouse out back where she grew her own herbs and vegetables along with marijuana. Em was an old hippie, and Kara loved her for it—even if she was a bit vacuous and Kara had to turn her back on her seventy-year-old grandmother's pot smoking. Legal or not, Kara didn't approve. Fortunately, Em understood that Kara was a cop and at least tried to hide her habit when Kara visited.

Em's long, mostly gray-blond hair was braided down her back and her bright blue eyes smiled when she saw Kara.

"Chicken noodle soup," she said.

"I'm not sick."

"It's not just for illnesses anymore. You've been antsy since you arrived."

"I told you, mandatory vacation. Though the plus is that I get to see you. You feeling okay? Maybe you shouldn't be cooking."

"I've told you a hundred times, Kara, I'm *fine*. The doctor changed my prescription and I'm feeling a million times better."

Em didn't like taking prescription drugs, but her vertigo had gotten worse with age. Kara was all for eating healthy and natural remedies if they worked, but sometimes, modern medicine was the only answer to what ailed you.

"I have an errand—do you need anything in Spokane?"

"No, honey, I'm fine. Go—the soup will be on the stove when you return."

She kissed her grandmother on the cheek and left.

11

Spokane
4:25 p.m.

Andy Knolls had told her the feds were briefing SPD this afternoon, and Kara needed to get to Agent Costa before he started stirring the shit down in LA. Lex was right about one thing: if Costa and his people started making inquiries about her with the local FBI office, it would disturb the hornets' nest. Kara was damn good at being whoever she needed to be and most everyone either completely forgot about her or respected her. But she'd pissed off one person in the FBI, and he'd unfortunately moved up through the ranks.

It had been her one big interpersonal screwup early on in her career. She'd learned her lesson, but she was still paying for her mistake.

She arrived before shift change and asked the desk sergeant where Andy Knolls was, fibbing just a bit that he'd asked her to be here for the federal briefing.

"If he's here, he's in the main briefing room down the hall, to the right. But it hasn't started yet." He checked her ID and badge, then handed her a visitor's pass.

She started down the hall when she saw Brian Maddox talking to two officers. He spotted her at the same time and grinned.

"Well I'll be damned, Quinn. Took you long enough to come see me."

She walked over to Maddox and he pulled her into a brief hug, which surprised the young cops.

"Maddox. I planned on calling."

"Bullshit." But he didn't sound angry. He introduced her to his officers. "Kara Quinn here is from Liberty Lake, left us for Los Angeles. Made detective young."

They exchanged pleasantries, then Maddox said, "I'll see you two in the briefing in—" he looked at his watch "—damn, it's about to start. Five minutes."

Maddox steered Kara down the hall to his small office. He left his door open—par for the course. He liked to hear the sounds and see the sights from his office. He'd always been a hands-on cop, and it didn't surprise Kara that he was a hands-on chief.

"You didn't come here to see me, did you?" Maddox said.

"Partly," she fibbed. She wasn't good with personal relationships—which made working undercover much better for her. But she liked Maddox. If it weren't for him, she might have landed on the opposite side of the law. He was the father she wished she had. "I'm here mostly for the briefing—I found the body."

"I read Andy's report. You've been here nearly

a week and didn't call—Julie's going to blame me, you know. Dinner? Sunday night. You can't say no."

"Going to issue a warrant for my arrest if I don't show?"

"Absolutely."

"Blackmail works. I'll be there." It would be fun to catch up with Maddox and see how the other half lived—meaning, cops *with* family and friends.

Maddox typed on his phone. "There, now you can't back out because I texted Julie that you're coming."

"Sneaky."

He handed her a slip of paper. "We lived in Spokane for a few years when I first took the job, but Julie missed being close to her friends and family, so a few years ago we moved back to Liberty Lake. Never thought I wanted to commute again, but it hasn't been too bad—except during a blizzard."

She looked at the address. It was up in the hills, a nice area.

"I know what you're thinking—we did really well on the Spokane house, bought low and sold high. We were able to afford the zip code."

"I wasn't thinking anything."

He laughed. "Anyway, Andy called and isn't going to make the briefing—one of his patrols found the victim's car near Newman Lake. He's heading out there now."

"Good—they need a break. Have you met the fed yet?"

"Costa? Seems less dicky than most feds."

"Dicky? Really?"

"Julie wants me to stop swearing. JP said *fucking asshole* the other day when a driver cut Julie off and they nearly got in an accident."

Kara burst out laughing. "I'm sure the driver *was* a fucking asshole."

"Yeah, but JP is six. Trevor and Teddy learned early on to keep their mouths clean around their mother." Maddox grinned. "Trevor got into University of Washington. Full scholarship. Can't believe he's moving out in the fall."

"You know they say this is the boomerang generation—he'll be coming back, just wait."

"Worse things could happen. He's a good kid, though, and smart. Smarter than Julie and me put together. Wants to go into genetic research."

"That's way over my head, Chief."

"Mine, too." He stood. "We should head into the briefing—don't want to throw Costa to the wolves just yet."

She walked into the room with Maddox, but made a detour to stand in the back. It was already crowded and she didn't want to draw too much attention.

Maddox went up to Costa, who looked from Maddox to Kara. She winked at him, then situated herself against the wall.

Maddox gave a brief introduction of Costa, and gave his blessing to his troops, though not in as many words. It was clear he expected his men and women not only to listen to the fed, but to fully cooperate.

The fed kept looking at her as he spoke, either trying to figure out why she was here at the briefing, or how she knew the assistant chief of police.

Good. Keep him on his toes. Even if he was less dicky than most feds.

Costa gave a quick rundown on the current homicide, then explained the connection to the other victims.

"Internally, we've been calling him the Triple Killer because he kills in threes. Not very original, but we are mere federal agents."

He was expecting a laugh, and a few people obliged. Costa obviously expected to be able to work a room. A diplomat? Maybe. Kara's assessment from yesterday was that he was far more hands-on than he wanted people to think, that he was a sharp tack, and he would do anything it took to cut through any roadblocks. Based on his tone here, he was willing to work with anyone he had to, but if the relationship impeded his investigation, he would mow them down.

She liked that and hoped her assessment was right.

She almost laughed at herself. *Of course* it was right. She read people better than most, which had saved her life—and her cases—more than once.

But she hadn't been able to save Sunny.

Block it, Kara. Block it out and focus. Triple Killer. Serial killer. Seven dead.

"Three victims in Portland, Oregon," Costa was saying. "A stay-at-home mom of three, a high school principal, an off-duty cop. Three years later in Missoula, he killed a nurse, a college professor, and another off-duty cop."

One of the officers said, "Did he target them because they were cops?"

Costa went through the case and Kara was immediately caught up in the mystery. Because the way he spoke, it *was* a mystery; they knew very little. The victims appeared random, but their profiler thought the killer stalked them and had a personal reason to single them out. They weren't certain whether the cops were specific victims because they were both out of uniform. There was no known connection between any of the seven victims, and they were now running far deeper backgrounds into their lives, starting with the first victim. He went through their names, races, and ages; how widespread the victimology was; and why that made this killer elusive.

All they knew was that on March 6 the killer would hit again if they couldn't identify him.

Yeah, she could see why the feds were all over this. Based on what Costa was saying, they had shit—but they had more now than they had two days ago.

"Our top profiler is working on this case, and I hope to have more information to help narrow our suspect pool later today," Costa said. "Profiling is not a hard science, but we've been extremely successful in the past, and we have a rough profile that we're honing as I speak. You can probably guess based on your experience that we're looking for a male. He's average in most every way, but he's likely a loner. Smart, has a job, but won't be working day to day with people. Highly intelligent, methodical. Just before this meeting, I got word that the Sheriff's dive team will be assisting us in searching the lake tomorrow morning to look for the murder weapon."

"Does that mean he uses a different weapon for each murder?" one of the plainclothes detectives asked.

"Local Portland law enforcement found two separate murder weapons, both generic double-edged knives, disposed of near those crime scenes. The knives were identical, but common. We believe that he uses the same type of knife with each victim—and possibly a different knife each time, suggesting that he gets rid of it immediately after the murder. The FBI only became involved after the fifth murder, and by the time we were caught up to speed, the killer took his sixth victim and then disappeared. Until now."

As Matt Costa looked around the room, Kara caught his eye. Why did he seem so suspicious that she was here? She had a vested interest, and she *was* a cop. She smiled at him, mostly to mess with his head because it was fun. He looked away.

He outlined how the killer grabbed Manners somewhere between work and home, and they believed she was taken directly from the parking lot of the hospital where she worked. He drove her to Newman Lake—where her car was recently found—and then had another vehicle to transport her to Liberty Lake, where he killed her. The timeline was precise—she went missing just after 8:00 p.m. on March 2 and she was dead between midnight and 3:00 a.m. on March 3, according to the preliminary autopsy report.

"Sexual assault?" one of the detectives asked.

"None of the victims were sexually assaulted."

"Tortured?"

"There is no evidence of pre or postmortem torture."

"Were the victims drugged? How?"

It was a good question—and it was also clear that Matt didn't have an answer.

"Because the initial investigations were all separate in different jurisdictions, and some of the bodies were found weeks after death, toxicology has been inconsistent. We believe based on lack of defensive wounds on the victims, that some were drugged or otherwise incapacitated, which facilitated their murder.

"We're extremely lucky that Ms. Manners's body was found so soon after her death. We have more time than we have had in the past—but it's still not a lot of time. He will kill again on March 6 and on March 9 unless we stop him. He has a set pattern. We all need to be extra diligent. Manners was taken from Spokane, but that doesn't mean the next victim will—or won't—be. The only thing I'm confident about is that the individual will be killed in Liberty Lake."

"And you're certain this is the same killer," Maddox asked.

"Yes," Matt said without hesitation. "I wish I had more information to share, but please, anything you see or suspect or just your gut telling you something is off, let your supervisor know. There will be a briefing sheet available shortly with these details, and I will make sure your department is kept up-to-date on our investigation. We need you all, and we're happy to work with you to catch this guy."

Maddox stood up. "I'm taking point with the feds from our office, and I'll make sure we have what we need—and they have what they need. You're the finest cops in the state of Washington, and we will stop this killer here."

The door opened next to Kara and she moved over and stepped back against the wall. Blending in.

A man in full uniform—the chief of police based on his stripes—stepped in along with another cop in plainclothes. Everyone turned and acknowledged him.

Maddox looked both irritated and uncomfortable. Interesting. Kara loved interdepartment drama—unless she was in the middle of it.

"Chief," Maddox said with a nod, "did you have something to add?"

"Quite a bit, as you're not chief of police yet, Brian."

What a jerk. Kara already hated him.

Kara leaned back to observe the exchange, plastering a blank, disinterested expression on her face.

The chief walked to the front of the room, extended his hand to Matt—who looked briefly blindsided and annoyed, but hid it well—and said, "I've read the report Agent Costa provided, and spoke to the Assistant Director of the FBI, Tony Greer. Of course our office will provide whatever assistance the federal government needs. This killer is in part targeting cops, and I don't want anyone to take that lightly. We will be diligent. Until this bastard is caught, no one patrols alone. I'm implementing a check-in system and already spoke to Chief Dunn in Liberty Lake, who concurs. Everyone will call in when you're home. When you leave for duty, you'll call in and then we'll check you off when you arrive. When you're off-duty and leave your house, we need to know where you are and who you are with. We need to have each other's backs. Understood?"

There were nods and agreements. Not a bad idea on the surface, but practically it would be a nightmare. Managing the work and private lives of hundreds of cops for days? A week? Kara didn't see how that was going to work smoothly at all. The riding with a partner—that was smart. But off-duty? Talk about creating a bureaucracy.

Costa looked like he wanted to say something, but didn't. He answered a few more questions and kept looking over toward Kara, so she left the room. She didn't want anyone to talk to her, and she was good at being a chameleon. She'd even dressed like a *real* detective, as Lex would sometimes say. *"Quinn, would you try and at least* look *like a real detective?"* Dark jeans, button-down shirt, blazer over her shoulder holster. She preferred wearing a belt holster, but she'd noted years ago that most of the detectives here wore shoulder holsters. It was all about blending in.

Kara waited for Agent Costa by his rental car. It was overcast and she thought it might snow tonight—probably not for long, and probably wouldn't stick unless the temperature plummeted. She should have stayed inside—the years in Los Angeles had made her soft.

But she'd wait right here.

The first thing Matt did when the briefing broke up was to find Maddox. "You said—" he began.

Maddox stopped him. "I thought I took care of it. It's my problem. I'll fix it."

Matt didn't want to know what was going on, but he asked anyway. "What's with your chief?"

"He's a lame-duck chief but doesn't want to leave. He's out at the end of the year. I'm in. So yeah, it a prickly situation, but I'll take care of it."

Matt was about to ask about Kara, when Maddox excused himself and approached the chief down the hall. He turned the other way and started to look for her himself. He didn't know if he was more irritated or curious that she'd shown up at his briefing as if she were just another cop. Finally, when he realized she'd bailed, he got angry.

The briefing was productive, but unnecessary, though making the connection with the men and women in uniform had been a plus. But he wished he'd known the LA cop would be there. He called Andy Knolls.

"Kara Quinn showed up at my briefing," he said.

"Okay."

"Okay?"

"Is that a problem?"

"Did you tell her about the briefing?"

Andy didn't say anything for a moment, then, "I told her I'd be there."

"She's a witness."

"I know. She's also friends with Maddox. He's the one who convinced her to be a cop, from what I heard."

What? She was buddies with Maddox? Matt was thinking about bringing her into the investigation anyway, so what was his problem?

Because she's putting herself in the investigation before *you asked. That's the problem.*

He shook his head. "Never mind. What'd you find up there?"

"Manners' car has been cleaned and bleached. We're securing it and taking it to the lab—they can go over it thoroughly. We haven't found the ATV. There are a lot of vacation homes up here and I've put together a team to inspect each one—but it's going to take time. Covering the area between Newman Lake and Liberty Lake is going to take days, even if I call in everyone."

Matt considered their resources. Finding the ATV would be terrific, but was that the best use of their time and energy?

"Start at the crime scene and move out from there. Go out two, three miles. You figure out the logical perimeter. But you're right—it's a matter of time right now, which is against us, and we're going to need your people. We can't focus on maybes."

"Are you sure?"

"No, but the guy jumped in the fucking lake—he had to be freezing. Do you think he'd go back twenty miles to where he dumped the car to dump the ATV?"

"Probably not."

How the hell was the killer getting around? From the very beginning, Catherine had said he worked alone, but this murder seemed to need two people if the car was miles from the body. Matt needed more people he could trust. He asked Andy, "You vouch for Quinn, correct?"

"Yes, why?"

"He's going to kill again, sooner rather than later. She sat through my briefing, she must be interested, and I can use another set of eyes, especially an experienced detective."

"I don't think she understands what it means to be on a vacation. Emily, her grandmother, plays Bunco with my aunt Dee, so I called Dee to check up on Kara. She says Kara hasn't had a vacation in years, that Emily calls her a workaholic with no social life."

"So if we need her, would you object to using her?"

"Not at all. Like I said, she's a good cop, has Maddox's trust."

"Good," Matt said.

"I appreciate your confidence in my department."

"I'm confident in you. I'll glad-hand the chief as much as necessary, but I'm relying on you and Maddox to cut through the bullshit and get what we need. Call me if you find anything."

Matt hung up and went outside. He called Ryder to ask if he finally reached Quinn's supervisor or the FBI office, then ended the call before Ryder answered when he saw her.

She was leaning against his rental car, eyes closed, her gray hat and scarf blending into the gray day.

"You must be freezing," he said, expecting to startle her.

She didn't jump. She smiled and opened her eyes. "It's not LA."

"What do you want?"

Her eyes weren't smiling. "You verified my credentials. Please don't call there again."

"Excuse me?"

"Whatever you want to know, I'll tell you, but if you start calling every agency in Southern California, I'm going to be burned."

"That makes no sense."

"I'll give it to you straight. I don't have many friends in the LA-FBI office, and I'd just as soon not have DC calling them and stirring the pot."

"Why would my inquiry cause a problem?"

"I might tell you sometime, but it's not relevant now. I assume you were following up—after verifying my ID—to see if you can read me in. I saved you the time by going to your briefing. Do you want my help or not?"

"Mierda, ya no sé." He really didn't know what he wanted from her.

"Fine." She started to walk away.

"Joder, no me digas que hablas español," he mumbled. It was his way of letting off steam.

She glanced over her shoulder with a half smile. *"Suficiente."*

Great, she understood Spanish. He was going to

have to bite his tongue or he'd get himself in trouble with his only witness.

"Stop," he said.

She did, turned, and faced him. "Matt, you want to know more about me to figure out if you can trust me. I get it. Your guy talked to my boss. Lex is not going to give you anything more than my basics, primarily to protect me, and secondarily because he doesn't like the feds. We work out of Special Operations, and I work undercover. I'm telling you this, even though I don't tell anyone outside of my unit anything about my work. But I'm stuck up here for ten more days. I'm a good cop—I can help."

It was a good speech, but she hadn't really told him anything. "You're not homicide."

"No."

She didn't expand, and that ticked him off.

"¿Por qué no puedes darme una respuesta directa por una vez?" he mumbled. *Why can't you give me a direct answer for once?*

He wanted a straight answer, and Quinn didn't give straight answers. And he really wanted to know what had gone on between her and the LA-FBI office.

"Trust me or don't," she said. "You're short-staffed and I would really like to stop this guy."

"Why?" Maybe that was the crux of his problem with Kara Quinn. "Why do you want to get involved with a 24-7 investigation like this while you're on vacation? It's a lot of grunt work."

"You know why."

"If I knew why, I wouldn't ask."

She looked like she didn't believe him. "Huh."

"Don't play games, Quinn—I'm freezing my ass off and I have work to do."

"I planned on visiting my grandmother for a weekend. My boss told me not to come back until March 15. That's sixteen days of not doing my job. Somehow, I don't think you'd be comfortable sitting on your ass for sixteen days."

She was right. He hated taking time off, and when he did he played hard, like when he decided to learn how to scuba dive a couple years ago. If he didn't have something challenging to do, he'd go back to work early. "Why'd your boss tell you to take a vacation?"

"I wrapped up a tough case and he thought I needed the time. First seventy-two hours were mandatory. And, I created a bit of a problem for the administration because my mouth opened before my brain engaged. But you know what? Time sucks. Time means you think about what you should have done or would have done. There's nothing that beats working."

"Case didn't end well?"

"Didn't end well for the bad guys."

Something flickered in her eye. Something definitely happened on her last case, and she was angry about it. But she hid her emotions better than most people. Her reaction was so subtle and well-timed that he wondered if she intentionally showed her anger, then covered it up so he'd be curious.

That thought was damn Machiavellian.

"If you want to help, call Andy and find the damn ATV this bastard used."

"Yes, boss."

She winked and walked away.

Matt watched Quinn slide into her car and drive away. There was something about her—she was infuriating because she wouldn't just give him a straight answer, but he didn't have the time to dig deeper into her. Andy trusted her, and apparently Maddox had mentored her. That should be good enough. He almost went back into the police station to talk to Maddox about her background, but he really had to focus on the case. They were running out of time, and he would do everything in his power to prevent another body from dropping.

If Kara Quinn could find the ATV, then more power to her.

He had a feeling she'd find it out of sheer determination and doggedness—because failure wasn't an option.

12

Washington DC
11:05 p.m. ET

Catherine was deep in her profile notes when her doorbell rang. She rose, closed her office doors—no sense terrifying one of her neighbors with the crime scene photos that now littered her office—and walked to the door. She looked through the peephole.

Chris.

Her husband had a key, of course. She'd owned this apartment since before they were married. She'd kept it because both she and Chris—a pediatric surgeon—often kept odd hours and needed a place to crash in the city instead of commuting the hour to their house in Stafford, Virginia. They'd bought the house when they first married thirteen years ago—when she had already graduated from the FBI academy, but was spending a year as a resident in a psychiatric facility for the criminally insane. Chris had just completed his residency. They'd known each other since medical school, but Catherine always kept people at arm's length.

Until Chris.

Stafford was close to Chris's new practice and his family in Fredericksburg, though as the demand for his expertise grew, he worked out of Georgetown more often than not. When you were the best at your job, you went where you were needed.

She loved this man but feared she would break his heart. They were legally separated because she had insisted, but Chris didn't want a divorce. He assured her that they would work it out. Matt had told her months ago that she walked out because she wanted to punish herself. She hated him for saying it, but he wasn't wrong.

She opened the door. "Chris. I wasn't expecting you."

"I drove up to check on a patient at GW who's being released tomorrow. Joshua."

The little boy who had lost his parents and nearly his own life in a tragic accident on the beltway. He'd had a collapsed lung, multiple broken bones, and extensive internal bleeding. The rapid response on scene coupled with Chris's talent saved Joshua's life. He would be living with his grandparents now, in Pennsylvania.

She opened the door wider and Chris walked in. "How are you?"

"I'm good. Really good. Just seeing that kid smile again after everything he's been through." Chris smiled. He looked tired, but content. "Joshua is a great kid—he's going to be okay. I gave his grandparents instructions, and they're bringing him back for a checkup next week. Referred them to a local doctor I trust for follow-up care, and the psychiatrist you recommended."

"I'm glad I could help in a small way."

"It's truly a miracle he survived, but he's a strong kid."

"I don't believe in miracles. You saved him—you and the paramedics on scene."

Chris didn't comment. The only thing she and Chris had fundamentally disagreed on—other than her work for the FBI—was religion. He believed in God; she didn't. It wasn't that she *disbelieved,* but she imagined a cruel God or an indifferent God; a bully, a brute, not the loving God of Chris's church. She didn't like how Chris deferred his accomplishments to someone else—even if it was someone who couldn't be seen, touched, or heard. When he gave a speech during his medical school graduation ceremony, he thanked God first.

She didn't understand. His parents had paid for his education, he did the hard work to graduate top of his class, he was smart—brilliant—and had more compassion than anyone she knew. Why credit a distant deity who anointed a few and cursed others?

But as a psychiatrist, she understood that some people—even smart people like Chris—were so humble that they couldn't accept their accomplishments on their face. Believing they were somehow blessed made their success easier to live with.

She closed the door behind Chris. "Would you like some wine? I have some food, but I'll admit I've been eating mostly takeout."

"Wine sounds good. Thank you."

She poured two glasses, handed one to Chris. He was looking at her closed office doors. "You're working again."

How did he know that? How could he see what was behind the doors?

"Consulting." She didn't want to talk about this now. She promised she would quit, make it official. "Just this one case."

He didn't say anything, but opened the den doors and looked at her work.

"Matt asked," she said lamely.

She felt the tension grow in the room. Chris and Matt had once been friends, good friends, but after eight months—she didn't expect them to mend fences. And that was as much her fault as theirs.

"It's an old case of mine," she said. "The Triple Killer, on the West Coast."

"I remember." He faced her. "You're not quitting, are you?"

"I already turned in my resignation."

"But you haven't left."

"My boss is stubborn. She ordered me to take a sabbatical before she'll accept my decision."

"Dammit, Catherine, that's what I told you to do in the first place! Take time. You can't quit unless you can be at peace with the decision, and you're not at peace."

He had suggested it, but Catherine knew he really wanted her to quit. When she broached the idea of private practice, he'd concurred.

"You want me home. You want me to leave the FBI."

"I want you *home*, but that doesn't mean I want

you to quit your job. I've *never* told you I wanted you to leave the FBI."

"You didn't have to."

"Sometimes, for someone so damn smart, you're deliberately obtuse."

"Chris—"

"I know you better than anyone, Catherine, and this is in your soul. You can't walk away from it, not like this. Not because of Beth."

She closed the doors again. Because part of her mind would be analyzing, thinking, coming up with questions. And that part of her mind would be closed to Chris and anything he had to say.

She walked over to her kitchen and topped off their wineglasses with the rest of the sauvignon blanc though they didn't need to be.

"How's Lizzy?" she asked.

"Come home with me tonight and see her in the morning."

"You know I can't do that."

"Why?"

"It'll confuse her."

"That's bullshit, Catherine, and you know it."

Catherine was taken aback. Chris never swore.

"She knows we're separated," Catherine said. Why was she nervous? She had wanted the separation. Needed it. At least, that's what she thought.

You want to punish yourself for Beth. You're a shrink, you know exactly why you left Chris. If your sister is dead, you can't allow yourself to be happy.

"I don't want to get her hopes up that I'll be moving back in," Catherine said.

"Lizzy is a smart kid. She gets it."

"She resents me."

"You do not believe that for a minute."

"I can't let this rub off on her. I know I'm not a loving mother. I want to be...but...*please.* Don't push."

She didn't want the darkness she dealt with every day to touch her child. What happened with Beth was the final straw—the pain on Lizzy's face at her aunt Beth's funeral had affected Catherine in a fundamental way. Lizzy was only ten. She shouldn't have experienced pain like this: deep, numbing grief.

She'd put the pain there. She'd brought the darkness to her family. And the darkness had taken her sister. The only good in her world, the only good left that touched her, was Chris and Lizzy, and Catherine would do anything to keep them far away from the dark side of humanity.

"Lizzy doesn't resent you," Chris said. "She knows what you do. She knows how the people you hunt affect you. Like me, she wants to be there for you."

"She's a child. She shouldn't know anything about this life. About the evil in the world. I'm supposed to be there for *her.*"

And that was the crux of her problem. She was never completely present because her mind was always working on tracking a killer. Getting into his head. Doubting her own morality. She couldn't let it go. She couldn't leave it alone. Why couldn't she turn it off? Others could. Chris did. He held life and death in his hands every day and sometimes death won—but he could see blessings where Catherine only saw pain.

"Lizzy has two strong parents who have careers in life and death. I don't shield her from reality, I put it in perspective. I don't have to tell you that she's an amazing kid. I'm not saying balance is easy—parenthood is not always easy. But kids pick up on everything. It's better to share from the heart than to keep everything bottled up inside."

"Share? *This?*" She waved her hand toward her den.

"Like I said, with perspective. You're not going to show her your crime scene photos, you don't have to share details, but she knows bad people exist in the world, and she's proud of you—*I* am proud of you—that you're one of the people with the compassion and skill to help put them behind bars."

"If only it were that easy."

Chris took the wineglass from her hand and put it on the counter. He put his glass next to hers, put his arms on her arms. Stared at her. For that moment, she wanted to go home with him. To their quiet green acres in Stafford. To forget murder, to forget violence.

But she could never get it out of her mind, never completely. And that's why she had left.

He leaned forward, gently pressed his lips to hers, then looked her in the eye.

"I love you. You're my wife, separation notwithstanding. I will be here for you, whether you return to the FBI, go on sabbatical, or leave. *I'm not going anywhere.* I've told you this over and over, but you don't listen. When you fall, I will pick you up. You will *always* have a home base, and I refuse to let you use our daughter as an excuse not to come home. We both take you as you are."

Her voice cracked. "I don't deserve a family."

"Stop." He kissed her again. She was so tense, so wound up; she was on the edge of destruction.

But for Chris. He touched her, caressed her, kissed her. It was new and familiar at the same time. They had loved each other for so long—that would never change. He was a rock, *her* rock. She returned his kisses, as if no time had passed. As if they hadn't been living apart for eight months.

He groaned, as if he, too, sensed her anguish, her fear, her hesitation disappearing. Groaned out of lust, of love, of need.

She melted under Chris's love, and they moved, entwined, to the bedroom.

"I will always love you," she told him. Then words weren't necessary.

Tonight, she could bask in the light.

13

Friday, March 5
Spokane
7:00 a.m. PT

Jim Esteban had flown in from Dallas so late the night before that Matt hadn't had the chance to touch base, but they met in the operations room Ryder had set up in the hotel at seven that morning. The war room—as Matt thought of it—was a regular room that Ryder had cleared of beds and other furniture and installed with four desks. It adjoined both Ryder's room and Matt's room. Matt didn't know how Ryder had accomplished this setup so quickly, but he was more than happy with his young analyst, who seemed also to be a logistics expert.

Jim drank coffee and munched on a pastry he'd grabbed from the continental buffet downstairs. "I talked to the lab tech before I boarded the plane, got his preliminary report on the crime scene. Read the prelim autopsy report. No tox screens have come back yet—wish my own lab was ready, I could run them faster."

"So far, the Spokane lab has been cooperative. I told the head tech, Miles Jordan, to expect you."

"I'm meeting with him at nine," Jim said. "Not many drugs can act almost immediately to knock someone out. There's usually a risk of the victim screaming or fighting back—even for a minute—or of someone seeing them. And an unconscious body is deadweight."

"Maybe you can light a fire under his ass this morning."

"I read him my creds. I think we're good. We'll go over everything, and I'm bringing over the files for the first six victims. The kid is high-strung, but he's smart. I'm smart. We'll find something. Whether it'll help locate the killer or convict a suspect, I don't know, but it won't be because we missed anything."

"Thanks for coming on board ahead of schedule."

"Once I told my superiors I was leaving for the FBI, I got the cold shoulder. I was already mentally gone. There's a case I'll need to follow up on—I trained my replacement, but it's a sensitive situation and I'll have to testify at the trial."

"Anything you need. After we're done here, you can go back, get things in order."

"My daughter and her family are moving into my house—it's in a better school district. She's a prosecutor—they get paid shit, but she doesn't want to go into private practice." Jim sounded proud. "Her husband's a cop. Good guy. They have three kids." He pulled a photo from his pocket. Two sandy-blond-haired boys who looked almost identical except for their height and a girl with dark pigtails and round

Harry Potter glasses. "The boys just turned eight and nine last month, and Trixie will be starting first grade in the fall. Boys look like their dad, Trix—my granddaughter—takes after her mom."

"Nice family."

"Yeah. There's a basement I never finished—my son-in-law is going to do the work, add a bathroom, put up a wall. I'll have my own space. And honestly, when I go home I mainly want to see the kids. We'd been talking about it when I decided to retire early. But this will work even better." He finished his pastry. "You don't have a family."

Statement, not a question.

"A brother."

"You close?"

Matt nodded. "I spend holidays with him and his family. He's a doctor in Miami."

Dante was brilliant, always had been. They were thirteen months apart, Dante older, and together they'd gotten in and out of trouble while growing up. He loved his brother and sister-in-law and their kids. But settling down wasn't in Matt's DNA—all the home and hearth genes had gone to his brother.

Then Michael Harris, the newest MRT member, walked in dressed impeccably in a dark suit and purple silk tie. He was big—bigger than Matt—and broad, former Navy SEAL. He'd joined the FBI after he served his country for eight years and been honorably discharged. He'd been in Detroit for six years, serving on their ERT unit as the munitions expert and on the SWAT team. Most FBI offices didn't have a dedicated SWAT team—agents cross-trained. Matt wanted someone with advanced tactical training by his side in case a situation got out of hand.

Matt raised an eye at Michael Harris's attire. "You know you're diving in a lake." He'd got it out of a colleague that Michael's nickname in the SEALs had been GQ. Matt hadn't gotten up the nerve to call him that yet.

"I have my gear," Michael said. He extended his hand to Jim. "Michael Harris."

"Jim Esteban."

Jim wore Dockers and a rumpled polo shirt. They couldn't be more different.

"You caught up?" Matt asked Michael.

"Read everything you gave me last night. Know what we're looking for at the lake. Play nice with SSA Torino because she has her nose out of joint. Thank the Sheriff for letting us use their equipment and make sure everything we find goes directly to Jim, who will be at the Spokane crime lab."

Matt made some notes and said, "Detective Knolls of Liberty Lake is looking for the ATV with a vacationing cop from LA—he's been solid since I arrived and may show up at the lake."

"Got it." Michael grimaced when he sipped the coffee. "This tastes like shit."

"You were in the military for eight years and you're complaining about hotel coffee?"

"We had better coffee in the Navy."

Matt's phone rang and he glanced at caller ID. "It's Doc Jones," he told his people. "I have to take this, but keep me in the loop, okay?"

He didn't wait for an answer before stepping into

his adjoining room and closing the door. It wasn't that he needed to keep the call private, but he wanted all his attention on Catherine.

"It's Matt," he said.

"First, I'm not coming to Spokane—you don't need me on-site."

"I already said you didn't need to be on the ground." He tried not to gloat that he had been right.

"You've given me good forensic information," Catherine said, "but I need more—specifically about the first murder. Anne Banks, the Portland stay-at-home mother. She's an outlier—at least with what we know right now. The background check went back five years, but we need to go further back, to her childhood if we have to."

"I got your email yesterday. Ryder is digging up the contact information for the detective in charge. You've always said the first victim is the key victim."

"It's standard in profiling, Matt. I was frustrated yesterday because I knew I was missing something. I spent all day reviewing every file, every photo, every interview…and realized when I woke up this morning that we have several major holes. Consider this—victims four and seven were both in the medical profession. Victims two and five were both in the educational field. Different jobs, but they were educators. Victims three and six were both in law enforcement. They *seem* random but they're not—not to the killer. He's choosing his victims based on their careers."

"Yet the first victim was a stay-at-home mother of three," Matt said.

"I believe she was in the medical profession before she had children. I looked through all the files in her case again this morning. There's nothing in there about where she was born, raised, what she did, where she lived—she'd been married for more than ten years and lived in the same house in Portland for all those years and no one went back further. They stayed local."

Matt took notes, then glanced at the Banks file. "You're right. I didn't notice."

"Anne Banks bothered me from the beginning because she was the only one who didn't fit the profile in any way, and we didn't even connect her until long after the sixth victim because she was killed in broad daylight, in a park, with dozens of potential witnesses, none of whom saw anything. She was the only victim who didn't have a full-time job. The only victim who was extremely affluent—her husband was a dot-com genius, made a significant windfall when he sold his company and then he started another. The only victim who had young children still living at home. She wasn't random."

"Are you saying that the killer targeted her specifically?" Matt asked. "Got a taste for killing, and just continued?"

"No. I think he has a specific motive for killing each person—meaning, they are not truly random—though we still don't know *how* he's choosing his targets. A minor slight? Does the individual remind him of someone who hurt him? Do the women remind him of his mother, the men of his father? Is there a more personal reason? We haven't established any personal connections between the victims, other than they were killed in groups of three. Perhaps they are all connected to the killer in some way—directly or indirectly—but not to each other."

Catherine cleared her throat and shuffled some papers; Matt heard her clicking on her computer.

"And?" He knew she had more.

"His murders are brutal, but well planned," Catherine continued. "*No one* has come forward as a witness. In seven murders, they don't even have a sketch, bad or otherwise, or anyone who saw the victim with someone immediately before they were kidnapped. My educated guess is that he calculated each murder for weeks, if not months. He knew their routines, patterns, schedule—and then planned exactly what time of the day—the right day—he could kill them. Those he killed in their homes—he knew they lived alone or would be alone. Those he took to another site, he didn't keep alive for longer than it took to transport them. He grabbed them, drugged them, traveled to his chosen location, then killed them. He didn't feel a need to explain himself and he didn't get pleasure out of torture or even from their fear. His victims were likely unconscious or otherwise incapacitated and couldn't fight back. His satisfaction comes from a cathartic relief when he kills."

"Except for the first victim," Matt said. "She was killed in public, in a park, found almost immediately."

"Exactly. That was bold—but it could have been that was the only place he could manage to get her alone. Her husband worked from home—they were together all the time. Her two older kids were at school, otherwise she would have been with them. And still—though she was killed in a public place—no one claimed to have seen anything."

That was truly frustrating. A mother killed in a neighborhood park and no witnesses. Did that make the killer supersmart or superlucky?

"When you talk to the original detective in Portland," Catherine said, "ask him to review all witness statements. Someone might have reported something that didn't seem relevant at the time. Anne Banks is, I believe, the key to finding this killer."

"After six years it'll be nearly impossible to get any actionable information from a witness," Matt said,

"Agreed, but the information could be hidden in the notes. I'm throwing ideas out there—but the detective will help you. I spoke to him three years ago and he was helpful then as well."

"You think the killer personally knew Anne Banks. That she knew him, maybe recognized him."

"Either directly or indirectly, he knew her and had a very specific—and very personal—reason for killing her. It wasn't random. *Something* set him off. He had to have stalked her for some time to know her schedule, when she would be running, how to get her alone. Matt—find out where Anne Banks worked and lived before she was married. My instincts tell me she was a nurse—not just any nurse, but a trauma nurse, just like victim seven Victoria Manners, just like victim Sophia Kwan, the nurse in

Missoula. I know you're short-staffed, but we need to go back further than the original investigations."

"Are you talking ten years? Twenty years?"

"When I initially got the case three years ago, I asked both the Portland and Missoula police departments to go back five to seven years on each victim. I received information haphazardly over the years, and some of the information is incomplete. Because this wasn't an official FBI investigation, I had no authority to push for more. But now? We go back to the victims' childhoods if we have to. To wait three years between his kills, that takes discipline and unusual patience. Yet in a sense he's escalating. He grabbed Manners on the second, killed her shortly after midnight. This shows he was anticipating the kill and couldn't wait until later in the day. Your next victim will be dead before the sun comes up tomorrow."

Matt had been thinking the same thing, but he was focused more on Catherine's tone.

"You have more, don't you?"

"I'm not going to jump to conclusions, Matt. The last time I rushed a profile, someone died. I don't have to remind you of that again, do I?"

Her voice was sharp, and Matt winced. "I'll run the backgrounds, Catherine. But we're on the clock here. If he's picking his victims by their profession, then a teacher is likely to die in sixteen hours."

"Don't put that pressure on me."

"I'm not. But give me one more thing—wait." He scribbled on a notepad, glanced at his own notes, then said, "The way the previous victims were all left in the city when several lived in the suburbs. Why transport them elsewhere? Shouldn't it be easier to kill them more remotely, like Manners? Less chance of being spotted?"

Catherine was silent for a moment. He heard her typing, and then quiet, then more typing. "Yes—it does seem odd, particularly in the case of Manners and the sixth victim—Deputy Boyd in Missoula. Manners lived alone, it would have made sense to have killed her at her home. Boyd was married, and he lived in a remote area east of the city, well outside the city limits. According to the original police report, his personal car was found abandoned on the road off the highway leading to his property. That means the killer must have another vehicle, either his own or one he stole to transport the victim to the city to kill him. In fact, based on the map of the area I just pulled up, the killer took him just inside the Missoula city limits."

"So that's part of his MO? That he kills his victims in a designated city?"

"The specific places where they live don't appear to have as much significance as the city where they were killed. Why, I can't even speculate." Catherine sighed and Matt heard the frustration in her voice. "I'll think more on this, but I need more background on Anne Banks."

"Based on your thinking, the next two victims will be killed in Liberty Lake, whether or not they are from Liberty Lake."

"Yes, without a doubt. There's obviously a strong

imperative for him in choosing the murder location—a specific reason I just can't see yet."

"You'll find it."

"I really hate to guess like this," Catherine said slowly, choosing her words carefully, "but at least one of the victims has a clear connection to each city. Given his pattern, that increases the chances that the next two victims will have a stronger connection to Liberty Lake, since there doesn't appear to be any connection to the lake with Manners."

"There isn't—nothing we can find. She is from Spokane, went to nursing school locally, lived and worked in Spokane. But Liberty Lake is only twenty minutes up the road—the local police are still working on old boyfriends, friends, neighbors, family. Maybe there *is* a connection we haven't found yet."

"Please let me know what you learn, even if it isn't complete. Even the smallest detail will help."

"I will. And this all gives me more than I had fifteen minutes ago. Catherine—thank you. This year has been hell for you, I get that. But sometimes, not working reminds us more of our failures than doing the job."

"Maybe I don't want to forget," she said quietly, and hung up.

14

Liberty Lake
8:15 a.m.

Kara showed up at the Liberty Lake police station at 8:15 a.m. with two large black coffees and handed one to Andy. With a wink, she tossed Abigail, the receptionist/dispatcher, a small bag.

"I love you," Abigail said when she opened the bag from Rocket Bakery. "It's an espresso hazelnut scone, isn't it?"

"You can shower Andy with your kindness when I'm gone. He's a good guy."

Abigail laughed and took a bite. Kara knew the scones were good—she'd eaten hers on the way to the station.

Kara always made sure anyone who controlled access to anything she might want loved her. Abigail was easier than most, but this was also Liberty Lake. Most people were friendly, and because everyone loved Kara's grandmother, she didn't even have to try all that hard. Sometimes, she just enjoyed making nice people happy—maybe because she met so few genuinely nice people in her line of work.

Kara followed Andy out to his police issue Bronco. He said, "Late night, early morning. My fiancée isn't too pleased with me right now."

"She knows she's marrying a cop, right?" Kara said, climbing into the passenger side.

"A cop in Liberty Lake, Washington, with regular hours and no real risk of getting shot."

"We're all at risk, every morning we strap on our gun."

"Not all risk is the same," Andy said.

Maybe not, but they were still cops, and Kara was surprised by Andy's comment.

They had planned on canvassing the lake, and since Kara was riding with Andy this morning, he put two other cops together to start at the other end. Like in Spokane, Andy didn't want anyone riding alone until they caught the Triple Killer.

"What happened with the victim's car?" Kara asked.

"It's at the crime lab. Miles will go over it, along with someone Agent Costa is bringing in. I canvassed everyone near where we found the car, but no one saw or heard anything."

"Par for the course."

"Not here, remember? Neighbors watch out for each other."

"Wasn't it found in the middle of nowhere?"

"Vacation house in Newman Lake. But the Madisons live on the same road full-time. I thought they might have heard the car coming, another car going. There's only one way to get to that house."

"One way? Really? Seems pretty dumb for the killer to drive in and out when he didn't have an alternate route."

"The ATV came from that vacation house."

"How do you know?"

"We contacted the owners last night—they live in Las Vegas. This is their second home. They own two matching ATVs. Only one was in their garage."

"You have a description?"

"Yep—sent out a sheet of what we're looking for. And ATVs are loud—we found a trail we think he went, away from other properties, which could explain why no one heard anything. The tracks are there, but unclear, and Miles doesn't think we'll get any usable evidence from them."

"So he took the ATV, somehow strapped her unconscious but breathing body on it, and rode through the woods all the way to Liberty Lake." Kara frowned.

"What are you thinking?"

"Why not kill her at the house in Newman? No one would find her body anytime soon, inside or out. Or anywhere in all that land between the house and the lake. Why drive twenty minutes cross-country with a body strapped to your ATV in the middle of the night?"

Andy didn't say anything.

"I'm just thinking out loud."

"I didn't think of it like that. Maybe to rinse himself off in the lake?"

"Did the toxicology report come back? Do you know what, if anything, he gave her?"

"Not yet."

"What if—and I'm just throwing ideas out there—he stole the ATV before he kidnapped Manners? Hid it closer to the lake? You can't get a car down to where her body was found, and the trail is too narrow to drive on. He could have hidden the ATV any number of places, or right in the open. Driven here—or even in a public parking lot, because they're generally closed after sunset. He could access them, but was less likely to encounter another person. She's stuffed in the trunk. He transferred her body to the ATV, took her a mile or two to the lake, drove the ATV back, took the car and hid it at the house."

"Which would mean he drove there well after midnight."

"When the Madisons were likely asleep."

"You could be right."

"I'm not a homicide detective." Though she had certainly worked her fair share of cases and tended to think like a criminal. Maybe because she'd been raised by two criminals. Though to her knowledge, neither her mother nor father had ever killed anyone.

"But how did he get from the vacation house—after he left Victoria's car—back to wherever he's living?" Andy asked.

"He had his car there." But as she said it, she realized that didn't make sense, either. Unless… "The question is, how did he get to Spokane."

"Explain."

"Here are the facts we know. The family in Vegas

is missing an ATV, but we don't know when it was stolen. We know that Manners' car was found on the same property as the missing ATV. We know that the killer transported Manners in the trunk of her car to the ATV. We believe he used the ATV to bring her body to the lake. A distance of roughly fifteen miles as the crow flies, or twenty miles using known roads—or he stole the ATV earlier and left it in a more convenient location."

"Which means that he stored his car at or near the vacation house." Andy shook his head. "We need to go back out there."

"Didn't Miles process the scene and not find it?"

"Yes—but we need to broaden the canvass."

"Probably a good idea," Kara said.

"I have to follow up on a call from last night—sorry to drag you along, I can leave you somewhere if you like—"

"No, I'm fine. What else am I going to do?"

"Relax?" Andy suggested. He sounded serious, and Kara laughed.

"Andy, I don't relax. My idea of hell is a spa day. I'm good, if you don't mind the ride-along."

"Nope, I enjoy the company. After we're done with our half of the lake, we can go back to the vacation home and expand the canvass. Also, I have a list of all the residences, including which are full-time vacation houses, which are being rented and which are vacant."

"Convenient."

"It helps when there's a break-in or suspicious people, and the rental companies are on board."

They headed out to the south half of the lake; the other officers had the north half. It would take all day to canvass properly, but Kara didn't care—Agent Costa had been a jerk yesterday in the parking lot, and at least looking for the ATV gave her something to do other than jog or trying to ignore her grandmother's pot smoking. Yeah, pot was now legal in Washington and California and half a dozen other states, but Kara had never quite gotten used to the idea that her grandmother was a pothead.

Aren't you the hypocrite.

Kara didn't do drugs for fun. Only when she had to in order to protect her cover or her informant. She'd seen drugs make too many people stupid, violent, or both.

Mostly, she thought, she needed to help with this case because she was a cop first and cops solved crimes. If her boss wouldn't let her go back to work yet in Los Angeles, she could volunteer her time here.

After all, she was on a paid vacation. And her idea of a perfect vacation was working.

Yeah, she thought wryly. *I'm as normal as they come.*

15

Spokane
8:45 a.m.

Michael Harris and Jim Esteban were both gone when Matt walked back into the war room, and Ryder wasn't around. Matt sent Ryder a message to do his own deep backgrounds on all seven victims, prioritizing Anne Banks, and to tap Tony Greer to pull in help from national headquarters. If Catherine Jones thought the killer was tied to Anne Banks's past, Matt would move heaven and earth to learn everything about her from the minute she was born.

It was nearly nine, and Matt needed food—he didn't care much about what he ate, as long as he ate. He left Detective Jacoby—the Portland cop who had run the Anne Banks homicide investigation—a message, and told the desk sergeant to mark it urgent. Then he headed to the hotel lobby where they still had the continental breakfast laid out. Not bad—eggs a little dry, bacon and toast, orange juice and coffee. He sat far away from any people so he could send Tony a status report, then review the old Anne Banks case file in semiprivacy.

Ryder Kim came downstairs twenty minutes later while Matt was getting seconds. He sat down and said, "Go ahead and eat. Working breakfast."

Ryder wrinkled his nose at Matt's plate. "I ate earlier."

Matt had seen the mini fridge in the operations room—Ryder had ordered it in for the team, but he was the only one who used it. Granola, soy milk, yogurt, and some fruit Matt didn't even recognize. Matt himself would eat just about anything—food was fuel. He'd probably even eat yogurt if there was nothing else.

Ryder slid over today's newspaper.

"Anything I need to know?" Matt said without picking up the paper.

"Uh, yeah."

"I'm not going to shoot the messenger." He picked up the paper but didn't immediately see anything he'd be interested in.

"It's about the briefing yesterday. You're not going to like the slant."

Matt rarely liked the slant the press gave anything. "You could have sent me a link."

"The hotel provides free copies." Ryder flipped the paper over.

The headline was front page, below the fold, followed by a worse secondary headline.

Serial Killer Targets the Spokane Valley
FBI Takes Over Investigation of Murdered Nurse;
More Bodies Likely to Follow

"Fuck," he muttered. He quickly skimmed the article. Someone who'd been at the briefing had talked. His first guess would have been the Spokane chief because he was an ass, but he hadn't attended the entire briefing. Still—he would have known all this information. "Did anyone call for a quote?"

"Yes, and I sent them to Assistant Director Greer—that's what you indicated two days ago until we get a spokesperson for the team."

Matt couldn't blame Ryder—that's exactly what he'd said—but he hadn't been thinking straight. He'd thought the press would want details on his unit or someone in authority to say *no comment.* But the amount of information in this article was staggering. Information about forensics, speculation about the connection between Manners and the Portland and Missoula murders, the fact that the FBI was on the scene in twenty-four hours and working with both the Liberty Lake and Spokane police departments.

But the biggest problem with the article was panicking residents. The reporter highlighted the fact that a local nurse was killed, and that the killer picked his victims at random. *Terrific.* SPD was probably fielding hundreds of calls from worried residents this morning.

"Any more press inquiries, send them to me—at least I can feel them out before I tell them to take a hike."

Who talked? Or, rather, who *didn't* talk, because the reporter had information both from the briefing and from the crime scene investigation that Matt hadn't shared at the briefing. He'd included photos of the lake and—shit, a photo of Matt in the parking lot of the SPD talking to Kara. Kara was visible only from behind, but Matt was clearly identified.

"¡Juro que voy a estrangular a quien haya hablado con la puta prensa! ¿Por qué la gente ya no piensa? ¿Creen que esto es una broma?" I swear I'll strangle anyone who spoke to the fucking press! Why don't people think? Do they think this is a joke?

Ryder frowned. "Do you, um, want me to create a digital news alert?"

"Excuse me?"

"So we see these things immediately when they're posted online. I should have thought of it before."

"Ryder, you've been doing the work of three people since we landed this case. Sure. Yes—do it, don't worry that it wasn't done. We'll be more organized next time."

"I'll get on it now." He left the lobby.

Matt called Andy. "Did you read the article by Greene?"

"Yep."

"Who talked?"

"Probably everyone. Packard likes to keep an open door with the press."

"I don't. How do I keep a lid on this shit?"

"That ship has sailed, Matt."

Andy was right. Matt should have also thought of this before—but he wasn't a press guy. He was a field agent. He did his job and let others deal with the media. How could he solve this case if he had to play politics? *"Odio la política,"* he mumbled.

"Excuse me?" Andy said.

Matt didn't translate. "Can you be at the station later for a possible press conference?"

"Just tell me when. Kara and I are working the ATV angle out here—she has a theory that's interesting."

Matt shifted gears. "What?" He was short-tempered, but bad press could do that to cops.

"She'll tell you. I'll put you on speaker."

"What do you know, Quinn? I don't have much time."

"The killer took a taxi or bus or Uber to the hospital sometime on March 2."

He was getting a headache. He refilled his coffee again and walked back to the war room, taking the stairs to release some of this frustration.

"What? How do you know?"

"You said you didn't have time, so I'm giving you my conclusion."

"I need more, Quinn. It's not even nine in the morning and the media already fucked my day. You didn't talk to the press, did you?"

"No," she snapped. *Sore spot?* "And if that reporter had posted my full picture in the paper, you'd be investigating another homicide because there's a reason I'm good at being an undercover agent—I don't let myself get tagged. He could have blown any future cover, me standing there with a fucking federal agent. Thank God it was just the back of my head."

"I apologize," he mumbled. She had a point—undercover cops were very peculiar.

"Here's my reasoning about the killer," Quinn said. "He knows Manners' schedule, grabs her in the hospital parking lot, immobilizes her quickly and shoves her in the trunk of *her* car. Drives to lake. Has an ATV stashed somewhere nearby. Why the lake? Don't know—he probably has his own whacked reason. It's quiet at night, no people, there's a lot of places around here just like that. But it's fifteen miles as the crow flies from Newman Lake, where the car was found, to Liberty and even at midnight, I'm thinking a guy on an ATV with a body somehow strapped on would attract attention. No trunk, no real way to conceal it. Plus, while she may have been unconscious, she wasn't dead. He would have had to cross the highway. He's too smart to expose himself that long."

All logical. "I'm with you."

"He stalked her earlier and knew she lived in a duplex where the walls are probably thin with lots of people nearby—not an ideal place to kill anyone, greater chance of being seen coming or going. So he comes up with this plan. Parks his own car earlier at the vacant house in Newman and takes the ATV to the lake. Leaves it…someplace, but I'm thinking within a mile or two of where he intends to kill his victim. A house, not a parking lot where it would have been found by the earlier canvass. Either he has a second car or he grabs a bus—there's three stops near the lake or he calls a taxi—we're near a major university here, so private taxis are thriving, too—and goes to the hospital. Maybe he transfers a couple times to cover himself, maybe he doesn't. He grabs Manners, drugs her, drives her car to where the ATV is at the lake, loads her onto the seat of the ATV and positions himself behind her, hightails it to the shore where he kills her, jumps in the lake to clean up, drives the ATV back to her car, drives her car to the vacant house in Newman, and takes his own car back to wherever he's staying."

Matt let Quinn's theory sink in. It seemed complicated—too detailed, too many factors could go wrong—but it also provided the killer with multiple outs. Yet the killer never used his own vehicle in the cases that they knew about. He always used the victim's car and he disappeared without a witness, suggesting he had a personal car or other transportation planted. Waiting for him. They already knew he was a meticulous bastard who stalked his victims. Having his car easily accessible to the crime scene—a predetermined location—was more than plausible. He needed to run this scenario past Catherine, get her take. She'd long ago ruled out a partner, but maybe they should rethink that possibility.

"Do you think I'm full of shit?" Quinn asked when Matt didn't immediately respond. "It's something like this—or he has a partner. And though I'm not a profiler, I listened to your briefing and this isn't a guy who shares his kills. He's a loner."

How'd she do that? Fucking mind reader? "I'm processing." Quinn was right—he was a loner. He'd just been thinking that Catherine determined he killed alone, and there was no evidence to suggest he had a partner. "It seems to be a convoluted way to get to the lake," Matt said, "but based on the limited information we know, it's plausible. But most likely not a taxi or Uber. Taxis maintain decent records, and an Uber you need a phone app and credit card."

"And I can tell you a half dozen ways you can clone a phone, steal an ID, and skim a credit card where it wouldn't be traced to him."

"Point taken," Matt said. The Triple Killer was smart, and if he had computer skills that would lend credence to Quinn's theory.

"Andy says they have an arrangement with the property management companies and know every rental property that's vacant or occupied within the town limits."

"Can we get it?"

"Yes," Andy said. "But if someone owns the place as a vacation house and doesn't rent it out, we don't always know when they're in town."

"But a rental agreement might help us in case some fucking defense lawyer wants to call this the poisonous tree," Matt said.

"Excuse me?" Andy said.

Quinn laughed. "I'll explain later."

"Don't tell anyone about your theory," Matt said. "Just us and my immediate team only. Okay?"

"Yes, boss," she said.

Matt ignored the veiled sarcasm—after all, he *was* the boss and he had a sense this was the way

Quinn communicated. And she'd already made it clear she wasn't a fan of any authority.

"Andy, my team will work the taxis and ride shares. Can you talk to the bus company and see if they have security disks from March 2? Actually—the entire week before. He might have come into Spokane early, checked into a hotel or something. Our profiler believes that he stalks his victims for a time, knows their patterns. We need to cover all bases. The rest of my team came in late last night. I don't know if you had a chance to meet them this morning, but Jim Esteban, my forensics expert, said there's only one other family on that road where you found Manners' car—and they didn't see or hear anything?"

"Correct—Miles Jordan with the Spokane crime lab processed the scene, but Kara and I are going to take another look around after we're done with the lake."

"Good—but I really need you both at the briefing. I need to nip this article in the bud, and the only way to do that is to control the message. This isn't my fucking job, but I have to do it," Matt said.

"Talk to Brian Maddox—he's good at this."

"Thanks." Matt hung up and made the call to Maddox to set up a meeting then another press briefing. Brian concurred that the article had far too much information.

"I thought Packard and I had an understanding yesterday," Brian said. "For him to do this—well, it's petty. I'll make sure he understands the situation."

Was he suggesting that the chief himself talked

to the press? That was bullshit, but Matt bit back his tirade. He didn't want to lose Brian's support.

"I'm counting on you, Brian," Matt said, swallowing his anger. "I need your department. I don't have the staff to manage a case of this magnitude. But listen to me—I am absolutely serious that I will pull everything if there's another breach. We have to control the message. Make sure Packard understands that, or SPD is out—and I don't want to do that."

"Understood, Agent Costa."

Maddox hung up. Matt didn't like playing hardball—well, truly, he did. It got the job done, but didn't make him a lot of friends.

"Ryder…" Matt turned to his analyst, who had returned to the briefing room while Matt was talking to Maddox. "We need to reach out to private and public taxis about any fares they picked up on March 2 and the week before, in Liberty Lake. A single rider, male. He wouldn't use his own name or phone or credit card, so focus on the description Catherine gave us. If we need to get a warrant, call Tony—he'll expedite it."

The killer may have made his first mistake. If they caught him because of this, Matt owed Kara Quinn a drink.

"Got it," Ryder said.

"And can you send me the contact information for Kara Quinn's boss? I need to mend a small fence there."

Ryder tapped a few keys on his computer. "You got it. Also, an ASAC at LA-FBI wants to talk to you about Detective Quinn."

Shit. He'd forgotten to tell Ryder to back off from the background into the detective.

"Dammit, I meant to tell you to drop that avenue. I talked to Quinn. I'm good with her assist. Send me his information, I'll follow up when I have time, but it's not a priority." He hesitated. Why would an ASAC reach out to him? LA had at least a dozen ASACs because it was one of the largest field offices in the country—they should all be overworked and not interested in a low-level inquiry. "What else did you learn about her?"

"We confirmed her identity and her hire date—she graduated from the police academy twelve years ago this coming July and received her gold shield five years ago."

"She's been a cop for *twelve years?* She's too young."

"She's thirty."

He'd figured she was closer to twenty than thirty. And she made detective when she was twenty-five? Not unheard of, but certainly rare for anyone, man or woman.

"Do you want me to get more?"

"No, if I need anything else I'll let you know. I had a heart-to-heart with Quinn yesterday and we have too many other irons in the fire to worry about why a vacationing cop wants to spend all her time investigating a murder. By the way, you're doing great. Trial by fire."

"Thank you, sir."

"Elimínalo con los malditos señores," he mum-

bled. Matt wished Ryder would just knock it off with 'sir.'

Ryder just smiled and went back to work.

Matt read the note with the LA-FBI contact information. He hadn't explicitly told Quinn he wouldn't contact the FBI, but he'd implied it, and he was a man of his word. He sent the ASAC—Bryce Thornton—a brief email—apologized for bothering him, that he got what he needed from LAPD, thanks anyway. Then he sent Andy Knolls and Brian Maddox a message that he wanted to meet with them before the press briefing to talk about the case because he had additional information from the FBI profiler.

He was in the middle of crafting the message he wanted to hand-feed to the press when his cell phone rang. Portland area code.

"Costa."

"Agent Costa? This is Detective Gino Jacoby from Portland. I worked the Anne Banks homicide."

"Thank you for calling me back. I won't beat around the bush. As you know, we believe that Anne was the first victim of the Triple Killer. We just caught another case here outside Spokane, Washington, but I was hoping to pick your brain more about the Banks case."

"You know there's disagreement about whether those six murders are truly connected," Jacoby said.

"Perhaps among some agencies, but not ours. We're not only positive the six murders were the work of the same killer, but he killed a nurse in the Spokane suburb of Liberty Lake two days ago. We believe he intends to murder two more victims before moving on. And I think we can stop him."

"How can I help?"

"We're doing a deep background on all seven victims, but because Banks was the first known victim, I wanted to reach out directly to find out everything you know about her life prior to her moving to Portland."

"I can pull that together. I don't think we went that far back, though. She was born in Idaho as Anne Goodman—that much I know—but she'd been married and in Portland for more than a decade, no prior marriages."

"That's good," he wrote down her maiden name.

"Her past didn't seem relevant to the investigation," Jacoby said defensively.

"I read your reports, Detective. I don't think you missed anything. You initially thought it might have been an attempted rape?"

"Yes—there had been a series of rapes in another part of the city, all in public parks, all at knifepoint."

Jacoby continued. "In those rapes, no one had been killed, though two of the victims had been cut. The rapist was caught a month after the Banks homicide, identified by two of his victims. We looked at him, but he had an airtight alibi the morning of Banks's murder. We also looked long and hard at the husband—I've been a cop for twenty years, I'm pretty jaded—but no one could fake that kind of pain. And she was killed in front of her baby—it's extremely rare that a father would do that. Plus he had no motive. No mistress, for example. Then we looked at her husband's associates—he was a wealthy entrepreneur who made a lot of people upset when he sold his first company. Some people didn't fare as well as he did and he'd received threats. But nothing of this magnitude, and nothing directed at his wife or family. It's been a black spot on my record, I have to say, Agent Costa. That little boy is almost seven years old now and never got to know his mother. The girls are twelve and eleven. Dad never remarried—I don't think he really got over what happened."

"Would you be open to speaking with Mr. Banks again?"

"If I can give him something. Three years ago the FBI came talking to him, and it didn't go well. I was angry that they didn't come to me first."

"I understand your frustration, and I need your help. Tell him we believe his wife's murder is connected to something that may have happened before they were married—I specifically need to know if she was a nurse at any point in her life, and if so, where she worked. This is a thin lead, but the only connection between the victims appears to be their occupation and the only outlier is Anne Banks—but if she was a nurse at one time, she would no longer be an outlier. It would also mean the killer might have some personal connection to her."

"I can tell you for certain that Mrs. Banks was a nurse when she met her husband—it's how they met. But that was…jeez, four or five years before they got married. He talked a lot at the beginning, rambled really. I don't know where she worked, I assumed Portland, but that makes me an idiot—I should have followed up."

"Not an idiot, Jacoby. Our profiler is thinking that the killer felt injured or slighted by one or more of his victims, but is killing others randomly who have the same occupation in some sort of sick substitution. But Anne wasn't a practicing nurse at the time, correct?"

"No—according to my notes, she hadn't worked during her marriage."

Matt continued. "Plus she was the first victim. If you can talk to the husband, find out anything that stands out as unusual given what we know now, even if he hasn't thought about his wife's nursing career in years. See if he remembers all the places she worked, how long, what area of nursing. I know I'm fishing—but it's a line that's still in the water and I might get a bite."

"I'll call him right now."

"One more thing—I've been going over all the original crime scene photos. The jogging stroller with her baby still in it was found about twenty feet from the body. I've read every report. They all indicate that the victim was stabbed and died in the same spot. Why was her baby so far away? If the killer had time to drag her off the path, why didn't she scream? The baby was *down* the path from the body. Did she push the baby away to protect him?"

"There's one thing not in the public reports," Jacoby said.

"I should have everything, though."

"It's a sensitive case, and like I said, the FBI were

jerks three years ago so I don't know that my boss would have been keen on jumping through hoops for you at the time."

Once again, interoffice jurisdictional bullshit made Matt's head ache. "Can you tell me now?"

"Every scenario we came up with didn't work with the evidence we had, except one. Anne was jogging on the path. It had started to rain. She had one earbud in her ear, the other out I assume to listen for traffic, as runners often do. The killer grabbed her from behind—we didn't believe he was following her on the path because none of the witnesses saw a lone man running behind or keeping pace with a woman with a stroller. The rain both helped and hurt our investigation—we didn't have much sign of a scuffle because the rain muddied the area, but we did have one good set of footprints, where we think the killer stood and waited for her to pass by. He must have known her route—from what we learned, she rarely deviated, which is why I've always told my own daughters never to run on a set schedule and to change their routes often. Anyway, we think she passed her killer but didn't see him—a tree obscured his hiding place. When he saw her, he sprinted, grabbed her from behind, put his hand over her mouth and pulled her into the foliage only two feet away. That was the basic MO of the rapist across town. Facial evidence indicated early bruising where he held Banks's mouth. But there were no torn clothes, no signs of attempted rape. The killer then reached around and stabbed her in the gut."

"He stabbed her from behind?" Matt tried to picture it.

"It's what the angle of the initial stab wound showed in the autopsy. Plus if he let her go, she would have stumbled, fallen back, screamed, done something. The thinking was, this was quick. Grab and stab. The angle of the initial stab wound lent credence to the theory. It wasn't straight on. But he pulled the knife up toward her sternum. Cut into her lungs. She wouldn't have been able to scream at that point. He didn't just drop her. He laid her down on her back as she was dying and sliced her three more times. Why? Hell if I know."

"It's his pattern."

"He must have pocketed the knife—we never found it—and shoved the stroller down the path. The murderer had blood on his hands. There was blood on the handle of the stroller."

"Why would he do that? Attempted kidnapping?"

"No idea. Maybe he didn't want the body discovered right away. Maybe the stroller was in his way, or the baby was crying… Hell if I know. We had no fingerprints—he wore gloves—and only one blood type, the victim's."

"Daytime, and no one saw a man with blood on his clothes walking out of the park?"

"I thought the same thing, Costa. It's bothered me. We had a dozen guys go through that park with a fine-tooth comb. I think I know what he did, but I can't prove it."

"Tell me. I'm willing to listen to any theory, no matter how wild."

"It was raining. Not heavy, just Portland drizzle. I think he wore a slicker, probably a poncho, something that wouldn't stand out. Dark, to hide the blood. Black, brown, navy. He puts his hands under the poncho and *voilà*! No one sees anything weird. He jogs from the scene to blend in and when no one is around, he pulls off the poncho, stuffs it in a backpack. Or, he has a car nearby. We scoured the scene and found trace amounts of blood on the trail in the direction he pushed the stroller, then they disappeared. We combed the area in a half-mile radius in search of the weapon, including every garbage can on public and private property. He could have disappeared on public transportation—which we thoroughly investigated—or had his own car nearby. I lean toward car.

"The body was found quickly," Jacoby continued. "She was dead, but the witnesses missed the killer by no more than seven minutes, based on our canvass of the scene and everyone who was in the park that morning. But in seven minutes he could have been to any of four streets that surround the park and driven off. There were no street cams, not in that neighborhood. It's busy, mostly young families and artsy types. Safe, low crime."

"It sounds like you did everything humanly possible," Matt said.

"I wish I weren't so human," Jacoby said. "Three kids are orphans because some bastard killed Anne Banks. I'll talk to her husband again. You have my number—keep me informed, Costa, okay? I have to know you get the guy—and that it's the right guy. I'll call you if I learn anything new."

Twenty minutes later, while Matt was putting together a large whiteboard of the seven victims and every common trait between them, Jacoby called him back.

"I don't know if this means anything," Jacoby said, "but Anne Banks, maiden name Goodman, was a nurse at Spokane General for seven years before moving to Portland to get married. That's where they'd met—her husband was speaking at a tech symposium at the college there and got food poisoning. She was on duty in the emergency room."

Matt nearly jumped out of his seat. "She was a trauma nurse?"

"Yes—does that mean anything?"

"The first victims in both Missoula and in Liberty Lake were trauma nurses. And get this—at least one of them worked at Spokane General. This has to be it, Detective. This is the connection. It goes back to Anne Banks when she was a nurse. Do you have anything else? Friends of hers from then? Anyone who is still in Spokane or knew her from the hospital?"

"One person—an Olivia Gunderson. She's still a nurse at Spokane General—runs the neonatal unit—and had been Anne's maid of honor. Mr. Banks said she visits the kids a couple times a year. I'll email you her contact information."

"Thank you, Gino. I'll let you know what comes of this."

Matt hung up. "Ryder," he said, "finish working

on the backgrounds, specifically the employment history for victim four, Sophia Kwan. See if she ever worked at Spokane General. Find out if any of the other victims have any connection to Spokane General, as a patient or a family member that was a patient or in any employment capacity, medical or not. Two victims are connected to the same employer—we have to dig deeper. Look at any connection between all seven victims and Spokane and the surrounding area. Did they work here, go to school here—we have a major university a stone's throw away. Did our professor in Missoula start here at Gonzaga? Call Tony and tell him we may need a warrant for any lawsuits that Banks was party to—I know hospitals and nurses and doctors are sued all the time. There might be something there."

"Sir, the hospital attorneys will think you're fishing."

"Just tell Tony I'm working on something tangible to give the fucking lawyers."

Matt wasn't positive he was on the right track, but he felt he was definitely in the ballpark. Two victims had been nurses at Spokane General. One, more than a decade ago. Did they know each other at some point? More importantly, had the killer known? And what was the significance?

Matt pulled out Anne Banks's autopsy report, keeping the conversation he just had with Detective Jacoby in mind.

The killer grabbed her and stabbed her from behind. Then he laid her body down and sliced her three times across.

No matter how he analyzed it, as Jacoby said, the kill had been fast. No drugs or sedatives had been found in the tox screen. The murderer stalked Banks, knew where she ran, stabbed and killed her without hesitation.

His instinct told him that Anne Banks wasn't his first victim. No one can be that quick, that meticulous, that prepared and able to kill without hesitation on his first kill. Matt supposed adrenaline might play a role, but normally there'd still be some hesitation, a mistake, no matter how small. This monster made none. The victim had no time to scream. No time to fight back. She had no defensive wounds. Even if she had tried to grab him, his slick poncho wouldn't have given her traction.

He called Catherine.

"I don't have anything else for you, Matt." She sounded weary.

He gave her the bare bones about what he learned from Jacoby.

"She worked at the same hospital where Victoria Manners worked?"

"Yes."

"That's good. That's a connection." Catherine now sounded more engaged, almost excited.

"That's not why I called. When you caught the case three years ago, did you search for any possible victims prior to Anne Banks?"

"There were no crimes that fit the MO, and no similar series of murders on those same dates in any previous year—I looked back fifteen years, not just in three year intervals."

"I'm looking at Anne Banks's autopsy report and the crime scene photos. He didn't hesitate."

"You're thinking she wasn't the first victim. It's certainly possible he killed before, but there would be another pattern. He is meticulous in the details."

"What do you mean another pattern?"

"Anne Banks was the first victim killed on March 3 in this manner. If he killed before...well, I'm making a leap here, but he prefers knives, I don't think he would deviate from his choice of weapon. Still, he may not have created this pattern until Banks."

"Such as he may have been practicing, leading up to this method."

"Possibly."

"Could he have gone from animal slayings to human and not hesitate?"

"Hmm."

"That's noncommittal."

"I don't have enough information. It's easy to say he started by killing animals, but not all serial murderers start that way. And it is a big jump from animals to people. I will say this—I'm fairly confident that he is motivated to kill for a specific reason. He's not a thrill seeker—meaning, he didn't set out to kill merely because it excited him. If that were the case, we'd see more violence to the bodies, less methodical precision, more time playing and cutting. It's almost—well, he's doing a job he thinks is necessary as quickly as he can."

Matt mulled that over. Quick, methodical, a duty. Duty... An obligation maybe.

"Anything else?" Catherine asked.

"I think it's possible Banks may have recognized him but didn't see him as a threat. She was with her baby. If he was a stranger, wouldn't she have screamed?" Matt said.

"I've always said that he would blend in, appear average and nonthreatening."

"I'm going to talk to her best friend," he said. "They worked together at Spokane General. I'm hoping she'll give me a path to follow."

"I'll look into unsolved homicides on the West Coast," Catherine said.

He heard her typing, and she said more to herself than to Matt, "Knife, double-sided blade, gutting or stabbing."

"What are you thinking?" Matt asked. "A lot of unsolved cases are going to pop."

"Not as many as you think, not with a knife. And I'm limiting the window. It could be he started with another type of vendetta, or he wanted to simply practice. I can't say—but I think you're right—based on the evidence, I don't think that Anne Banks was the first person he killed. But still, she was important to him. She may have been the first person he killed for a specific reason and her death initiated this pattern."

"I'd like you to give my team a profile this afternoon. I also need something for the press."

"You can't quote me."

"I won't—you know me better than that. But the press is all over this. Someone at SPD talked, most likely the chief himself. I need to calm the waters."

"I understand, but I'm piecemealing this. Send

me everything you've learned about Banks. Let me know after you talk to her friend if you learn anything important. I guarantee, the killer targeted her as some sort of retribution. Punishment. I haven't quite figured out the motive, but it's personal."

"And the others?"

"Possibly. But Anne Banks will link directly to him in some way, while the others may be surrogates."

"Did you get my email about Quinn's theory on how the killer moved about?"

"Quinn?"

"Detective Kara Quinn. The LAPD cop on vacation who's been helping us."

"Right. I saw it, didn't connect the name. It's entirely plausible, though it seems extravagant for his purposes. Is there something else about that property that could be important to the killer? You might want to run a property check going back at least thirty years. I'm sure he picked it for a reason. Like the victims, it might seem random, but to him, it's not."

She didn't say anything else. Matt said, "And?"

"And what?"

"I heard you thinking."

"I'm wondering why Liberty Lake. The other locations—Portland, Missoula—the victims had a connection to the town. They either worked or lived there. Victoria Manners has no connection to Liberty Lake—she lived in Spokane and worked in Spokane, correct?"

"Liberty Lake is a suburb."

"The killer had to transport her twenty miles. The

other six victims were killed either at their home, at their work, or a location between the two. Manners is her own outlier, just like Anne Banks. He picked Liberty Lake for a reason. Unless she has a connection to the place, he picked it specifically for her murder. Why?"

Matt didn't have an answer. But he felt closer to finding it now.

16

Liberty Lake
12:05 p.m.

"I'm hungry," Andy said. "Gracie owns a sandwich shop on the other side of the lake—let's get a bite."

Kara hadn't thought much about food since the scone this morning—and they were nearly done with their side of the lake.

"Thirty minutes and we'll be through," she said. "Then it's my treat."

"Gracie is my fiancée. She doesn't charge me."

Kara had guessed that, and sometimes Andy's deceptively simple manner threw her, but she liked him.

Andy pulled over at the end of a cul-de-sac high off the main lake road. There were three houses here, all with steep drives and framed by trees. "I'll call her and tell her we'll be late—she knows I take my lunch at twelve-thirty, and she'll worry, what with everything that's been going on."

"I'll talk to the people on the right—these are all occupants, right?"

"Yeah—full-time residents. I don't come up here much, but I think they're all working folks in Spokane. Don't know that I've met them."

Andy had previously met nearly everyone they'd spoken to this morning, which was both charming and time-consuming. No one would call this cop Speedy, but he was thorough and there was no doubt in her mind that if anyone saw anything remotely suspicious that they'd call Andy immediately.

Completely different than being a cop in LA where the only people Kara recognized were those she'd arrested twice.

No one responded at the first house, and Kara went up to the middle house. The stairs were exercise in itself—she certainly wouldn't have to run or go to the gym today. She and Andy had done plenty of walking.

Kara heard two dogs bark as soon as she knocked, then the squealing of young kids. From the porch, she couldn't see the two neighbors on either side, but there was an amazing view of the lake below.

A happily frazzled woman answered the door. She didn't look old enough to have kids. Two labs—one black, one yellow—tried to escape and she held them each back. Two kids who looked identical except for a six-inch height difference ran behind their mom, chasing a third kid who couldn't be much older. Three kids under five? Kara would shoot herself.

"Boys! Leave your sister alone for five minutes, okay?"

The woman stepped out, pushed the dogs back

through the doorway, and closed the door. "Six months," she said.

"Excuse me?"

"Six months and the triplets start kindergarten." She looked at her FitBit. "Five months, twenty-six days. What can I help you with?"

Kara was still hung up on *triplets.* She'd definitely shoot herself. Or never have sex again.

"I'm Detective Kara Quinn assisting the Liberty Lake police department on the—"

"Kara?"

Kara generally remembered people—99 percent of the time—but she didn't recognize this woman. "Do I know you?"

"My God! I haven't seen you in *years.* Your grandmother told me you're a big cop down in Los Angeles."

Kara ran through everyone she'd known in high school—Central Valley High School served the Spokane Valley, mostly the areas east of Spokane, including Liberty Lake. It was a large school and Kara hadn't been particularly social.

"Ranie Anderson. Used to be Woods. Thank *God* I married someone with a normal last name. I still haven't forgiven my parents."

Ranie Woods. The name…

"Your hair used to be blond. And you didn't wear glasses."

"I used to bleach my hair to within an inch of its life and contacts because, you know, glasses were for nerds." She rolled her eyes, then smiled and adjusted her stylish frames. "Glad I grew out of that. I met Charlie in college—UW, in Seattle. He's from Tacoma. We settled here after graduation. I run into your grandmother at the store all the time—I didn't know you were back!"

"I'm just on vacation."

"Vacation? Your grandmother didn't mention."

Good, Kara thought, because she didn't like anyone knowing her business, and Em didn't know the meaning of the word *private.* Which was the primary reason Kara never talked to her about her work.

Kara motioned toward Andy's truck at the base of her driveway. "I'm helping Detective Knolls with his case—we're talking to everyone who lives around the lake about whether they saw something suspicious on March 2 or 3."

"Poor woman! I read about it in the paper. The FBI is working on it."

"Yeah, they're all over the place," Kara said. "So March 2—a Tuesday." She didn't need the small talk, she needed information.

"Right. I was home all day. I'm going stir-crazy—Maddie's been sick for over a week—she's better now, so we're going hiking tomorrow—supposed to be a beautiful day." She froze. "Unless we shouldn't go out. Should we stay inside? Is the killer still at large? The newspaper said he killed nurses and cops. Charlie is a civil engineer."

"Go out, have fun. Don't let the papers freak you out. Where's Charlie now?"

"He works for the county—they had some pipe issues near the border—I don't know exactly what he's doing out there. Probably drinking coffee and getting away from the little monsters. Just had an idea—maybe I'll have my mom come over and watch the trips and I'll make Charlie take me to a nice dinner tonight." She nodded at herself.

Kara still only vaguely remembered Ranie Woods—they had been in the same grade, but Kara didn't think they had any classes together. Kara had straight As, but stayed out of the advanced classes Ranie was in because she never planned to go to college. She wanted to keep a low profile because she didn't trust that her mother or father wouldn't come back and pick her up just as easily as her mom dumped her here. She was surprised Ranie remembered her—again, low profile. Blend in.

"Did you hear or see anyone on an ATV Tuesday or Wednesday?" Kara asked again. She glanced over her shoulder. Andy was approaching the third house on the cul-de-sac.

"I don't—well, yeah, you know what? Early Tuesday morning the dogs started barking. Like before five—before Charlie has to get up for work, so it pissed him off. We thought it was deer or fox—but I heard what I thought was a truck. I couldn't go back to sleep—stupid, I know. I made coffee and told the dogs to knock it off. It sounded like a truck behind the house—which wouldn't be possible because there's no road back there—it's all forest. But with the echoes and stuff, it could have been on the road."

"Before five in the morning you heard what sounded like a truck. Could it have been an ATV behind your house?"

"Yeah. That's possible."

"Are there any trails back there?"

"Lots—you know the area."

Kara didn't. She'd lived in Liberty Lake for only three years and couldn't wait to get out. She wasn't much for exploring the mountains. The path around the lake? Sure, that was fun, but hiking? Never.

"Thanks for your help, Ranie."

"There's a few of us from high school who've settled in the Spokane Valley—we get together every Thursday for coffee, and once a month for drinks. You should join us while you're here—catch up with everyone."

Kara almost said *Why? I barely know you, I didn't socialize with you, I didn't socialize with anyone.*

But she smiled warmly. "Thanks, Ranie—I'm not going to be here long, but I'll see."

The woman brightened. "Great! I'd better check on my rug rats—you'd be amazed at how much trouble three kids can get into in five minutes."

Kara laughed, waved her goodbye, and thought *no way in hell am I having three kids.* She didn't even want one. How could she go out and do her job, risk her life every day, if she had a kid who depended on her for everything? No, thank you. She didn't want that responsibility.

Andy was already back at his Bronco. "No one home. Who lives there?" he asked.

"Someone who remembered me from high school. Ranie Anderson, nee Woods."

"Woods—I know the family. She must have been your age, a few years younger than me."

"She may have heard an ATV early Tuesday

morning—that would be March 2. Around 5:00 a.m. Her dogs barked, woke her up. Are these trails wide enough for an ATV? Though, a trail might not be necessary—this part of the mountain isn't too steep."

Andy pulled a map out of his visor and unfolded it. Found the street they were on, then figured out the most likely trail the ATV would have traveled. "Well I'll be damned."

Kara was trying to read the map upside down. "What?"

Andy took a pencil from his pocket. "You found Manners here." He made a small X. "And this is the Anderson house." He made another X. "This trail—" he ran his pencil lightly along a path on the map "—goes directly down to the lake. It has to cross the road here, but at that time of morning or night, no one would have seen him."

"Wouldn't more people have heard the ATV?"

"Possibly. But except for this little road, he wouldn't be close to any other residences."

"Where does it end?"

"It goes all around the lake, but it's steeper in some places. For hiking more than running or biking. But—" Andy studied the map, then circled an area. "Here's a narrow trail that heads back down to the bike trail you were running along. And here…and here…he could have parked a car."

"Would someone have been suspicious?"

"Not really. Remember, half these people don't live here year-round, so they're not going to know what's familiar, and the people who do live here year-round, they're used to strange cars coming and going because of the rentals, and half the people have ATVs. I had one since I was a kid."

"Let's check it out."

"You think the ATV was there?"

"I do. How far a walk to the closest bus stop?"

Andy looked. "Four, almost five miles. It's half the bike path, plus a hundred yards or so. First stop is 6:20 a.m. for the commuters—the buses stop there every forty minutes until sunset."

"Gives him plenty of time to walk to the stop and blend in."

"I hear doubt in your voice."

"I don't think he took a bus. Bus drivers have set routes, know the regulars. A stranger in a small area like this? Early in the morning? He'd stand out."

"Wouldn't a taxi also notice a stranger?"

"Not the same way—but taxis tend to keep better records."

Five minutes later, Andy pulled over to a small parking area on the south side of the lake. "Not here," he said as he drove slowly through it.

"It is. Somewhere nearby." She felt it in her bones, and she always trusted her instincts.

He glanced at her. "We can come back with a search team."

"Leave me here, have lunch with your girl, and pick me up in an hour."

Andy shook his head and parked on the far side of the lot. "No solos. We have time."

"If he parked here," Kara said, "he could drive the ATV along the bike trail… Shit, Andy, her body was found less than a mile from here."

There were no cars parked here, but it wasn't exactly lake activity weather, and it was after noon on a Friday. By tomorrow, dedicated outdoors people would be on the lake fishing, hiking, having a picnic. During their canvass, they'd passed a few bikers, but the kids were all in school. Those who drove to the lake to hike parked at the main entrance, closer to the highway. If Kara wanted to park somewhere and not be seen, she'd do it here.

"What's the closest vacant cabin?"

He looked at his list. "We'd have to drive—oh, wait, we *can* walk. The mountain trail would go right by it."

They only had to hike fifty yards from the turnout before they reached the cabin from behind.

And there it was. An ATV, covered with a canvas tarp.

"Call the crime techs," Kara said.

"We should verify it's the missing ATV."

There was no doubt in Kara's mind that it was. Though time and weather had disappeared discernible tire treads, this was it. She felt it in her gut. Maybe she *should* have been a homicide detective.

Andy pulled out latex gloves and slipped them on. He walked around the ATV, pulled back the canvas from the front, and looked at the small license.

"You're right, Kara, this is it. I'll call it in."

17

Spokane
12:45 p.m.

Matt ended the call. Andy and Kara had found the ATV—he really didn't think they'd do it so fast, but he was pleased. Jim Esteban was hitching a ride with the prickly crime scene tech, so his own person was out there, and Michael Harris was still at the lake, unreachable. Matt hoped he was right and the weapon could be recovered, because it would be one more piece to their puzzle. But right now he was focused on Olivia Gunderson and what she might know about Anne Banks.

Anne's friend still worked at Spokane General and was on duty, but as soon as Matt said he was with the FBI and investigating both the Anne Banks and Victoria Manners homicides, she got someone to cover for her and met Matt in a private office.

Olivia was the same age Anne would have been—forty-three. She was tall and willowy, with a short haircut and no-nonsense attitude.

"I was really upset that the newspapers mentioned

Anne this morning—I'm just glad it was here and not in Portland, where Craig could read it. Her murder destroyed him. He's never been the same."

"I spoke to the detective in charge of Anne's case, and he gave me your name. He also confirmed that Anne had worked here prior to moving to Portland."

"Yes. Is that important?"

"It may be. Did you work here at the hospital with her?"

"Yes—we went to nursing school together. Shared an apartment until she moved to Portland. She was my best friend." Her voice cracked, then she rubbed her eyes. Matt let her collect herself, didn't push her.

A moment later, Olivia took a deep breath and continued. "We were hired right after graduation. I did a rotation of several floors before settling on neonatal, and I went back for advanced training. Anne always wanted to work in the emergency room—she didn't like to be bored..." Her voice trailed off as nostalgia hit her again. "I almost moved to Portland with her, but I got a promotion here right before Craig proposed, and my family is all in the Spokane Valley. And she and Craig needed time to be newlyweds. But we talked nearly every day. I was there when each of her kids was born. I still miss her. I was engaged when she was killed—we were planning my wedding together." She looked down at her wedding band. It was simple, Matt noted, like the woman sitting in front of him.

Matt had let Olivia talk freely to make her comfortable sharing with him. But now he needed to focus her.

"Olivia, I know this is hard for you, but I need you to dig deep. You've worked with law enforcement before, right? In your capacity as a nurse?"

"Of course."

"So you know that sometimes, we don't have all the information we need about the victims. I'm still in the investigation stage. You heard about Victoria Manners and how she was killed."

"I saw her picture in the paper. Read the article. It was awful."

"Did you know her?"

"No. We have hundreds of nurses. I know everyone in my department, a few others, but I'd never met her. She was a temporary employee, right?"

"Yes, a trauma nurse with a staffing company. I'm going to be blunt with you, Olivia," Matt said. "We don't have a suspect. We're using every resource at our disposal to identify and stop this killer. Victoria had been here for three weeks, and we have reason to believe the killer targeted her because she worked here, specifically, in the emergency room."

"Oh God—do I need to warn the staff?"

"No—the killer has a pattern. The first victim in each city is a nurse."

"But Anne wasn't a nurse anymore!"

Matt didn't have to say anything before Olivia figured it out on her own. "You think it's someone who knew Anne when she worked here? Why? Everyone loved Anne."

"Could be a staff member—former staff member—or a patient. Or someone who gave her undue attention. We've gone through police records and

Anne never took out a restraining order against anyone. But you were her best friend. Did she ever think she was being followed?"

"No—not like that."

"Like what?"

"Well, like a stalker."

"It could be anything—even just a feeling."

"I can't think of anything—we did everything together. Worked, had the apartment, we both loved cross-country skiing. She wasn't close to her parents and ended up spending more holidays with my family than hers."

"Okay—we'll come back to that. I'm fishing around here, but we think the killer knew Anne when she was a nurse. Did she have any male friends? Or an ex-boyfriend?"

"Ex-boyfriend? Who'd wait so long to kill her? In front of her b-baby?" Her voice cracked and she cleared her throat. "The guy she dated before Craig was kind of a jerk. He was a doctor, and I told Olivia not to date him, but he was really cute and did the whole knight-in-shining-armor shtick. He cheated on her, broke her heart. Jason Tragger. Still single, still dating nurses—but in Seattle."

It didn't fit, not Catherine's profile, but Matt made a note. "What kind of doctor?"

"Oncologist. Specializes in childhood leukemia. I mean, he's a jerk to his girlfriends because he can't keep it in his pants, but he's a really great doctor."

"How long did they date?"

"Six or seven months. Then she didn't see anyone until Craig rolled into the ER. He looked like death warmed over, but she said he had a sparkle in his eye and she knew he was the one." She sighed. "They loved each other from the beginning. I mean real, soul mate kind of love. My husband and I were together for years before we talked about marriage, and it's comfortable, you know? I mean, I love him, and we have a great marriage, but it's a comfortable love, like cozy blankets by the fire and a dog at your feet. When Craig looked at Anne, he saw nothing but Anne. From the minute they met until the day she died. It's been six years but he'll never remarry. It would be romantic if it weren't so damn sad."

"What about problems at work? Someone who didn't like her, who thought she did a poor job, or maybe too good of a job and outshone them?"

She looked confused. "That was so long ago. I really can't remember anything specific. We rarely worked together, but if there was something that bothered her she would have told me. And why would someone kill Anne because of something she may have done or said? Or all those other people the newspaper mentioned?"

"We don't know. Between you and me, we think each victim may have slighted the killer in some way, very possibly unintentionally. Like for example, if you cut someone off on the road but don't notice and you get a horn in your ear. Or you get a promotion when someone else thought they should have gotten it. It could be completely innocuous, but something that festered in a person with a psychopathy."

"I see what you're getting at," she said, though

she sounded confused, "but Anne was a great nurse. Patients loved her. Doctors loved her."

"But the emergency room—she probably dealt with tragedy. Some people don't take tragedy well."

"Like losing a patient?"

"Sure."

"I couldn't possibly remember every patient she lost. She worked in the emergency room—there were people who were dead when they came in, or already dying. It can get crazy down there."

"What about her immediate supervisor."

"She had several during the time she was here. Administration should be able to help you there."

Matt already had Ryder working with administration. "Olivia, you may remember something after I leave—and so I need you to call me, even if you think it's small. Anything about the time that Anne worked here that gave you pause, or that she mentioned that bothered or disturbed her in any way. It may be a colleague, a patient, a patient's family—anything." He handed her his card and wrote his cell number on the back.

"I will." She stared at the card. "So the newspaper was right—Anne was killed by a serial killer."

"Yes, that part they got correct. But much of what they wrote was exaggerated. I can tell you this—we have a team dedicated to finding this killer and giving Anne and the other victims justice."

"Is it true a teacher might die tomorrow?"

"Not if I can help it."

Matt was still angry that the press had so much information.

"I hope you find him, Agent Costa."

So do I.

Matt had a missed call from Michael and hit redial. "News?"

"Big news. The jackpot. I found it."

Michael sounded winded but excited.

"You found the knife?"

"Yes. I found the knife approximately sixty feet from the shore. Jim and Miles from the crime lab are here—they wanted to package the evidence specifically. It's not the knife they're interested in."

"You lost me, Harris."

"Shit, sorry—I got distracted. Thirty-five feet from the shore, I found a large plastic bag full of clothes. The bag had been deliberately cut—likely by a knife—so water could get in. Jim figures the killer was disposing of the clothes he wore, said no other set of clothing has been found at the previous crime scenes, so this could potentially be huge."

"He's right. But it's wet—what can they get from it?"

"That's why Jim rushed up here. They want to contain the clothes and bag in sterile conditions, immediately start the drying process—which is going to take time. He said even with water contamination if there's a lot of blood, he'll be able to find some and match it to the victim. And possibly the killer if he somehow nicked himself through his gloves. But there could be other evidence—like a receipt or a note or credit statement. Depending on the ink and paper, they might be able to read it if it's dried properly. Maybe even hair wrapped around a button. We'll at a minimum get the clothing sizes, brands. Anything that can narrow the suspect. Hell, he could have left his driver's license in the bag. Remember the idiot in New York who dropped his wallet next to his victim?"

Matt wasn't holding out hope that this killer made that big of a mistake, but he'd take the smallest lead they could get. "All good. I need you back here before the press briefing. But first, we have a conference call with Catherine, then we're going to SPD early. I want you to make the Public Information Officer your best friend while I make sure Maddox took care of the leak."

"Wish I could watch that."

Matt wasn't in the mood. "Anything else?"

"No. I'll hop a ride back with Torino—I made her my best friend, too, considering you pissed her off yesterday."

"Maybe you can be the fucking team diplomat," Matt mumbled and hung up.

Matt went back to the operations room in the hotel, which was only ten minutes from the hospital. Ryder was juggling two calls and typing. The kid was solid, and not for the first time Matt was glad he'd brought him on board. He might not have FBI experience, but Matt suspected that someone with more experience and a set way of doing things wouldn't be able to adapt well to a fast-paced environment that required multitasking, from mundane chores—like running background checks and setting up the war room—to high-tech processing and information analysis. Ryder had been required to jump from task to task without a break, and learning to prioritize was difficult for the best of agents. Ryder seemed to have an intuitive grasp of what was most important and work from there. Matt barely had to tell him how to do his job. They'd worked together for a month at national headquarters, and already Matt found him indispensable.

Matt sent Tony an updated report, sent Catherine the information on the knife and clothing, then reiterated that he wanted her to brief his team before the press conference. She responded that she would be available at two-thirty Pacific time. Less than an hour from now. He sent Jim a message and asked if he could be here at two-thirty, or be somewhere where Ryder could loop him in—he wanted Jim's impression as well as Michael's.

As soon as Ryder got off his call, Matt said, "We need to set up a Skype call with Catherine at two-thirty, then Michael and I are going to SPD to talk to the chief. Press conference is at four. I'm not happy about it, but there's not a damn thing I can do at this point except mitigate the damage." And maybe—just maybe—save someone. He looked at his watch. Damn, damn, damn! He didn't have enough time. He didn't want another victim dead, and he didn't want to think about what would come next.

Ryder made a note, then said, "Lawsuits with the hospital that went to trial are public—I'm running a program to pull out all lawsuits during those seven years plus the year after Anne Banks left where either Banks or the emergency room was named."

"You can do that?"

"I had a guy in the cybercrime unit at headquarters help me write the algorithm," he said.

"Great. But I sense a problem."

"Lawsuits that are settled or dropped for lack of standing aren't in the database. If a lawsuit was filed and dismissed, we need to pull it from another field, and often the names of the defendants—such as if Anne Banks was named as a defendant—are redacted because the suit was determined to be without merit."

This was why Matt never once considered being a lawyer. Shit like this would drive him insane.

"I've reached out to the legal department at the hospital and they claim their lawyers are figuring out what they can give us," Ryder continued, "but I don't think they'll share anything. I asked Tony to expedite a warrant for any complaints against Anne Banks or the emergency room during those years."

"Outstanding," Matt said. His phone rang. It was Andy Knolls. Matt answered. "Good job on the ATV."

"Credit Kara, not me. We're heading to Spokane—but we have time before the press conference. When is it scheduled?"

"Four—swing by the hotel first." He could use as many people as possible right now."

"Almost there."

"Room 310."

Matt used the few minutes he had to update the whiteboard with information about Anne Banks and how she connected to Spokane. But she *didn't* connect to Liberty Lake. Just like Victoria Manners.

So why Liberty Lake? Why not kill her in Newman Lake where he left her car? Why not kill her any number of places in Spokane? There were parks, lakes, a river that went through town, wide-open spaces, mountains, flatlands—there was a specific reason the killer chose that spot. Matt had to figure it out.

Matt pulled out the maps of Portland and Missoula where he had already marked the locations where the bodies were found. All within the city limits, but not clustered together. He stared, willing the answers to come to him, but he didn't even know the right questions.

A knock on the door interrupted his thoughts. Ryder jumped up and let Andy and Kara in. Andy looked around. "You could have used my office. We have room."

"I appreciate it," Matt said, "and we may need to expand there, but we're still on a learning curve—and a time crunch. It helps to have my room right there." He jerked a finger toward the adjoining door. Plus, at the time Ryder set this up they didn't know how cooperative the local police would be. The jury was still out on Chief Dunn, who Matt had yet to meet but had been quoted in that damn newspaper article.

To Ryder he said, "Find out Harris's ETA."

To Kara he said, "You were right."

"I usually am," she said, then winked. "You mean about the lake or the ATV?"

"ATV?" Matt questioned.

Andy said, "That was all Kara. I was ready to go to lunch, but she had a hunch and it paid off."

"I was thinking about the lake—they found the knife and the clothes."

"What does it mean?" Kara said. "Other than he knows how to destroy evidence."

"My forensics expert thinks they might get something, even with the clothes saturated."

"Jim, right?" Kara said. "I liked him. Sort of had that gruff but smart Colombo thing going for him."

"He got Miles on board right quick," Andy said. "Good idea putting them together, Matt."

"I had a hunch—and not any choice. We need as many forensic people as we can get in a fast-moving case like this, plus access to the Spokane lab."

Ryder said, "Agent Harris is five minutes out."

"Get Jim and Miles on Skype first, then dial-in Dr. Jones. By the time we get it all working, Michael will be here."

Kara was inspecting the whiteboard where he had the seven victims laid out. "The first victim is a nurse, too?"

"Not only that, but she worked for seven years in the same hospital where Victoria Manners was working when she was abducted."

"No coincidence there."

Matt snapped his fingers. "Ryder—as soon as you can, send photos of each victim—our public photos—to Maddox. I want to get them on air and in the paper. Locally for certain, as well as the other jurisdictions if we can swing it. If we can shake our killer up a bit, I'm all for that. And maybe someone local will recognize the other victims. From college, work, fucking childhood best friend, whatever we can get will help."

"Any word on the killer's means of transportation from Liberty Lake on March 2?" Andy asked. "If we assume that he left his own vehicle there to use after he killed Manners, then he would have to get to Spokane another way before then."

"We're still working on it," Matt said with a glance at Ryder.

Ryder said, "We know he didn't take a bus, we're working on the taxis—Yellow Cab and private."

"We expanded it to the morning of March 3 as well," Matt said, "in case he drove his car to Spokane after stashing the ATV and needed to get back after the murder. But most people would remember picking up a lone guy the same day as a body was found. My guess is that he had his own vehicle hidden at Liberty Lake and used public transportation until he grabbed Manners and had access to her car."

"Maybe he's staying in Liberty Lake," Kara said. "He could have walked to his place."

Matt stared at her. "I hadn't thought of that."

"He would still need to get to Spokane to grab the nurse," Kara continued.

"I can reach out to the property management companies and ask for any lone men who are renting property this month," Andy suggested.

"Do it. I'm not certain he's that close, but it would explain why he picked the lake to leave the body."

Michael walked in and Matt introduced him to Kara and Andy.

"We met at the lake," Michael said.

Ryder said, "I have Dr. Catherine Jones, Mr. Jim Esteban and Mr. Miles Jordan all ready."

"Let's go," Matt said.

Ryder adjusted the largest monitor so that Catherine was the main focus and Jim and Miles were a smaller box in the corner of the screen.

"Catherine, can you hear me?" Matt asked.

"Yes."

"Everyone, Dr. Catherine Jones, a forensic psychiatrist with the FBI's Behavioral Analysis Unit. She wrote the first profile of the Triple Killer three years ago with minimal information. It took months before we connected all six murders to the same killer. But we did, thanks to Catherine." Matt introduced everyone to Catherine, and then said, "Before you begin, Catherine, I wanted to ask Jim about the evidence found at the lake today."

Jim said, "We found a knife that could possibly be the murder weapon based on the size and type. We also found a large plastic bag of clothing, intentionally saturated with water. Miles and I have already started drying the clothing in a sterile, controlled environment and if there is any remaining evidence, we'll find it. However, the biggest find was the gloves."

"Were they with the clothing?" Catherine asked.

"No—they were in a smaller plastic bag and weighed down with a rock. The lake water cleaned them somewhat, and the killer may have assumed if we found them they would be completely devoid of evidence. But there was still a substantial amount of blood on the gloves. There's no real current in the lake—no recent storms. No flowing water. Over time, the evidence would have been destroyed, but we found it sixty hours after he disposed of it. The Spokane lab has a pretty good setup—we're going to focus on processing the gloves at this point while we wait for the clothes to dry. If there is any physical evidence from them, we'll find it. We're also processing Manners' car—her missing shoe was found in the trunk. He may not have noticed—or didn't care—that it had fallen off. Plus, I just received word back from the ME that he reviewed all the autopsy records that you sent over, Costa, and said that preliminarily, all the wounds are consistent and most likely created by the same person. The outlier is Anne Banks—her autopsy results are different enough that he wouldn't commit."

"Great news," Matt said. "None of the other crime scenes have collected so much evidence in such a short time."

"True," Catherine concurred.

"Regarding Banks—we already have a theory as to why her stabbing is slightly different. The killer cut her initially from behind when he grabbed her."

Jim nodded. "That's consistent with the report."

Matt continued. "I asked Catherine to give you all a rundown on the person we're looking for—a basic profile. I've already filled her in on the new information about Anne Banks, the first victim, and her connection to not only Spokane, but Spokane General, where Victoria Manners worked."

Catherine said, "The information I received three years ago was incomplete. I've been going through everything that we have from then and now, and we still have some big holes, though the information about Anne Banks is extremely valuable." She cleared her throat and picked up a coffee mug, took a sip. "I've spent last night and today reviewing all the files I do have and confirming information. I'll put that together in a formal report and send it to you, Matt, but to get you started I'll go through the problems and tell you where we are."

Catherine gave a rundown on information they already knew about the first six victims and how she connected them, but as she spoke it became clear that she was leading them toward the pattern. Nurse. Educator. Cop. They hadn't seen it before because they didn't have the background on Anne Banks, and had only begun to suspect it yesterday—but now it was clear.

She detailed the type of personality they were looking for: high-functioning, intelligent, introverted, but not openly antisocial.

"He waits an unusually long time between his triple murders," Catherine said. "We call this a cooling-off period, but it's more than that for him. He's methodical, disciplined, extremely organized. We have always assumed that his victims are random, and they *appear* to be random, but it's important to understand that they are *not* random, not to the killer. He has a specific motive for choosing his victims. It is irrelevant that they are different genders, different ages, different races. This has bothered me for some time, because serial murderers generally have a defined victim pool. Prostitutes, for example. Or homeless men. Or young blonde women. And generally, serial murderers will both build up to murder and have an identifiable tipping point, something specific that set them off, that made them 'snap' for lack of a better word…though they haven't truly mentally snapped."

"So he's not crazy," Michael said.

"I can't say with any confidence what his mental state is," Catherine said, sounding more like a lawyer than a doctor. "But I would deduce, even considering that I haven't interviewed him, that he is completely sane."

"Where's his home base?" Kara asked.

Matt glanced at her. He hadn't forgotten she was in the room, but he hadn't expected her to speak up. Why, he didn't know—Kara didn't seem to be a person to keep her mouth closed if she had an opinion or observation.

"I don't understand the question," Catherine said.

"Well, he killed in three different cities. Does he move to one city, find a place to live, get a job, stalk his victims, kill and leave? Or does he come in for a short time, a month or so, to target his victims, kill them, then go back to wherever he comes from?"

"That's a good question," Catherine said. "I don't have an answer. I will go out on a limb and suggest that he's been in town—if not for the three years since the last murders, at least for a few weeks. He definitely stalks his victims, knows where they're going to be and when they'll be there. To be able to kill seven people so violently, so brazenly, he is confident that they will be alone."

Matt made a note to follow up on rentals, but he didn't think that was going to help—there had to be hundreds, or thousands, and no central database. Still, they could contact property companies for male renters within the last three years.

Jim spoke up. "I think it's relevant that none of the victims fought back, except one of the male victims." He glanced at his notes. "The off-duty cop in Missoula had blunt force trauma to his head, otherwise, no signs of physical violence."

"Sedatives?" Michael asked.

"Nothing has been conclusive so far," Jim said. "But we're rushing the tox screen on Manners and should have results by the end of the day. My guess is it'll be a common sedative, but the dosage he uses is particularly potent leading to an immediate loss of consciousness. Possibly fentanyl, which acts quickly and in high dosages can be deadly. Unfortunately, not all victims were given broad tox screens. We're covering every base with Manners."

"Does that mean he has a medical background?" Matt asked.

When Jim didn't answer, Catherine said, "No—he could learn what he needs on the internet. But how does he get close enough that these people don't consider him a threat? Remember—Anne Banks was running through the park with her infant when she was killed."

"Why March 3?" Kara asked.

Silence fell.

"Well," Catherine said, "that's the million-dollar question. The date is significant to him, and the number three. I keep coming back to March 3. Violence done to him or to someone close to him—someone very close, like a parent or sibling. But this is important—he would have exhibited sociopathic signs as a teenager."

"Isn't that a contradiction?" Jim asked. "If he's a sociopath, would he have that close of a connection to anyone, even as a teen?"

"Yes—sociopaths are not purely those who don't feel normal emotions. Sometimes, they feel too much emotion, and they shut everything down in order to function. I don't think that's this killer—he's too methodical. But that doesn't mean he can't feel for someone he bonded with as a young child."

"If three's important to him," Matt said, "why does he slice each victim exactly four times?"

"Four?" Catherine hesitated. "Oh—I see. I'm looking at only the three horizontal marks, none of which were necessary to achieve death. The vertical cut on each victim is the cause of death—the other three are his personal signature, for lack of a better word. That's the three. The initial cut is to kill. But all this shows that he has complete control—slice the victim down the middle to ensure that they die, then three cuts across the body. Three is key. Three events, three people, three cuts. But I don't know why."

Catherine flipped through papers. "As I said to

you before, Matt, if you have the time and resources to pursue it, it would help to dig deeper on all the victims. But the first victim is *personally* important to the killer. I'm pleased you found so much information about Anne Banks so quickly."

"You lit a fire under my ass," Matt said.

"Hardly necessary since you don't sleep," Catherine replied. It was phrased as a compliment but sounded like a slight.

Matt decided to ignore it. He asked, "Is the Triple Killer disciplined enough to wait that long to enact revenge?"

"Revenge—why do you say that?" Catherine asked.

"Because that's what it feels like. Revenge, punishment for a perceived crime. Justice not done."

"First—yes, he could wait a long time to enact revenge, especially if the trigger occurred when he was a child or young adult. Second, you may be right and this is revenge, but then I would think the victims themselves would be more connected—something we would have already seen, beyond occupation. Likely, it's more the victims are surrogates for someone he wants to kill, but can't. Someone who did him wrong, in his mind."

"So—punishment," Kara said. "Either the person who wronged him or a surrogate. Still reads like revenge any way you slice it."

Catherine didn't say anything, but a tiny twitch in her neck told Matt she wasn't particularly happy with Kara's blunt pronouncement. Probably because it lacked Catherine's class and nuance—though that didn't make it any less true.

Ryder said, "Sir, it's three-fifteen—you need to meet with Chief Packard in fifteen minutes."

Matt needed more. "Anything else, Catherine? Anyone? I'm meeting with the press soon. I need to give them something without tipping our hand."

Silence all around. This wasn't going to help.

"Anyone," Matt said. "We're running out of time."

Catherine spoke first. "Keep tabs on the audience. I guarantee he's following the news on this investigation. Fifty-fifty, he'll show up at a press briefing if he's in the area. Zero chance if it's indoors or sparsely attended. But if there are a lot of people, he may come to watch. If he doesn't, he'll watch it on TV or online or read about it in the paper. He'll want to know everything about what the police are doing, what they've found—and he'll crave more."

Matt glanced at Kara. Out of all of them, she looked the least like a cop.

As if she'd read his mind, she said, "I'll do it."

"Do what?" Catherine asked.

"Work the crowd. Blend in. Assess the audience. I know what you want."

"Thanks," Matt said.

"I have a question," Kara said.

"Ask."

Ryder tapped his watch and pointed at Matt. Matt nodded—he knew they were on the clock, but Kara had insight that had already proven valuable to the investigation.

"What happens if we screw with his pattern?"

"Explain," Catherine said.

"He kills on specific days. What if his intended target is unavailable? Or has a friend over? Or goes out of town? Does he pick another victim? Does he kill the friend? Does his head explode because his pattern is fucked-up?"

Matt hadn't thought of that—he was focused on simply finding and stopping the predator. "What do you think, Catherine?"

"It's an interesting question. I think it depends on whether the individuals he picks are representative of the person he wants to kill—such as if Victoria Manners was chosen *specifically*, or simply chosen because she was a nurse. If he's targeting occupations, then yes, I think he'll find another victim. He may have a backup in mind, or he'll grab someone who fits his criteria. Definitely a greater chance that he'll screw up at that point because it goes against his established plan. But if the victims are personal, then he could have some sort of psychotic breakdown. If he can't complete his pattern, then I can't predict how he'll respond. He'll certainly go after his intended victim, but there could be collateral damage—friends, family, colleagues—or he could change his MO, such as the weapon he uses."

"So we're damned if we do, damned if we don't," Jim said.

"Not necessarily," Catherine said. "If you throw him off his game in any way—take one of his would-be victims off the playing field—he'll react. Until now, he's been driving the train, so to speak. He plans and executes his plan. He is in control. He is acting—the police are reacting. You make him react to something he's not expecting, he'll reveal himself—either intentionally or accidentally. Just be careful, Matt—once his pattern is destroyed, he can and will do anything to achieve his goal."

"Which is?" Kara asked.

"You said it earlier, Matt, that this feels like revenge. Maybe retribution, or punishment for past crimes or perceived crimes. So even if his pattern is interrupted, he's going to continue down the same path. Nurse. Teacher. Cop. Watch yourselves, please."

Matt heard the emotion in Catherine's voice, though she tried to conceal it.

"Matt—be careful with this guy," Catherine reiterated.

"Catherine, I have some ideas on what to say at the briefing, I'll call you while I'm driving."

He nodded for Ryder to disconnect the calls.

"That was enlightening," Andy said.

"Andy," Matt said, "get one of your people to put together a list of every teacher, substitute, principal, or administrator in the Spokane Valley."

Everyone stared at him.

"What? Isn't there a master list somewhere? The state's Department of Ed? The local school boards? Anything?"

"I suppose."

"I don't want to lose someone else. This is the closest we've gotten to this bastard's pattern in advance of his next murder. I want to throw a wrench in his plans. Get the teacher list and everyone you can to start calling with personal warnings. If they don't watch the news, we need to reach them somehow. Door-to-door will take too long."

Matt turned to Kara. "I can tell you're carrying. If you're going to blend, you can't carry. It'll peg you as a cop."

"I promise," she said with a smile, "you won't be able to pick me out of the crowd."

He doubted that.

18

Spokane
3:50 p.m.

Matt sent Michael to track down the public information officer and make her his other best friend while he waited for Chief Packard.

And waited. The press conference was inching closer, and Matt needed Packard on the same page. He was going out on a limb with what he planned to do, but if Catherine was right and the killer would say or do something to reveal himself if his victim were taken away, he had to try.

Because they had next to nothing, and the clock was ticking.

Matt was used to getting the shaft from local law enforcement, but he'd been emboldened and optimistic after the reception he'd received from Andy Knolls and Brian Maddox. Packard reminded him that every department—and every cop—was different.

Fortunately, he had plenty of work to do while he waited. He sent Andy a message:

Can you run property records on that Newman Lake house? Go back as far as you can. Our profiler is wondering if there is something important or special about the house, at least to the killer.

It was ten to four by the time Chief Packard walked up to where Matt waited outside his office. "Sorry to keep you waiting." He shook Matt's hand and motioned for him to join him in his office.

Sorry my ass.

The trappings of the office bordered on ostentatious egotism. Plaques, photo ops, commendations, framed medals. It wasn't the awards per se that bugged Matt, it was the display—lights highlighting the more prestigious awards, pictures of Packard with politicians, including four different presidents in two political parties. No family, no friends, no fishing expeditions or hunting trips. Half a minute and Matt had a profile of the guy. No wonder he petitioned the city council to extend his term. He was nothing without his job. Matt wondered if he'd once been a good cop—hence the commendations—but as he saw his own mortality and retirement looming, he clung too tightly to the past.

Matt might be looking at himself twenty years from now—but that would still be twenty years from now.

"I know you're busy," Matt said, using his most professional and conciliatory tone, "but I need to talk to you before the press briefing about the article in the paper."

"You should have called me directly about the briefing, not gone through Maddox."

Matt was having a difficult time containing his temper. "Sir, we've been working eighteen-hour days since I arrived, and I apologize if I'm not up to speed on your jurisdictional protocols."

"Maddox said you have a statement. I've called in print, radio, and television. There are also two neighborhood watch organizations who are concerned—that's why I was late. I met with the groups. The public should be concerned. They need to be diligent to protect themselves and their families."

"This killer has a very specific agenda. We've been here for two days. We don't have all the information we need, but we have a lot more than we did when he hit in Montana three years ago. Our top profiler briefed my team an hour ago on several key facts, which has led us to finding a connection between the first victim in Portland and the most recent victim, Ms. Manners."

"You had an internal briefing and didn't include me?"

"Sir, with all due respect, you're missing the point here. Someone in your department leaked information to the press without vetting it through me."

"Agent Costa, you are making an unverifiable leap that it was my department that spoke to the press. You've also been working with Detective Knolls and Liberty Lake. And a detective from LA has been riding along with Knolls. You have the FBI all over town, and a not-so-discreet search of the lake. It seems to me that any number of people could have leaked information to the press. Perhaps if you had been more forthcoming from the beginning there wouldn't be this need to play catch-up."

Matt knew it was the chief, the way he averted his eyes, cast blame everywhere but himself. But if Matt called him on it, he would be cut out of all resources and lives were on the line. Swallowing his anger, he said as calmly as possible, "I informed your office as soon as I was assigned this case. My team is newly formed, but we're working day and night to stop this guy."

"Everything goes through me, understood? You want to brief my men, you talk to me. You want to use my crime lab, you talk to me first. I found out secondhand that the head of my lab went to Liberty Lake to process evidence retrieved by your diver."

So that's what it came down to. Power. The chief wanted to be the damn gatekeeper. Where was Maddox and his promise to fix the situation? But if this was the way Matt got what he needed, so be it. "Understood," Matt said. "On one condition—you make it clear to your people that no one talks to the press without consulting me. We have to be careful about what we release."

Packard nodded. "Do you have a statement for this afternoon?"

"Yes. It's a well-crafted statement to prompt both public diligence and let the killer know that we're close."

"Are you close?"

"No." Matt hated to admit that they didn't have a handle on the guy. Knowing the profile was not knowing who this bastard was. "However, we believe that the first victim—Anne Banks—was a personal target. She worked at Spokane General, where Victoria Manners also worked. I have an associate in the audience who is going to watch the crowd. There's one thing I want to keep in-house."

"What?"

"That we found the gloves. My diver found the gloves in a bag weighted down by a rock in a different location from the other evidence. My forensics guy thinks that's the greatest possibility of getting viable DNA from the killer—hair or blood if he nicked himself."

"Very well. I'll lead. This is still my city."

Matt nodded, and hoped he wasn't making a huge mistake. "My profiler suggests that we hold the conference outside, that the killer might show up and stay if the venue is outdoors and he see us."

"Front steps. Give me five minutes and I'll meet you in the lobby."

A dismissal? Matt wondered what Packard planned on doing in those five minutes.

He strode toward the lobby and found Michael chatting with the desk sergeant. When Michael spotted him, he pulled Matt to the corner, where there was some privacy.

"What'd you learn?" Matt asked.

"The PIO is hot," Michael said.

Matt wasn't in the mood. "And that's relevant how?"

"Just a comment. She wouldn't tell me squat, only that she didn't talk to the press at all yesterday, which is odd in and of itself because she's the PIO. She gave them the brush off, trying to get a statement from the chief, so when she saw the paper she was stunned. Doesn't know who leaked the information, but implied the chief is buddies with the crime beat reporter."

"Did you see who was out there?" Matt gestured toward the front steps.

"About forty people, not all press. Two television crews. A couple radios. A group wearing some American flag insignia—looks like an anticrime group."

"Neighborhood watch or something, per Packard. We need a unified message, and more important, I need to control what gets out there. The killer is going to be watching the news, reading the papers, checking the internet. Hell, he might have a Google Alert set up so he gets informed of every damn tidbit as it happens. Did you know there's already a Twitter hashtag? Ryder told me about it. Hashtag Spokane Triple Killer."

"Welcome to the new era of policing."

"It sucks."

"It has its advantages. Maybe the killer is monitoring Twitter. Maybe he'll interact with someone."

"He's been smart—would a smart killer do something that could get him so easily caught?"

"To gloat? Because he knows he's smart so he creates false accounts? To correct the record?" Michael shrugged. "I don't know."

"Hmm. Maybe." He sent an email to Catherine about social media. She'd already confirmed that the killer would be tracking the investigation. How might they be able to use that to their advantage? Then he forwarded the message to Ryder. The kid probably had already thought about tracking social media, he seemed to be up-to-date on modern policing.

Ryder called as he hit Send. He had the public transportation tapes they'd asked for and would be reviewing them while Matt was at the press conference. No dice on the taxis—nothing fitting their profile. Private rides were harder, and Tony was working on that angle from DC. Would the killer be so bold as to take a private taxi all the way to the hospital? Or would he jump around? Walk? Take a combination of public and private transportation? Where was he all day after hiding the ATV at the vacant house?

Matt wrapped up the conversation, confident that if there was anything to find with transportation, Ryder would find it.

He glanced at his watch. It had been more than fifteen minutes since he left Packard, and they were ten minutes late for the scheduled press conference. Where the hell was he?

Matt glanced through his messages. He had a response from the ASAC in LA, Bryce Thornton.

I would like to discuss Detective Quinn with you at your earliest convenience. If she's assisting on one of your cases, you need to know who you're working with.

Matt ignored the message. He couldn't be bothered with interagency bullshit right now, and he'd promised Kara he wouldn't pursue it. It wasn't relevant to his case, and she was helping, and that's all that mattered: finding this killer before someone else died.

A female cop approached with a warm smile for Michael. He reciprocated and touched her arm as she passed by. Great. Matt didn't need a sexual harassment lawsuit when his team was barely out of the gate.

"Agent Costa?" the cop said. "I'm Sergeant Diana Jackson, the PIO. Chief Packard is ready. Please follow me."

They followed Jackson around the side of the building to the front steps. As soon as they arrived, Packard stepped to the podium and spoke briefly about the murder of Victoria Manners and detailed that SPD was working closely with Liberty Lake and the Sheriff's department gathering and processing evidence from the crime scene. He wasn't doing bad, and he didn't give away any key details—which was a plus.

While the chief was talking, Matt got a text from Jim that they had confirmed that Manners had been drugged with an opioid.

Fentanyl is an opioid and we're testing now for that and a broad range of narcotics. It's likely a compound. Once I get the results, we can ask Portland and Missoula to test their victims—if they properly collected samples of blood, tissue, etc. I also asked the ME to go over the body again looking for an injection site. If small, it may not be obvious.

Fantastic, Matt thought. One more piece to the puzzle, and one he could use in this briefing.

Matt looked out at the crowd. Forty plus people congregated, some tight together near the front, others loosely in the back. He couldn't see Kara. Had she bailed on them? In hiding? What was her game?

Packard then introduced Matt.

Matt presented the timeline of the Triple Killer succinctly, outlining the three murders in Portland then the three murders in Missoula.

"Victoria Manners is the seventh victim of this killer. We believe she was targeted because she was a trauma nurse. We also believe it's not a coincidence that the first victim—Anne Banks—had been a trauma nurse also at Spokane General before leaving to raise her family in Portland, and that the fourth victim, Sophia Kwan, was also a trauma nurse.

"At this point, we have a working theory that I'm ready to share with the public in order to promote public safety and vigilance. This killer kills in threes in three different cities. Three victims in Portland. Three victims in Missoula. But we want to stop him here, in Spokane. We believe he chooses his victims at random, though with a clear methodology. The first victim in his chosen city is a nurse. The second victim is an educator. The third victim is in law enforcement."

He let that sink in. He looked out into the crowd and still didn't spot Kara.

Matt continued. "If you are a teacher, an administrator, a college professor, be diligent over the next few days. Do not leave work alone. If possible don't go out alone, and if you have friends or out-of-town family you can stay with for the weekend, all the better. Change your routine. If you jog every morning at 6:00 a.m., jog at eight. And change your route.

"To date, this killer has chosen victims who were alone and isolated. Driving on a quiet road late at night. Living alone in a remote home. Leaving work by themselves after dark. I do not want to cause alarm or panic. I *do*, however, want everyone to be aware of their surroundings."

He focused on what Catherine believed would set the killer off. Matt was always nervous about taunting a killer, but this time he agreed with Catherine—it would likely cause him to make a mistake. Catherine had told him privately, *"The killer believes he's in charge, that he is smarter than the police. Talk about how weak he is. How inferior. Make him seem like a brute, a bully, but powerless. The more we can get under his skin, the greater chance he'll slip up."*

"The killer targets victims who are alone because he is a coward," Matt said. "He drugs his innocent victims—telling us that he's physically weak and unable to overpower most of his victims."

True, they only had confirmation on Manners, but it reasoned that if he drugged Manners, he drugged the other victims—outside of Anne Banks, whom they knew he had killed quickly. The press didn't need to know all the details.

"He kills his victims when they're unconscious and unable to fight back," Matt said, "again confirming that he is weak and believes that he is powerless.

"We also believe that his first victim knew him—that she may have recognized him, or would have if given the opportunity. He killed her in front of her infant son, leaving the child in a stroller only feet from his dead mother. He's cruel, without concern for others, and he will not stop until we stop him.

"My team will stop him. The FBI has devoted people and resources to ensure this cowardly killer is caught and prosecuted to the fullest extent of the law. We have hit the ground running because Ms. Manners' body was found quickly, only hours after she was so brutally murdered. We've found more evidence at this crime scene than at all the other crime scenes combined. We've found the knife used to stab her, the clothes the killer wore when he killed her, and the vehicle used to transport the victim to Liberty Lake. My top forensic criminalist is working closely with experts at the Spokane crime lab, and together, we'll process the evidence quickly and efficiently, with the goal of apprehending this killer before he strikes again."

19

Spokane
4:20 p.m.

Kara only half listened to the cops as they did their talk. She was watching the crowd. She'd done this dozens of times in a variety of circumstances, looking for small signs that someone was *off.* That someone was just a bit too interested or a bit too angry.

She started by analyzing the press. If she were a bad guy who wanted to check on the progress of a criminal investigation, she'd take on the role of someone expected to be in attendance. Press was logical. But each person had the reporter vibe. Some had a cameraman or another person carrying equipment. The dress, the mannerisms—she dismissed everyone in the press pool within minutes.

She looked at the larger group of anticrime activists, who stood on the grassy area outside the police department, or next to the narrow road. She sidled up to a young woman carrying a toddler on her back in one of those kid backpack things. No chance she was the killer, so Kara asked her about their group.

There were seven, all wearing the same American Flag shirt. The mom knew all of them, and would have chattered on the entire conference if Kara didn't get away from her.

Several too old. A lone teenager holding a skateboard—much like the skateboard Kara had tucked under her arm—looking more amused than anything. That kid was up to something, but he wasn't the killer, so Kara put him in the back of her mind. Two lone men. She photographed them discreetly. They were the right age—thirties—and looked normal in every way. One of them approached the woman with the baby and kissed her—okay, husband, anticrime group, dressed like a businessman. The other walked away to the side. She approached, stood three feet behind him, and half listened to the speech while watching him.

He was a possible. Yet he wasn't trying to hide his identity. He was dressed in business casual, didn't strike her as off. But some killers were crafty, and just because her instincts were better than most didn't mean that they were foolproof.

Then he turned and looked right at her. His eyes were moist. "Excuse me," he mumbled.

"Are you okay?" she asked.

He shook his head. "I don't know why I came here. I'd hoped for something—I don't know."

"You knew Victoria Manners."

He nodded. "I run the staffing agency she worked at. I was hoping this press conference was going to tell us who killed her—but it's nothing that wasn't in the paper. I need to go."

She let him leave. Verifying his story would be easy enough, and she had a picture of him, but she didn't doubt him.

No one else fit the profile. She dropped her skateboard and rolled down the sidewalk, looked at parked cars. No one sitting in a vehicle and watching. No one on the periphery or trying to hide. Still, she took photos of every license plate within visual distance of the press briefing. She looked at the buildings—a government office building on one side of the main street, a mix of houses and small businesses on the other side. No one looking out windows. She returned to the conference. Two cops were in the crowd. Had Costa sent them in? Or Maddox? Didn't matter, she had them both pegged quickly. One was obvious—his gun was partly visible under his blazer—the other was trying to blend. Jeans, loose T-shirt, windbreaker. But he had that cop vibe.

Her eye fell back on the teenager with the skateboard. He was certainly up to no good. She kept an eye on him. Discreetly, but the kid didn't even notice because of how she was dressed.

Just one of the boys, aren't I?

She almost laughed out loud as she watched the kid pick the pocket of the baby daddy. So smooth, so clean she was almost impressed. But what really impressed her was when the kid slipped the wallet out of the pocket of the undercover cop in jeans and the cop didn't even notice. Well, shit. She couldn't let a badge get burned like that. And the killer wasn't here. Of that she was certain.

She caught up with the kid not even a half block

later. Helped that she, too, had a skateboard and could keep up. Most of the time, no one paid attention to teenagers, which was why it was her favorite undercover disguise.

Kara stuck out her foot and tripped him. He fell on his ass with a foulmouthed complaint. His skateboard slid under a parked car.

"Bitch, watch it!"

"You're good, but I'm better," she said.

He jumped up and retrieved his skateboard. She didn't give him time to get back on.

"You're under arrest," she said.

He laughed. "No fucking way you're a cop."

She pulled handcuffs from her pocket—always a risk to carry when undercover, but she felt they might come in handy—and cuffed him. The conference was breaking up. She dragged the kid in through the side door and found a uniformed officer.

"Hey, buddy, can you take this kid off my hands? He picked a couple pockets at the press conference." She'd only seen him pick two, but when she cuffed him she felt at least three wallets in the deep pockets of his cargo pants. "Including this." She slipped the cop's wallet—with his badge—out of the punk's back pocket.

The officer looked suspicious. He opened the wallet. "Detective Theodore Coleman. I'll be damned."

"She planted that wallet! I didn't steal nothing," the kid said.

Kara rolled her eyes.

"I need you to write out a report," the officer said.

"No problem, but I have to talk to someone first."

"I haven't seen you around. New?"

"Detective Kara Quinn. LA, not Spokane. I'll be right back—" she glanced at his name badge "—Officer Sherman."

Sherman took the kid from her, a perplexed look on his face, and she walked down the hall to where Matt was walking in with Maddox.

She'd missed most of the Q&A, but figured she wouldn't learn anything new, and she was certain the killer didn't show up.

Matt spotted her and did a double take. He said something to Maddox, then walked over to her.

"Where have you been?"

"Watching the crowd."

"From in here?"

"No."

"Why don't you ever give me a straight answer?"

She raised her eyebrows and kept her voice calm. "Do not yell at me."

Matt motioned for her to follow him. She did. Happily, because he was obviously irritated, and Costa was fun to mess with. He was so damn serious but she saw something more in him than most cops. Maybe it was brains. Maybe it was drive. Whatever it was, she knew he was pissed, and she was going to enjoy the confrontation.

He found an empty conference room and closed the door behind them. It was just them, a table, and two chairs, though neither of them sat down.

"What happened?" he demanded.

"I mixed and mingled. The killer didn't show."

"How do you know? You were in here."

"No—I came in when I caught a teenage pickpocket. By that time, I'd already assessed everyone in the audience—you'd just started Q&A. The killer wasn't there. Manners' boss showed up, from the staffing agency. The anticrime group had met with Packard first—they know a lot more than he said to the crowd. I ID'd everyone in the group that was in attendance—they were known to the chapter secretary. Every male who fit the profile in age didn't fit in other ways. I took pictures of every license plate in the area, which I'll send to you."

"I didn't see you."

"You were looking for me, not a teenager on a skateboard."

He opened his mouth, closed it. Mumbled, "*Voy a ser condenado.* I did see you."

She smiled. "Told you I could blend in."

"Catherine is certain he's tracking the news—and a public, outdoor press conference would be ideal for him." Matt was frustrated, but Kara tried not to take it personally.

"She's a smart shrink," Kara said, "but there are other ways to track news. He wasn't in the audience."

"You can't know that."

She raised an eyebrow. "I caught a pickpocket who was so good he slipped a wallet out of an armed cop's pocket, complete with his badge. I assessed everyone in the audience, and I'm telling you, he wasn't here."

"You caught a pickpocket."

"You doubt me?" Costa was going to be so much

fun to play with. Kara hadn't had so much fun in a long, long time.

"I don't have time for games, Quinn."

"No games. Look, you said Anne Banks knew the killer. If he's after someone who knows him, he's not going to get caught in action. Meaning, he's not going to show up if he thinks a cop might recognize him."

"Makes sense." He sat on the edge of the table and assessed her. She pulled out one of the chairs and sat down, giving him the physical upper hand, but she had been in charge since they walked into this room—and he didn't realize it.

Yeah, Matt Costa was going to be fun.

"Maybe he's just playing around," she said. "Waiting for his true target to be available, or to throw off the investigation."

"So he kills Anne because she slighted him, but killed a couple more people so she wouldn't seem like she was a specific target?"

"Exactly," Kara said. "And he may have other specific targets, and everyone else is just window dressing."

"You might be onto something," Matt said. "I'll run it by Catherine."

"You do that." She got up. "In the meantime, I gotta go give a statement on the thief and then convince Maddox to quash my name." She smiled and handed Matt back his wallet. "You were too easy."

Matt took his wallet, looking both surprised and angry, but also impressed. "You stole my wallet?"

"You gave me shit because you thought I'd bailed

on you—I was just having fun. Don't take it personally. I've been picking pockets since I was a little kid."

Matt stared at Kara as she walked out of the conference room. He looked down at his wallet, then flipped through it to make sure everything was still there. Nothing appeared to be missing.

Well, damn. He probably walked right into that. But he was tired and frustrated, and he hoped that the press conference would save a life, but feared the killer was ten steps ahead of them.

He took a deep breath, then stuffed his wallet back into his pocket. Closed his eyes and tried to picture when Quinn had pulled it. He'd opened the door to the conference room and let her enter first. That was the only time they brushed against each other. He hadn't even felt her extract his wallet, but that was the only time she could have done it.

Yes, he was impressed. But if she did it again, he'd cuff her. Not for long, but long enough to show her who was in charge, and that this wasn't a game.

Detective Kara Quinn was like no one he'd met before. He didn't know whether that was good—and would help him solve this case—or if he should just cut her loose.

20

Spokane
4:40 p.m.

He stared at the cop standing behind the podium. He didn't hear anything the FBI agent was saying, all he saw was *him.*

The man who had destroyed his father.

The man who had taken everything from him. *Everything.*

He took a deep breath and realized the FBI guy was saying something important, and he needed to listen and focus. He stopped the recording, pressed Rewind, and started from the beginning. Nothing he didn't already know. Until the federal agent spoke.

He closed his eyes so he could pay attention to his words.

Okay, he knew they'd connected the murders—he'd read the articles out of Missoula, but they hadn't gotten very far and everything died down after a few weeks. There was one local article on the anniversary of the cop's death and no new information.

You knew this day would come.

He wasn't done. He hadn't finished his mission. How much did they really know? How much did they have?

They don't have anything. You're not stupid. You've covered all your tracks. Stick with the plan. It has served you well for years. It's still the perfect plan.

He breathed deeply, controlled the fear that crept up. The fear that he had *made a mistake.*

He hadn't made a mistake. He needed to focus. There was more here, more for him to do!

Tonight, late tonight, he would kill again. That kill would calm him down.

He picked up his knife and flipped it in the air. Caught it. Flipped it; caught it. A dozen times and he was calm.

Why are the feds here so fast?

Damn, he missed what the agent—Costa, his name was—said. He rewound the news report a third time and listened. Focused.

Weak? He called me weak?

He frowned. He wasn't weak. He lifted weights nearly every day. He ran regularly. He was strong—very strong. How *dare* the FBI call him *weak.*

You are a coward. You're a coward because you never stood up to your old man. You never told him to go to hell. You did what he told you because you were scared. Weak. Just like he always said.

No. He wasn't weak. He didn't give in to the destruction of alcohol. He didn't lose his job, lose his house, lose everything!

"You're an idiot, and I'm glad your mother is

dead so she can't see what a weak, sniveling brat you've become. She's rolling over in her grave right now, watching you cry like a fucking baby."

He shook his head, trying to get his father's voice out of his head. What he said wasn't true. *It fucking wasn't true!*

He kicked the coffee table and it toppled over, spilling his soda and chips everywhere. Dammit, it's all that FBI agent's fault.

His jaw clenched and he shut off the TV. He couldn't watch anymore, not now. He would later—when he was calm again. He paced the length of the house. Back and forth. Thinking.

It didn't seem like the police knew anything. So what if they found the knife? That meant shit. It had been sitting in the bottom of the lake for two days. He'd worn gloves. And even if they managed to get prints or DNA or anything else, it wouldn't matter. He wasn't in the system. He'd never been arrested.

He'd just have to be very, very careful never to put himself in a position where someone might get his prints or DNA.

Back and forth, up and down the hall.

Everything was fine. It was all *fine.* He was careful, very careful.

What if that principal didn't show up? What if he listened to the news? What if he ran away? Who would be the coward then?

The idea that he couldn't finish what he started made him itch. He *would* finish.

Ogdenburg was next. He was at the top of the list but there were two other backups if Ogdenburg fell through. It wasn't like tomorrow's kill was essential It was a placeholder.

Sure, it wouldn't be as easy to go after his backups, but he was up to the challenge. He had notes on all of them. Ogdenburg was first, but if he ran away, he would go to the next. Then the next.

He had a plan. That's why he always had a backup plan, because something might happen he couldn't control.

He stopped pacing and stared at the blank television.

What if you can't get to any of them? What if they all run and hide?

Why borrow trouble? His aunt used to say that all the time.

Why borrow trouble, honey? Don't worry about what-might-be; focus on what is.

He breathed deeply. In. Out. Calm. Peaceful. Walked back down the hall. Then back to the television. Two, three, four times.

Better.

If Ogdenburg wasn't at his house tonight, then he would move on to Plan B. If Plan B wasn't home, he'd go to Plan C. Plan C was a bit more trouble. Plan C had a family and didn't live in Liberty Lake. He would have to wait until C was alone, which would be more difficult on a Saturday. He'd have twenty-four hours, though. He would find a way. He always found a way.

He realized he was pacing again, that his agitation had grown as he contemplated everything that could go wrong on March 6. This was no good. If he didn't get his head in the game, he would make a mistake. And he couldn't afford to make *any* mistakes when he was *so damn close* to finishing what he started.

He had to get out of this house, just *run,* like he'd done after his old man went to jail. Run to get away from his well-meaning aunt, who had *no clue* what the real world was like. Run to clear his head. Empty the pain, the defeat, the fear. In the end, all he felt was cold anger. Cold. Deliberate. Purposeful anger.

An hour later he was back at the house, hot, invigorated, the demons that had been fighting for attention, suppressed. The anger was back, and that was what he could control.

He'd always been able to control his rage. It was the fear—the fear of failure—that made him weak.

He showered, made a sandwich, ate, and watched the recording of the news again. This time calmly, with a clear head. This time with focus.

The FBI agent had sent out a warning to everyone who worked in education. That annoyed him, but he had his contingencies. It was okay.

It would be okay.

He'd never had to use one of his backups before; he didn't expect to now. But if he did, it would be okay. That's why he planned things out.

So what if someone tried to stop him? That almost made it more fun.

He looked at the clock. Seven p.m. He wanted to leave now, but he had five hours. Five hours before he could kill.

But it wouldn't hurt to follow up on his contingency plans. Make sure that everything was in place, should he need it.

He picked up his knife; stared at it. Balanced it on the back of his hand. Three fingers. Two fingers. One.

The calmness returned; he was at peace. He carved three marks into the table.

One for his mother.

One for his father.

One for him.

21

Spokane
7:20 p.m.

Anne Banks had worked exclusively in the emergency room of Spokane General for seven years. The first four were as a trauma nurse, the last three as a supervisor and head of triage. Most of the staff Matt spoke to hadn't been there long enough to remember Anne, but he talked to one surgeon who remembered Banks very well. She'd been smart, competent and well respected.

Human Resources wasn't open—it was after seven on a Friday night, and they wouldn't be in until Monday. But after an hour of running around and talking to half a dozen people who couldn't get him anything, one administrator finally promised to contact the head of HR and have staff come in personally first thing Saturday morning to pull all of Anne Banks's employment records. If there had been any complaints against her from staff or patients, they'd share—provided that Matt produced a warrant.

"I'll pull everything together," the administrator said, "but HIPAA laws are serious. I need a warrant before I can turn them over to you."

That was all they could do at that point. Driving back to the hotel, Matt stared into the darkness, frustrated. Tony was working on the warrant. It shouldn't be taking this long—but it was three hours later on the East Coast, meaning ten at night. Matt hoped he had the warrant in hand first thing in the morning.

Michael Harris was right—Matt needed downtime. He was on overdrive but nothing good would happen if he had no sleep. He'd taken four hours each night, but two nights and a cross-country flight had taken its toll. It was the night of March 5 and Matt felt helpless. They'd done everything they could to warn educators, but in Matt's experience, most people didn't take warnings seriously. They would think, "Oh, that couldn't happen to me."

What more could they do?

¿A dónde diablos vamos desde aquí?

Where the hell do we go from here?

He called Andy Knolls. It took the cop several rings to answer.

"Knolls."

"Andy, it's Costa."

"What can I do for you?"

"Teachers. Administrators. Do we have the list? Have you started calling them? Particularly those who live or work in Liberty Lake."

Silence.

"You there? Did I lose you?"

"I'm here. We're working on the list. It's not comprehensive because we're dealing with multiple school districts, plus the university, but we're close."

"It's after seven. He could kill in five hours. I want to stop it. Send me names, numbers—my people will work on this, too."

"Abigail in my office is taking the lead. She has a dozen volunteers working out of Liberty Lake PD and estimates they'll be done with the calls by ten-thirty."

"Oh. That's good." But by Andy's initial tone, Matt was worried that they didn't have the resources.

"Anyone we don't reach, we'll make a house call. Then follow up again with everyone in the morning."

"Okay. You have it under control then. Thanks."

"Is everything okay, Matt?" Andy asked.

Did he really sound that lost? Maybe he was. With every passing moment, he felt like they were losing ground. Even though they had gained so much intel in just two days, they didn't have the killer in custody. They didn't even have his name. Matt didn't want to see another victim. He didn't want to talk to another grieving family.

"Yeah. I'm just making sure we're doing everything we can short of putting every teacher in protective custody." Matt could just see his boss's head explode at the thought of the FBI housing *thousands* of potential victims just to keep them off the killer's radar. "If we can stop him *this* time, he'll screw up. I'm certain of it."

"I hope you're right. I'll call you if we learn anything."

"Thanks. And if you need my help, call. Anytime—day, night, I don't care."

"I figured that."

Matt ended the call and felt marginally relieved. Andy Knolls was a good cop, but he was still a small town cop. Knowing that he had jumped on Matt's suggestion to get the phone lists told Matt that they had a chance. They might just stop the Triple Killer now. Tonight.

Still, there was so much they *didn't* know. How did Anne Banks end up on this killer's radar? Every sign, every interview, pointed to Anne being a good person, a respected nurse, a loving mother, a desired wife. She had friends and family, a normal life. Did it go back to her childhood? Her home life? Her best friend said she was estranged from her parents. Didn't have a good relationship with them. Was there a sibling? Something criminal in her family? And what did these three cities have in common, if anything? Did the cities mean something to the killer—or was it because specific people lived in these cities?

Anne was the first of many, which told Matt that the killer had an agenda. Revenge. The kill itself—violent but efficient. He didn't play with his victims, he didn't torture them, but the murder itself was brutal and bloody.

There were easier ways to kill someone.

But the killer chose a knife.

The killer chose the method.

Kill—the first, fatal slice.

Mark—the three horizontal slashes.

Gloat.

Watch the investigation from afar.

Relish his superiority.

His intelligence.

Seven dead and he hadn't been caught.

He would bask in that fact, Matt thought, no matter what Matt had said to the press today—and to the killer he hoped was listening.

Maybe taunting him had been the wrong move.

But there was no going back now.

22

Spokane
8:30 p.m.

Matt walked into the war room to touch base with Ryder, when all he wanted was a shower, a double shot of Scotch, and a good night's sleep. He'd settle for four hours, uninterrupted, but hoped for six. He needed a clear head in the morning and already planned to be up before dawn.

But before he did anything, he wanted to make sure again that Andy's people had reached every teacher and administrator in Liberty Lake.

He was surprised to find Kara, Michael and Ryder in room 310 eating pizza and drinking beer. Well, Ryder wasn't drinking beer—he was drinking bottled fizzy water or some such thing.

"Eat," Michael told Matt.

He was starving, and there was more than enough. He grabbed two slices and sat down. Ryder looked nervous that he'd been caught relaxing.

"Do you need something, sir?" Ryder asked.

"We've done everything we can, Ryder. Andy

Knolls and his staff are personally reaching out to every educator who works or lives in Liberty Lake. He expects to be done by ten-thirty. If we can just keep them safe for the next twenty-four hours, we'll go a long way into screwing with the Triple Killer's head."

"And get him to fuck up," Kara said. "I like the plan."

Matt did… And didn't. The unpredictability could put more people at risk, yet it might be the only way they could stop the killer. "For my team, we'll be starting early in the morning, so eat and drink and get a good night's sleep."

"As much as we can in six hours," Michael said.

"I'm sure your SEAL training prepared you for times like this."

"Yes, sir, it did."

Matt narrowed his eyes at Michael, who grinned. Matt almost laughed. He needed this. Just an hour to decompress.

"You talk to Andy?" Kara said. "He okay?"

"Yes, why wouldn't he be?"

"Well, I may have created a problem for him with his fiancée, and he wasn't really happy with me. Andy brought me over to her sandwich shop tonight—I had to go back to Liberty Lake to pick up my car after the press conference—and she said something about how she was worried about him getting shot, and I said she didn't need to worry because our killer prefers knives. My joke didn't go over too well."

Michael laughed, though Matt didn't see the

humor. Maybe that's why Andy had sounded off when he was talking to him earlier.

Michael said, "Quinn was telling us how Maddox arrested her when she was a teenager, then convinced her she'd make a better cop than criminal."

Matt wished he'd heard that story.

"Did you really catch a pickpocket at the press conference?" Ryder asked. "I heard Jim and Miles talking about it earlier. Someone pickpocketed a cop?"

"A punk, couldn't have been more than fifteen," she said. "I only saw him grab two wallets—but when they processed him, he had three on him. Of course, I was a bit busy determining that the killer wasn't on-site watching your boss speak." She winked at Matt.

He didn't know whether to laugh or continue to be irritated with her.

"We're starting early tomorrow," Matt said. "Oh-six-hundred. It's going to be a long weekend."

"And that's my cue to leave," Kara said.

"I'll walk you out," Matt offered.

"I'm a big girl with a gun."

"I want to pick your brain about something. Do you have ten minutes?"

"I have as much time as you need. I'm on vacation after all."

Right, Matt thought. As if Kara Quinn would ever take a real vacation.

They took the stairs to the lobby. "I'm getting a drink," Matt said. "Join me? After today—I can't shut it off. I asked Andy to send me names, but he says they have it covered."

"Then they do," Kara said. "I know how you think, Matt—you want to do everything. A case like this, you have to trust your team."

"Would you?"

"No, but that's why I work undercover. I'm more like the *I have to do everything myself* kind of cop." She paused. "Though, I have a good handler. Lex has never let me down when I've needed him, but he gives me enough room to do my job."

They sat in the hotel bar, in a corner booth where they both had a visual on the entrance. Matt was still hungry and there was bar food, so he ordered an assortment of appetizers and a double Scotch for him; Kara ordered a tequila shot and beer. He watched her salt the rim, then down the shot.

"Better," she said with a wink. She was going to have to stop winking at him—it was distracting. "So." Kara leaned back into the booth and sipped her beer. "Pick my brain, Agent Costa."

Suddenly, he didn't want to talk shop. He wanted to find out what she'd told Michael Harris about her recruitment into the police academy. But he didn't ask. Because that would be going down a path he desperately wanted to be on, a path he shouldn't be on, a path that would lead directly to bed, a path that would cause numerous problems.

"I've always been good at delegating and using my team's individual strengths. You have uncanny observation skills. And honestly? I was looking for you this afternoon, at the press briefing in the crowd and became angry that I didn't see you. There were only forty-five people there, and I didn't see you."

"Because you were looking for me, not a unisex teenager. Put my hair up in a cap, take off makeup, wear a loose jacket, I can pass for a fifteen-year-old boy."

He snorted. "Hardly."

"You see what you expect to see. A young person carrying a skateboard doesn't draw your attention. Just a kid trying to figure out what's going on. Unless you're that little punk who saw a crowd and thought it was time to make a quick buck."

"The next potential victim—I want to do more, and I don't know what, other than putting a cop outside every house."

"And is that realistic?"

"They don't have enough cops in the county to cover every teacher and administrator."

"Look, Matt, you've done everything you could. Andy is doing everything he can. We thwart the killer this time, we win this battle."

"I still can't shake this feeling that it's not going to be enough. That we won't win the war."

The appetizer platter came and they each ordered another round of drinks. Matt ate for a bit, then said, "We've done everything physically possible to warn teachers. But even if we save this victim for now, we still have to think about the cop who may be next. And whether he'll strike again. This killer is smart and methodical. If he sees our presence, he might just back off. And if I'm wrong and he still gets to a teacher…"

His voice trailed off. He refocused on what he could control. "Either way, I can save the cop. I need your eyes, ears, instincts. Anything about the first two cops who were killed—anything in there that might tell us about who he's going after now? One cop was white—Boyd in Missoula—and Nakamura in Portland was Japanese American, so race doesn't help us."

"Both were men."

"And that might mean something—except that the first educator who was killed—a principal in Portland—was a Caucasian female named Rebecca Thomas. The college professor in Missoula was an African American male named John Marston. All three nurses were female, but nursing is still predominately a female profession. And while they were all trauma nurses, the educators were in completely different fields. A vice principal and a college professor."

"Yet the first victim was a *retired* trauma nurse. No longer working. Maybe there is something else in common with the second victim in each set."

"Ryder and our analysts in DC are running deep backgrounds on all seven victims. Catherine thinks there's something connecting the victims to the killer, but until we can connect more than two victims together, I have no idea what. And do these locations even mean anything? I think it's his way to fuck with us. Different states, different jurisdictions, almost impossible to put everything together into a cohesive investigation."

"You're worried about the cop."

He hadn't said it, but Kara was right. He was worried, really worried.

"March 9. This Tuesday. Probably early morning because this guy doesn't want to wait anymore. He killed Victoria Manners early in the morning before dawn. Catherine concurs that he's going to kill someone in the next few hours, before dawn tomorrow, if he can get to them. He's antsy. Growing impatient. But he won't deviate from the day. So even if we get everyone under wraps tonight, we'll have to stay diligent until midnight tomorrow. And then worry that we missed something and there's a dead teacher somewhere, while also trying to protect every damn cop in the area."

"You feel helpless."

"Don't you?"

She didn't say anything for a minute. "The cop is going to have a connection to Liberty Lake. Either he lives or works there—now or in the past. Maybe Andy's fiancée has a right to be concerned."

"I hated Chief Packard's idea—logistically—of pairing up every cop and keeping track of their off-duty movements, but honestly, I think it might be the only way to keep these guys safe," Matt said.

"And we take his prize off the table and he gets reckless. He'll make a mistake. And he may get reckless sooner if we take his second victim away from him."

"*If* we can protect all the cops—not just Spokane PD, but Liberty Lake and all the other communities in the Spokane Valley, plus the Sheriff's department." Matt pulled out his phone and made a note to write a memo first thing in the morning. "I'll alert everyone in the area that a cop connected in some way to Liberty Lake is in danger and to be extra cautious this week."

"Except Victoria Manners had no connection to Liberty Lake."

"I'll prioritize the risk. And we're still running a background on her—maybe her boyfriend lived there, or she went to school there, or she summered at the lake. Or the killer is just fucking with us—or giving us a clue we're too stupid to figure out."

"Hardly stupid."

"It feels that way."

"I'll observe. Talk to Maddox. He knows everyone—he worked out of Liberty Lake for years." She frowned.

"You're worried about him?"

She shrugged. "Him and Andy. And all the other cops in Liberty Lake. But Maddox is a friend."

"He recruited you."

"In a manner of speaking."

"What story did you tell Harris?"

She raised her eyebrows. "You really want to know?"

Hell yes. He shrugged and smiled. "If you want to tell me."

"I was a junior in high school. I didn't have a lot of friends—didn't want them. I was in and out of different schools my entire life."

"Army brat?"

She laughed, a real, honest-to-goodness laugh. "I wish. My parents were con artists. Common thieves.

We moved a lot. Then my father got tossed in prison and my mother started hanging out with similar losers. I swear, if my mother and her steady stream of boyfriends had spent their energy actually working for a living rather than thinking up get-rich-quick scams, they *would* be rich. Half the time I didn't even go to school. Transcripts? What are those? And pickpocketing? I learned those skills when I was still young and cute."

Kara was still young and cute, Matt thought, then tried to push the thought out of his head.

"So," she continued, "my mother and her boyfriend of the month came up with some new scam on tourists in…where were we? Vegas, yeah. Anyway, I started fucking with their plan, and when they realized I wasn't going to play along anymore, my mother dumped me on Em in Liberty Lake. My mother was a piece of work, and I never trusted that she wouldn't show up one day and pack me up. Before I turned sixteen, I'd become an expert on emancipation. She did show her face once and said she had a job that I was perfect for, and I told her to go to hell, I was filing for emancipation and would tell the court everything she had me do for her. She pouted and left. Of course, that didn't stop her from calling me three years later when she needed to be bailed out of jail."

Kara frowned at her beer.

"I don't care about your criminal past. You obviously overcame it."

"I just—well, I don't usually talk about my parents or my personal life. You must be a monster in interrogations."

"I hold my own. I suspect you do, too."

She simply smiled.

"And?" Matt prompted. "Did you become emancipated?"

"No need to. She didn't come back before I turned eighteen. So—all that goes into me not liking to take shit from anyone. I didn't have a lot of friends—who could I trust with any of that crap? But there was another girl my age who had a rough life. Hell of a lot rougher than me—my parents were assholes, but they never hit me or starved me or pimped me out. Anyway, like me, Jamie was living with her grandparents. We became friends. She went to a party. I told her not to go." Kara paused for a long minute and Matt wondered what she was thinking. About the past or what to share with him? Then she shrugged and said, "She was drugged and raped. A common story. I didn't take it well."

"You—?"

"Not me. I mean, I wasn't drugged or raped. But Jamie was so twisted up and I wanted to kill someone. Instead, I killed his car. Maddox didn't so much arrest me, as detain me. I told him everything, and he told me I should be a cop, because if I continued down the path I was on I'd be in prison." She paused. "I didn't tell your friends upstairs all that. Just the end result. And described in detail what I did to the Corvette that prick owned."

"You've led an interesting life. And you're what? Thirty?"

"You've been checking on me."

"Your boss gave the basics. I figured you went to the academy right after high school and since you've been a cop for twelve years, that makes you thirty."

"Turned the big three-oh in January. Now your turn."

"I'm thirty-seven."

"I meant, what's your deep dark secret."

The waitress came over and asked if they wanted a last call—it was eleven and they were shutting down the bar, even though it was a Friday night. So it was with cheap hotel bars in the middle of nowhere.

Matt shouldn't, but he ordered another Scotch. Kara smiled at him—damn, she was sexy—and ordered another tequila shot.

"I have no deep dark secrets," he said. He had some dark stories, and he didn't want to talk about Beth. "And I doubt that's your deepest or darkest."

Why had he said that? What was he asking for?

"I tell you my parents are petty criminals and you led a perfectly normal life?"

"My dad was career military—he came over from Cuba when he was a kid. My mom is first generation. My dad was so proud to be an American. He enlisted when he was eighteen, planned on serving for six years then going to college. But he loved the Navy, stuck with it."

"So *you* were the Army brat. Or, rather, Navy brat."

"In a manner of speaking—though my dad wasn't moved around. He was stationed most of his career in Florida. He was killed in action, according to the official files, but it was an accident on base. Training accident. His CO really liked him and marked it KIA so his family could get better benefits. I was fifteen, my brother was sixteen."

"Did either of you serve?"

He shook his head. "I wanted to, but my mom would have been crushed. She worried all the time about Dad, but knew he loved what he did. She was also wise—she knew I would be going into the military only as a tribute to my father, not because it was in my heart. She was a big believer of following dreams."

"Is she around?"

"She died five years ago. Cancer. My brother is a big shot doctor with a gorgeous, smart wife, two kids, and another on the way. Still lives in Miami."

"And you decided to become an FBI agent."

"It was roundabout, but basically, I'd planned on being a cop. Ended up being recruited into the FBI out of college. No deep dark secrets."

"We all have secrets, Matt," she said.

He almost told her about Beth and what happened last summer. And worse, he could tell that she knew he had something he was holding back, as if she could read his mind. When he told her she had uncanny observation skills, he'd meant it—but it went way beyond that. Maybe that's why she was so good as an undercover agent, why she had made detective at twenty-five, why she was on mandatory "vacation."

"Maybe we do," he said quietly. "Some things are harder to talk about than others." Because he wanted to tell her about Beth, he deflected. "Why undercover work?"

She shrugged.

"That's not an answer."

"I'm good at it."

"I'm a good scuba diver, but you don't see me diving for treasure."

"That sounds like fun, though."

"You dive?" he asked, surprised.

"Never learned, but I'm a wicked swimmer. Always wanted to take a class, but I don't really like rules."

She'd totally changed the subject. Smoothly, expertly. But he wouldn't let her. He really wanted to know what made her tick. "Hence, undercover work."

She raised an eyebrow. When she did that, it was so damn sexy. Did she know? Did she know that she was exactly his type? Hell, he didn't know he had a type, but if he had to pick a woman now, it would be Kara Quinn. It was the contradictions. Young, but not young. Petite, but strong. Sassy, but smart. But mostly, she was mysterious. The more he learned, the more he realized how much there was to learn.

"Maybe, in part. Maybe I just like being a different person." Kara jerked her head toward the bartender who'd just finished closing down the bar. "They're closing up. I'm going to call a taxi. One tequila too many."

"You can stay with me."

Don't go there, Matt.

She gave him a sly smile, leaned forward, and

said quietly, "If I go to your room, we're going to have sex."

Too late.

"Are we?"

He wanted to. He couldn't explain why he was drawn to Kara. Maybe because they were both outsiders. Maybe because she was sexy in an oddly wholesome way. Maybe because he hadn't been in a relationship—short or long—in months. Maybe because it was temporary—they both had careers in different states.

She smiled and for the first time since he'd met her, the smile reached her eyes. They sparkled and he went from simmer to boil.

Hell, Mathias, you've been turned on since the minute you saw her.

She leaned forward and said, "Or we can just... *cuddle.*"

He barely resisted kissing her right there in the bar. He whispered, *"Como el infierno, cariño."*

Matt took her hand and led her to the elevator. It was late; they were alone. Before the doors even closed, his mouth devoured hers.

He was about to ask her if she was really okay with this when her arms went around his waist and she pulled his body against hers.

The door opened way too fast, but he was only on the third floor. He jumped back, not wanting anyone on his team to see him like this. Kara was a witness as well as a temporary team member. Taking her to bed... He shouldn't.

"Stop thinking," she said.

How the hell did she know what he was thinking?

"Are you sure?"

"Are you?"

Matt was normally confident in everything he did—at work and at play—but Kara's confidence had him hesitating, as if she knew something he didn't.

His room was at the end of the hall next to the staircase. Jim and Michael were across the hallway. His room adjoined the war room, but he doubted anyone else was up at midnight. He hoped.

Still, he entered quietly. He made sure the door was locked to the adjoining room so no one could surprise him. Out of the corner of his eye he saw Kara slip the *Do Not Disturb* sign on the door and close it.

"Where were we?" she said.

Here he thought he was seducing her, but the tables had turned, and she walked over to him and kissed him. He hesitated again because this was happening too fast. His head was in a whirl, his body was primed, but his duty kept getting in the way.

Kara stepped back, but still had her hands on his arms. "Matt," she said, "we're attracted to each other. We're both single. And if you make love half as well as you kiss, we're going to have a lot of fun. Stop thinking about the case—it's midnight, and unless you have some psychic connection about what the killer is going to do and when, you can't do anything right now. Stop thinking about your people finding out that we're going to get naked and have some fun. I don't care, but you do, and I respect that.

I don't kiss and tell. I like you, Matt. I want to be here. And I know you want me here."

He did. He wanted Kara right now. She was an LA cop and he was a virtual nomad, but he wanted her.

Maybe that's why he was so attracted. Whatever they did, whatever they had, would by necessity be brief.

She unbuttoned her flannel shirt. Flannel had never looked sexy to him before tonight. Underneath was a thin black tank top. She started to take it off, too, but he grabbed her wrist and pulled her to him.

Then he saw the scars.

The first was on her upper right shoulder, a bullet wound. He knew because he had one of his own, on his left calf. He'd only been shot once. It hadn't been serious, but it had hurt like hell.

He kissed her, then tilted her head and kissed her scar.

Then he saw the second.

It was on her left shoulder, in the back, and it wasn't a gunshot. It was a long, narrow white scar, older than the gunshot. A knife wound, and it had been serious.

"Stop thinking," she said.

"You were shot. And stabbed."

"More than once, but I'm alive, and I can prove it."

She pushed him back on the bed and took off her tank top. She had another knife wound on her left breast, a long, narrow scar. A gunshot on her left side.

"Kara—"

"I'll turn off the lights if you say one more word, Costa."

She reached for the lamp, but he took her hand and kissed it, then licked from her palm to her fingers. She closed her eyes and sighed.

"Don't you dare turn off the lights. I want to watch you." He reached for the back of her neck and pulled her down on him, holding her tight as he kissed her.

Matt had every intention of finding out how she got so many scars. While he didn't know Kara Quinn well, he knew her well enough that if he pressed now she would leave or… Or what?

He had never met a woman who was both completely mysterious and extremely open at the same time. He didn't think it was possible.

And yet here she was.

"You're still thinking," she whispered into his ear, then nipped his lobe to the point of pain. Her tongue shot out, her hands reached under his waistband, and as soon as she touched him, he was done thinking about anything for the rest of the night, except making sure that Kara Quinn had just as much fun as he did.

23

Saturday, March 6
Liberty Lake
12:05 a.m.

Grace hadn't wanted Andy to leave that night. Kara's joke about the killer preferring knives didn't go over well *at all* and Grace was worried.

But out of all the teachers and administrators that Abigail and her people had called, there were only three they couldn't reach. One they confirmed from the school district was out of town for the week; the second was a principal who worked at Central Valley High School—where both Andy and Kara had graduated—but lived at the lake. The last, an English teacher who worked at the elementary school, but had a home just outside the town limits. Andy would go to her house next.

Andy arrived at the lake house with two officers. He didn't want to think that anything was wrong, that Jeffrey Ogdenburg was already dead—it was only five minutes after midnight. But the feds had him worried, and listening to the profiler earlier in the day had disturbed him on several levels.

Andy loved being a cop, but he was a small town cop. Vandalism, theft, a few domestic violence situations that weren't fun but at least predictable because Andy knew most everyone in town. Murder was way out of his comfort zone. This investigation had made him think long and hard about his future, and whether he was cut out for a law enforcement career.

Except that Victoria Manners was the first murder victim in Liberty Lake in more than a decade, and he couldn't expect to have another serial killer in his town in his lifetime.

The cops—a rookie and an experienced cop—stood on the path watching while Andy knocked on the door of Ogdenburg's cabin.

At first, he didn't hear anything, and he grew worried. He was about to tell the officers to check around back, when a light came on in the entry. "Coming, coming," a voice inside said. "Who is it?"

"Detective Andy Knolls from Liberty Lake PD."

"The police?"

He heard a bolt slide and then the door opened. Andy realized then how easy it would be for a killer to pretend to be a cop and get anyone in this small town to open their door.

Ogdenburg was in his late thirties and Andy had clearly woken him up. He showed his badge and said, "Mind if I come in?"

"Is something wrong?"

"You didn't answer your phone."

"I get crappy reception up here. Is it my sister? My parents? Are they okay?"

Now he was worried, as Andy would be if a cop came to his house late at night.

"Everyone is fine. We're reaching out to everyone in the educational field who lives in the area to notify you of a potential threat. My officers are going to walk around the property and check things out, if you don't mind."

"Threat? Um, no, go ahead." Ogdenburg rubbed his face. "Come in."

"Do you mind if I look around?"

"Not at all, but what's going on?"

Andy asked him if he'd heard about the woman who was killed. He had, and Andy filled him in on the basics of the investigation. Nothing that hadn't been said at the press conference, but reiterating that they believed that the killer would be targeting a teacher or administrator in Liberty Lake.

"We're recommending that you find another place to stay. Maybe with relatives, or out of town. After a day or two, it should be safe for you to return, but for the next twenty-four hours we have some concerns."

"Why me?"

"We don't know that you are a specific target, but the FBI believes that his next target is a teacher, someone who lives or works in Liberty Lake." Andy didn't get into the profile details, that some of the victims may be specifically chosen, while others might be surrogates for someone else. He didn't know if he agreed with the psychological assessment, but again, that was way outside his comfort zone. Nothing about this case made sense to him.

"But the nurse was from Spokane, wasn't she?"

"Yes."

"So you really don't know."

"I wouldn't be out here at midnight if I didn't think that there is a threat to you, however small."

"I'm going to my sisters' tomorrow morning. I'll stay with her for the night. Okay?"

"That's good, but maybe you can go there tonight?"

"I'm not going to wake her up in the middle of the night. I'll check all my doors, keep them locked, not open them for anyone."

"Even if someone says they're a cop."

Ogdenburg looked at him oddly. "Oh. I see your point."

"Are you certain there isn't any place you can go tonight? I can escort you."

"I mean, if you really, really think so, I guess I could find a hotel or something."

It was clear he didn't want to leave. Andy was torn. Should he insist? He had no real authority. And hadn't the profiler said that if the killer couldn't get to his specific target, that he may have a backup? Andy's head ached.

"It's up to you, Mr. Ogdenburg. We are fully staffed tonight and we'll patrol your street regularly, but I am happy to take you to your sister's or a hotel, if you want."

"I promise, I'll keep all the doors locked, and if anyone comes to the house, I'll call 911, okay?"

"Please do. Even if you think it's nothing, better safe than sorry."

Andy finished checking his house, looking in every closet and large cabinet, checking the doors and windows, and ensuring that Ogdenburg was alone. The two officers came to the door. One said, "No sign of anyone. We checked all the cars parked on the street or visible in a driveway—there were six. All registered to local addresses."

"Did you take down the plates?"

"Yes."

"Okay." Andy glanced at his watch. It was nearly twelve-thirty. Ogdenburg was safe for now, and he was aware of the threat. "Please be alert, Mr. Ogdenburg," he said.

"I will. Thank you for coming out. I really do appreciate the alert."

Andy left, told his officers they needed to check on one more person, and then they could all go home for the night.

Everyone would be back working bright and early in the morning. The killer was still out there, and Andy didn't know if these warnings would deter him. If not early in the morning, the killer still had the rest of the day—and night—to kill.

Andy took a final look at Ogdenburg's house and drove off.

Jeffrey Ogdenburg checked all his doors and windows again. Liberty Lake was a safe town, but he considered that if the police had come out at midnight to check on his well-being, they had cause to be concerned.

He poured himself a glass of milk and pulled two cookies out of the jar—homemade chocolate chip, from his sister. She had never cooked when they were growing up, and still didn't cook well—except for baking. Somehow having kids had jump-started her baking genes and she made amazing cookies, pies, cakes—he gained five pounds every time he went over for dinner because of dessert.

Not that he was complaining—Jenny was happy, and that's all he cared about.

He watched a half hour of news on the twenty-four-hour cable channel and became drowsy. He hadn't heard anything outside, not even the wind—though a storm was supposed to be coming to town early in the week.

He turned off the television and went to his small den, pushing aside work he'd brought home for the weekend. He moved his mouse and his screen popped to life, then he googled information about a killer in Spokane. An article had been published late that afternoon, after the police had a press conference. Pretty much what the cop who'd come to his door had said. Some guy was randomly killing teachers.

Why Liberty Lake?

A former student?

The police didn't have any real information, and there were a lot of teachers in the Spokane Valley.

Still, it made him uneasy. He knew many of the teachers in the area—he'd worked with them, socialized with them. And the reporter pointed out that the nurse who had been killed at the lake wasn't even from here. She lived and worked in Spokane.

Jeffrey was a nice guy, and he knew it. It's probably why he was still single. He didn't particularly like dating, and he was more of a homebody. His idea of the perfect woman was a teacher who loved working with kids, who liked coming home after work and watching television or sitting on the couch curled up with a book. Someone who liked long walks and an occasional hike or camping trip, but still preferred being home in front of a fire. Maybe have kids, maybe not. He'd considered getting a dog—he'd had one when he moved out of his parents' house, but Rollie died two years back of old age.

There were no updates to the news article.

Jeffrey was beat; he didn't really want to listen to the press briefing—the reporter had been clear about what was going on. It was now well after one in the morning, and he had a full day planned tomorrow.

Today, he reminded himself, he'd be careful—he wasn't an idiot. He'd hang out with his sister and family all day. Maybe even spend the night. In fact, if his sister had heard the news, she'd probably insist. That didn't bother him. He liked her kids and her husband. They could make a game night out of it.

He turned off all the lights except the small light above the kitchen stove, then went back to bed. He'd been reading in bed when the police came to his door—well, he'd fallen asleep reading in bed. He picked up his book, but his eyes were drooping, so he marked his page, turned off the lamp, and drifted off to sleep.

24

Liberty Lake
After Midnight

Rage burned beneath his skin. The killer wanted to tear that FBI agent apart limb by limb. Cut him into tiny pieces and throw them in the *goddamn fucking lake!*

He'd almost been caught at Ogdenburg's house. He'd been outside, waiting for the principal to turn out his light. It was safer that way, easier. In the dark, in the shadows.

Then the Liberty Lake Police Department showed up and screwed with everything.

He didn't wait around to see what was going on; he walked the half mile down the trail to his car and left. Sped toward the second target…

And she wasn't home. Not only was she gone, but she had left quickly. She'd worked Friday morning—he'd made sure of that—and he'd confirmed that she had no plans, no reason to leave town. She'd gone because of that ridiculous press briefing and warning!

Not ridiculous if she listened.

He walked through her house, the rage slowly building. He knocked over her television. Kicked her couch. Pushed over her bookshelf. She wasn't here!

He left before he became reckless. Drove slowly to try and control his adrenaline. He couldn't risk being pulled over, not tonight. Because when the police found the body—and they would find one, because he would succeed—they might remember him.

Initially it wouldn't be a problem—he wasn't in the system. He hadn't been drinking—he didn't drink. He refused to be a drunk like his father. He had a local address—and a license to prove it—and he had a reason to be out, at least one that would stand up to any stupid cop who asked.

He didn't want to go to Plan C, which would mean waiting until tomorrow night. He didn't want to wait. Besides, it would be too close, too close to the deadline. He'd never—not *once!*—had his plans go so completely off the rails.

Because of the fucking FBI.

Because of that FBI Agent, Mathias Costa.

He should kill him just on general principle.

Don't be a fool! He's not part of the plan. You go after him, you'll never complete your mission. It would be chaos.

Focus!

He considered his options. Wait until his third target returned at the end of the day, or go back to Ogdenburg.

He'd been driving on the freeway for the last hour. The twenty minutes from Spokane to Liberty Lake back to Spokane and now heading back to Liberty Lake.

His hands clenched the steering wheel. He found the needle on the odometer topping eighty-five—he slowed down without braking. Took a deep, cleansing breath.

He itched to find a drunk and take out his rage, but that would be dangerous. He never swerved from his path, *never*. It's why he was free. It's why he could walk the streets nameless, faceless. It's why he could return home and breathe. He wanted a drunk because he needed to kill… He needed to release these demons, this overwhelming craving to punish those who were weak. Pathetic. Losers.

Like his father.

It's not about him! This is about your *retribution.* Your *vengeance. And you will have it.*

Be patient.

Every mistake his father had made was because he was rash and reckless, acting with anger instead of cold logic.

He was not his father. He would never be his father.

"You are my sunshine."

His mother's angelic voice crooned in his head. If only she were here. If only she hadn't left, nothing bad would have ever happened to him.

It's not her fault she had to go...

His memories of his mother were small bright lights in a sea of dark, raging waters that surged through him. Beacons of what could have been, what should have been, what would have been had the world not conspired to take her.

He breathed deeply and found himself circling back to Ogdenburg's house.

Be careful.

His anger at being thwarted by the police earlier had dissipated. He regained his focus, his calm. He had time. He had hours to complete his mission.

He turned his lights off and drove slowly past the target's house.

Ogdenburg's lights were on, and he saw the flicker of the television behind the closed blinds.

Somehow, that made him feel better. He had a plan for this. If Ogdenburg was awake, he had his syringe ready. If he was asleep, he wouldn't need it. He would be able to enact Plan A just like he planned.

But he had to make sure the police were truly gone.

He drove through the winding streets and didn't see a police car anywhere. But Ogdenburg's lights were still on.

He left the neighborhood and drove through side streets and over the freeway, to his childhood home.

He would take just one look, then go back.

He had to see *the* house again. *His* house. He'd thought he'd be able to ignore the urge, but his second night here, he drove by.

He thought one time would be enough. It was far from enough. He'd driven by eight times in the two months he'd been living in Spokane. He would have driven by every day, but he refrained. He had things to do, to prepare, and he couldn't risk having someone recognize his car.

He meandered through streets that he'd once known so well. There were more houses now, more people, but the streets were mostly the same.

This was dangerous, he told himself. Long after midnight and police would wonder why he was driving through a neighborhood when he didn't live here.

I'm from out of town. I missed my exit.

I got lost.

I was visiting my mother on Vine Street...

He turned on Vine and slowed the car to a crawl.

He'd wanted to drive by every day, but he resisted. Barely.

This was the ninth time in eight weeks. A good number, nine.

The last time. It would have to be the last, until he finished his retribution.

He stopped the car in the middle of the street and turned his head. The streetlights were dim, clouded by the growing fog. No lights were on in houses. It was nearly two in the morning; everyone slept.

He stared at the house. *His* house.

The new owners had painted the house a very pale green with cream and dark brown trim. He couldn't see it now, in the dark, but the first time he'd driven by was in daylight and he would never forget the betrayal. Much different from the white house with rust trim that he'd grown up in.

They'd added on in the back—a second story, in brick. They'd added brick pillars to the front.

He hated it.

They'd also taken down the evergreen in the yard and planted two smaller elms. Had the tree died? Had it come down in a storm?

They had children. Three girls and a boy. Two older kids in school and two little kids, one of them a baby.

His research told him they hadn't bought the house fifteen years ago when it had been stolen from him. They'd bought it nine years ago. But they'd been the ones who had taken out the permit to add on. They'd been the ones who had changed the color of the exterior.

They had been the ones who had torn out his mother's garden. The tree. Put up a stupid mailbox on the street with painted daisies and the name RICHMOND.

He hated them, the bastards. They had ruined his mother's house. They added an addition that went up and back, and thus her garden was gone. Bright flowers she coaxed out every spring from the cold earth.

They had taken, destroyed, the last part of her on earth.

He flipped his knife in the small space. Flipped, caught. Flipped, caught. Balanced it on the back of his hand.

Three fingers. Two fingers. One finger. Perfectly balanced, and a plan started to form.

This house on Vine was not the Richmond house. It was *his* house, and he would make certain that they damn well knew it.

He flipped the knife again and put it down. Then

he drove down the block out of the neighborhood and went back to the freeway heading east, exited the next off-ramp, and returned to Ogdenburg's house.

The lights were off now. A faint light shone in the kitchen window. But the house felt asleep.

Still, he had to be sure. He parked around the corner in a driveway where the house was set far back, so he wouldn't wake the owners. Turned off his car.

Waited.

Waited.

Just after two in the morning, a patrol car drove past his parked vehicle, which was now covered with a thin layer of moisture from the damp night. Drove up the street, around the corner. Slowly. Looking for him. Not seeing him.

He was hiding in plain sight, and it gave him a perverse sense of pleasure that he was only yards from the police, but they didn't see him. Didn't know he was waiting, watching.

The patrol left. He'd wait ten minutes.

Nine.

Eight.

He pulled out his knife and flipped it.

Seven.

Six.

The countdown excited him, reminding him that when he hit zero, when he killed the principal, that he would be three days away from his final justice.

How long did he have before the cops returned? Thirty minutes? Sixty? Were they patrolling at regular intervals, or trying to trip him up?

He breathed in; he breathed out.

One more minute...

He smiled, started his car, and drove three minutes to a street that had no road access to Ogdenburg, but had a trail that went right to his deck.

He parked his car so it was not visible from any of the scattered residences, then opened his glove compartment. Inside was a key ring. He'd been to this house before; Ogdenburg had never known. Why would he check for his spare key? He hadn't needed it in the last two weeks.

Besides, even if he did, he would never have thought someone had broken into his house and taken it, because the killer hadn't left a trace.

He was good at that. At being invisible. At being smart.

Quietly, he exited his car and walked down the wooded trail that led to the principal's house. Cold. Clear. Focused. His breath wasn't even visible because it was so dark, but he'd been through these woods enough times that he didn't get lost.

Six minutes later, he let himself inside the house with the key.

Silence.

This penultimate kill was going to be easy.

25

Spokane
6:15 a.m.

Matt's phone rang and he groaned. He hadn't drunk that much last night, but he also hadn't gotten much sleep.

Not that he was complaining about what had kept him up.

He grabbed his phone, in an effort not to wake Kara. He glanced over to the other side of the bed.

She wasn't there.

He flipped on his light. "Costa," he said gruffly.

Kara was gone. He didn't hear her in the bathroom, and he didn't see her clothes anywhere.

"It's Catherine."

He shook his head, cleared it. "Sorry. I forgot to set my alarm." It was six-fifteen. How had he slept in?

"I have something. I emailed you, but I wanted to call, too. The deep backgrounds—there's a connection between the college professor in Missoula and the city of Spokane. Before he started teaching in Missoula at the University of Montana, he was the principal of Spokane High School."

Matt slipped out of bed while still holding the phone. He was naked and the room was cold. He turned up the heater and slipped on sweatpants. "John Marston, right?"

"Yes. Victim number five. I then looked at the other victims. No one else graduated or taught at or worked at Spokane High School, but I feel this is important. I think the killer knew Marston personally—just like he knew Anne Banks. And if he's as young as I think he is, the killer could have attended high school back when Marston was principal there."

"I'm on it."

"I copied Ryder Kim on my findings. But listen—I have a theory. It's not clearly formed, I'm working out some kinks, but I think I'm close. Anne Banks *had been* an ER nurse in Spokane, but left nursing when she moved to Portland to get married. Yet, the killer still saw her as a trauma nurse—which is why he also targeted Sophia Kwan and Victoria Manners, both who *were* trauma nurses at the time of their deaths. An insatiable rage? We just don't know why yet. And the killer still viewed Marston as a high school principal—even though he moved to continue his education and had become a college professor by the time he was killed. That's why he also killed Rebecca Thomas in Portland—she was a vice principal, a person in authority. And that's why the victim you will most likely find today will be a high school principal."

"But Spokane isn't Liberty Lake, remember.

Though they're both in the Spokane Valley, they're twenty miles apart. They're different jurisdictions, different towns, schools, everything."

"Which tells me that the law enforcement officer the killer has already targeted worked or works out of Liberty Lake. He's laying these victims on his own doorstep, so to speak."

Andy Knolls was Matt's first thought.

"That's exactly what I was talking about with Kara last night."

"Kara?"

"Kara Quinn, the detective."

"Right—I forgot. From LAPD."

"I said that the cop would be connected to Liberty Lake. There's only a handful of cops who work out of the PD here—plus the police chief, who's more a figurehead than cop," Matt said. "I'll have everyone called in for a mandatory meeting today and maybe one of them knows these other victims."

"Good—if we can disrupt the killer's pattern, he's bound to expose himself. So be prepared—what I said the other day still holds. He may change his MO. He may take out more than just the one cop he has targeted. But my sense is that he has a specific victim in mind and he will do *anything* to get to him. I suspect he personally knows the cop, just like he knew Banks and Marston. But *the victims* may not have remembered him, and the cop may not, either. Especially if whatever happened to set this killer down this murderous path occurred when he was a child."

"I'm going to jump in the shower and get working on this. Thanks, Catherine, this is exactly the break we need. And the press conference was a success. Andy Knolls and the other Liberty Lake cops personally spoke with everyone who works in the education field and lives in Liberty Lake. Many left town or stayed with friends. Keeping potential victims alert is half the battle."

"I agree—just be careful, Matt. You're putting yourself out there, and this psychopath is not going to like it if he can't get to his target."

"Que es exactamente lo que queremos." Which is exactly what we want.

"Not if he becomes erratic," Catherine said. *"Ten cuidado, Mathias."*

"I promise to be careful. Glad to know you still care."

Matt hung up, half hoping that Kara was in the bathroom. But she wasn't. He turned on the water, then found a note on the mirror.

> Matt ~
>
> I don't normally kiss and run but didn't think you wanted to explain my presence to your team. Catch you later.
>
> ~KQ

He frowned. He was glad she left a note, but he expected something more than this informality. After last night... Hell, he was horny again just thinking about her.

Shut it down, Costa.

He stepped into the shower cold, which cleared

his mind and his libido, then heated up the water and two minutes later stepped out. Five minutes after that he was dressed and entered the war room. Ryder Kim was, of course, already working.

"When did you get up?"

"Five o'clock, sir."

"I should have set a wake-up call. I crashed hard last night and forgot to set my alarm. I just got off the phone with Catherine."

"I read her email. I have a list of every high school principal in Spokane and Liberty Lake, public and private. There are twenty-eight."

"How'd you get them so fast?"

"The internet, sir. I had the larger list that the police put together, then narrowed it down to this subgroup. I have a secondary list of assistant principals if their information is listed on the district website."

"I'm going to call Maddox and Knolls, get them on this right now. Reach out to every principal again. I don't know that they can spare twenty-eight units today, but we need to sit on everyone we can. Maybe convince them to spend the day at the police station. Time is running out. Actually, you call Maddox—I need to talk to Andy Knolls. Catherine is certain that the next victim the killer stalks will be a cop from Liberty Lake."

Knolls answered on the third ring.

"Hope I didn't wake you, Andy."

"No. Eating breakfast."

"How'd it go last night? Did you reach everyone on the list?"

"Yes, everyone who was in town. Your press conference had an impact. But we cleared every house and warned each person to be extremely security cautious, and encouraged them to spend the day and night with others—change their routine."

"Good. We have a breakthrough of sorts. We believe that the target today is a principal at a Spokane or Spokane Valley high school. Ryder has a list, and he's calling Maddox to start doing the rounds on all of them. Can you go back to the principals only? Maybe we can put them up in a hotel or something. Do you have the budget for that? One night."

"I can make it happen."

"Great. We're getting that break, Andy, I feel it."

"I'll be in the office in twenty minutes, split the list with my officers."

"That brings me to the other issue. Based on what we already know, our profiler believes that the killer will target a law enforcement officer who works in Liberty Lake. Do you understand what that means?"

"But wouldn't he be targeting a Spokane cop? Because Victoria Manners is from Spokane?"

"We considered that, but he left Manners' body in Liberty Lake. That tells me that he's targeting either a Liberty Lake principal or a Liberty Lake cop, depending on who his primary target is and who his surrogate is."

"Yes, but—"

"Listen to me carefully, Andy. John Marston left Spokane sixteen years ago, Anne Banks left Spokane seventeen years ago. Catherine feels that whatever set the killer on this path happened before either of them left."

"I don't really understand where you're going with this," Andy said.

How could Matt explain? "Meaning, they lived here in the area a long time ago. Whatever grudge this killer has, he's waited ten, fifteen, maybe twenty years before tracking his victims down. He may have been a student at Spokane High School during Marston's ten-year tenure there. We're looking at long-ago conflicts. Can you pull old records? Both in your department and any sheriff or officer from any law enforcement agency who lived or worked in Liberty Lake…let's start ten years ago and go back twenty-five years. Both current and retired cops."

"My department will be easy—we have personnel files readily available. I'll call the Sheriff's department. They'll pull their own," Andy said.

"This is our first real big break. Anything you need, let me know."

"Thanks, Matt."

Matt ended the call.

Andy had checked everyone last night, and now they had narrowed down the potential targets. They were going to throw a wrench in this killer's plans—he knew it. They were now in the driver's seat, forcing the killer to react.

With that goal firmly in mind, he crafted an email to everyone involved—the two police chiefs, plus Maddox, Knolls, and every member of his team—including Kara. She was from Liberty Lake, she knew the area and could help keep an eye on Andy.

"Where's Jim and Michael?" he asked when he was done, surprised they weren't here.

"Mr. Esteban is at the Spokane lab—he left here at six and will update you when he has something. He and Mr. Jordan ran some cultures, I believe, that needed time to cultivate and should be ready this morning. Agent Harris came in at six-ten, said he would be eating elsewhere and back in an hour."

"What's wrong with the hotel's continental breakfast?" Matt asked.

Ryder wrinkled his nose and Matt grinned.

"I for one am fine with the cheap eats. I'll text Harris and have him pick me up—send me part of the list, whatever Maddox and Knolls can't cover."

"Yes, sir."

Matt sighed. He decided changing Ryder Kim's formal behavior wasn't going to happen overnight.

Matt went downstairs. Since it was the weekend, the hotel had added more food to the breakfast options; he had a Belgian waffle with his eggs and both sausage and bacon. Nothing wrong with that, as far as he was concerned. So what if the bacon was overcooked? It was edible and tasted like bacon.

He sat in the corner, texted Harris, then read Catherine's memo more carefully. He highlighted the key points.

> Nurses Kwan and Manners are surrogates for Banks.
>
> Banks was the real target; the others are a mere diversion for the police. Likely he would have considered how the police would take time to investigate each crime and he knows the other

victims would distract law enforcement away from figuring out his true motive.

He's killing Banks again, each time he kills a nurse. But he also understands that because there is no connection between him and his surrogate victims, their murders will divert resources and misdirect the investigation.

Rebecca Thomas, the murdered vice principal in Portland, is a substitute for the killer's real target, John Marston. Why she's a female I can only guess—he may simply have wanted someone in authority at a high school and she was convenient. Again, Thomas was a diversion, as will be the victim he has targeted for today, unless your team can stop him.

A pattern is emerging here—even if complicated. It reveals the killer's sociopathic, yet logical, thinking. Anne Banks was the first target, the first of three. John Marston was the second of three. That gives us the last—the third of three—a cop, as the specific target.

Get the names and faces of Banks and Marston to all law enforcement in the greater Spokane community.

Whoever knows them—or thinks they know them—needs to be debriefed immediately. These people may have slighted or hurt the killer in some way, maybe even indirectly, in his formative years—or at least he believes they did… Perhaps when Marston was the principal in Spokane High School, he punished the killer for something he did as a student at school. Maybe the killer felt he was wrongly accused.

Perhaps the police were called.

Perhaps he had to go to the hospital for injuries.

There may have been a lawsuit.

Someone will know the killer… If my theory is correct, he was a young teenager whenever these events occurred and thus his physical appearance has probably changed and may not be recognizable to those who once knew him.

Maybe the victims connect somehow to the killer's family life. Serial killers are often developed in the prepubescent/early puberty years when a major event severely disrupts their home life. Without any corresponding support, coupled of course with early signs of sociopathy that may or may not have been documented, a sociopath can turn into a killer.

Matt forwarded the memo to Maddox, Knolls, and Kara, and told them to focus especially on the last two paragraphs. They might have more insight.

He emailed Ryder instructions to follow up with Tony Greer about the warrant for Anne Banks's legal records at the hospital, and that he wanted as many agents as Spokane and Seattle could spare first thing Monday morning.

If we don't catch this bastard today, I will need all the people I can get to protect an unknown number of cops—and we both know how cops feel about taking protection.

Matt was not writing off the principal. So far, so good. If they could throw the killer off his game, he would make a mistake—and Matt was ready to capitalize on it.

He went back for seconds at the buffet and was on his third cup of coffee when Michael Harris walked in, dressed impeccably as usual.

"Ready, boss?"

"Don't call me that."

Michael grinned, his teeth sharply white against his dark skin. "You didn't come back to the war room last night."

"Kara and I had a drink."

Damn, why had he said that? He didn't want everyone to know they'd slept together.

"She's something."

"She's smart."

"And hot."

"What did I say?"

"Not hot. Got it."

Matt grabbed a cup of coffee to go and followed Michael to his rental car. "Ryder divvied up the list of twenty-eight principals, and we have four—let's hit them fast. You drive."

"Never pegged you as one to give up control of the transpo."

"I need to work—can't do it while driving." Matt slid into the passenger seat and typed the first address into the GPS, then pulled out his phone to follow up with Jim, Maddox, and Knolls.

"Let's go, or I will be driving and you'll be taking dictation from me."

"Roger that."

26

Liberty Lake
7:30 a.m.

Kara walked into Liberty Lake Police Department only minutes after Andy. She knew when he'd arrived because she'd waited until he showed up before she came in. The office wasn't technically open until eight, but she'd received Matt's memo and called Andy, who said he'd be there early.

Last night was fun, and she wouldn't mind sharing Agent Costa's bed another night or two before she returned to LA. She suspected, however, that there was something else going on with him—something that might move past the *let's have fun for a few nights*.

He was intense about everything he did—the job, conversation, sex.

All good, because having 100 percent of his focus on her personal enjoyment was just fine. She didn't do relationships; it wasn't in her skill set. Plus, she had a job in LA and she was itching to get back to it. *Needed* to get back to it.

So what if the hot Cuban Agent Mathias Costa interested her? So what if he was hunky and smart? He was an alpha male trying very hard, and failing, to be a beta—the way he kept asking her if she was sure she wanted to go to bed… Yeah, she was sure—she voluntarily went to his hotel room. She put her hands down his pants. Finally, she had to tease him a bit so he would let go of propriety—and then *wow.*

Yeah, she wanted another night or three.

But sex was sex, and just because she enjoyed it—and enjoyed it in particular with Matt Costa—didn't mean there was a future, and that was A-OK with her. She was hardly relationship material, and she was pretty certain Costa would disapprove of many of her undercover activities. Plus, his intensity struck her as real, but he was also a bit of a player. He certainly had plenty of experience, and absolutely knew exactly how to set off her libido.

None of that meant that if he had time off, and she had time off, that maybe they should share time off down the road. The whole friends with benefits thing had worked well for her in the past.

"You look worried," she said to Andy as he made a pot of coffee.

"I became a cop fifteen years ago."

"That's why I'm going to stick to you like glue."

He didn't so much as crack a smile.

"I don't know what I could have done."

"You didn't do anything."

"I read the memo. The killer feels that Banks and Marston hurt him in some way. Maybe they did. Maybe I did something and didn't realize it. Arrested an innocent man. Said the wrong thing at a traffic stop."

Kara put her hands up in the time-out gesture. "Whoa. Stop. Don't even go there. You are straight up one of the most honest cops I've met in my life. I'm a damn good judge of character, Andy, and you are an all-around good guy. You did *nothing* wrong. Got it?"

He still looked concerned.

"This guy is loony tunes," Kara said. "Yeah, I know, the shrink thinks he's sane—and maybe *legally* he's sane, which is a good thing so we can lock him up for the rest of his fucking life. But whatever twisted sense of *injustice* he feels, *none* of that is on you or whatever cop he has in his sights. Did Anne Banks deserve to be stabbed and carved up in front of her baby? Did John Marston deserve to be sliced and diced in his own home? Hell no.

"I don't care if Marston was a prick who expelled kids for no reason. He didn't deserve to be gutted. And Anne Banks…she was a nurse. She saved lives. What if she didn't save someone? Is that her fault? What if they couldn't be saved? Does she deserve to die because some guy comes in after a heart attack and flatlines it on the operating table? *No*."

Andy nodded and shrugged at the same time. "What do you really think? Over and above the fact you say he's a loony tune."

"Let me rephrase that. I'll side with the shrink on this one—the guy is sane. I think he has an agenda, a very specific agenda, and we're going to stop him. You and me and the FBI goon squad."

She was trying to get Andy to lighten up a bit—sure, be diligent—but if he started second-guessing himself or losing himself remembering every collar he'd made over the last fifteen years, he would be in greater danger.

"Confident, aren't you?"

"Always. I'm ready when you are."

Andy poured two to-go cups just as Abigail walked in. "I got here as soon as I could."

"Abigail, I need all personnel files of any sworn officer who worked out of our department between the dates I sent you. If you can please pull them and make a list—current, transferred, retired."

"Of course, sugar. What's going on?"

"The FBI thinks the Triple Killer is going to go after one of our people."

"No! Why on earth?"

Kara piped up. "Because he's a nut job. But this is important, okay?"

"I'm on it. It won't take me long—I'll get you the list before lunch. I can retrieve current officers in five minutes—just need to run the report."

"Send the info to me as you get it. Kara and I are going to check on a few people—we talked to all the teachers and principals yesterday, but the FBI narrowed down the potential victims to principals and vice principals only. We're still going to touch base again with those, offer protection."

"Do we have that many people?"

"If I have to haul everyone in here and put them in jail, I will," Andy said.

Not practical, but Kara liked the sentiment.

Andy continued, "I'll need patrols to ride double today, no exceptions, no one goes out alone. Detective Quinn will be with me, so that should free up someone else."

"Okay—does Chief Dunn know about this?"

After hanging out with Andy for the last couple days, Kara realized that he ran the office and the staff looked to him for guidance, not the chief. She wasn't surprised. Andy instilled loyalty among his people.

"He was included in the memo—but I don't care what he says, for the next four days at a minimum, no one is to ride alone. Agent Costa is going to debrief our office sometime today with more information about the killer, but we have to watch out for each other. And—just in case—keep the door locked when you're alone."

Now Abigail looked freaked, and maybe she should be, Kara thought.

They left the station. The first two principals they checked on were alive and well—one they woke up, and one was tending to his yard.

Andy explained to each what was going on and suggested that they not be alone for the rest of the day and night. The first was divorced and lived alone. Two other cops had spoken to him the night before, and he had already made plans to visit his daughter in Seattle. Andy got her contact information and his cell phone number.

The second, a vice principal at the elementary school, felt they were overreacting but finally—after thirty minutes of conversation and arguments—

agreed that he would cancel his standing golf game that morning and stay home with his wife.

Andy was frustrated. "He didn't take us seriously."

"You did what you could," Kara said.

"I'll have patrol drive by every hour. It's all I can do—I can't force them to leave town or hire a bodyguard."

He called in the order.

"Andy—you can't take this personally."

"Wouldn't you? This is your town, too. You may not live here anymore, but your grandmother does. You have friends here. There are seven thousand people, take or leave, who live here full-time. They live in Liberty Lake because it's safe. A good place to raise kids. A good place for recreation, to start a family, to be happy. And this person has stolen that security from us. From everyone. No one is going to feel safe again."

Kara didn't want to tell him she didn't have many friends, and none here, other than her grandmother. And maybe Maddox. In fact, Andy was probably the closest thing she had to a friend and they'd just met.

And safety? It was relative and never a given.

"Andy, Liberty Lake has you. And they'll have you when this is over. *You'll* make them feel safe again."

"I don't know how you live and work in Los Angeles. So much violence and hate and anger. Senseless violence. I love my town, Kara. I don't want it to change."

It was a naive but sweet idea. Kara didn't want to

destroy Andy's optimism, so she said, "Then help it stay the same."

She saw people for who they were—the good, the bad, the very, very ugly. She didn't see a lot of good, but so what? That was the way the world worked. Violence might seem senseless to someone who had a good soul, but she understood it. She knew why the people she went after hurt and killed people. For money, for power, for control. To make themselves feel superior.

She didn't fit in here—Liberty Lake was too good for her.

When she met someone like Andy, she didn't initially believe that they were as noble and good as they seemed. But he was exactly as he came off. She hoped that he kept that spark of optimism and joy because so few people had it. In fact, she knew only two people who didn't have an ounce of hate or violence in their soul—Andy and her grandmother.

Andy was the reason she did what she did—people like Andy Knolls and her grandmother Em. And damn if she'd ever let them down.

They were driving to the third name on their list when Matt Costa called Andy.

Andy answered and put Matt on speaker. "Kara is here with me. She's riding shotgun today."

"Good. Harris and I are at a spread in the county, about halfway between Spokane and Liberty Lake. Joanne Grant. She's the principal of St. Elizabeth's."

"Is she—?"

"She's not here. Her place has been tossed. I'd think she was robbed, but nothing valuable appears to have been taken. Cushions are torn open, a mirror's broken, a bookshelf knocked over. There's no blood, but we need an APB out on her."

"Grant left town yesterday," Andy said. He typed on his onboard computer. "Right after the press conference."

"How certain are you?"

"My officers followed up on the phone. I have her contact information—Abigail also has it. She's in Yakima with her sister."

"I'll get it from Abigail."

"You think she was the target."

"Very likely. Dr. Jones said if we screw with his plans, he may crack or deviate. This house? He's definitely cracking."

"That's great."

"Hold that thought."

"I mean, we saved the principal."

"It's still only eight-thirty in the morning. He may very well have a backup plan, and we need to make sure everyone is accounted for."

"Of course. Kara and I just cleared two, are heading to the third on our list."

"I need a favor—can you call in the crime scene investigators? I need this place gone over and I already called Jim, but we have to jump through the goddamn hoops Chief Packard put in place."

"That's county—"

"I'm not dealing with another jurisdiction. This is the Triple Killer. My team would normally take care of it—when we're fully staffed. But right now I need help, and Jordan's people are good."

"I'll get it done."

"Thank you. Be careful out there, Andy, Kara."

"Always," Kara said.

Andy called Brian Maddox and relayed the information. He'd navigate the jurisdictional issues and get the job done.

When Andy hung up, he said, "We talked to Grant yesterday. She left because of the press conference. It worked."

He sounded relieved and happy all rolled together, but Kara was still worried. Matt was right. They may have taken one target off the table, but he would have a second or third target in his sights.

Until the cop. According to the shrink, he had a specific person in mind. A person he would be compelled to kill. But considering he'd escalated—nowhere in the reports had she seen *trashing a house* as part of his MO—maybe he wouldn't wait until March 9 to go after the cop. Maybe he would speed up the timetable. They all had to be diligent from here on out.

"We're here," Andy said, and pulled in front of a small A-frame cabin on a slope. "I was here last night, just after midnight. Jeffrey Ogdenburg, principal of Central Valley High."

"Our alma mater."

"Was he there when you graduated?"

"No, it was Susan Carpenter. Bitch."

"She wasn't that bad. I had her for English my senior year, before she was the principal."

Kara glanced at him. "You were never in trouble."

"How do you know?"

"Because you would hate her, too."

Andy glanced at his patrol computer. "Odgenburg is thirty-nine, single, lives alone. He said he'd be going to his sister's this morning, would keep the place locked up. The patrol drove by six times between midnight until now—no sign of trouble."

They got out and approached the door, rang the bell. No answer. It was already after nine in the morning, but some people liked to sleep in.

Kara wasn't one of those, but sleep had never been her friend.

Andy knocked loudly. "Mr. Ogdenburg, this is Detective Andy Knolls with the Liberty Lake Police Department. We talked last night."

No answer.

He knocked again.

No response.

Kara said, "I'll walk around, see if his car is in the garage. Maybe he already left."

She took out her gun. Andy seemed surprised, but she wasn't one to take chances, especially when a killer was out and about. They didn't know what to expect, but she had an itch—and she always trusted her instincts.

She walked around to the side and looked in the garage window. As her eyes adjusted to the dark, she spotted a lone car. A Toyota Land Cruiser.

She went back to the front. "He own a Land Cruiser?"

"There is one registered to his name."

"It's in the garage."

Andy looked stricken, as if he knew what they would find inside.

"I need to call it in."

"We have probable cause," Kara said. "I have your back, Andy."

She doubted that Andy had ever drawn his gun in the line of duty. He would likely go to the range, practice every month, but it was clear he didn't think he would ever have to shoot. Small town cop with a small town girlfriend and a small town life.

Kara almost felt sorry for him. Like he still believed in Santa Claus and she was going to burst his bubble.

Andy radioed in their intentions, then pounded on the door. "Police! We're coming in!"

Kara tried the door. It wasn't locked.

She opened it and went low to the right. Andy entered.

She smelled blood.

"We need to clear the house," she said.

"He's dead."

"We don't know what's dead yet," she said sharply. "We need to clear the house now."

Andy pulled his gun—belatedly, she felt, which irritated her—and went left, toward the living area and kitchen.

That left the bedrooms for Kara and dammit, she knew that's where the dead body would be. Because most likely the killer sliced open Ogdenburg while he was sleeping.

The house wasn't large, a two bedroom, two bath spread far from any other houses.

Ogdenburg's door was open. And though she knew he was dead—the smell of the dead was something you never forgot—seeing him flayed in his own bed startled her.

She shook her head, checked the room—closets, bathroom, under his bed.

"Clear," she called out.

Andy said nothing.

"Clear!" she shouted, and left the bedroom, heart pounding.

She should never have left Andy by himself. He had never faced a situation like this before, and she would never forgive herself if something happened to him. The killer could still be here, hiding, waiting to attack.

"Andy!" she called, the hair on her skin rising, as she held her gun up, but close to her so no one could grab it by surprise. Checking each doorway, behind each door, hesitating around corners, expecting a killer or a dead cop.

"Kara."

She heard his voice—barely. Andy was standing outside on the porch, his face white and drawn.

"I shouldn't be a cop."

She wasn't in the mood to counsel or coddle or correct him. She was angry that he'd scared her, and angry that he didn't have her back. She'd been alone in that house when no one should leave their partner alone.

You're an undercover cop for a reason. You don't

trust anyone. Why did you think you could trust this cop?

"Call it in, Detective," Kara snapped. "I'll secure the scene."

27

Liberty Lake
11:15 a.m.

Matt went out to the crime scene in Liberty Lake. He was surprised to find Kara directing cops and talking to Miles Jordan and Jim Esteban.

He approached. "Where's Andy?"

Anger flashed in her sharp blue eyes, then she suppressed it. For a cop who kept her emotions in check, he was surprised she let him see anything and wondered if it was deliberate.

A second look told him it was raw anger—it was real, and it was directed toward Andy. Matt wouldn't want to be on the receiving end of Kara's rage.

She jerked her finger toward the street. Andy was standing in front of his truck, not looking at the house or cops, but gazing into the woods beyond.

Matt would talk to him later. He asked Jim, "Anything new?"

Jim shook his head. "Same MO; sliced down once, across three times. Killed in his bed, probably didn't even know what was happening until the knife came down. No struggle. Killer cleaned up in the vic's bathroom, which may give us a huge break. He cleaned up after himself, but bathroom surfaces are fantastic to get prints or other biological matter. Blood in grout and cracks is really hard to erase without dousing the room in bleach."

Kara said, "Forensics will confirm, but he entered through the front door. No sign that he picked the lock—he may have had the key, or was as good as me at picking a lock. No telltale scrapes. The door was unlocked when Andy and I arrived. We had probable cause to enter. Ogdenburg's car was in the garage, he wasn't answering the door, and his name was on our list."

"No complaints from me," Matt said. He would have done the exact same thing.

"We cleared the house. I found the body in the master bedroom. Andy called it in."

"Is the coroner still in there?"

"Yes, but he hasn't removed the body. I thought you might want to take a look so asked him to hold until you arrived," Kara said.

Matt wanted to ask who put her in charge of the crime scene, but there was something in her tone that had him backing down.

He walked through the house. It was exactly as Kara had described, in her brief, efficient manner.

But she was right, he wanted to see. He wanted the image in his mind so he could better understand the Triple Killer. This scene—it wasn't violent. A lot of blood, a dead body, but it was… Simple. Enter the house in the middle of the night, kill a man in his bed—no other assault, neither sexual nor physical—clean up in his bathroom, leave.

Bastard.

The coroner said, “Can I take him?”

Matt nodded and left the house. “Coroner’s done. Do your thing,” he said to Jim. He glanced around. “Where’s Quinn?”

“Helping with the canvass,” Jim said.

Yet Andy was still standing by his truck. While Jim and Miles brought their equipment inside, Matt approached the cop. “Detective.”

“You don’t want me on this case, Agent Costa.”

“Yes, I do.”

“I’m resigning.”

“Like hell you are. In the middle of a homicide investigation?”

“I could have gotten Kara killed.”

Now Matt *was* confused, though Kara’s irritability made a little more sense. “Explain,” he demanded.

“We got here and she went in, gun drawn, told me to clear the house with her. I smelled his body. The violence done to him. The blood…” Andy wasn’t looking at Matt.

“We knew this was going to happen…yet, I didn’t believe it. And it happened. I couldn’t stop it. I was here last night, I talked to him, warned him. Made sure every door and window were secure. And then I left.”

“That’s not on you, Andy.”

“I froze. I left her in there, alone. What if the

killer was still inside, hiding? What if he attacked her and I couldn't stop him?"

Conflicted emotions rolled through Matt. Andy was a small town cop. Kara was a big city detective. Now he realized why she was mad. She expected Andy to back her up, and he didn't. Dangerous for anyone, but especially for cops.

It would have pissed off Matt as well. As a cop, you had to trust your partner. There could be no doubt, otherwise you couldn't do what was needed to save lives—and protect your own.

"That's ultimately your decision, Detective Knolls, but not now, not when we're in the middle of this investigation and I need all hands."

"I don't know that I can."

"You can and you will. You sit on this house until everyone is done with their job. Talk to the neighbors. Ask if anyone has seen anything suspicious in the last month. Talk to Ogdenburg's staff, anyone who knows him. Did he think he was being followed. Have conflict with former staff or students. I'll notify next of kin." Not Matt's favorite part of the job, but he had questions, and right now he didn't trust Andy to get answers.

"Was Joanne Grant the primary target? And because she left town, he came here to Ogdenburg?" Andy asked.

"I don't know," Matt admitted, though knowing who had been the original target could help get into this killer's head. He had trashed Grant's house, telling Matt he'd been furious that she wasn't there. "We won't know until we find the killer and ask him. But we're processing both scenes and he *is* getting reckless. Trashing Grant's house proves it. We're jerking his chain and we *are* going to find him. This killer stalked his victim, knew his pattern, knew that he would be here, at home, at night, alone. He knew there was no boyfriend or girlfriend or spouse. He knew which bedroom was his. Someone had to have seen something. They might not know it, but they know you, Andy, and they trust you."

"I graduated from Central," he said, forlorn. "So did Kara. So did nearly everyone who lives here."

"Stop feeling goddamn sorry for yourself. Maybe you should resign, but you're not going to do it until we catch this killer." Matt didn't want to be hard on him, but maybe he needed some tough love. "I need you, and you will step up. Detective Quinn isn't a member of your police department, and she's been running this crime scene, which a defense attorney might be able to exploit." He doubted it, because Kara was a sworn officer, but Matt would say anything to get Andy's head back into the game.

"I didn't think about that."

"And remember—whatever your problems, it's nothing that can't be fixed with more training. You're a damn good cop—and like all of us, you can get better. When you're done here, arrange a meeting with all past and present law enforcement. I don't care if they're eighty years old living in a retirement home, any cop with *any* connection to Liberty Lake—however minor—I want in a meeting at your station tomorrow at noon. No exceptions. You put together the list and check it twice. Someone here knows this bastard, and we're going to brainstorm until we figure it out."

"If I may offer a suggestion?"

"Offer."

"We don't have enough room at Liberty Lake PD to host that many people. But the main briefing room in Spokane would work."

The less Matt had to deal with Chief Packard, the better, but Andy was right. "Fine, you make it work. Talk to Maddox. He promised to run interference with his boss."

"That, I can do."

28

Spokane
1:00 p.m.

Matt finally got word that the warrants had come through for the hospital lawsuits. He asked Ryder to get Ogdenburg's next of kin information to him, while he and Harris drove back to Spokane.

Four large boxes awaited them. He wanted to call bullshit, but the administrator explained that this was common for hospitals—more cases were dismissed or settled than ever went to court.

"But I only want the cases that name Anne Banks."

"That's what you have. Fifty-one cases that were settled or dismissed. In the box labeled A I included a summary sheet, and a list of each case that did go to trial where she was a named defendant or where she was called as a witness. There were only four. Your assistant said he was getting the documents already through the online file system with the court."

"Thank you," he said. He didn't know where to start.

"If I may," the administrator said as if she'd read his mind, "I would start with wrongful death accusations. They are the bulk of the lawsuits, to be honest. The others are nuisance cases or minor complaints. One mother sued because she waited in the emergency room for twelve hours before her daughter was seen. We were in the middle of a multicar accident, numerous victims, and she brought her daughter in for a cough that turned out to be nothing more than the common cold. I don't see someone like that killing anyone, but the warrant was clear that you needed every case where Anne Banks was mentioned."

True.

"I took the liberty of separating the cases into wrongful death or injury and everything else. Hopefully, that'll help?"

"It will. Thank you."

Michael helped Matt put the boxes in the trunk. "I know that look," Michael groaned.

"Shit rolls downhill, buddy. Ryder will help, but this is yours. I need someone competent that I trust, not a rookie cop who doesn't know what to look for. Spokane PD is already running through students who had issues with Marston during his tenure. I can't ask them for more. And I'm notifying Ogdenburg's next of kin. You want that job? I'll swap paperwork for a death notification."

"No, no you do that. Maybe I can ask the hot detective to help—I mean, Detective Quinn."

"Go ahead," Matt said. "She's probably still at the crime scene, and somehow I don't think even a guy as charming as you will be able to convince a workaholic undercover cop to spend her vacation sitting at a desk going through paperwork."

"Yeah, maybe not. She sort of scares me."

She sort of scared Matt, too, but for different reasons.

After Matt dropped Michael and the boxes of medical lawsuits at the hotel war room, he headed downtown to tell Jeff Ogdenburg's sister that her brother was dead. He hated this part of the job, but it had to be done. Plus, she might be privy to information about anyone following her brother, or anything he might have said about a prowler or former student.

Brian Maddox called while Matt was driving. "I talked to Andy," he said. "We're meeting tomorrow at noon in our auditorium. It'll fit everyone, and it's secure. You think this is necessary?"

"Yes. And you said you live in Liberty Lake, right? You need to be at the meeting."

"Andy said the same thing. And that house in Newman Lake? I didn't know it when I heard the report that the ATV had been stolen from there, but Andy told me that the house had been in my family years ago. My parents owned it, and Julie and I lived there early in our marriage, before I took the job in Spokane. My parents retired to St. George—in Utah—and sold it when I moved to Spokane."

"I don't like coincidences."

"Nor do I, but I think this is truly one. Newman is smaller than Liberty Lake with more vacation homes."

"I'm going to want you, in particular, to study the two victims' case files."

"I already have. I honestly don't remember Anne Banks. That doesn't mean much of anything, because whenever I would go to the hospital on the job, it's generally chaos. And it was a long time ago. I could have crossed paths with her, because I certainly went there often enough during the years she worked there, but nothing stands out."

"My staff is culling through dismissed and settled lawsuits where Banks was named. Nothing may come of it, but right now our only lead is looking for a connection between Banks and Marston. I'd like you to look at them, too. They're at the hotel, if you can stop by there at some point today, or tomorrow before the debriefing."

"I'll go there today. Marston I remember. He came to a couple community meetings we had between the police department and school districts in the wake of Columbine. He was instrumental in making sure that schools and law enforcement are all on the same page in the event of a hostage situation or school shooting. And I led a tactical drill at his school when he was still principal, for training purposes, years ago. So I've talked to him, but only in those capacities."

"It's a start. Have you run any complaints against him? Assaults? Other charges or accusations? I know your people are working on school discipline reports during that time."

"Yes, and there's nothing in our system on Marston. I contacted the Sheriff's department. They don't have him in their system, either. The guy was clean."

In the initial investigation, if Marston had a restraining order or had been party to a lawsuit, it should have popped. If he had any criminal record it would have popped, too, but a major felony would preclude him from serving as a teacher, not to mention a principal. Yet Matt didn't believe in making those kind of assumptions, so it was always best to double-check.

"I have one more thing," Maddox said. "Two of my officers interviewed a teacher who worked with Marston. She's now retired, but she said there was a former employee who had threatened him shortly before he left Spokane to get his PhD."

"Name?"

"She doesn't remember. I have her contact information. Maybe you can get more out of her."

It sounded like a waste of time, but he couldn't let it pass by unanswered. "Send me her info. I'll stop by after I talk to Ogdenburg's family."

"Andy should do that."

"Yes, but he's not going to ask the right questions. He misstepped this morning and he's taking it hard."

"He told me. He's not used to this level of investigation. But he's a good cop, Costa. I vouch for him."

"I told him to get his head in the game, that I'm counting on him."

Matt hung up. Ryder was analyzing so many reports and Matt kept adding more to his workload. Ryder needed help. They were running press reports, crime reports, court documents, full background—it would take days to sort through. After Ogdenburg's sister, then talking to the retired teacher, Matt would go back and devote time to the tedious chore.

¡Mierda, estamos demasiado delgados!

They were spread far too thin. They needed more people. He'd been stubborn with Tony about who was on his team because he knew what the job entailed and how close they would by necessity need to work. Maybe he'd been too stubborn. As soon as he pulled up in front of Ogdenburg's sister's house, he sent Tony a message.

Save this email because you'll rarely hear this again: You were right. I was being picky about my team. I'm still picky, but you know who we need. You pick the rest, just give me veto power. One of them has to be able to work with the press and locals, but they need to be more than a mouthpiece. I'm already tired of playing middleman. I know we have ultimate authority and jurisdiction, but we're going to need the help of local law enforcement to effectively run this new unit.

As he walked up to the door, Tony responded.

I knew you would come to your senses. Trust me. I have your back.

Matt got his first break that afternoon.

Talking to Ogdenburg's sister had been difficult. Death notifications always were. She was unable to help answer any questions.

Jeff hadn't said anything about being followed or

harassed or feeling uncomfortable—not to his sister, and she was certain he wouldn't have bothered their parents about anything that might worry them. Matt vowed to find the killer and left, his gut twisted, fueled by anger over a senseless death.

He almost didn't talk to the teacher, Bollinger, that Maddox told him about, because there was so much work to catch up on. The lawsuits were the most likely to point to someone who had a grudge against Anne Banks, and he wanted to help go through the files—the more hands the better.

But Dorothy Bollinger didn't live too far from the Ogdenburg's neighborhood. It was an older, well-kept area with tree-lined streets, wide yards and raised porches.

He knocked on the door and introduced himself to the tall, gray-haired grandmother. She invited him into her too-warm house and offered him water or coffee.

Pictures of family of all ages and from all generations took up every inch of wall space.

"Actually, coffee would be great." He rarely accepted hospitality from witnesses, but he was running on fumes after visiting Ogdenburg's sister, and he could smell the rich brew filling the quaint home.

She brought a tray into the dining room and motioned for him to sit. "Black? Light?"

"Black, thank you."

She'd also put out a tray of grandma cookies, as he thought of the small shortbread circles with fruit in the middle. He took one of those, too. He hadn't eaten since breakfast.

"Ms. Bollinger, I'm following up on your conversation with two Spokane PD officers earlier today."

"Oh yes, they said someone might have additional questions. It's *so* awful to hear what happened to Mr. Marston in Missoula. He was a wonderful principal. I was sorry when he left to get his doctorate. Tough, but fair. It was usually the difficult kids who ended up liking him the most because he held them to a high standard. Too often, parents and even teachers don't expect teenagers to be accountable—to society, to family, to school. They dismiss bad behavior as if it's something they all will grow out of, when if they're not corrected, they will generally come to believe their bad behavior is acceptable."

Matt didn't need the sociology lesson, though he didn't disagree with her. "You mentioned another teacher who had a conflict with Mr. Marston."

"No—not a teacher. It was an employee. And ever since those nice officers left, I've been trying to remember his name. I can *almost* picture him."

"*Him*. That's good. What was the conflict?"

"Mr. Marston fired him—and I honestly don't think I ever knew the circumstances around it. But it must have been egregious. Mr. Marston rarely fired anyone. Teachers are hired by the school district, and he wouldn't be able to specifically terminate any, though I'm sure he would have a say. All serious discipline was handled by the school board. But he had discretion over other hires."

"Like?"

"Maintenance, teaching assistants, some of the support staff."

That's good. That narrows it down, Matt thought. "How are you aware of this?"

"It was winter. I remember that much, because we had just come off three snow days in a row. We're used to snow and ice here, but this was a particularly bad storm. This man pushed Mr. Marston when he was getting out of his car. Just pushed him down into the snowbank. He was belligerent, yelling at Mr. Marston. I had just driven into the parking lot—I got out of my car and told them I was calling the police. Mr. Marston said no, don't. A couple other teachers were there and we were talking about calling the police, regardless of what Mr. Marston said. We didn't know if the man had a weapon, or if he was going to use his fists. The man yelled more, pushed Mr. Marston down, then left. Stomped through the snow to a car on the far side of the lot. Later, I asked Mr. Marston what had happened. He said he had to let the man go because he'd come to work drunk again. The way he said it, it was clear it wasn't the first time. I asked why he didn't go to the police, and Mr. Marston said the man had lost his wife a year ago, and hadn't been the same since."

Matt leaned forward. "You didn't tell the other officers that."

"I guess I didn't remember this morning." She smiled. "You're very good at your job."

"You just had more time to think about it. And you don't remember his name?"

"No, I recognized him, but I never had interactions with him, if that makes sense. I taught American History to high school juniors for thirty years, until I retired eight years ago. This happened—well, fifteen, sixteen, seventeen years ago. Maybe longer? I haven't lost my mind, thank the Lord, but I don't remember everything well."

Sixteen years ago—that was when Marston left Spokane to get his PhD. That would help. "I can find out exactly when because you had three snow days in a row, correct?"

"Oh my, yes! You would. The school district would have records of that. And it was February, I'm almost positive. I drove to school irritated because the neighbors didn't take down their Christmas lights yet and I had lost a bet."

"A bet?"

"My husband and I used to make these silly little bets. He told me the Lawtons wouldn't have their lights down before February. I said of course they would, they're responsible folks. And that morning must have been early February because they were still up and I had to cook dinner every night for a week. And Agent Costa, I don't like to cook."

When Matt left Mrs. Bollinger's house, he called Brian Maddox and relayed the information to him.

Maddox remembered the storm, down to the day and year—eighteen months before Marston left.

Matt said, "We need all employment records from that school—any male who was fired in January or early February that year."

"I can do that, but we might not get anything until Monday."

"Can't you light a fire under the school district? This is our single best lead."

"I'll see what I can do on a Saturday. I know the superintendent—he might do it himself."

"Thanks, Brian. I'm going to check in with the forensics team, then go to the hotel to help with the lawsuits I have my team going through. We're getting closer."

Matt hung up. He'd been so certain they'd thwarted the killer after the warnings they issued. So certain that the killer wouldn't be able to get to someone… But he had. Whether Ogdenburg was the intended victim this time or a backup because the killer couldn't get to Joanne Grant, Matt didn't know. But destroying Grant's house suggested someone with barely controlled rage.

But he calmed down. Ogdenburg was killed just like the others. One deep cut, three slices. Methodical, and he cleaned up after.

They had less than three days to find the answers—when their psychopath would target a cop.

Damn if Matt was going to lose someone else.

29

Liberty Lake
3:00 p.m.

Kara had sent her boss Lex to voice mail three times; each message said, “Call me when you can.” Nothing more, nothing less. But three times?

She was still angry with Andy. He was a cop; he should act like it. She wasn’t a coddler; she didn’t tell people that it was *okay* when they screwed up. She expected a certain level of competence, and being a good backup was required. Hell, she screwed up plenty and took the knocks for it, but she’d never failed in her duty. She’d never put another cop’s life in danger.

She worked the scene because Andy didn’t. She wasn’t a cop in this town; she would have bailed if she wasn’t already invested in the outcome.

If she wasn’t worried about the cops in Liberty Lake.

The feds knew what they were doing, but they were sorely understaffed. Spokane PD was more than competent, in particular Maddox, but this wasn't their jurisdiction and they had other cases to attend. They were pulling out all the stops, but for how long? Would it take another dead cop before they found this nut job?

Kara couldn't just sit by and kick back while every cop in eastern Washington was looking for this killer. If something happened while she zoned out, she would never forgive herself. People she cared about lived here—were cops here—and she had to put aside her frustration with Andy Knolls. Focus on his strengths—and he had them. Hell, she had liked him until he walked out of that house while she searched it high and low. It didn't matter that nothing happened and the killer was long gone; it was the moment of panic when she called for him and he didn't answer—she thought he was dead. Then the moment of disbelief and rage that he had walked out and didn't have her back.

Calm. Down.

Andy needed more training. This was Liberty Lake after all—he'd probably never seen a murder victim in his life.

Forensics had found one small piece of evidence, but Kara didn't think it would lead anywhere. They determined that the killer hadn't parked on the street, but had used the trail system on foot. There was evidence of footprints leading up to the house from the back. There were many other footprints—but Andy had brought out cops to check the house last night. These were distinct because they went to and from a trail that edged the back of Ogdenburg's unfenced property.

A team of two officers were following it, but Kara didn't hold out much hope that they'd find a witness or evidence.

Once forensics had cleared the scene and the cops came back from their canvass of neighbors—none of whom could be seen from Ogdenburg's house, and those who were home couldn't recall seeing a trespasser—Kara left. She drove back to Em's, had a very late lunch, and called Lex.

"Planning to transfer to Spokane now?" Lex said, irritated.

"You didn't say it was urgent."

He sighed. "Kara, we have a problem."

She hated Lex's lead-ins. "Just tell me."

"Chen's working on a plea deal with the feds."

"What the fuck? What are the feds even doing in this shit storm? This is an LAPD case! It's our jurisdiction, our evidence, our undercover sting. You damn well know that when I shot Chen's thug that it was justified."

"I know that. You were cleared internally. But the feds want Chen's supplier. And Chen says that Xavier Fong wasn't armed when you shot him."

"He threw a fucking *knife* at me!"

"And missed—"

"I have a scar."

"Mostly missed. And then wasn't armed and you shot him."

"He threw a knife at my back and if his aim was any better you'd be talking to my corpse. He was reaching into his belt for another weapon and I shot him."

"The feds are listening to Chen."

"He runs a sweatshop. Brings in slaves to do his work for him. He killed Sunny!"

"I know, Kara—and believe me, we're doing everything we can—"

"I'm coming back. Right now. You can't let them do this!"

"That would be the worst thing you can do right now."

This could *not* be happening. "I spent the last fourteen months building a case against David Chen. We have him. I handed the DA a damn good, prosecutable case. Against Chen and a dozen of his associates and three businesses!"

"Kara, you did what you were supposed to, and we rescued hundreds of people. *Hundreds*. Feel good about that."

"I do feel good about that," she snapped, "and I'll feel fucking *amazing* when I know David Chen will never see the light of day."

"I just wanted to tell you what was going on before you heard it from anyone else. I'm doing my best here—I've taken it all the way to the top. The chief knows that the feds only got involved when your name came up."

"Shit. Because I pissed off a couple fibbies years ago they're going to let a predator like David Chen get a walk?"

"He won't walk. But…yeah, they're thinking about a plea and reduced sentence. And if they take the case from us and make it federal, we're screwed. The DA wants it—he's fighting for it. You do have friends down here, and DA Dyson is one of your biggest fans. I'll let you know what happens."

"I should be there." Dear God, she was whining now. This wasn't fair!

"Dyson might call you. You can talk to him, but being a thousand miles away from LA is a good thing."

"Call me when you know anything," she said. "Please," she added. She sounded desperate. She *was* desperate. She *hated* being stuck up here when her entire case was falling apart because the fucking federal bureaucrats had their nose out of joint because she embarrassed them *years* ago.

"You still helping the Liberty Lake PD?"

"Doing their fucking job is more like it," she muttered.

"You okay?"

She rubbed her eyes. *No.* "Just tired. Our killer took a second victim in Liberty Lake. A high school principal. If pattern holds, his next victim is supposed to be a cop. But damn, I'm going to help catch him before a cop dies."

"Sounds messy up there."

"It is, but there are some competent feds. They seem to all be in Spokane."

"Good to know, because I haven't met any that I liked. Be careful."

"Anything for you, boss." She hung up.

Damn, damn, damn!

"Honey?" Em said from the doorway. "Is everything okay?"

"Peachy."

"You can talk to me. You know that, right?"

Kara looked at her sweet grandmother. Emily Dorsey didn't have a mean bone in her body. She didn't watch the news because she thought it was sad; she didn't watch violence on television. She liked the shows where unknown people sang, where stars danced, where there was always a happy ending.

No way was Kara going to introduce her to a dark slice of humanity. Em had enough of that shit from her own daughter.

"Thanks, Em," Kara said. She got up and hugged her. "I love you."

Em seemed surprised. "Are you sure you're okay?"

"Yeah."

"It's just—you haven't said *I love you* in, well, since you told me you were moving to Los Angeles."

"That can't be right."

"I'm old, not senile."

"Maybe I don't tell you enough. But I do."

"I've always known that, pumpkin." Em smiled and touched her cheek. "Are you going back to Spokane tonight?"

She had been thinking about it. Because if she stayed here, she'd be thinking about what was going on in Los Angeles. If she started thinking about her case against Chen falling apart, then she would get on a plane and confront whichever bastard was screwing with her. And *that* would probably not help Lex or the DA keep jurisdiction within LAPD.

"Is that okay?"

"Honey, working makes you happy. And all I've ever wanted was for you to be happy."

30

Spokane
8:30 p.m.

The killer followed the federal agent—Special Agent in Charge Mathias Costa according to the news reports—from the Spokane Police Department. He had been waiting for his target to leave at his usual time, but he didn't. Maybe he wasn't even there.

Which bothered him. He made a point of keeping his targets under tight watch in the days leading up to the kill.

He told himself it didn't matter. He'd seen him yesterday; he'd see him tonight. Maybe drive by his house, watch him turn off the lights.

But when he saw the head federal agent, the killer was compelled to follow him. Learn everything about him. Where was he staying? How many people did he have with him? Did he have a bad habit or two? Drink too much like his old man? Pick up a prostitute because he was in a town far from home?

The newspaper itself didn't have as much information as the online blog the newspaper ran. They'd done a big article on Costa and his team and interviewed the Assistant Director of the FBI. One of the very top, most important people in the FBI.

All thinking about *him*. They called him the Triple Killer. He didn't care much for the name, but he *had* a name, a special FBI code name.

It was kind of scary and kind of exciting, all at the same time.

According to the blog, Mathias Costa was in charge of the Mobile Response Team, a new squad of the FBI that traveled to areas that had minimal law enforcement presence.

> "Our goal," Assistant Director Anthony Greer said, "is to provide support and assistance to local law enforcement in rural and underserved communities. We have some of the sharpest minds attached to the Mobile Response Team with advanced training in forensics, investigations, interrogation, and psychology."

One interesting note, he saw, was that the MRT unit wasn't fully staffed yet. But he read the article three times and it was clear that the team had been sent here half-staffed because of *him*, because *he* was that important, because his *case* was crucial.

How exciting!

Still, the killer couldn't afford to get sloppy. After seeing the cops at his target last night, and going to Plan B and the bitch not even *being* there, he had to be smart. He shouldn't have gone into her house when he realized she had run away. That had been a mistake, though he wore gloves and his hair was under a cap and he had been careful. Now? He had to be smarter than he'd ever been. So what if they had figured out his pattern. They didn't know what these people had done to him. They didn't know who was *really* important.

He couldn't be stopped now. The best for last. The most guilty would die, and then he had a new plan. A new, perfect finale that would atone for all that had been stolen from him.

He followed Special Agent in Charge Mathias Costa to a hotel off the interstate, just outside of the downtown area. It was neither a fancy hotel or a dive.

Calling it quits early, are you?

He frowned. He saw Deputy Chief Brian Maddox's car in the parking lot. Were they all having a meeting? Why would they be meeting here, at the hotel? That seemed rather odd.

He had to take the risk. He *had* to know what they were doing. No one would recognize him, but he was always careful during his killing week not to do anything that would draw attention to himself. People were generally stupid, but some people weren't.

Some people might remember a face if they saw it twice.

He needed to wait for a count of ten before he followed Costa.

His palms itched to open the car door. He wondered if the federal agent would know him if he saw him. Would he know that he was looking into the eyes of a man who had killed?

Had Costa killed? He was a cop. How many cops had pulled the trigger in the line of duty? How many had pulled the trigger just because they felt like it? Had Costa been in the military? Had he fought in a war?

Ten.

His subconscious told him it was time. He opened the door, casually closed it. Didn't lock it. He left nothing of import in his car. He'd only had it for two months. He always bought a different car before he started hunting. Then when he left Spokane, he would sell it and get something else. Another nondescript, five-year-old reliable sedan that looked like half the cars on the road.

He didn't want to stand out.

He entered the lobby. It was a nice lobby, but not crowded. He would definitely stand out if he stood here for too long.

Look like you have a purpose.

There was a lounge to the right. Only a dozen or so people were in the bar, probably all guests. He walked in purposefully. Sat at the bar. Ordered a beer. He hated drinking—his father had made sure of that—but he could tolerate a beer.

The bartender said, "Charge to your room?"

"No, cash."

The bartender rang up the receipt and slapped it down on the bar. He examined it. Six fucking dollars for a bottle of beer. No wonder they had no money while he was growing up. His dad spent it all on liquor.

He paid and sat there, sipped his beer, discreetly looking around.

A couple other people drank alone, watching the muted news behind the bar, the words scrolling up; a few of the guests sat together at tables.

He almost did a double take.

In the corner of the bar was Deputy Chief Brian Maddox and a blonde. A young blonde who was not his wife. She was very pretty, but she was a cop. He didn't know how he knew that, but he did. Maybe it was because of how she seemed to know he was looking at her and glanced in his direction. He pretended to be watching the news.

New cop? A fed? He didn't recognize her, and he'd been watching the Spokane Police Department for two full months. Didn't mean much—there were a lot of cops here. But it was clear that this lady cop and Maddox were friendly. Why hadn't he seen her before? If Maddox was cheating on his wife—the bastard—why hadn't he picked up on it?

She must be a fed. She wasn't in town before, now she was, and maybe she and Maddox knew each other from something or were just working together to find him.

He almost smiled at the thought that here he was and they had no idea.

Still, he didn't like not knowing all the players he might encounter.

He almost walked out, but then Maddox and the blonde got up and left. They talked in the lobby for a minute, then Maddox left the hotel and the blonde went up the staircase.

He breathed easier. He was right; she was with the feds. He hadn't screwed up his surveillance.

He took another sip of his beer and said to the bartender, "I noticed a couple police cars outside. Trouble?"

He shook his head. "Not here. We've been getting a lot of them in and out this week. With the murder up in Liberty Lake and all. A couple of the federal agents are staying here."

"How exciting," he said. A couple of the feds? Wouldn't they all stay in the same hotel? Did that mean there were only a few working this case? That would confirm the information in the paper. But how few were a couple? Two? Four? Six? "I read about the murder in the paper."

"There was another one, early this morning."

"Really? I didn't hear anything about it."

"Was on the news, right before you walked in."

Perceptive bartender. He wasn't going to be able to stay long, didn't want to be remembered.

"Another nurse?"

He shook his head. "Some guy. I didn't catch the name. It was up in Liberty Lake."

"Wow. Spokane used to be really safe."

"Where you from?"

Careful.

"Born here, but left for college. Stayed in California for the weather, just here on business."

"I hear ya. If my parents didn't need me here, I'd be down south so fast. Arizona. The desert. I've been trying to convince them to move."

Fortunately, another customer wanted a refill, so

the bartender walked away without any more small talk. So he left a buck on the bar—not too large or too small a tip to be remembered. He walked out, got in his car. He almost drove away.

This is where the FBI is staying. This is where they are plotting against you. They don't know you, but they think they do.

He bit his lip. It was risky, but he prided himself on always having another plan. And being here, in this hotel, could be useful.

He walked back in with his backpack and smiled at the clerk. "I need a room for a couple nights. Do you have anything available?"

"Yes. I just need an ID and a major credit card."

He slid over both. The clerk barely looked, ran the card, handed everything back to him.

It didn't really matter. His ID was a good, high-quality fake, and his credit card was a business, one of the three shell corporations he'd set up when he first set out his plan of retribution.

"How many nights?"

"Four—but I might be here all week."

"That's fine. You can let us know the morning you're supposed to check out."

"Anything on the top floor?" he asked casually.

"Do you want to be close to the elevator?"

"Not really."

The clerk typed, smiled. "All set."

He signed and got the key. He went up to the room, looked around. It was on the top floor—the fourth floor—next to the stairwell. Perfect. Were the feds on this floor? It almost made him giddy to think about.

He took a book out of his backpack and put it on the nightstand. He pulled down the comforter and rolled around on the bed. Just in case anyone talked to the housekeeping staff. Washed his face and used three towels.

Then he left.

31

Spokane
9:45 p.m.

When Kara walked into the war room, Matt did a double take. He hadn't expected to see her tonight.

"You didn't have to come down. It's getting late."

Michael—who still looked like he walked out of a *GQ* magazine even though he wore sweatpants and a T-shirt—said, "Kara's been here for hours."

"Just talked to Maddox in the bar for a few," she said. "He stopped by on his way home."

"I didn't see you when I came in."

He should have noticed, though the bar *was* off to the side and not all seats were visible from the lobby.

"She may have found something." Michael was at a desk reading a thick file.

"It just seemed…interesting," Kara said. "GQ here told me what you learned from the teacher who worked with Marston—about an employee who lost his wife, then his job. And then I got the luck of the draw."

She called Michael GQ. Why? Did Michael actually tell Kara that had been his nickname in the Navy? Or did she pick up on it intuitively?

Or was she flirting?

Don't go there. She doesn't owe you an explanation.

"Don't sell yourself short, Quinn," Michael said. "Both Ryder and I had already gone through all these files."

She dismissed his comment. "I made a leap, and it paid off."

"Details," Matt said.

Michael said, "So there's this lawsuit that was dismissed. It was filed, had depositions, then deemed without merit by the court. The plaintiff appealed. That appeal was also denied. Eighteen years ago, there was a horrific multicar pileup on Interstate 90. Nine vehicles were involved and the nineteen injured were split between Spokane General and Mercy which is farther out. Because Spokane has the trauma ward, the most serious injuries were brought there. Eleven people total at Spokane—three had been declared DOA at the scene."

Matt asked, "That was in the lawsuit?"

"No, Ryder pulled up the press reports on the accident."

"Okay. Sorry, just trying to picture it."

Michael nodded. "They were all in the same vehicle. Went straight to the morgue. Two victims died en route to Spokane. The remaining nine were brought into the emergency room and triage was performed by the head RN—Anne Banks."

Matt closed his eyes so he could picture the scene. "I'm with you."

"According to the lawsuit, a Zachary Hamilton claimed that Anne Banks prioritized patients who were less critical than his wife, costing his wife her life. She died in the emergency room. The hospital responded that triage is difficult in the best of circumstances, and the hospital will always prioritize patients they believe have the greatest chance of survival with medical attention. Lorna Hamilton had already lost a tremendous amount of blood, had been unresponsive in the ambulance, and suffered severe head trauma. An autopsy was performed that indicated that it would have been extremely unlikely that she would have survived her injuries even with immediate surgery, coupled with having a rare blood type."

"And Anne Banks made that decision."

"Yes. And she, and the hospital, were sued." Michael paused, and Matt opened his eyes.

Something in his tone had Matt asking, "What?"

"I've been in situations like Banks. Where you have a dozen bodies, and you have to make split-second decisions. I wasn't a medic, but in the field you have to make the call. Who gets out first. Who has the greatest chance of survival—but won't without medical attention. It's the worst feeling. Makes you feel like you're playing God, and you feel wholly inadequate."

Michael was internalizing—which was good and bad. Good because he could put himself in Anne Banks's shoes, and in the shoes of a grieving family.

Bad because, being a soldier who had some PTSD issues when he got out, Matt hoped the memories wouldn't cause him sleepless nights.

Matt prompted, "And the court dismissed?"

"Said there was no merit to the lawsuit."

"Hamilton. We need to find out everything we can about him."

"We know at the time he lived in Liberty Lake, on Vine Street. No longer there. He was in prison for a year—drunk driving, third time's a charm. Ryder is trying to find out what happened to him after his release."

"This is good." Matt glanced at Kara. She was sitting in a chair, eyes closed, and he wondered if she was sleeping. "Send his name to Maddox and Knolls. They might recognize it. Liberty Lake is the connection—his old stomping grounds."

"Yes, sir."

Matt saw Kara's mouth curve up, just slightly.

Matt asked, "Is that all we have?"

Michael shook his head. "There are a couple other potentials, but that was the only lawsuit that had a man who lost his wife within a year of Marston firing an employee of the high school."

"And where did Hamilton work?"

"We don't have that information yet."

"Maddox is working with the superintendent," Matt said. "Did you tell him all this?"

"Yes," Michael said. "Maddox is on it. He's a solid cop."

"Good. This might be it. What were the other cases that you flagged?"

"The lone survivor of a family in the same pileup outside Liberty Lake sued the hospital—and the Sheriff's department and Liberty Lake PD and FD—for wrongful death. I don't quite understand the reasoning here, but it was a young guy, sixteen, and he would have had to have had an adult working this for him."

"Fucking lawyers," Kara mumbled.

"Guy's name is McCafferty, and we're trying to track him down, too. Another lawsuit that Ryder flagged happened early in her career, where a pregnant woman died while Anne Banks was attending her. She had preeclampsia, came into the hospital, and they were trying to get her blood pressure down to perform an emergency C-section when the woman—and child—died."

"Why Banks? She wasn't in the OB department."

"Emergency, I don't know. Husband's name is Holloway."

"That's it?"

"Nothing else stands out, but Ryder is running all the plaintiffs. It just takes time."

"Where *is* Ryder?"

"His room. Said Kara and I were too chatty." Michael laughed.

"I can multitask," Kara said. "Read tedious lawsuits *and* play games."

Ryder ran into the room waving a printout. "I think I have something."

"Spill."

"March 3—that was the night of the pileup. The

one where Hamilton's wife and McCafferty's family were killed."

Ryder handed Matt a printout of the newspaper article the day after the tragic accident. He skimmed it and his gut twisted in excitement. This was it. He knew it.

"It's one of them," Matt said.

He sent Catherine a text message, though she'd be sleeping right now. "It's after eleven on a Saturday night. We're not going to get anything on them now. But start the ball rolling—I want to know where those two men are before the briefing tomorrow. And if we can locate them, I want to talk to them. Understood?"

"Yes, sir." Ryder sat at a computer and started typing.

"I left Jim Esteban at the lab," Matt said, "I don't know that he's going to get back anytime soon. He and Miles Jordan are working on the forensics from Ogdenburg's bathroom and think they might have something. Plus they're going back to Joanne Grant's house to make sure the CSU didn't miss anything when they processed. The guy was in a rage—he might have left blood, hair, his fucking wallet."

"That would be nice," Michael said, "however unlikely."

"Point is, we don't have anything else until morning. Go to bed. Meet here at oh-eight-hundred. Everyone needs sleep—including you, Superboy," he said to Ryder.

"I will," Ryder said with no reaction to his new nickname. "I'm just starting the criminal search on the names, and sending a note to Tony to assign someone to run a thorough background on both of them. I can do it, but not as fast as headquarters."

"Delegate. I'm fine with that." Matt turned to Kara. "At noon we're having a debriefing with every cop who has worked in Liberty Lake or has a strong affiliation with Liberty Lake—retired and active."

"Good."

"You're welcome to join us."

"Thanks, maybe. Liberty Lake's my home base, and this guy is really pissing me off."

Matt left Kara, Ryder and Michael in the war room. He didn't know what was going on between Michael and Kara—nothing, he was sure, except that they had this rapport that he was a bit uncomfortable with.

¡Me resbala!

Who was he trying to fool? Himself? Yes, he did care.

Why, Matt? Why do you care? Kara is a big girl, just because she slept with you last night doesn't mean there's anything between you but mutual lust.

He liked her. He wanted to spend time with her.

Estás actuando como un adolescente cachondo.

You're acting like a horny teenager. Grow up, Costa.

Yeah. Easier said.

He kicked back on his bed and hoped that he would drift off, but his mind was working double time.

"Well, shit." He sighed, got up, and took a long, hot shower. When he got out, he wrapped a towel around his waist and looked at the digital clock by the bed.

It flipped to 12:00 a.m.

It was March 7.

Hamilton? McCafferty? Was the Triple Killer one of them? Or were they completely missing the boat?

He didn't think so. Not when that pileup happened on March 3. They were close. *Very* close. But were they close enough? Even if they identified him, if he had changed his name, if he was in hiding, if they didn't have a good photograph of him—they just didn't have the time. Everything had to come together, and fast.

He was about to pull on sweatpants when he heard a knock at his door. He glanced through the peephole.

Kara?

He opened his door. She looked as exhausted as he felt.

She stepped in and shut the door behind her.

"Kara—" he began.

She silenced him with a kiss. A hard, passionate, desperate kiss. His towel fell to the floor and he took her to bed.

"Are you okay?" he asked, breathless, when their lips parted.

"Very," she mumbled. "Shut up."

"Demanding."

"You don't even know the meaning of the word."

She flipped him over so she was on top and he couldn't talk if he tried. Every thought left his mind as she took charge.

After they had sex—mindless, passionate, very physical sex—he slept like a rock for five hours. He didn't even hear Kara leave.

32

Sunday, March 7
Washington DC
10:30 a.m. ET

Catherine Jones made a point of having brunch every Sunday with her husband and daughter. When she was still living with them in Stafford, Chris and Lizzy would go to church in the morning and Catherine would cook. She loved trying new recipes, but there were a few go-to dishes that everyone loved. She and Chris would have mimosas and enjoy a leisurely morning that would spread to a leisurely afternoon—unless one of them was called into work. Often, her sister, Beth, would join them, occasionally Matt if he was in town, and less often, Chris's family.

Sundays had been her favorite day of the week because of her family, until Beth was murdered and Catherine couldn't pretend anymore. Pretend that her job didn't affect her. Pretend that she was normal.

Still, even though they were separated, Chris brought Lizzy into the city after church and they would go out for brunch. Not the same as before, certainly, and she was never as comfortable as she had been when they were still together, but she loved them. She loved them so much that it hurt, and if she lost them like she'd lost Beth she didn't know how she could survive it.

Which was why she had to step away. No one seemed to understand that. Chris tried—and she loved him for it—but he didn't realize that if she lost him, she would be dead inside.

But she couldn't live like his, in a half-packed condo. Late last night she'd unpacked most of her boxes. She realized she wasn't going to sell. Maybe Matt was right. Maybe working again would give her other crimes to focus on instead of Beth's murder. And she couldn't very well live with her mother, who had made it perfectly clear that she blamed Catherine for Beth's death.

Catherine had enough blame and guilt of her own.

After unpacking, a couple hours' sleep, and a half pot of coffee—Catherine sat at the computer, her alarm set to remind her when Chris would arrive. She pulled up her emails, thrilled that Matt and his team had uncovered so much information about the potential killer. Catherine spent the morning reading the two lawsuits that had been brought after the pileup on Interstate 90 in Liberty Lake. She didn't have a sense of who the killer was from those two men—an older man, perhaps, still grieving for his wife, angry that the hospital—that the nurse, Anne Banks—had chosen to save someone else over his beloved. Catherine could picture the grieving husband going after her—but so many years later? And why the other victims?

She still felt the murders were committed by a younger man, based on several factors, not the least of which was his chosen murder weapon *and* the time before the first kill. She wouldn't rule out Hamilton, but McCafferty fit better. The lone survivor in his family. The lawsuit itself was tragic. He'd been trapped in the car with his dead family for an hour. What could that have done to a teenager? The lawsuit was clearly filed by an ambulance chaser. They had sued everyone, and no case had merit. But the young man could have believed that the hospital, the police department, the fire department, that everyone was to blame. He'd been impressionable and facing a horrific loss. If he didn't have the support of extended family, he could have internalized his pain and yes, years later, taken it out on those who he twistedly decided to blame. And he was younger than Zachary Hamilton. Catherine's entire profile had been built on skewing to a younger killer. McCafferty would be thirty-four now, right in the middle of her profiling sweet spot.

Yes, she leaned toward McCafferty. On paper, he worked. And she firmly believed that whatever happened that March 3 out on the interstate so many years ago started this string of murders. The police responded. Anne Banks—the trauma nurse—had made a difficult decision. The principal? Was there a principal involved in the accident? The cause of the accident? Or maybe in the aftermath, a principal hurt McCafferty in another way.

Catherine sent off the memo to Matt and realized that Chris would be here any minute. She had several files that came late yesterday about unsolved stabbings in the three states involved, plus bordering states. She sensed that there might be something there—that there were no hesitation marks on Anne Banks's body told her that Banks wasn't his first victim. He could have been perfecting his style, or just growing comfortable with killing, before he went after his real target.

But it would take her hours to go through these reports and if she started now, they'd be on her mind for the rest of the day, and she wouldn't be fully engaged with her family.

Two hours. She could turn her back on violence for two hours.

Chris called her from downstairs, right on time. She grabbed her purse and shut the doors of her office, as if shutting a door in her mind. She wished it were that easy.

She slid into the front seat and turned to look at her beautiful daughter, Lizzy. The girl unbuckled her seat belt, leaned forward, and hugged Catherine so tightly it brought tears to her eyes.

"Hi, Mom! I have *so* much to tell you."

Catherine kissed her. "I can't wait to hear." She turned to Chris. He leaned over and kissed her.

She wanted them back.

She didn't know how she could make this work.

"I was thinking," she said as they drove off. "Next weekend we have the party on Saturday. Maybe I should stay over and cook brunch like old times."

"Really?" Lizzy said, bouncing in her seat.

"It's your birthday. It's whatever you want. We can go out, of course—"

"No! No, no, no! I really, really want you to make brunch. Please? That's all I want for my birthday."

Catherine said, "Chris, maybe we should return *the present* if we can get away with just feeding our child."

"Maybe we should," he said with a grin.

"You wouldn't," Lizzy said, and laughed. "This is going to be great. Can I make the menu?"

"Sure. I'll go shopping on Friday."

Friday… Because no matter what, the killer would be captured or gone, and Catherine would have succeeded or failed to stop him.

Damn, she wished she could just put it all aside for *two hours*! What was wrong with her? Why was she thinking about the Triple Killer when she should be thinking about Lizzy's birthday and the sheer joy in her daughter's voice when Catherine said she'd be home next weekend?

Chris reached over and took her hand. He kissed it. The simple affection almost made Catherine cry. "I'm on vacation for a week starting Friday," he said. "Not on call, no patients to monitor, free and clear."

"A week? But what if someone needs you? What if there's an accident. You're the best pediatric surgeon on the East Coast."

Chris laughed. "I like that you think that, Cat, but there's one or two other qualified doctors out there. This was a good time. For me. For us."

She didn't know what to think.

"Maybe," he said, "it's time for you to take that sabbatical, for real. When you're done with this case."

"Maybe," she said.

Maybe he was right. Maybe everything would be better if she came home.

33

Liberty Lake
9:00 a.m. PT

"You didn't sleep here again," her grandmother said as she came into the kitchen. "That's two nights."

Kara was making oatmeal. She was probably one of the few people who actually liked oatmeal, but she only liked it when she made it herself. She had her favorite oats—not instant—and blueberries and honey. Sometimes when she was in the mood she'd add bananas and pecans.

"Want some oatmeal, Em?"

"You made it from scratch? Yes, thank you."

But the distraction didn't work. Em set the table and said, "So where have you been sleeping?"

"Sorry, Em. I didn't think you'd notice. Late nights working."

"Of course I noticed. You're supposed to be on vacation."

"I don't like vacations."

"Honey, you're tired."

"I'm fine." Sleep was overrated. She rarely got

more than four hours a night. Four hours was fine. Less than that and she was a zombie, more and she felt restless, like she'd missed something while she slumbered. She poured another cup of coffee. It was her third. She poured coffee for Em, with lots of cream and a heaping teaspoon of sugar.

"Thanks, dear."

Em didn't ask again, thankfully. She was very liberated about pretty much everything, but if Kara told her she'd spent two nights in bed with the same man, she'd want to meet him. Em would think there was something special, and Kara couldn't explain to her grandmother that it was just really good sex.

This morning, she hadn't wanted to leave Matt. She wouldn't have minded enjoying a leisurely day, including morning sex in the shower and going back to sleep and then sex in the afternoon. But of course she left—Matt was in the middle of a murder investigation and while he might be able to spare an hour at midnight for hot sex, he would be hitting the ground running as soon as he was up.

Going to Matt's room last night had been stupid and oh-so-right. No talking, just sex. Hot, satisfying sex. And she slept—she slept hard for four and a half hours, longer than any night since she arrived in Spokane. But her internal clock woke her at five. She watched him sleep for a few minutes, considered waking him for morning sex, then didn't. He needed sleep because this case was intense, a ticking time bomb, and she needed to leave before she—or he—developed an attachment neither of them really wanted. She had one more week here, and he'd probably be gone before then.

Yesterday had been a really shitty day, until last night. Finding the body, first off. It wasn't lost on her that she'd found both bodies attributed to this psycho. Then Andy falling apart and questioning his career choices. That had come out of left field. But she was also angry because she thought he had her back, and he didn't. That anger had fueled her for the rest of the day, leaving her both melancholy and frustrated.

Why did she even attempt to trust anyone? She should know better. Years of watching her own back should have taught her that.

Then the clincher—Lex calling and telling her the case she had painstakingly built was falling apart—yet he wouldn't let her come back to fix it. That fucking bastard David Chen was going to walk—she knew it, in her gut—and there was not one damn thing she could do about it. She wanted to throttle the feds. Why were they being such dicks? Who was behind it? She'd pissed off a few of them, but she never thought she'd made them so angry that they'd negotiate with a human trafficker in order to nail a use of force charge against her.

"I'm having dinner with Brian Maddox and his family tonight." She needed to change the subject and get her Grams off the topic of where she had been spending her nights—and who she had been spending them with.

"That's nice. He's such a nice man. And his wife, Julia—"

"Julie."

"Right, Julie, she always brings me homemade cookies for Christmas, and a bottle of that port I love so."

"They're what you've always called good people."

"I'm sure Mr. Maddox would hire you. He's in Spokane now. That's a big city."

She would have laughed if it wouldn't have insulted her grandmother. "I like Los Angeles, Em."

"It's so far away."

"Maybe you should move to Santa Monica. There's lots of things to do there, it never snows, and there's a seniors community not far from my place."

Emily scowled at her. "I'm not that old, Kara Leigh."

She winced. Emily rarely disciplined her, but when she did, she called her by her full name.

"I didn't say you were old."

"I'm not leaving. This is my home, young lady, and I don't want to move to California."

"I'm sorry, Grams."

Emily refilled their coffee and sat back down. "I worry about you."

"Likewise."

"Will you visit again?"

She almost sounded like a child. Kara felt guilty—she'd spent most of her time working on a case she wasn't even getting paid for, doing things she didn't have to do. No one would blame her if she stepped away and spent time with her grandmother.

"I'll be here for a whole other week."

"Working."

"Not the whole time. I think the FBI is close—they've been pulling out all the stops."

"You never liked the FBI."

"No, because most FBI agents I've met are assholes. But the ones here, not so bad."

"They're lucky to have you helping."

Kara grinned. "I'll tell them you said so."

"You do that because I mean it."

The doorbell rang, and Em said, "I'll get it. You finish that oatmeal."

Kara was almost done, and dished up two bowls. Em loved bananas, so Kara sliced a banana and drizzled honey on top. She fixed her own and turned to see Andy Knolls standing in the threshold, in uniform, his hat in his hand.

"Your grandmother said you were in here."

Kara called out, "Em! I have your oatmeal ready!"

Emily came in and picked up her bowl. "I'll eat in the sunroom."

"You don't have to—"

"I want to. I don't want to hear about this case. Everyone is talking about it, and I'd rather not think about those things." She shuffled off.

She didn't want to talk to Andy, or offer him breakfast, but realized she'd have to do both.

"I made oatmeal. Fresh."

"I'm fine. Gracie and I had breakfast after church."

She glanced at the clock. It was after ten.

"I wanted to come by before the briefing. Are you going? Do you want a ride?"

"I don't need to be there," she said. She sat at the kitchen table and motioned for Andy to sit.

"I'm sorry about yesterday, Kara. I really am. I couldn't sleep last night thinking about how I disappointed you, how I let down my entire department."

She was fine with him not sleeping.

"I've seen dead bodies—car accidents, mostly. A man who shot his head off, suicide. That was three years ago. It still haunts me, but it's not the same."

She didn't see the difference. To her, the only difference was if you knew the victim. When you saw the dead eyes of someone you had spoken with, someone you liked, someone who trusted you—yeah, that was fucking hard to deal with. She felt bad that Jeffrey Ogdenburg had been murdered in his sleep, but his death was her job. In a manner of speaking. It was a *cop's* job. She could separate her emotions from the scene.

"Andy," she said, "you grew up in a quiet town. Murder isn't pretty. It's violent and vicious and usually the reasons are stupid. A guy gets popped for ripping off his drug dealer. A girl gets strangled for leaving her boyfriend. A husband beats on his wife and kids because he's a fucking asshole. It happens."

"It doesn't happen here."

"It has now. And it will happen again. If you can't handle it, yeah, you should quit."

His face fell.

Damn, she was no good at this psychology shit.

"Look," she said bluntly, "you're a good person, and you can be a good cop. Everyone here in Liberty Lake likes you. They trust you, they listen to you. And they no longer feel safe. You can fix that, but you're going to have to want to. You're going to have to work for it. And that means sucking up whatever fear is inside and dealing with this psycho. That means going back to training so you don't leave your partner high and dry at a crime scene. You have to want it. If you'd prefer to stand around feeling sorry for yourself and your town, go ahead. Just give your badge to that idiot Pierce Dunn and be done with it."

She leaned forward. "Remember this, though. If you resign, you're still here in Liberty Lake, and this will fester in your gut for the rest of your life. The guilt. The failure. Do you really want to live like that?"

Slowly he shook his head.

"You'd better get to the briefing. Let me know if there's anything new. I was with the feds last night going over the lawsuits from the hospital where Banks worked, and we pulled out a couple names to run. Maybe there's something there, maybe there isn't. But you need to be at the briefing."

"The next victim is going to be a cop. It really hit me last night."

"No. There are going to be no more victims because we're going to find this guy and lock him up for the rest of his fucking life."

"You believe that?"

"Yes." She did. She had to believe with every case that the good guys would win. If she didn't believe it, she'd turn in her shield.

"I'll let you know if anything new comes up. Thanks, Kara. For everything."

34

Spokane
12:00 p.m.

Michael Harris was running down the individuals they'd identified last night so he wasn't at the briefing at Spokane PD. Matt had enough information to share with the group of cops and former cops, and hoped they had information for him. Nearly fifty men and women were in the room, and Maddox said the only people who were missing had moved from the area. "I called them all yesterday and spoke to them personally," he said. "They will be extra cautious for the next few days."

That was the best they could do for now, but Matt suggested that Maddox assign someone to follow up with them again tomorrow and Tuesday. "Considering that our unknown subject brought Manners from Spokane to Liberty Lake, he could very well go to another state to grab a cop." Though he didn't think that was likely. Matt had a sense that the killer was leaving the victims on the doorstep of his next target.

Matt had everyone settle down and jumped right

into his presentation. He brought Ryder with him because he wanted to show pictures, and Matt's advanced tech skills were nonexistent.

"You all know that the Triple Killer struck again yesterday—sometime between 1:00 a.m. and 4:00 a.m. on March 6."

Matt looked around the room. He spotted Andy in the back, standing. Good, because Matt needed him—he knew everyone in this room, which was an advantage.

Matt went through all the information they had to date, starting with the first victim, Anne Banks. He wanted to make sure that each cop in this room understood that they could be the next target. Showing the victim in happier times—then the crime scene photos—put the situation in perspective.

"We've made a lot of inroads to identify this killer, and while we don't have his name or address, we may have found his motivation. We have two possible suspects—but again, we have no evidence against them other than a possible motivation. Anne Banks was a specific target—the other two nurses were killed based solely on their profession."

Ryder swapped out the photos of Banks for Marston. Matt explained their theory that John Marston was the specific target, and that the vice principal in Portland and the most recent victim were, essentially, distractions.

"We believe that the killer not only knew Marston, but that they may have had a run-in at some point. A witness said that a former employee had attacked him at school one day, but Marston didn't file charges because the employee had recently lost his wife. While that may not be connected to our killer, we can't discount it as possible, and Deputy Chief Maddox is working with the superintendent to find out the employee's identity."

Ryder swapped out Marston's photos with the photos of the first two cops who were killed. "Based on the pattern," Matt said, "the Triple Killer kills first a nurse, then a principal, then a cop. Since we now believe that Banks and Marston—both living in Spokane at the same time—were specifically targeted, we think that the cop who is next on this guy's list is also from this area."

A cop in the front of the room said, "But we're all from Liberty Lake. Why isn't every cop in Spokane listening to this?"

"Good question. Maddox sent out a memo to all Spokane cops to be cautious, and Chief Packard instituted the partner ride-along for the duration of this investigation. But *where* the killer leaves the victims is the key. In Portland, for example, the murdered cop lived in the suburbs, but he was killed in Portland. In Missoula, the cop lived in the county, not the city, but the killer killed him just inside the city limits. They were substitutes for the person the Triple Killer intends to kill. This tells me the location is important to him. He brought Victoria Manners from Spokane to Liberty Lake. Ogdenburg lived there, so he killed him in his own home. The cop—or retired cop—he's targeting either lives in Liberty Lake or works in Liberty Lake. That's why we asked your retired officers to come down today. You might hold the key to identifying this murderer and bringing him to justice."

Matt nodded to Ryder, who brought up the two primary suspects. "I need to stress that these two men are wanted for questioning only. The FBI is tracking them down now. Both were parties to a lawsuit after a pileup on I-90 in Liberty Lake on March 3, eighteen years ago, took the lives of nine people. Zachary Hamilton lost his wife. She died in the hospital, and he felt that Anne Banks prioritized other patients over his wife, resulting in his wife succumbing to her injuries. The autopsy indicated that no medical intervention could have saved her life, but as we know, grief can twist people's emotions.

"McCafferty was sixteen and lost his entire family in the wreck. His case is a lot more complicated because he sued multiple parties. The profiler working the case feels that McCafferty best fits the personality for our killer because of what happened and his age. He was trapped in the car with his dead family, and based on the lawsuit, Dr. Jones believes that an ambulance chaser convinced McCafferty or his guardian—we don't yet have that information—that others were to blame for the accident. We've distributed packets on each man and victim. Look at them carefully. Really think about if you know them. Even if you just saw them once or twice. We know that the killer stalks his victims, knows their routine. Very likely you could have spotted him, though you may have not recognized him. Hamilton has a record. McCafferty does not."

One of the cops asked, “Why wait so long? Why these elaborate setups?”

“Good question. Dr. Jones believes that the killer is of above-average intelligence and killed others along with his intended victim in order to throw the police off his trail, to obfuscate his true motive. And it worked—until now. In addition, we’re looking at any unsolved stabbings in multiple states—we believe that the killer may have practiced or started killing with a different MO because there were no hesitation marks on his first victim, rare in such a violent attack.”

Maddox said, “I know Hamilton.”

Matt did a double take. “How?”

“It was…oh gosh, years ago. Fifteen, sixteen maybe? I can look it up. When I was still in Liberty Lake. The bank foreclosed on his house, he refused to leave. My partner and I had to forcibly remove him. It wasn’t pretty. He was an alcoholic—like you said, he’d been in jail for drunk driving. He’d lost his wife, lost his job, Child Protective Services sent his kid to live with a relative after the second drunk driving arrest because the kid was in the car. His whole world was falling apart, and then he wouldn’t leave the house.”

That could definitely be a trigger. “Do you know where he is?”

“No. He was in jail for three days while the house was emptied and all the contents put in a storage locker. The bank paid for the locker for one month, I don’t even know if he claimed his things. He left the area and I never interacted with him again.”

"We need to find him. There are usually a series of triggers—stressors in someone's life—that leads them to become a serial murderer."

"What about the homeless stabbings?" a cop in the back said.

"What homeless stabbings?" Matt asked.

"You asked about unsolved murders, right? There was a series of stabbings a few years back."

Another cop nodded. "Detective Whitman caught the case."

Maddox said, "Whitman retired a few years back, but I remember the homicides. Three homeless men, stabbed to death in the middle of the night in Spokane, most likely while they were sleeping or passed out. Whitman thought they were thrill killings, possibly more than one perp, possibly teenagers. Little evidence at the scenes, and much of it was contaminated because of the location. No discernible pattern. One victim was killed in the winter, out by the river, and no one found his body for months. The other two were in the summer, about a month apart, found within hours."

"I need everything about those murders," Matt said. "And they just stopped?"

"Yeah. Three dead over eight, nine months? Nothing since."

"If you can pull me the files, and any forensics, and the contact information for the primary detective in case I need to talk to him."

"No problem."

Matt called Catherine as Ryder drove them back to the hotel. "There was a series of three murders, homeless men, stabbed to death, about fifteen years ago. Unsolved."

"Hello to you, too, Mathias."

He rubbed his eyes and sighed. "Hello, Catherine. How was brunch?"

"Good. I've been back for a few hours."

"And Chris? Lizzy?"

"Well, thank you."

"Are we done?"

"I saw those homicides in my files," she continued as if they hadn't attempted small talk. "I was writing up a report about unsolved stabbings. There are three more stabbings of homeless men that I think is the work of the same killer."

"You think the three in Spokane is the work of the Triple Killer?"

"I think it's possible, but what I meant was that the three in Spokane are connected to three other stabbings."

"All the same city?" he asked eagerly.

"No. Santa Barbara, California. Eugene, Oregon. And Reno, Nevada. All in the two years before Anne Banks was killed."

"And nothing in the last six years?"

"I'm still processing the information, but nothing that matches this MO. All the victims were homeless men, all addicts. The first six victims—the three in Spokane, and the three spread out six years ago—had multiple stab wounds. A lot of rage, very disorganized. There was also a man stabbed to death nine years ago in Bozeman, Montana. Same basic wound pattern. He wasn't found for months, and the remains were compromised. But the investigator believes that the killer intentionally hid the body, unlike the other similar murders. And while they believe the man was homeless, they don't know for certain. Only that no one was reported missing of his age and general appearance at that time."

"Why would he do that? Could he have left evidence?"

"Possible. Or the victim connects to him in some way. They couldn't ID the body because of advanced decomp, though the ME is certain that he was the victim of multiple knife wounds, including a blow that nearly decapitated him. Do you realize how difficult it is to decapitate someone?"

"Yes."

"There is nothing that suggests it's the same killer. The MO doesn't match the Triple Killer, but because these murders were all earlier in his life, he may have been experimenting before deciding on his more disciplined approach. However, though TOD was virtually impossible to determine, based on advanced entomology, the ME believes the victim died the first week of March."

"March, nine years ago."

"Exactly."

"You know what I think of coincidences."

"I'm going to dig around into these findings a bit more, see if anything else pops. But I'm going to go out on a limb."

"You? A limb?"

"You're not funny, Matt."

But there was a bit of humor in her voice, which

told Matt that the brunch today with Chris and Lizzy had gone very well, and maybe they could—finally—find a way to deal with Beth's death.

He said with mock offense, "You wound me."

"While the six homeless stabbings may or may not be the work of the Triple Killer, I'm confident that they are the work of the *same* killer."

"So you're saying there might be a second serial murder case."

"It's possible. However, looking at these forensics I think it's the same guy, and the three murders in Spokane were his first. The one in January, he gets a taste for it, but it scares him. He waits. Builds up his courage, then does it again. Twice, close together, only weeks apart. Then he waits. For what? I don't know. There could be other victims we haven't identified yet. But I think it was around this time that he started thinking about retribution. About people he felt deserved to die. Starting with Anne Banks. It took him time to build up to that."

"You are brilliant, Dr. Jones."

"I'm going to send all the forensics to Jim Esteban and put him in touch with the ME in Bozeman."

"Great."

"And be careful, Matt. You're now the face of this investigation and if the killer thinks you're in his way, he won't hesitate to come after you."

They were close. Matt felt it in his bones.

When they were back at the hotel, Matt started going through the lawsuits more carefully, looking at the statements of both Hamilton and McCafferty. "Ryder," he called out.

"Yes, sir?"

"Do we have current addresses on these men?"

"No, sir. Hamilton left Washington State after he lost his home. I was able to trace him to Montana. He had a job there for a while, then nothing in more than ten years. McCafferty went to college on the East Coast and there's no record of him returning to Washington. I have headquarters looking for him and working on finding local family."

Maddox had sent over copies of the first three crime scene reports of the murdered homeless men. Matt was reading through them when his phone vibrated.

"Costa."

"This is Assistant Special Agent in Charge Bryce Thornton. Is this Special Agent Mathias Costa?"

Shit. He'd avoided Thornton's calls for two days because he didn't want to create a problem for Kara when she went back to LA. He'd thought the email he'd sent on Friday would suffice.

"Special Agent in Charge," he said. He'd pull rank early if he had to because he wanted to get out of this conversation as soon as possible. Not just because of his promise to Kara, but because he had a lot of work to do.

"I'm sorry, sir."

"What can I do for you? I'm in the middle of a high-profile investigation right now. Sunday isn't my day off."

"I'll make it brief. Your assistant inquired about

LAPD Detective Kara Quinn the other day, and I was following up."

"Did you not get the email where I told you I had what I needed?" Of course he had, but Matt would play this game any way he needed to.

"Yes, but as I indicated, there are things you should know if you're working on a joint operation."

"We're not. I spoke to her boss and got the information I wanted. My assistant was just going through channels, which was ultimately unnecessary."

"With all due respect, sir, you need to know that Detective Quinn has been under investigation by the FBI twice in the last five years, specifically related to her undercover work. She's also currently under federal investigation regarding use of force and violation of federal law during her most recent undercover investigation. It's why she's been placed on administrative leave—though her boss, Sergeant Popovich, may have told you that she's on vacation."

Matt tensed. He didn't want to know this information, but he needed to. Yet, why would Thornton be calling him out of the blue when Matt explicitly said he didn't need anything from him?

"Explain," he said sharply.

"Yes, sir." Bryce's kiss-ass tone grated on Matt, but he let him talk. "On February 15, Detective Quinn used deadly force during an undercover sting operation involving an illegal sweatshop in Los Angeles. Witness statements indicated that the suspect was unarmed and complying with orders. Our office was brought in for a possible civil rights violation—the suspect was Chinese American. This isn't the first time Quinn has used deadly force in the line of duty—nor is it the first time she's been under investigation."

"This information is irrelevant to my current situation, so—"

"You need to understand that this woman should never have been a cop," Thornton interrupted. "The LAPD has been cleaning up her messes for twelve years, and this may be the final straw. Any good deeds she may have done during her tenure are washed away by her blatant abuse of authority and continuing violation of state and federal law. The fact that she's trying to move laterally into another agency while this is hanging over her head is proof she knows her days are numbered."

"Excuse me, what position is she up for?"

Silence. "Your assistant—Mr. Kim."

"Did Mr. Kim say we were vetting her for a job?"

"No, but he is with the FBI Office of Recruitment, according to his file."

Very, very interesting. Ryder had been initially assigned to the OOR, even though Matt tapped him directly out of Quantico for the MRT unit. It had to do with how he got paid and a lot of other bureaucratic crap that Matt didn't care about, but his boss, Tony Greer, understood well. But how would Bryce Thornton know that unless he researched Ryder after the initial inquiry?

"Thornton, you have it wrong. I'm the SAC of the newly formed Mobile Response Team. You probably didn't hear about it because we were recently commissioned and work in rural communities. Detective Quinn was a witness in one of my cases, and Mr. Kim was calling to verify identity and credentials."

"I see. Well, sir, everything I said still holds. Watch her. And I hope you don't need her witness statement for the prosecution, because by the time your case comes to trial, she won't be a cop—and may in fact be in federal prison."

Matt ended the call, but he was definitely concerned about what Thornton said. No wonder Kara Quinn said most feds she knew were dicks—Thornton was the definition of a dick. Yet, he must have *something* to back up his claims. He couldn't just open a federal investigation without *some* evidence of wrongdoing.

Matt itched to call Popovich, Kara's boss, but he put that aside when Michael walked in, holding out his own cell phone. "Jim has something and needs to talk to you now."

Matt took the phone from Michael. "Jim?"

"We got something. And we're going to have more, but damn, we're going to nail him."

"I'm waiting." He shouldn't snap, but he was still fuming over Thornton's call.

Jim didn't seem to notice. "You get me a suspect, I'll match him to DNA."

Matt nearly did a dance. "You have his fucking DNA? How?"

"Remember what I said about bathrooms? The guy was good. He cleaned up well, and he poured bleach down the drain. Smart, because we shed a lot of hair when we shower. But he cut himself. He cut himself when he killed Ogdenburg. Might not have even noticed it. I believe he took one of his towels off the rack—and took it with him, because no used towels were found in the house. There was a small drop of blood behind the metal rack. We swabbed it—it doesn't belong to Ogdenburg."

"This is great. Prints?"

"It dripped. He didn't touch the bar. Probably grabbed the towel only. The blood dripped from his finger is my best guess."

"Have you run it?"

"What do you think this is, Hollywood? It's going to take me a couple of days, minimum. But I already sent it to our lab in California. Spokane has a good setup, but they're not equipped to handle DNA, and you said if they can't do it here, send to our lab." The main FBI laboratory was at Quantico, but they had a smaller forensics lab in California. "Called, talked to the director, explained that this was the only physical evidence of a serial killer who targets nurses, teachers, and cops. He's on board. But it's still going to take a couple days. I have a blood type and basic markers. Type is uncommon—B positive. Less than 10 percent of the population. And I got something else for you."

"Shoot."

"There's evidence from the three homeless murders in Spokane. Maddox came by, said you wanted me to take a look at the files. And there is blood evidence that doesn't match the victims on two of the bodies."

"B positive."

"Bingo."

"Catherine was right. Send her the info. It'll help with the profile. Thanks, Jim. This is terrific."

Matt turned back to the lawsuits, finished up his notes, followed up with Ryder about McCafferty to find out when he left Spokane. If he wasn't here when the three homeless men were killed, then he wasn't the Triple Killer.

Though one was killed in January, and two in the summer. If he was in college, he could have killed if he came home for breaks.

He planned to meet with Andy Knolls in Liberty Lake that afternoon to discuss each cop who'd attended the briefing and review their cases during the years that overlapped when both Banks and Marston lived in Spokane. All Matt could think about was that the three of them—Banks, Marston, and the potential third cop victim—had all encountered the same person, possibly at different times. Matt also matched up the murders of the three Spokane homeless men—though they occurred the year *after* Marston left for Missoula.

When Matt drove into Liberty Lake, he made a detour. He needed to find out what was going on with Kara. He didn't know that he fully believed Bryce Thornton, but there was no reason for the agent to lie to him. Still, Matt was certain there was more to the story. And he needed to know what it was.

35

Liberty Lake
3:45 p.m.

Kara spent most of Sunday reviewing all her notes from her investigation into David Chen and his associates. She called her closest friend on the force, Colton Fox. She and Colton had often worked undercover together, and he helped her with Chen. He wasn't working on anything new, and it was probably killing him as much as her.

"What the fuck is going on with the Chen case?" she asked after a brief hello.

"You talked to Lex."

"And? You couldn't call me?"

"And say what? Thornton is an asshole? You know that."

"Thornton? What are you talking about."

Colton paused a beat. "Lex didn't tell you."

"He didn't tell me about that prick. Fuck. Thornton has had it out for me for years." It figures Thornton was behind whatever federal bullshit was coming down in LA.

"You broke his nose."

"I'll break it again."

"It's not going to hold. No one is going to believe Chen's statement."

"In this day and age? When cops are put out to take the fall for everything? I swear, I wish I could twist the nuts off every bad cop out there who has set us all up for this bullshit."

"You're preaching, sister."

"Do they have anything but Chen?"

"Not that I know. I'd tell you."

Colton was one of the good guys. He could be a hard-ass at times, and he sometimes crossed the line, but he did a great job, and he took bad guys off the streets. The real bad guys, like Chen.

"Will you keep me in the loop?" she asked.

"As much as I can."

"What the hell?"

"I'm building another cover. Going in tomorrow if we get the approval."

"I should be there to watch your ass."

"It's a nice ass to watch, isn't it?"

She rolled her eyes, even though he couldn't see her. "Be careful out there, Colt. I don't want to break in another partner."

"Never. I hear you're working hard."

"Found a dead body. Serial killer. Interesting investigation."

"You always loved that shit."

"Hobby. I much prefer playing in the mud."

"Playing in the mud" was how Lex, their boss, referred to undercover work. Because criminals were scum, but they were fun to put in prison.

"Maybe I should be telling you to be careful up there."

"I'll see you in a week. And seriously—if you need backup, let Lex know. I can be there in twelve hours—you know that. For you, I'll take my lumps with IA and the FBI and any other alphabet agency they throw at me."

"I know. See you later."

She hung up. She and Colton had a long history. Friends, sometimes friends with benefits. It worked for them. But first and foremost, they were cops. They loved their job. And there was no one else in LAPD that she'd rather work with.

She looked at her notes again. Talking to Colton helped, but she didn't like knowing that Thornton was driving this train. That bastard had it out for her; always had, it seemed. Even before she popped him in the face. Earned her a seven-day unpaid suspension, but the applause of every cop on the force who'd had to put up with Thornton's bullshit since he'd arrived in LA.

Dammit, she'd built a good, solid case against Chen and his associates, and the DA himself had been thrilled when she turned it over to him. She was always great on the stand and had experience winning juries over when there was a complex case like this one. She'd had to take the mandatory three days because of the fatal shooting, but it was justified. Even IA, after she'd given her official statement, turned off the recorder and told her it was a no-brainer, knife thrown from less than twenty feet she should be lucky she'd survived. She had a fucking inch-long scar on her back to prove it.

The human trafficking angle *might* be federal on the surface, but the sweatshops were under LAPD purview, and Dyson had prosecuted two high-profile cases over the years just like this one, one of which Kara had been instrumental in tying up.

But she had to get this case to trial *first*, to put Chen behind bars for life, and the FBI was going to screw everything up if they took the case from LAPD and cut Chen a deal.

Frustrated because she was stuck here in Spokane for another week, she grabbed a beer and sat back down at the kitchen table.

Emily walked in and sat down across from her. Her grandmother smelled like she had just been smoking weed. Kara couldn't get too angry with her—she was seventy and had chronic arthritis. And it was legal—now. It hadn't been legal fifteen years ago when Kara moved in with her.

"You look so sad," Em said.

Kara wasn't going to talk to her stoned grandmother about her messed-up case in Los Angeles.

"I'm good."

"Who were you just talking to? I didn't mean to eavesdrop, but you told him to be safe. Another cop?"

"A friend. Colton. You met him a couple years ago."

"Your boyfriend?"

"No. A friend and colleague." Though her grandmother was very hip about most everything, she really didn't want to get in a conversation about her and Colton and how they occasionally had fun in bed but it didn't mean anything more than they needed to let off steam and they trusted each other. As much as two undercover cops could trust. Besides, if there was something serious going on between her and Colton, she certainly wouldn't have slipped between the sheets with Matt Costa. She was no saint, but she didn't two-time her lovers.

"You sounded worried."

"I can't really talk about it."

Em frowned.

"He's working undercover. It's a sticky situation."

"You work undercover."

How did she know that? Kara painstakingly avoided talking about work. She would have to be more careful around Em.

"Grams, I can't talk about what I do."

"I worry about you."

"I know you do. I'm good at my job."

I need my job. I am my job.

Fortunately, the doorbell rang, saving Kara from any further explanations—which she couldn't give, and would end up hurting Em's feelings. The last thing she wanted to do was hurt her grandmother.

"I'll get that," she said, motioning to her grandmother to sit. She walked through the cluttered house to the front door—surprised and pleased that Matt Costa was on the stoop. She smiled and said, "You could have called."

"Andy told me you were taking the day off. After

yesterday, I don't blame you, but I had hoped you'd be at the briefing."

"I had some work to take care of, and it was easier to do it here. Related to my last case in LA."

"Oh. Right. Sometimes I forget you're out of your jurisdiction. You've really been a great help to my team. I mean that. Ryder and Michael sing your praises."

"They're smart," she said with a grin. "Come in." She closed the door behind him. It was cold—and she wondered if snow would be hitting in the next day or two. She knew a storm was coming in, just didn't know how fierce it would be.

Costa took off his coat and frowned, glancing around.

"Not me," she said, knowing exactly what he was smelling. "My grandmother. I run the 'don't ask, don't tell' program when I visit."

"I guess that was the last thing I expected to hear." But he smiled. Definitely not a by-the-book fed.

She walked through the kitchen, where Em was washing vegetables she'd pulled earlier from her small greenhouse. "Grams, this is Matt Costa with the FBI. Matt, my grandmother, Emily Dorsey."

Matt extended his hand. "Pleased to meet you, ma'am. Your granddaughter has been a great help to us this last week."

"Of course she has. She doesn't know the meaning of the word *relax* or *vacation*."

Grams was testy today.

"I took today off, didn't I?"

"Working from home is still working." She waved

her hand. "Go on, offer your guest a beer and take it outside. I don't want to hear about any of this stuff. It upsets me."

She kissed her grandmother on the cheek. "Love you, Em." Then she grabbed two beers from the refrigerator and went outside. Matt followed. She turned on the fire pit and it roared to life. The heat felt good.

"I know you're busy, Matt, so spill it. You must have a reason for stopping by."

"Andy is struggling with this case."

"I know. I told you that yesterday. I talked to him this morning. I didn't exaggerate or downplay it. He's not used to this level of investigation."

"I had Michael Harris stick with him most of today."

Kara realized why Matt must be upset. "Shit, I'm sorry."

"About what?"

"I'd been partnering with Andy and I bailed on you today. If you needed me, I would have been there. All you had to do is ask."

"No—that's not it. I mean, maybe—partly—I expected you at the station when I got there this afternoon. But you're on vacation. I can't expect you to devote 24-7 to this case."

The way he said it made Kara think there was something more, but she hoped she was wrong.

You're not wrong about these things.

"I promised to help for the duration," she said. "But today I needed to take time to go over my last case. It's—well, it's a clusterfuck right now and my boss needed specific information."

Not completely true. Kara needed specific information so she knew that she hadn't left any holes in her case.

"I know we're on a clock here," she continued. "In fact, I'm having dinner with Brian Maddox and his family tonight. He worked in Liberty Lake during your window of time, and he lives here. He's one of the smartest cops I know. I was hoping we could talk things out informally."

"He mentioned the dinner earlier."

"You want to come? He wouldn't mind," Kara said.

"I would—but I can't. We believe that the Triple Killer also killed three homeless men fifteen years ago. And this time, he screwed up. We found blood in Ogdenburg's bathroom that doesn't match the homeowner. We're getting closer."

"But."

"But a cop is at risk and we're not close enough. I reiterated to Andy, and earlier on the phone to Maddox, that they both need to be extra careful—and be particularly sensitive to anyone watching them. Even if they just feel like they're being watched."

"I'll make sure Maddox takes it seriously. He's a good cop—he knows he's not invincible."

"I'm frustrated," Matt said. "It's March 7. End of day. That means not only does the killer know who his next victim is, he's been stalking him. Ogdenburg was killed early the morning of March 6. The coroner puts TOD between one and four—said the

ME can probably narrow it down. The guy was in his bed. Didn't fight back. The killer came in and killed him while he was sleeping. Only a short time after Andy was there."

"I know," Kara said, her voice tight.

I found his body after all...

But Matt didn't seem to read between the lines, which was probably a good thing. She didn't need to be coddled.

"Our guy could kill a cop at midnight March 9... up until 11:59 p.m. This guy knows his next victim's schedule. He'll see that the cop has deviated from pattern."

"He's been reading the newspapers. He knows cops are riding in pairs."

"What if we're wrong and the victims *are* truly random? And it's only their profession or the location that matter to the killer? He could grab a cop in, hell, Boise, Idaho, and drive eight hours here and kill him in Liberty Lake."

"Matt—I don't think your Dr. Jones's profile is wrong on this. It's a weird pattern, but it *is* a pattern. It may not make sense to us, but it makes sense to the killer."

"You sound just like Catherine."

Kara finished her beer. "Another?" she asked him.

He shook his head. "I need to work through this tonight with Andy. We've gone through so much paperwork, even with everything we did yesterday, but there's still more." But he didn't make any move to get up.

"What else?"

"Nothing."

He spoke too quickly. He knew it. She knew it.

"I'm getting another beer. I am on vacation after all." She got up.

When she was almost to the back door, Matt said, "Are you on vacation? Or mandatory administrative leave?"

She hesitated only a fraction of a second, then opened the door and went inside.

Kara stood at the refrigerator and stared at the beer bottles. Her grandmother didn't drink beer—wine, Em was all over it, but beer was Kara's preferred beverage. Staring wasn't going to do her any good—they were all the same beer, a local craft beer she liked. She didn't even want another beer.

Matt had talked to Bryce Thornton. Whether Matt dug around or Thornton heard about Kara's adventures in Washington through one of the traitors at LAPD, Kara didn't know. Did she care?

Yes. She *did* care. She'd asked Matt not to talk to LA-FBI and he had.

She grabbed two beers and went back outside.

She slammed down the beer in front of Matt. "What do you want to know?"

"I don't know."

"Don't insult me by lying."

"Everything."

"I can't tell you everything."

"What can you tell me?"

"What did Thornton say?"

Matt was a good cop, but he didn't have much of a poker face. She'd read the situation correctly.

"That fucking bastard."

"Well?"

"I don't know what he's saying about anything. I never do. I'll find out, but I skipped town before I had to deal with that federal bullshit."

"A federal investigation into a deadly force accusation is not bullshit, Kara."

"What?" Kara—who always controlled her reactions, even when she was angry, hadn't even suspected. She would have laughed if she didn't want to hop on a plane and punch that scumbag Bryce Thornton in his too-perfect jaw.

Break it, to go with the broken nose she'd given him eleven years ago when he was a measly, low-ranking agent. Damn, why did the pricks always rise to the top?

"Thornton said there was a federal investigation in your use of deadly force against an unarmed suspect."

"Thornton opens an investigation into me every chance he gets. I'm his pet project."

"It doesn't work that way, Kara. The FBI is a bureaucracy. He would have to jump through hoops to open and reopen investigations into one individual."

"Every time he comes after me, he loses. He'll lose this time."

"Do you want to tell me about it?"

"No."

"Dammit, Kara—this is serious."

She fumed. She would have told Matt—on her own terms—if *she* wanted to. She refused to discuss anything with a federal agent when she wasn't 100 percent positive she could trust him. She'd thought Matt was one she could trust.

She was wrong.

And being wrong just pissed her off.

She said, "You either trust me or you don't."

"I met you four days ago, Kara."

"And you've known Thornton for how long?"

"That's not the same thing!"

"I'll tell you one thing. I have used deadly force seven times in my twelve years as a cop. Yes, more than most cops, but most cops don't work undercover and with the scummiest of the scum. It's the nature of my job—it's dangerous and necessary. Every single time, I've been cleared. They were all just. *Every. Single. One.* I already told you that I was forced to take a vacation. Bryce can call it administrative leave all he wants, but it's my vacation time I'm cashing in. But the reason Lex told me to take a hike was not because of my use of force."

"Then why?"

She wanted to tell him—not to justify or explain herself, but because losing Soon Chi Chu hurt. Kara didn't get emotional about her cases—she couldn't and still do what she did. Lex told her she was getting too close to the young Chinese girl Kara called Sunny, and Kara had dismissed him as being the overprotective father she didn't want. But he was right. Because he was *always* right about things like this.

When that bastard David Chen killed Sunny, Kara compartmentalized her murder like she did every other victim she'd ever come across. But it was hard.

Too hard. Okay, down right *impossible.* Sunny gave Kara information because Kara pushed her. Sunny had never wanted to get involved, but Kara was good at getting people to do what was against their best interests.

They were so close—so damn *close*—to Sunny being free. No human being should ever be in captivity. No human being should suffer slavery. No human should be subjected to the pain and humiliation of being treated worse than cattle in a sweatshop where they made pennies a day.

And then Sunny was dead, and her blood was on Kara's hands. Literally and figuratively.

"Call me if you need my help on your case, otherwise, goodbye. Show yourself out."

"Don't—" Matt said as Kara walked inside.

She kept going.

She would destroy Bryce Thornton as soon as she was back in LA, and he would never see it coming.

36

Liberty Lake
5:00 p.m.

Matt regretted his conversation with Kara. What had he been thinking? He hadn't. Why had he thought she'd just explain? She was hostile and defensive, and under normal circumstances he'd think that was a sign of guilt, but with Kara, he didn't think so.

Dammit. He'd fucked up again. He shouldn't have slept with her in the first place. If he hadn't, would he have reacted any different? Maybe. Maybe not. He couldn't put the genie back into the bottle, so he was going to have to suck it up and deal. He'd offended her, and that wasn't his intention. She'd devoted nearly as many hours as he and his team had—and certainly more than any of the local cops except maybe Andy—to working this case. She'd even come by last night and helped read through the dozens of lawsuits, a tedious and time-consuming chore that he honestly hadn't expected her to volunteer for. He owed her—and yet he'd pissed her off.

"Fix it," he mumbled to himself, though he didn't know how.

First, find this killer.

He met Andy at the police station. Andy had sandwiches, chips and coffee waiting. "My fiancée, Gracie, thought we might be hungry."

"Thanks."

"Abigail spent all day pulling the hard copies of every file from the years in question, then she went the extra mile and organized them by arresting or responding officer. They're labeled in the conference room. I've already started going through them and weeding out those that don't fit."

"Great."

"I'm surprised you came yourself."

"Jim is forensics, and Michael's getting two agents who came in from Seattle tonight up to speed. Maddox is home working with the superintendent to get all the files for Marston and identify that employee he fired. The fact that he knows Zachary Hamilton—had a run-in with him—makes me nervous. Catherine thinks Hamilton is too old, but I'd still like to find out what he's been doing since he got out of jail."

They sat down and started reading reports. Matt pulled the stack that was labelled *Maddox*—he wanted to read the report on the foreclosure in particular.

Andy said, "I went to see Kara this morning."

Matt didn't want to talk about Kara. But he said, "She forgave you."

"Not really, but I guess in her own way. Told me

to, essentially, grow a pair. To either quit or stop feeling sorry for myself."

"Sounds like her."

"Reminded me why I became a cop. I like to help people. To listen. To have a safe community. I wasn't expecting this violence, but it could happen again. Abigail is researching some training programs for me."

"You're not quitting. Good."

"No. But I recognize now that I have work to do. People do feel safe here and I helped with that. After this, I'm going to have to make them feel safe again. You're probably not used to that—you're from a big city. But here, it's important."

"It's important everywhere."

Matt frowned as he flipped pages. Included in the report was a list of contents that the bank prepared when they took possession of the house, and a note that a relative came over to retrieve personal items for Hamilton's son.

"Do you know anything about Hamilton's son?"

"No. Just that Maddox mentioned his son was sent to live with his aunt, I believe."

Matt made a note. "We should find out what happened to him. I don't have a name or age, but he would have been a minor."

"CPS will have records. I'll work on that first thing in the morning."

Andy made his own notes.

"The place was a mess, according to the reports. Guy loses his wife, loses his kid to the system, loses his job. I can see him doing something out of anger and hopelessness, but this level of planning? Not seeing it."

"I have the report from the accident on March 3." Andy got up and retrieved a box. "I was going to ask Kara to join us, because this is a lot of work, but I think she's still upset with me."

"She's fine," Matt said. She was more upset with Matt than anyone. "But I'll take it back to the hotel with me. I want to finish going through these reports and then we can tackle that. Why is no one else in your department helping?"

"Chief Dunn has everyone doubled up and keeping the police presence. No one has time off until after the ninth. I kind of agree with him, because right now we're looking for a needle in the haystack." He made a note about something. "However, I assigned the patrols. They're doubling up at the lake—since both Manners and Ogdenburg were found near the lake. And doing regular patrols by every cop who lives here."

"Good."

Matt paused to take a call from Jim. He was processing the cold case homeless murders, and so far, forensics matched up with the limited physical evidence they had in the Triple Killer case.

"You get me a suspect, we have him solid on Ogdenburg and two of the three homeless men," Jim said. "Spokane has an excellent system, state-of-the-art storage facilities, so no defense lawyer is going to be able to cry contamination or degradation."

"They'll try," Matt said.

"And fail. Be safe, Matt."

Matt ended the call and went back to the Hamilton file, making notes. There were a few oddities and he had some questions. Maybe Maddox would know. He'd call, but since he didn't live far from the Liberty Lake PD, Matt decided to drive by on his way back to the hotel.

Kara never felt comfortable in a family setting, even with people she liked. And she really liked the Maddox family. Julie was down-to-earth and never made Kara feel like an outsider. She had her own in-home business that she started after her second child, Teddy, was born. First, she made wooden puzzles for kids and sold them at craft fairs. Then a few years later, she started selling on the internet. Recently, she'd branched out into a collection of beautiful cutting boards in the shape of states. She had a website and went to craft fairs in the summer and currently employed two people full-time to help her keep up with orders. Julie gave Kara a tour of the garage, which they'd converted to her workspace. "We're going to build an add-on this summer when the weather is nice, so we can put the cars inside, but this is what it's been like for the last two years. Kind of crazy." But she clearly loved it. Julie was the single most organized person Kara had ever met. "Brian wants to work with me when he retires. That's quite a few years from now, but I think we'd want to kill each other. I'll convince him to get his teaching credential."

"A teacher?"

"He loves working with teenagers especially.

But he'll be chief of police next year, and while it's a lot of hours, it's not as physically demanding. He'll probably stay until mandatory retirement age—which is the same year JP graduates from high school."

JP was their youngest, six years old. Brian told Kara that he was a "oops" baby, but kept them on their toes.

If only she had parents like Brian and Julie, she wondered how different her life would have been.

Or maybe, she was exactly who she would have been no matter who her parents were.

Somehow, she doubted that.

They went inside. Brian was grilling steaks on the patio, even though it was freezing and Kara was pretty sure by this time tomorrow there would be snow. His oldest son, Trevor, was helping, and Kara watched them through the glass. Brian was a good dad. He was a cop, through and through, but be loved being with his family.

"Hey, Kara! I made a racetrack in my room! Wanna see?" JP did nothing quiet or slow. He ran upstairs, expecting Kara to follow. Which she did. She wasn't a kid person as a rule—the kids she encountered were damaged. Lex had always said she was good with kids—and maybe she was. Mostly because she didn't put up with their bullshit and talked to them on their level. But most of the kids she encountered were in gangs, running drugs, abused, in the system. Not fun and carefree and happy like Brian's family. So to watch JP be what she thought of as a normal kid—when she hadn't been one, and she didn't see normal kids in her job—it was good. Good for her to remember that she did her job to give these options to more people. The option to be safe, to have a family, to live a happy life.

After inspecting a rather death-defying Indy 500 track complete with loops and hairpin turns, Kara went down to eat with the family. She listened to Trevor talk about college and Teddy talk about his girlfriend—who he was going to see right after dinner. For two hours only, because it was a school night, per his mother. It was so normal. So…natural.

She didn't feel like she belonged.

"Trevor will help me clean up," Julie said. "You two talk. You don't get a lot of time to chat."

Kara and Brian went out to the back patio with a couple of beers. He turned on two heat lamps, which was nice. They had a pool, now covered for the winter—a luxury here in Washington because it only got hot enough to swim in the summer. There was also a lot of space—no houses behind them, only an open field sloping up to the mountain.

"This is nice," she said.

"It is."

"Julie's business is doing well."

"Yep. She makes as much money as I do," Brian said.

"No shit?"

"By next year she'll be making more, even after my raise. I'm really proud of her. She started it as a one-woman shop, and now has this amazing business. And she loves it. Pays Trevor and Teddy to help, especially during Christmas when it gets hectic."

"You didn't tell her that you might be a target."

"No."

"Brian."

"She doesn't need to know."

"Yes she does. This is serious."

"I know it's serious, Kara. I've been a cop almost as long as you've been alive."

"Then tell her."

"She knows that there's a killer out there. She knows that the killer may target a cop. She doesn't know that it's a cop connected to Liberty Lake."

Unbelievable. "Fucking *tell* her, Brian."

"You've gotten bossy."

"I've always been bossy."

"If I truly thought that I was the target, my family wouldn't be here."

"You have to consider it, Brian."

He didn't say anything.

"I am." He paused. "This guy isn't going to come after me until Tuesday. If I get any sense that I might be on his list, I'll send them away tomorrow. Okay? But it just doesn't make any sense."

"He's a psychopath. It doesn't have to make sense to us. It makes sense to him because his brain is twisted."

The sliding glass door opened and Matt stepped out. "Your wife said I could come out. I hope I'm not disturbing anything."

"Not at all. Just in time for dessert," Brian said.

"I don't want to put you out."

"You're not."

"Well, I have something to discuss before we go inside, if that's okay," Matt said.

"Give it to me straight. You found something?"

"Maybe."

Matt felt intensely uncomfortable under Kara's gaze. It wasn't that she was looking at him in any specific way, just that he couldn't read her.

He wouldn't have come over at all, if he didn't think it was important.

"Brian, I am concerned that you may be the target."

"We were just talking about that," Kara said.

Brian shook his head. "You're going to have to have some damn solid proof."

"I don't have proof—yet. But Zachary Hamilton, the Liberty Lake guy you evicted after the bank foreclosed some years back? I went through the file completely—including everything that the bank had submitted as part of the documentation to get the warrant. The house is located at 369 Vine Street."

"You're basing your threat assessment on the address having a three in it?"

"No. It's just one piece. Hamilton was fired from Spokane High School only a week before a terminated employee attacked Marston in the parking lot—based on a witness statement. I don't think that's a coincidence. So now I have confirmation that you, Marston, and Anne Banks all had a confrontation with Zachary Hamilton."

"What about the cop who arrested him for his third drunk driving charge? I just put him in county lockup for three days. The other cop put him in prison for a year."

"Andy's talking to her now—that was Spokane PD. That cop has no connection to Liberty Lake. She's never lived here, never worked here."

"But you're still just making a guess that the Triple Killer is targeting a cop from Liberty Lake."

Before Matt could argue, Kara said, "For shitsake, Brian, you're deflecting. This is real."

"I just don't think this is enough to put me on the list. Hamilton is older than me. Your initial report said the killer would be under forty. I'll be fifty next year."

"Criminal psychology is not perfect, but it does give us a place to start. Hamilton is fifty-five. But what bothers me is that I can't find him. I've found McCafferty, the other guy I was looking at. He's living in Massachusetts. Is married, has two kids. First thing in the morning I'll talk to him, but if he's in Foxborough tomorrow morning, I don't see him traveling cross-country to be home with his family in between killing a couple of people."

"But it might not be Hamilton at all. It could be someone else."

"You're right. But too many things are lining up with him. I need you to take it seriously."

"I am."

"I'm moving in," Kara said.

Brian sighed and rubbed his eyes. "Look—just let me talk to Julie before you dump this on her, okay?"

"Of course," Matt said. He gathered up his folder. "And I hope I'm wrong. But if I'm wrong then we have a complete unknown out there and we'll be starting at square one. I have the box of reports from the pileup. My people and I are going through everything again tonight, along with two additional agents sent in from Seattle. Fresh eyes, to see if something else jumps out. I'll talk to McCafferty in the morning. And we're working on tracking Hamilton down. He moved to Montana after the house was foreclosed, but there's nothing on him for the last ten years. He could be anywhere."

"Can I go through that tonight?" Brian gestured to the folder.

"Of course. It's a copy." Matt handed it to Brian.

"May I?" Kara said.

Brian gave it to her. "Let's get some dessert," he said.

They all went inside and Julie Maddox dished up apple cobbler, which was delicious. Kara was quiet—unusually so. Matt was distinctly uncomfortable. He wanted to talk to her about earlier today, but he had a whole bunch of work to do, and it was already after eight.

Brian walked him out thirty minutes later. "You have a nice family," Matt said. "Thank you for your hospitality."

"Your job doesn't afford you much of a family life, does it?" Brian said.

"It's why I was picked—no personal attachments."

"Don't you miss having a home base?"

"I was in Tucson for five years early in my career and have a little house down there. That's where I go to relax. For quite some time I've been moving from office to office, then working out of headquarters in DC for the last two years. And I have a brother who stayed in Miami, a niece and nephew, and another on the way. Christmas with Dante and Layla and Layla's huge family holds me over. Dante's a successful doctor and I have an apartment over his garage whenever I want it. It works for me."

Mostly. Sometimes, Matt wondered what it would be like if he had something like Dante had. He would get antsy. He always did. It's why he couldn't commit to a woman. He'd once cared for Catherine's sister, Beth, but there wasn't anything deeper than a basic affection. He saw true love when his brother looked at his bride. That, Matt had never felt.

He didn't feel comfortable discussing his personal life with this man. He had a great respect for Brian Maddox—he was one of the good cops, one of the people Matt felt he could trust, though Matt wished he took this threat more seriously. But Matt liked to keep his personal life to himself.

As if Maddox sensed what he was thinking, he said, "I'll read over your notes. Talk to Julie. Send her to visit my parents in St. George. Or down to Scottsdale—my boys love baseball, and they'd love to get out of school for a couple of days to watch spring training."

"So far, the killer hasn't gone after families, but we definitely don't want to risk anyone. I can put a patrol on your house, or an agent inside."

"Kara said she'd watch my back. She's a good cop, Matt. You can trust her."

"I'm sure she is, but she's here on vacation. Pulling bodyguard duty for a couple of days?"

Kara walked up to them.

"I'm doing it," she said. "I wasn't joking earlier."

Matt hadn't seen her step out of the house.

Brian laughed. "A patrol will be sufficient, Kara."

"Like hell. Your house is remote. Access from all sides, including the backyard and a thousand acres of open space behind you. I'm good, I'm not letting anything happen to you. I think Costa's right—and I think you're a fool if you don't think so."

Brian was irritated. "I already told Costa that I'm sending Julie and the boys away."

"Good. I'm going to Em's. I'll explain to her I'm moving in with you for a day or two, and I'll be here bright-eyed and bushy-tailed in the morning. I'm your partner in this, I owe you."

"You don't owe me, but—"

"You think because I'm a girl I can't watch your back?"

"Of course not."

"Then shut up."

She glanced at Matt and he wanted her to wink at him like she'd done the other day, but she didn't. All he saw was the cop Kara. Because that was all she wanted him to see.

She walked over to her car and drove off.

"Are you sure this isn't overkill?" Brian asked seriously.

"It's not. I can put the agents on you."

"I trust Kara. She knows what she's doing. I don't think she ever stops working. But having a couple agents to relieve her or watch the house—if you really think I'm the target, I won't object. I don't have a death wish," Brian said.

Matt needed to go, but Brian Maddox was probably the only person in Liberty Lake who knew Kara Quinn—really knew her. "What does Kara owe you for?"

"Nothing."

"Because you convinced her to become a cop?"

"She's always said if any other cop had arrested her after she trashed the rapist's Corvette, she would have turned to a life of crime."

"Arrested? How could she be arrested and still be on the job? She told me you detained her."

"Yes, in a way. I convinced the asshole to drop the charges on the condition that she paid restitution. It burned her to do it, but she did destroy the Corvette, and it could have been a felony conviction. But she was still a minor, and I went to bat for her with the judge. Even though the rapist dropped the charges, the judge wanted a bench warrant. Ended up with probation, no ding on her record, erased at age eighteen. And the bastard still got part of what was coming to him—a year in prison. Should have got more, but I had to manipulate him into taking a plea."

Matt was perplexed, and it must have showed. "Kara said a friend of hers was raped and Kara trashed the guy's car."

"Yeah—that's the truth, but sort of the simple version. Kara didn't have an easy childhood. Rather… unorthodox, let's say, until she moved in with her grandmother when she was fifteen. But even though her parents were less than law-abiding, Kara always had this steel spine to protect the underdog. She just wanted to do it herself. Her friend was date-raped, and Kara knew who did it. She's lucky she broke his car instead of his neck, which I wouldn't have been able to get her out of. It was a classic he said, she said—and the victim's part was vague because she didn't remember anything—but I convinced the asshole that I had a witness, and Kara played probably her first undercover role. Or maybe not, considering what her parents had her do when she was a kid."

Matt had a million questions, but remained silent.

"We essentially gaslighted him, he caved, made up a lie about not knowing the girl was drugged, agreed to a plea deal. I made him serve the full year, too.

"If I had a daughter, I'd want her to be like Kara," Brian continued, "but with a healthy dose of fear. I worry about her. She got her GED and enrolled in the police academy in LA, though I was trying to get her to go to college. Maybe she needed to get away—the Spokane Valley isn't very big, and Kara has always felt uncomfortable with people knowing her business. She visits now and again, and we talk from time to time. I had a conference down in LA a couple years ago and met her boss. Good man, keeps her alive."

"I'll admit I was surprised that she's an undercover cop."

"Worries me, doesn't surprise me. Not in the least. I don't think Kara likes herself—or at least, she doesn't really know herself. She's much more comfortable playing parts. If only she could see what I see—or what you see."

"Excuse me?"

"I see a solid cop who wants to change the world taking out one scumbag at a time. You see that—and more. You must have gotten under her skin, because I haven't seen her so prickly in…well, ever. That takes some doing. Nothing breaks through Kara's Teflon exterior."

Matt didn't believe that for a minute. He'd made her angry, and he felt like shit for it. He may have even hurt her feelings, and he felt even worse if he did.

But he hadn't broken through her surface. He didn't think anyone could.

37

Monday, March 8
Spokane
7:00 a.m.

On Monday morning, Ryder set up a Skype call between Matt and Charlie McCafferty, the man who'd lost his family eighteen years ago, when he was sixteen. He'd left Spokane for Boston College two years later, graduated with honors, went into graphic design for a start-up company that he was still with, married nine years ago and had two young children.

He definitely didn't fit Catherine's profile, but Matt needed to talk to him.

It was ten in the morning Eastern time, and McCafferty was in his office.

"Thank you for taking the time to talk to me," Matt said, assessing the man over the computer. He was pleasant looking, thin, and wore thick glasses. He had on a cable-knit sweater and behind him on a coatrack was a long wool coat and scarf. "Still cold out there? It was freezing when I left DC last week."

"Snowing. I kind of like it. What can I do for you, Agent Costa?"

"I'd like to talk to you about the car accident you were in years ago when you lost your family. I know a lot of time has passed, and I know that it was a horrific experience for you, but it would greatly help me if I could ask about the lawsuit you filed."

McCafferty's expression didn't change, but his shoulders leaned in just a bit and he glanced down at his keyboard.

"I don't know what you want from me, really. I left for college and haven't been back—well, once, for my cousin's wedding a few years ago."

Travel would be easy enough to verify, but Matt made a note. "Several lawsuits were filed after the accident. I'm investigating a series of murders that may be connected to that."

He looked confused. "Murders? From the accident? I don't understand. Are you saying that the accident might have been a murder?"

This was confusing, so Matt took a gamble and explained it outright to McCafferty, in as few words possible. "Let me backtrack. A series of eight murders have occurred over the last six years, all starting on a March 3, the day and month of your accident. The first victim was a trauma nurse at Spokane General who lost one of her patients that night eighteen years ago. In the course of our investigation, we uncovered several other lawsuits against that nurse and other people who may now be at risk. That's why I wanted to talk to you."

"About murder?" Charlie said.

"About your lawsuit. I read the file, the transcripts, I cannot begin to imagine what you were going through as a teenager."

McCafferty didn't say anything for a long minute.

"Charlie?" Matt pushed.

"Let me understand this. You think because I sued the hospital and lost that I killed someone?"

Pretty much, but Matt didn't say that. "Not you specifically, but one of the accident survivors—the dates aren't a coincidence."

"I haven't killed anyone, I promise you that."

"The lawsuit? Were you disappointed at the result?"

"I haven't thought about it in a long time. It wasn't even my idea. I don't really remember much of anything that year, to be honest. But my uncle insisted, and I just went along with it. I can't even tell you who we sued or why. That was the worst night of my life. I woke up and I just knew my whole family was dead. My parents. My little sister. And I thought, why me? Why me?" His voice trailed off and he looked at something next to his computer, then refocused on Matt. "I really don't know how I can help you. I've never killed anyone—I can't even imagine it. Maybe if someone broke into my house and threatened my wife, my kids? Even then… I'd defend my family and try to talk them out of it. Or give them what they wanted before I even thought about fighting back. I don't even own a gun."

"I have to ask, just to check the boxes, but have you ever traveled to Portland, Oregon."

"I don't think so. Maybe as a kid, we once went

on a road trip down the coast all the way to Los Angeles. I was twelve or thirteen. But I don't really remember."

"You went to Spokane High?"

"Yeah."

"Did you know the high school principal, a John Marston?"

"Big black guy? Yeah, I remember him. He was actually really cool to me after the accident. He came over to my uncle's, where I was living, and we worked out a study at home plan. Both my legs were broken, and I didn't want to go back to school and talk to anyone about what happened. I was depressed and miserable and my uncle was all focused on getting the money. He didn't mean anything bad by it—he lost his sister after all and he thought I deserved something. My mom and uncle were really close. He was angry, and I guess sometimes people need someone to blame when bad things happen. That accident was no one's fault, really. It was an awful night. Sleet. People were driving carefully, but someone spun out on black ice, and someone else hit them, and there were big rigs and everyone was sliding. Anyway, I might never have gone back to school, except that Mr. Marston convinced me to return for my senior year, said it would be good for me. He was right. I ended up with a scholarship to Boston College, and that was really the best thing that could have happened to me."

"Did you know Mr. Marston was murdered three years ago?"

"Murdered?" The expression on McCafferty's face was shock. "That's awful. What happened?"

"That's what I'm trying to find out. I'd like to talk to your uncle. He might remember something about that time that could help."

"But Mr. Marston had nothing to do with the accident. I really don't understand."

"I can't go into the details, but I'd like to know more about your lawsuit and whether your uncle knew anyone else who was suing the hospital at the same time."

"We didn't win or even settle. It was dismissed and I was relieved. I didn't want to relive it anymore."

"How are you doing now?" Matt asked. "You like Boston?"

"I love it. I work in the city but live in the suburbs. It's nearly a two-hour train ride, but I only have to come into the office twice a week. I do most of my work at home."

"You're married, with kids, right?"

"Yeah." He smiled, a genuine smile. "Boy and girl, a year apart, couldn't have planned it better. They just turned four and five. Best day of my life was when I met Megan, my wife. Next-best days were the births of my kids."

Matt sent two FBI agents from Seattle—Diana and Carl—to Liberty Lake to assist Andy with following up on all the police reports they'd gone through the night before. Verifying information, dismissing complaints, following up on tips generated by all the press the Triple Killer had garnered—some of which Matt himself had asked for after the press conference. And Matt needed Michael with him. While Matt didn't believe that the killer would target any of the federal agents, Catherine's comment the other day about what would happen if they messed with the killer's pattern stuck with him.

Matt had been the face of the investigation—something he didn't aspire to but couldn't avoid. Michael was well trained and former military. Matt trusted him to have his back more than two agents he'd never met.

Early on in his career, Matt recognized that while all FBI agents had the same training and had to meet the same minimum level of qualifications in every area, some agents were head and shoulders above the others. Better at the gun range, better physically, smarter, sharper, shrewder. One of the reasons he had such a difficult time filling the slots on the MRT unit was because he wanted the best of the best—he had one of the top forensics people in the country with Jim Esteban. He had the top profiler at BAU if Catherine agreed to work with him. Ryder was one of the smartest, most organized analysts Matt had ever worked with, even though he was still a rookie. And Michael Harris was former Navy SEAL, SWAT trained, and a methodical cop. He wanted more like them on his team.

"Michael, with me," Matt said, then turned to Ryder. "Be alert, Ryder. We don't know who this guy is yet. Stay here in the hotel. If there are any issues call the cavalry."

"Yes, sir."

Matt turned to Michael and rolled his eyes. The "sir" crap was getting under his skin, but he didn't know how to fix Ryder. Maybe he should just let it go.

"Where are we headed?"

"To talk to McCafferty's uncle and then CPS."

"I hate CPS."

Matt wasn't surprised. He knew Michael had a dicey childhood.

"Andy Knolls contacted them this morning and I need to light a fire under them. Tony Greer is expediting a warrant for CPS records, but I don't have it in my hot little hands yet. I'm hoping by the time we're done with the uncle, we'll have it."

The entire reason Matt wanted to meet with Charlie McCafferty's uncle was to make sure he had had no cause or inclination to kill Banks or any of the others. Almost immediately upon meeting him, Matt crossed him off the list. He was retired and babysitting his three young grandchildren. His wife was baking cookies. He had pictures of his family everywhere—four kids, seven grandchildren, and his sister and her family including Charlie from years ago, plus recent photos of Charlie and his family.

Not that a close, happy family would preclude someone from murder, but after a five-minute conversation, Matt didn't think the uncle had it in him. He got the sense that a lawyer had convinced the family to sue after the accident, and the uncle regretted that decision.

"I was grieving and I wanted someone to blame.

I just didn't realize how my actions impacted Charlie. He had to keep reliving the accident, talking about it, and it wasn't helping him. I was relieved when the judge threw it out, because if he didn't, that would have meant more years of stress on Charlie. I think the lawsuit was one of the reasons he decided to go to college on the East Coast, and I blame myself for that."

His wife came over and put her hand on his shoulder. "Don't, honey. Charlie needed to start fresh." She smiled at Matt. "We go out there for a visit every fall now. Charlie doesn't like to visit here. He came in for Karen's wedding—they were always so close. It hurts, but we don't want him to have to relive the accident. Going to Boston was good for him, and that's where he met Megan. It was meant to be."

Matt thanked them for their time and left.

He called Tony on his way to CPS. "I need that warrant. You know how these bureaucrats are."

"I'm getting there. I'll email it as soon as I have it."

Matt hung up.

"Not good news?" Michael asked.

"He's working on it. Let's see what we can get without it."

Michael drove to the county administration building where Child Protective Services was located. He was quiet, but Matt didn't intrude. Michael had a tough childhood in Chicago and the Navy had saved his life. Matt knew this from the personnel file, not because Michael talked about it. He'd been in and out of foster care from the time he was nine until he enlisted.

Fortunately, the warrant came through as Matt was talking to the director. And because Andy Knolls had paved the way, CPS had already started researching the file. Matt didn't have the kid's first name, but with his father's name they were able to pull up the records digitally.

The director printed out a copy of the record for Matt. It was thin, but it gave them what they needed—a Glen Vincent Hamilton, now thirty-one. He'd been twelve when his mother was killed, nearly fourteen when he was taken from his father and sent to live with his mother's sister in Kennewick—two hours away.

"Is this all you have on him?"

"He wasn't in the system as a juvenile delinquent—he came through here only because his father went to prison. I wasn't here at the time—this was years ago. We facilitated locating his closest relative, an aunt. Followed up—" she looked at the file, flipped a page "—twice to make sure that he had adjusted. He did tell the counselor he didn't want to visit his father in prison. We don't force kids to see their incarcerated parents, but if they choose to, we will arrange for regular visitation."

"You've had no contact with the son since."

"No, Agent Costa, there was no need. There's a notation here that he continued to live with his aunt even after his father was released, but that's all."

"Thank you."

Matt and Michael walked out.

"Shit," Matt muttered.

"You want to drive down to Kennewick?" Michael said as he slid into the driver's seat.

It was noon. Two hours there, an hour of conversation, they'd be back before dark.

"I don't know. The killer is most likely here."

"What other leads do we have?"

"We're going to waste half the day. But if this is our guy…we need to talk to his aunt in person." But should he call her and give her a heads-up? Or make a surprise visit, even if that meant she might not be available? He sent Ryder a note that he needed to confirm the information about Glen Hamilton's aunt in Kennewick.

He then called Catherine.

"Hello, Matt."

"I'm stuck. We have twelve hours till midnight and McCafferty didn't pan out."

"What's his story?"

Matt briefly told her. "It's not him. I have the Boston field office verifying he didn't travel to Washington in the last week, but I talked to his family who's still here, and I don't get the vibe that any of them had the motivation or desire or even the capacity to kill methodically in cold blood. McCafferty is employed and settled in a Boston suburb, married with kids."

"Unlikely."

"It's not him."

"And Hamilton?"

"We can't find Zachary Hamilton anywhere. It's Ryder's number one priority right now—we traced him to Montana where he disappeared ten years ago. He has a son named Glen, who went to live with an aunt after Hamilton was sent to prison for drunk driving—not his first arrest. But the kid is thirty-one now, and I don't know where he's living or what he's doing. There's one relative—Hamilton's sister-in-law, the kids' maternal aunt."

"She may have insight into her brother-in-law Zachary, as well as the son. It's something."

When Catherine didn't elaborate, Matt said, "What is?"

"We need to know more about this family, Matt. I've read through the lawsuit. In Hamilton's deposition, he blamed the Spokane hospital and specifically ER nurse Anne Banks for his wife's death. But it was the words he used." She shuffled papers. "He said, 'She killed Lorna. She left her to die.' Later, he repeated that Banks had 'killed' his wife, and that she 'chose' to save others instead of Lorna. A lot of rage there. Hamilton's attorney should have made it clear to his client only to state the facts and the emotional impact his wife's death had on his family. But the rage was clearly pent up, and where there's rage, there can be the motivation to kill."

"Enough to kill more than a decade later?"

"He had been in prison at one point. Maybe Banks had moved by the time he was out and he couldn't initially find her. A series of events could have happened and by then he located her, right around the anniversary of his wife's death—a death he believes could have been prevented."

"So we should talk to the sister-in-law."

"Do you have another suspect?"

"No. Hell, we could be going at this all the wrong way."

"Do you believe that?"

"I don't know what I believe at this point, but right now this is all we have."

"Psychology is not a hard science. This pattern is so clear now that we've identified it. I agree with your assessment about Brian Maddox being the likely target because so far he's one of only two law enforcement officers from Liberty Lake who had a run-in with Hamilton. You also need to make sure the officer who arrested Hamilton for his third drunk driving offense is covered, too. Officer—" she flipped paper "—Theresa Corrigan. That arrest led Hamilton down the path where he lost his job, his freedom, his son, then his house. That's a lot of losses in a short period of time, on top of the rage he felt at the death of his wife just the year before. He seems to have had no other support structure besides his son and sister-in-law—both of whom lived hours away—no one else, no close friends, no church or civic organization. So he moves out of state…then disappears. You need to find him. Before he finds you."

"I have two agents from Seattle who came in to help. They're working with Andy Knolls on all the arrest files from Liberty Lake to make sure we haven't missed something, but I'll pull them tonight to sit on Corrigan. She has a partner for the duration, but I can spare the agents."

"Are you on Maddox? Or local cops?"

"Detective Quinn is staying with him. He's sending his family out of town today, and two of his own officers are going to watch his house 24-7 for the next two days. But Corrigan has no connection to Liberty Lake—she lives in Spokane, she works in Spokane, and has never lived or worked in Liberty Lake."

"Except she arrested Hamilton," Catherine said. "Remember that Manners worked in Spokane, but was killed at the lake. Ogdenburg worked in Spokane, but was killed at the lake. I don't think you can take Officer Corrigan off the potential target list, not yet."

"Point taken."

"And remember—don't go anywhere alone."

"I have Michael with me. I took your warning to heart. Now that I'm the face of the investigation, if we thwart him, he could come after me. I get it."

"Good to know. Be careful."

"I knew you cared."

"You're impossible." Catherine hung up.

Matt grinned. *I'm wearing her down.*

Michael said, "I guess we're going to Kennewick."

"Yep. I'm going to call the Seattle agents and tell them they're on Corrigan, starting at ten tonight. Andy's people can relieve them in the morning."

"If I may?"

"May what?"

"They got here at eight in the morning. You and I have been putting in almost twenty-hour days—this is what we signed on for. Quinn has her own reasons for doing it, but most anyone else is going to balk at working more than a twelve-hour shift."

Matt hadn't thought of that, maybe because he didn't do much else except work. "I'll have them relieve the Spokane detail in the morning."

"Better."

Matt called Andy, explained what he needed. Andy would make sure that not only was there a cop in the house with Corrigan, but that a patrol with two cops were watching her when she got home.

"My people will relieve them in the morning. How are they working out?" Matt said.

"Fine," Andy said in a tone that suggested otherwise. "I wish I hadn't made Kara mad. She's really good at this."

"She decided she's protecting Maddox." Matt said. "I don't think anyone, even Maddox himself, can convince her to walk away from that assignment."

38

Kennewick, Washington
3:10 p.m.

Nadine Montclair was sixty-one and worked as an administrative assistant for a paper product company. Matt decided not to call ahead because he didn't know what to expect, though he had verified her employment and that she was in the office. Unfortunately, he'd seen too much during his career to make any assumptions about an individual's guilt or innocence. He also found that when he wanted straight answers, it was best not to give a potential witness or suspect too much time to think. And if Montclair was still in contact with her brother-in-law or her nephew, Matt didn't want her giving either of them a heads-up.

Montclair had her own office adjoining the CEO; she brought Matt and Michael inside. She was petite and casually dressed.

"FBI?" she asked. "I must have heard that wrong."

Matt and Michael both showed their badges. "We

won't take too much of your time, Ms. Montclair. We're here about your nephew, Glen Hamilton."

"Glen?" She seemed confused. She motioned for them to sit, and she sat behind her desk. Her office was small but orderly, just enough room for two chairs, other than hers. She reached into a bowl of wrapped butterscotch candies and took one out. "Help yourself," she said as she unwrapped hers and put it in her mouth.

"Thank you," Matt said, but didn't take one. He said, "Glen moved in with you when Zachary Hamilton went to prison for drunk driving. He was fourteen at the time?"

She nodded. "Zach would never admit that he was an alcoholic," she said. "He drank when my sister Lorna was alive, but kept it under control. She threatened to leave him once, and he promised to do better. I think he did, for a while. He loved Lorna. It was probably his only redeeming quality. But everyone loved my sister. She was truly a kind and caring person."

She looked from Matt to Michael and back to Matt. "I don't understand what you want to know. Lorna has been dead for eighteen years. She died in a car accident—in fact, the anniversary of her death was only a few days ago."

"We're in the middle of an open investigation, Ms. Montclair. I can't share many details right now, but I need to talk to your brother-in-law and nephew right away. I was hoping that you might know where I can find them."

"Is Glen in trouble?"

"We just want to talk to him."

"My nephew has been through so much."

"When was the last time you saw him?"

"Not for a while. He moved to Seattle, got a good job for a computer company. He's a smart boy."

"How long ago was that?"

"Six, seven years? He calls me on my birthday and a couple other times a year. He's always been quiet, reserved, a little bit of a loner. Especially after my sister, his mother, died."

Michael picked up a picture from her desk. "Is this you and Glen?"

She smiled. "His high school graduation."

Michael snapped a photo of the picture, and Ms. Montclair frowned.

"What is it you really want from Glen?" she asked.

Matt didn't want to tell her that he was a possible suspect in multiple homicides, not yet—she may not believe it possible, and then decide not to talk to them. "We really need to find your brother-in-law Zachary Hamilton, and we're hoping that Glen might be able to lead us to him."

"Zach?" She shook her head. "I've never forgiven him. I never liked him when Lorna was alive, but he was her choice and he was good to her. But after she died? He neglected Glen. Instead of taking care of him, Zach drank more, lost his job, went to jail. Even when he got out, they never talked. His son wanted nothing to do with his father, although he went up to Spokane a couple times to see him—before Zach lost the house and moved out of the area.

It never went well. I'd hoped after sobering up in jail that Zach would change, but he went back to his old ways. Couldn't keep a job. Couldn't pay the mortgage."

"And Glen lived here with you until he graduated high school?"

She nodded. "I never married, never had kids, and he was an easy teenager even given his circumstances. Never gave me any trouble. Respectful, polite, did chores for me without being asked."

"Can we trouble you for his phone number? Or the name of the company he works for?"

She turned to her computer and brought up her contact list. She wrote down Glen's information and handed it to Matt. "I doubt very much that he knows what happened to his father. And I don't think he cares, to be perfectly honest. I never talked to Zach after Lorna's funeral—unless I absolutely had to, usually because Glen needed something."

"Did Glen ever talk to you about his mother's accident?"

"No, that was a tough subject for us. Lorna was my only family—our parents died when Lorna was nineteen. I was a few years older so we lived together until she met Zach in Spokane. Then I got this job and moved down here.

"I've been with the company for almost thirty years. Lorna had Glen. Her world revolved around her little family—her husband and son. Zach blamed everyone for Lorna's death, but it really was just an awful accident. Whenever I talked to Glen about it, he would become so sad. I suggested that he talk to a counselor, but he didn't want to. And I didn't push it—time usually heals."

"Thank you for your help, Ms. Montclair."

"Of course. But Glen—he's not in trouble, is he? He's never been in trouble. Not so much as a fight at school, at least when he lived with me. Never had detention, all his teachers liked him because he was so polite and studious."

"He sounds like he was a good kid," Matt said, noncommittal. "Again, thank you. I'll call if I have any more questions."

They walked out and Michael said, "Wasn't Scott Peterson, the guy who killed his wife and baby, also described as a perfect son? Polite and respectful?"

"A lot of kids are polite without turning into killers."

"It was just the way she was talking, Costa. Even my little brother, who was damn close to perfect, got in trouble from time to time."

"I didn't know you had a brother."

"He was killed in a drive-by when he was twelve," Michael said.

"Man, I'm sorry. I didn't know."

Michael shrugged and slid into the driver's seat. "Long time ago. Back to Spokane?"

"Yes. As fast as you can."

Matt had a few calls to make, one to Glen Hamilton's employer. Hamilton lived in Tacoma, south of Seattle, but his employer was a major computer company in the city. It took several minutes before Matt got through to his supervisor. He learned that

Glen worked remotely from home and was only in the office twice a month for staff meetings. The last time Glen had been in was the end of February. He was a valued employee who did his work well and on time, according to his boss, but had no real desire to move up or take on more responsibility even though he was capable.

Next Matt called the Seattle FBI field office. He asked that they send two more agents, this time down to Glen Hamilton's residence and talk to him, then assign a car to sit on him for the next forty-eight hours. If he didn't budge, then he wasn't their killer. It was a four-hour drive from Spokane to Seattle. Hamilton could fly in an hour or less, which was possible but unlikely. It would leave a paper trail.

The phone number might be the best chance of locating him, but they needed a warrant for the records or to ping it. And right now, they didn't have enough information for a warrant. If they couldn't get it, Matt might call the number and hope Hamilton would pick up. It was definitely worth a shot.

Matt called Catherine and filled her in on what the aunt said.

Catherine didn't speak for a long minute.

"Hey, did I lose you?"

"I've been going over forensic reports," she said, "and the timeline from the homeless men in Spokane who were stabbed to death, and the man who was stabbed to death in Bozeman. Do you realize that Glen Hamilton would have been seventeen at the time of the Spokane murders?"

"Your point?"

"His father was foreclosed on fifteen years ago. Glen would have been sixteen. Zach then disappeared, correct?"

"There's no record of him buying or renting in the Spokane Valley after that. We tracked him to Montana, up until ten years ago."

"But Glen went to visit his father while he still lived in Liberty Lake, correct? Before he lost the house?"

"Yes, but I don't have dates."

"My guess would be shortly after he got his driver's license. And before his father had lost the house on Vine Street—and lost everything inside. Everything that had been his mother's. That had been *his*."

"Okay, but I don't see where you're going with this."

"His father lost the house because he lost his job because of his drinking. This was all after he lost his son because of his drunk driving arrest, correct?"

"Yes—he went to jail and that was when Glen was sent to Kennewick. He was nearly fifteen."

"When the father got out of jail, he went back to his job—but couldn't hold it down. He went back to drinking. That's when he lost the house. Glen was sixteen. Perhaps he finally got the courage to confront his father, or perhaps he just wanted to retrieve what belonged to him or his mother. But he was too late. It was all gone. The house, the personal items, his father. He had nothing to take out his rage on… except homeless alcoholics who couldn't fight back."

"That's a stretch, and it's going to be difficult to prove."

"Consider that this boy was the recipient of his father's rage for at least two years before he went to live with his aunt. And from what you learned from the aunt, he may not have been a model father and husband even before his wife's death."

"Are you saying Zachary abused his son?"

"Maybe, maybe not, but he must have heard his father blame everyone for everything. The ER nurse for his wife dying. The school principal for him losing his job. The cop for arresting him and sending him to jail. Going to jail put him behind in his payments. Maybe the aunt helped, maybe he had savings or a life insurance policy, but not working for six months had to have hurt his finances. Everyone was to blame, except himself, Zach Hamilton."

This was the old Catherine—she had gotten into the killer's head. Matt knew she would be able to do it, if she just focused and put aside all the shit that happened last summer.

Brian Maddox wasn't the cop who put Hamilton in prison for a year; that was Corrigan. But Brian had arrested him when the house was foreclosed on and Hamilton refused to leave. Which cop did Zachary Hamilton blame the most?

"Are you thinking that they're in this together?" Matt asked. "A father-son killing team?"

"No. I think Glen killed his father in Bozeman."

"Whoa, I am completely lost."

"Remember I told you earlier that there was a stabbing victim in Bozeman nine years ago? His remains were severely compromised—there wasn't a lot to work with. Because it was obviously a homicide, and the victim was unidentified, the ME stored the body in cold storage—as required by state law. So we still have the remains to work with. And your team traced Zachary Hamilton to Montana. I'm going to contact the Bozeman medical examiner to have them send the remains of their stabbing victim to Jim Esteban. I'll expedite it—and if I can't, I think Esteban needs to fly to Bozeman ASAP."

"So you think John Doe is Zachary Hamilton."

"I do. If you follow the killer's pattern—the homeless alcoholics were substitutes for his father. Glen Hamilton killed those men in a rage. I've viewed the autopsy results, and they indicate a lot of anger, multiple stab wounds. And the first Spokane homeless murder was only months after the father, Zachary, lost the family home and left the city. Hamilton hated his father, but at the same time, he adopted his father's cause—the need to punish those who took from him.

"If his mother had never died, none of this would have happened," Catherine continued. "His rationale is that if his father wouldn't have drank too much, he wouldn't have lost his job, wouldn't have lost his house. That was the final trigger. The house. Stability. Where Glen grew up. Where all the memories of his mother were. I was looking over the reports you sent—the bank put everything from the family home in storage. I followed up on that, learned that no one claimed the goods, so after 120 days, they were auctioned off. Everything that Glen had—everything that had been his mother's—gone."

"Believing your theory and proving it are two different things," Matt said.

"That's why we need the body from Bozeman. If we can confirm that it's Zachary Hamilton, it will certainly give us enough for a warrant to trace Glen's phone, search his home, travel records, credit card receipts—whatever we need."

"You think so?"

He could hear the smile in her voice when she said, "If I make the argument, absolutely."

Welcome back, Catherine.

Michael and Matt were still driving back to Spokane when Matt received a call from an unfamiliar number.

"Costa."

"Hello, is this SAC Mathias Costa?"

"Yes."

"This is Special Agent Tammy Sherman from the Seattle field office. I was sent to Tacoma to follow up on Glen Hamilton."

"Did you make contact?"

"He wasn't home. His neighbor said that he travels a lot for work and she hasn't seen him since the middle of February, and then only for two or three days. Before that, it was January."

"I need a current photo of Hamilton, if you can get that for me. And follow up with his employer—I'll text you the information. I talked to them briefly. He works from home, but they didn't say anything about travel. I want to know if his company is aware that Hamilton hasn't been in Tacoma in nearly two weeks. Is he on vacation? Or possibly lying to them about his work location? If he works remotely on a company computer, his employer may be able to track him that way. I want to know anyone he may be close to in his office. Talk to them—find out everything you can about this guy."

"I'll do that and get back to you."

"Thanks, Tammy."

Matt hung up and considered his options.

"APB?" Michael said.

"I'm thinking yes—but let's keep it internal for now. Cops only. Not the press. I want every cop to have this guy's picture. A person of interest—no trigger fingers on this. I don't want anyone getting the idea that they're getting justice for two dead cops by killing my suspect. And dammit, I want a warrant for his phone."

He sent Tony Greer a priority text message that they had a number for Hamilton from his aunt. He wasn't asking for a phone tap, just a warrant for records, so maybe Tony could craft an argument that would get it.

"I'm going to tell Maddox and Corrigan that we have our guy," Matt said. "They in particular need to be on alert, Michael. We need to get back pronto."

"Thirty more minutes, boss. I'm busting past eighty."

Matt sent the information he learned to everyone on the team. He didn't want anyone caught unawares.

"We're close. I feel it."

But time was running out—Matt feared they wouldn't find him before he struck.

Failure is not an option.

39

Liberty Lake
6:45 p.m.

Glen Hamilton's plan was simple in its brilliance.

He'd had to make adjustments because of the newspaper article that said all cops would be riding with a partner until the Triple Killer was caught.

Triple Killer. What a stupid name. What did it mean? Nothing.

But they had given him a name. He was important enough for that. That had to mean something, right?

Deputy Chief Brian Maddox was his last prey; there would be no substitute. Maddox had taken everything important from him. If it weren't for Maddox, his father wouldn't have been evicted from the only real home Glen ever had.

He had been given no chance to intervene. He was never even aware the bank took all their stuff—no one had bothered to contact him! Maddox should have told him, giving him a chance to retrieve his things. But no one told him all the family belongings would be sold. *Everything!* No one gave him a chance to save anything.

His mother's sewing machine.

His mother's pretty vase collection where she would put the roses she'd cut from her garden, beautiful flowers that added hope and cheer to a dark house.

His mother's clothes. They were only things that Glen imagined might still smell like her.

He didn't care about his own things—toys he'd outgrown, outdated video games, broken furniture, his sagging mattress.

He wanted his mom back, and the house *was* his mom.

And then everything was gone. Stolen from him, just like his mother.

Originally, he'd planned to wait for Maddox at his house when he came home from work. The cop didn't park in the garage, and there was a perfect hiding spot among the trees that separated the Maddox property from his neighbor. Because Maddox was a large man, Glen wasn't certain if the drugs would take effect quickly enough, and he couldn't risk having him struggle or cry out or try to go inside before he collapsed. So he had bought a Taser, practiced with it. It was the most powerful Taser he could buy, and he was pretty certain it would take a big man down instantly. Then he'd poke him with the drugs, drag him into his car, and keep him under lock and key until midnight. Until 12:01 a.m. when he could slice him open and watch him bleed out.

He wouldn't use Maddox's own car to transport

him, because Maddox always drove home in a truck from Spokane PD. That meant there would be GPS tracking, and he would be far easier to find. Hamilton would have to use his own car—not ideal, but he was confident he would be far away from Spokane before the FBI figured anything out.

Then he'd lie low for a long, long time.

But only after you take care of the intruders first. They don't deserve the house. No one deserves Mom's house.

No, he would wait awhile before returning to his family's Liberty Lake house. He could disappear a long time—he had the skills, the patience. Hide close by, like in Coeur d'Alene. Wait for everything to die down. Quit his job—he had enough money to live on for a year, or more. His three shell companies, where he'd put half of every paycheck; his savings account, which he had wisely invested.

He was smart, frugal, patient.

And he could adapt to anything they threw at him. Brian Maddox would not survive the next twenty-four hours.

The first sign that Glen had to change his original plan was when Maddox came home with a female cop. He was quite a distance away, so he couldn't make out her features. The air had turned icy and she had a hat and scarf on. Snow would be coming, sooner rather than later.

But the setup was still the same. The best place to grab Brian Maddox was still on the other side of the garage, where he parked his truck. As he'd done every morning when he went to work, Maddox would first go out to the vehicle and turn it on to let it warm up five to ten minutes, then go back inside to get his coffee, before he came back out to leave.

Every. Single. Morning.

When Maddox didn't work, he would go through a similar ritual. On Sundays he and his wife and kids went to church, then out to breakfast at a diner in Liberty Lake that had been around since long before Glen was born. Everyone went there. Glen had only gone once since he'd been back in town because he didn't want to stand out. The food was good, but not as good as his mother's cooking.

Maddox worked half days on Sundays and was off Saturdays. Mondays through Thursdays he worked the early shift. On Fridays he started his day a little later. He'd take his youngest son to school, then run errands.

His wife worked from a home office in the garage, and had a couple people who helped her. They would come after Maddox was gone and the kids were off to school, sometime between nine and ten. Not really on a tight schedule. One woman worked until two-thirty because she had kids to pick up from school—he knew, because he followed her once. The other was a guy who left between four and five. He was not much older than Maddox's oldest son. He wore his hair long and took a lot of smoke breaks.

Glen hadn't been here earlier today, but it had been the same ritual for weeks, and he didn't expect it to change.

Now the only real window of time to grab Maddox was in the morning before he left for work. Kill him quickly there in his driveway. It had to be done and done fast.

Glen considered grabbing Maddox now, but with his family home and the other cop inside his house he had no guarantee he could get to him.

Glen did not like the odds. His previous successes had all been because he attacked his victims when they were alone—when they were weak, distracted, vulnerable.

He didn't want to storm the house. Too risky.

He circled in his car, then parked in a driveway far down the street. He'd surveyed the neighborhood many times. The owner of this particular house was an airline pilot; his schedule was erratic. He had left two days ago and would likely not return for another day or three. The houses were spread far apart, and there were many trees, but Glen couldn't risk any neighbor spotting an unfamiliar car and calling the police. He had to be quick.

He left his car and walked in the shadows across the street, through the open space between two houses, and into the open field behind Maddox's house. The snow from the last storm had all melted because there were few trees in the field to provide cover, but tomorrow's storm would bring it back. The grass was long enough to obscure him in the dark of night from the prying eyes of neighbors as he made his way to Maddox's house.

The house had a pool in the back with a safety fence around it. There were enough trees and shrubs to hide in, so he edged closer. Though he wore a thick jacket, gloves, and a hat, the cold seeped under his skin. He couldn't stay out here too long.

But he'd stay as long as he could.

Glen watched the house from just outside the property line. Maddox and the female cop were in the living room. The back blinds were all open, and when they turned on the lights, it was easy for Glen to see inside. No one else was home. If the wife was home, the lights would have already been on. He glanced toward the garage, which was dark—no one appeared to be working late.

No wife, no little kid. The youngest boy was never left home alone.

Glen frowned. The wife wasn't there. The boys weren't there. This was unusual. They were always home at night. Sometimes the older boys had things after school, but it was late, well after the dinner hour. The family always ate together… Just like Glen had eaten with his parents every night until his mother's senseless death.

The female cop walked to the back of the house and closed all the blinds. Glen could no longer see in. She looked familiar, but Glen wasn't surprised—he'd spent a lot of time over the last two months watching the police station, and all the cops that went in and out. She wasn't in uniform but she could have changed at the station, he supposed. Or maybe she was a detective.

He took a deep breath, let it out. Cold enough for snow. It might snow tonight, and definitely tomorrow, according to the forecast. A major storm coming in quickly. Snow would make it easier for the cops to track him.

Maybe there was a logical reason that the wife and kids were gone, not because Maddox was suspicious. Because they could not know whom he intended to kill. They. Could. *Not.*

He should have grabbed Maddox earlier tonight as he went into the house. Hit the female cop over the head, drugged Maddox. Or, maybe he could find a way to lure the female cop outside, zap her with the Taser, then go in and get Maddox.

Too risky. If Maddox heard anything, he'd have his gun out.

Glen didn't want to die.

Tomorrow morning. That was the only real option now, he was sure. When Maddox came out to warm up the car, zap.

Waste no time. Kill him right there. Stab him in the gut and slice him all the way through.

Fast. He had to do it fast before the female cop came out.

Simple. Effective. Dead.

He closed his eyes. Rage would not serve him well, and he felt it creeping in, eating at his gut. He had survived so long doing what had to be done because he learned to control his actions. He learned patience and self-denial. He learned that he couldn't act without thinking through every possible outcome, planning for every contingency.

He learned the hard way, fifteen years ago. When he finally had the courage to confront his father…

* * *

Glen walked up the weed-strewn path of the house he'd grown up in, pulling his jacket tight around his body. It was so cold he felt he'd never be warm again.

A For Sale sign was on the lawn. No way would he allow his father to sell this house. It would not happen! He couldn't let it happen...

He knocked on the door.

No answer.

He pounded.

No answer.

He tried the knob. It was locked.

Anxiety bordering on panic, he ran around to the back door and tried it. Locked. He twisted and shook the doorknob, but it wouldn't budge. "Zachary!" he shouted. "Let me in!"

He wasn't afraid of his weak, drunk father. He came here to do what he should have done years ago. Maybe if he'd had the courage to kill his old man when he was thirteen, his mother would never have been out in the car that night in the storm. She would never have died and left him.

Glen broke the window of the back door, reached in and unlocked the dead bolt. Then he entered his family home and stopped in the middle of the kitchen.

It was empty.

There was nothing inside. No kitchen table with the red-checked vinyl tablecloth.

No whimsical plates of kittens and puppies over the threshold to the dining room.

No food, no dishes, no curtains.

Slowly, he walked from room to room, his knife twisting in his hand. It wasn't a large house; it didn't take long to realize there was nothing here. Not one piece of furniture. Not one family photo. Everything had been stolen.

He would learn later that the police had arrested his father and the bank foreclosed on the house and all his belongings had been sold. He would learn later that when his dad got out, he left town.

Glen felt a deep loss. As great as losing his mother again. Everything that was Lorna Hamilton was gone. Her body. Her home. Her scent.

Glen left, a dark pit forming in his chest. A thick, growing, overwhelming rage that had only teased him in the past. Now it took over. Now it was part of him. Woven into his nerves like a snake, clutching, squeezing, suffocating him...

He planned to drive back to his aunt's house, but he couldn't, not now. He didn't want to hurt her, and he had to hurt something. Someone. If not his father, someone else.

Glen never remembered how he got to Spokane, or why it was now dark, or why he was driving up and down the streets slowly, looking. He didn't know why until he saw the drunk stumbling down, falling behind a dumpster.

Pathetic, drunk fool.

Just like his old man.

He stopped his car and got out. Approached the man. As he neared, he didn't see the old bum with the red bulbous nose or the long, greasy gray hair. He saw Zachary Hamilton, the man who had sired him, the man who had scared his mother, the man who drank himself out of more jobs than Glen could count.

"Do you need a ride? The church down the street is offering beds for the night."

"Go away," the drunk slurred.

"Really, I don't mind. I'm doing community service and want to help. It's going to be ten degrees tonight. You'll freeze to death. Literally."

Maybe because he looked normal, he looked nice, the bum pulled himself up and staggered over to Glen's car. Glen helped him into the back seat, where he lay down. Glen looked around. It was so late, so cold; no one had seen him. Still, Glen drove as far from town as possible. The drunk didn't even notice. He was passed out.

He stopped in a park near the river. As soon as he opened the door and started to drag the bum from the back seat, the old man woke up.

"Stop that," he mumbled.

He was weak. He pushed at Glen, but Glen held fast and pulled the man from the back of the car, dropping him unceremoniously to the ground.

The man grunted, pulled himself up. Swore at Glen, staggered away.

Glen watched him sit up against the closest tree, pulling his coat against the cold.

And all he could see was his father.

And the knife in his hand.

With a scream, Glen lunged toward the stranger, arm raised, and stabbed him in the chest. So deep that the hilt was buried. He wrestled the knife out of the man's chest, warm blood coating his hand, his arm, spraying across his face.

"I hate you!" he screamed, and plunged the knife again into the body.

And again. And again. The drunk didn't fight back. Couldn't. Weak, pathetic.

He'd stolen everything Glen loved. Now Glen had stolen his life.

And it felt good.

It felt so damn right.

When he was done, he didn't feel the cold. Not at first, then it seeped back in and logic returned.

He needed to hide the body where it wouldn't be found for a long time.

He needed to clean up, get rid of the knife, his clothes. Clean his car. Go back home, to his aunt's house. Wait. Make sure no one saw him. No one found the body. No one could trace this murder to him.

He was so damn cold…

Glen shook his head and came out of his memory. How long had he been sitting back here, among the trees, watching Brian Maddox's house, but not seeing anything but his past? He couldn't be this irresponsible!

He was about to leave when the female cop came out of the house. She walked around the backyard.

She had her gun drawn.

No way she could have heard him out here. He wasn't even on Maddox's property and he knew Maddox didn't have a security system. He knew this spot where he hid couldn't be seen from the house at night. He wore dark clothes and a dark hat.

Why was this girl cop with him tonight? What were they doing? Paranoid? Did someone suspect his plan?

Nothing connected him to any of the murders. Nothing! He was sure. He'd been so careful.

The female cop walked behind the pool and looked out into the field. She might as well have been looking right through him. He was hidden well.

Now he knew where he recognized her. She was the blonde who had drinks with Maddox at the hotel where the feds were staying. She was *that* fed. She had to be. Why was she here? Why would the feds be guarding Maddox? Because he was the deputy chief? Because he was oh-so-fucking-*important?*

"Fucking fishbowl," she said, her voice faint, carrying over to him on the cold breeze. Then she walked around the rest of the yard and back to the house.

He breathed easier, then left.

He didn't like to deviate from his plan, but he had to. What was more important, killing Maddox or killing him the right way?

Glen scratched his palm. He needed to do everything the *right* way. His mother had always told him there was a right way and a wrong way. A right way to fold the towels. A right way to bake a cake. A right way to make a bed.

The knife, his knife, was the *right way* to kill.

But he also needed to kill the cop. Which was more important? Doing it *right* or just getting it done?

As he walked back to his car, his head began to ache. He left Maddox's neighborhood and drove the twenty minutes back to his rental house in Spokane. Once he was outside of the Liberty Lake town limits, he breathed easier.

He had some more planning to do; he was so close to fulfilling his goal. He could picture Brian Maddox dead. That was all the motivation he needed.

40

Liberty Lake
7:30 p.m.

Brian was grouchy now that they were back at his place. Kara checked the outside perimeter, searched the entire house, and secured the doors. "Why don't you go to bed?" she said. "Your grumpiness is driving me crazy."

"I should be out there protecting my fellow cops, not locked in here hiding." He glanced at the clock. "It's only seven-thirty."

"Do you have food? Because you don't want me cooking."

"We should be on patrol."

"I agree with the feds on this one. You are one of two possible targets. The other one, Theresa Corrigan, is under lock and key at her place—do you think she should be out on patrol?"

"No, but—"

"You're the boss *yada yada.* I get it—you don't like being sidelined any more than I do. But Glen Hamilton is a serial killer, and he's got your number.

Everything we learned about him today confirms that Hamilton is our guy. You saw his DMV photo, you're not going to miss him, no matter how ordinary he looks. By the way, you're sleeping in one of the kids' rooms tonight."

"What?"

"I checked the house from top to bottom. Went out back—there are plenty of places to stake out. Tomorrow morning when the sun comes up I'm going to send a couple of cops out there to look for signs that Hamilton has been watching you. Because Costa said this guy stalks his victims, and if I were going to stalk you, I'd do it from the rear."

"We have a safe neighborhood. We watch out for each other. And everyone here owns a gun. They hunt, they protect their property, they wouldn't let some prowler just walk around."

"*If* they see him. We have to assume he knows where you live. Could have followed you from the station. We have to assume he has probably figured out which room is yours. Maybe he's like Spiderman and can scale walls. Or a normal human and brings in a ladder. Isn't one of the kids' rooms downstairs?"

"Trevor."

"So if he does get in upstairs, we'll hear."

"Fine," Brian snapped.

"If you'd just have stayed at the hotel with the feds, we wouldn't be dealing with this bullshit now."

"I can't sleep this early."

He went into the kitchen and rummaged through the refrigerator and cabinets. He brought crackers and salami and cheese to the dining table, plus cans of soda. "I really could use a beer."

"So could I. But you don't always get what you want. After this is over we'll split a six-pack and toast to a job well done."

"Confident, aren't you?"

"Always. Rummy?"

"I've never beaten you."

"I promise not to cheat."

"I wouldn't even know if you did."

"You wound me."

They played cards. Kara won and didn't even cheat. Then they ate ice cream and watched a movie. It was eleven when Brian said, "I'm going to try to sleep."

"Remember, two of your best officers are outside as well. They're down the street in an unmarked car so Hamilton might not spot them, if he's planning on coming here tonight. Costa and Harris will be here in the morning. Tomorrow you stay inside the station. It's the safest place you can be. You go on no calls—*none*. And then if we haven't found him by end of day tomorrow, you're not coming back here. You're going to hotel headquarters for the night."

"Damn bossy badge," he muttered.

She grinned. "It'll throw him off."

"And then what happens?"

"That's the million-dollar question. Maybe his head will explode. We can hope, right?" Kara started up the staircase. "I'm going to make a show upstairs—turn on the lights, walk around, turn off the lights. If Hamilton is watching from the field out back, he'll think that you're going to bed."

Brian rubbed his face with both hands and sighed. "Thanks, Kara. I'm sorry for being so stubborn earlier."

"I know how to wear people down."

Fifteen minutes later, Kara came back downstairs. She checked on Brian—he was reading in Trevor's room. She'd already checked all the windows—twice. She saw Brian's gun on the nightstand. "I'm leaving the door open," she said.

"Hope my snoring doesn't keep you up."

"Why do you think I slept on your office couch this afternoon? I'm not sleeping tonight. Already started a pot of coffee."

She went to the kitchen and poured herself a cup. She wasn't tired, but a steady infusion of caffeine would keep her alert. Not too much, not too little. She'd done this many, many times before.

She had turned off all the lights except for one in the living room. The blinds were closed, and if Hamilton *was* watching, he knew that Brian came home with a cop. She didn't want to make it easy for him.

Her phone rang. It was Matt. She didn't want to talk to him, but she had to because this was now a job, and no way in hell was she letting Brian Maddox get sliced and diced by a psycho nut job just because she was angry at the lead investigator.

"Quinn."

"It's Matt. I'm outside."

"Relieving SPD so soon?"

"No—I want to come in. I just didn't want to knock and send your adrenaline through the roof."

"I don't think Hamilton will knock." She hung up, looked through the peephole anyway to make sure Hamilton didn't have a gun on Matt. He stood there alone, and she opened the door. He walked in, bringing a rush of cold air with him. She looked up and down the street. Nothing suspicious. She closed and bolted the door. "Brian doesn't have a security system. But this is Liberty Lake—most people don't. So why are you here? Think I can't handle an all-nighter?"

"I didn't call Thornton."

"I don't care."

"I think you do."

"I called Lex, my boss. He didn't tell me everything about the investigation when I talked to him yesterday—but I knew the feds were trying to take my case away. So I called him on it. He didn't want to tell me the details because he planned on squashing it before I returned, but he spilled when I told him what Thornton said. Bryce Thornton has had it out for me since I called him on the carpet for fucking up one of my other investigations. So I'll tell you this—David Chen—the bastard I arrested—is the only witness to my so-called deadly force against an allegedly unarmed suspect. Thornton wants to call it a civil rights violation because the guy I popped was Chinese American? What about the civil rights of all the people Chen *owned*? Chen runs what some people call a sweatshop but I call slavery, and so would you. He killed my informant. *My* informant, who I cultivated and protected."

Couldn't protect.

"I should have shot that bastard when I had the chance."

"What happened?" Matt asked quietly.

She didn't want to talk about it, but she was already agitated—at Matt because he listened to Thornton, at Thornton for trying to work with the bastard Chen to take her down, at herself because Sunny was dead and she couldn't stop it.

"I was undercover as a buyer for a big box store. We had the store on board with us, vouching for me. I worked it for over a year. Chen was good. Wined and dined me. Took me fucking forever to get inside, but when I did I recruited Sunny. She didn't want to help. She was scared. I pushed. I'm good at that. I'm good at getting people to work against their own self-interest. She helped, got me exactly what I needed to take down that bastard. Then he killed her before I could get her out. I arrested Chen because I had the evidence, I built the case, I didn't need her to testify. But she's still dead."

Matt was watching her closely. She didn't care. Maybe the feds all had a cushy life, never seeing the underbelly of society. Never looking a predator like David Chen in the eye and knowing he would kill her as soon as look at her. Thornton certainly never had.

"So he fell off a roof evading arrest and broke his fucking leg," Kara said. "Boo hoo." If only the roof had been taller, he'd have split his head open instead of only breaking his femur. "He was down and out and I was taking him into custody. His goon came after me with a knife. Fortunately he had bad aim or it would have been in my back rather than slicing my arm."

Though he'd seen all her scars the other night, she pushed up her sleeve and turned around to show Matt the latest. It still itched, it was still red, but it was healing.

"I turned and fired. Completely justified." She leaned forward. "And if Thornton wants to go toe to toe with me because I shot a man who had thrown a knife at my back, and I didn't wait until he got out his gun or his backup knife, both of which I found on his person when I searched him, I'll fight him. And now Chen is testifying against me to the feds? I call bullshit when I see it. And hear this—Chen killed my informant in cold blood. He was responsible for trafficking more than *five thousand* Chinese nationals—women, children, old men—to serve in sweatshops throughout the country for the last *ten years*. He ran the entire operation and *I took him down* along with a dozen of his cronies. And Thornton wants to give him a plea deal in exchange for testifying—for *lying*—against *me*? No. Never going to happen."

She was pacing, a sign that she was both angry and nervous. She hadn't wanted to tell Matt all that. But she was so damn *mad* that he listened to Thornton, that he called her on it, that he thought he had some claim to her what? Her life? Her integrity?

She was her own person. Always had been. Figured that out really early when her parents put her out to con people. Cute little blonde girl couldn't be a pickpocket. Cute little blonde girl couldn't be faking that injury. Cute little blonde girl could cry on cue.

She had hated herself for a long time for going along with all the stupid scams and cons. And when she put an end to it—when she finally stood up for herself—she vowed she would never be used again. By anyone. By her parents. By her boss. By any man she chose to sleep with. She didn't need anyone to do it for her. And *fuck* everyone who tried to use, manipulate, maim or kill those around her. They would pay.

"Forgive me, Kara," Matt said. "Please forgive me."

He sounded sincere. He looked like he actually felt bad for what he'd done, but she didn't want his pity.

"Nothing to forgive," she said. "You're a fed. You believe other feds. It is what it is."

"I didn't believe or disbelieve him. I listened, then I asked you."

She tried to calm down. She usually did much better at keeping her anger under control. "Look, Matt, I'm happy to have this case. You know that—I wouldn't be here if I didn't want to be. I wouldn't be helping you if I didn't want to help. This psycho needs to be stopped, and if I can protect my friend Brian from getting a knife to his gut, I'll do it, no question. But this time next week you'll be back wherever it is you're from, and I'll be back in LA battling to save my case or working my next one. Maybe one day our cases will collide and if you're unattached and I'm unattached I would be happy to share your bed again. But I'm not naive, and neither are you."

"And that's it?"

"It is for now." She pointed to the clock over the fireplace. "One minute to midnight. Showtime."

41

Tuesday, March 9
Spokane
6:00 a.m.

Matt didn't sleep much when he got back to the hotel—he crashed around three in the morning and woke up just after five, but immediately he was thinking that they needed to catch Glen Hamilton today and started running through a variety of scenarios on how to do it.

Matt's team—and most importantly Catherine—believed that he was the Triple Killer, but they had nothing more than a theory—which meant they had no warrant. They couldn't run his credit, they couldn't look at his bank statements, they couldn't grab his phone records. The AUSA said if they could prove that the John Doe in Bozeman was Hamilton's father, Zachary, they *might* be able to get a limited warrant for Glen Hamilton's travel, phone, and credit statements. If Matt's team could prove that Hamilton was in the same cities at the same time as the Triple Killer, the warrant could be expanded. They'd called his phone through a secure, private line. No answer. The voice mail was automated. Matt hadn't left a message.

The only thing the team could get now was Hamilton's DMV record, which was accessible to local law enforcement without a warrant. No tickets, no accidents, but they had a copy of his most recent photo, taken six years ago. Yesterday, they'd sent the photo to every cop in the Spokane Valley. A black Honda Civic was registered to his name, but Seattle FBI confirmed that it was housed in his garage in Tacoma. He was probably renting a car—hell, he could have bought a second car, registered it in any of the other states—but they wouldn't know for sure until they could access his records. He had Spokane PD send out a notice to all other law enforcement agencies to run the name, but so far nothing had popped.

Sometimes playing by the rules was frustrating. One piece of solid evidence and he could get a warrant for everything he needed—but that solid piece of evidence was elusive.

Matt sent Ryder a message to bring everyone in ASAP to discuss how to flush Hamilton out. *Maybe* they were wrong about this guy. But the fact that they couldn't find him—couldn't talk to him on the phone or sit down face-to-face—was damn suspicious.

Just not suspicious enough for their lawyers to fight for a warrant.

As soon as he stepped out of the shower, Matt called Chief Packard. Though they'd had a rocky start—Matt still didn't like the guy—Packard had definitely stepped up to the plate this weekend. Matt had Brian Maddox and Theresa Corrigan under twenty-four-hour surveillance all day yesterday and certainly today. The teams had been checking in regularly. But if they were wrong about the killer's motive and potential targets, then the other cops who simply were using the buddy system might be at risk. They needed to verify that no one was missing at regular intervals throughout the day. The first check in was 6:00 a.m.; it was six-fifteen now.

"I was just about to call you, Costa," Packard said in lieu of a greeting. "I've heard from every officer and civilian on payroll, and just received notification from Detective Knolls in Liberty Lake and the Spokane County Sheriff—all is clear among our men and women in blue. No one is missing."

"Good to know," Matt said. "Debriefing at eight?"

"Everyone will be here—on or off duty."

"Thank you, Chief."

It was nearly 6:30 a.m. by the time he stepped into the war room. Ryder and Michael were there; Jim was not. He was already at the lab preparing to meet the assistant ME, who was driving in John Doe's remains from Bozeman through the night because of the pending storm. It was going straight to the morgue, where they could perform a second autopsy, if necessary.

"Brainstorm," Matt said, and poured himself a cup of coffee. "How do we catch Glen Hamilton before he gets to a cop?"

"Release his photo to the press," Michael said. "Someone has to have seen him if he's in town."

Matt had thought of that. And he was still thinking about it. "Pros and cons."

"He'll go to ground," Michael said. "Disappear."

"But he can't hide forever," Matt said.

"He could go after anyone, because he may feel trapped or desperate," Ryder said. "He might change his MO."

"Catherine raised that concern after Kara initially posed the question the other day. Still, if it's Hamilton, he's been here for weeks, if not months. He's originally from Liberty Lake, and he knows the area. He can hide. Bide his time. The million-dollar question is, if he doesn't claim his victim today, before midnight, what will he do?"

"I think the more information out there the better," Michael said. "Don't say he's a suspect, just that he may be a witness, and we're trying to talk to him."

Matt nodded. "That's good. We can work with that. Maybe he'll walk in on his own, thinking he can one-up us."

It had happened before. It wasn't common, but sometimes the smartest criminals were the ones who thought they were *too* smart to be caught, no matter what they said to the police.

"He could have a friend in the area that he's staying with," Michael said.

"Catherine feels confident that he's a loner, but it's possible," Matt said. "We'll craft the press release to make it clear that we are concerned for his safety. Not make it seem like he's dangerous, but that we're looking for his father as a person of interest. If he's cornered, even a friend or family member could be in danger."

Ryder said, "Since he has an employer, you could have the employer contact him, tell him that he needs to come in for a meeting."

Matt appreciated the out-of-the-box thinking. "Not bad. He might be suspicious, but that could buy us some time. Or have his aunt call him."

"Tell him what?" Michael asked. "That we were asking about him?"

"Exactly. We went down to talk to her. Have her reach out and ask him if everything's okay. We'll call Catherine on our way out to Liberty Lake and get her take on it, but I like the idea." He glanced at his watch, finished his coffee. "In fact, we need to head out there now to escort Maddox into the Spokane station preferably before the roads turn to ice. Ryder, while we're gone, keep in contact with Jim and let me know the status of John Doe throughout the day. And keep working on tracking Hamilton through all means at our disposal. Tony is going back to the judge to try and spin this another way, even a limited warrant would help."

His phone rang as they were walking out. It was Andy Knolls. It was frigging cold and Matt missed Miami, missed Tucson, missed every warm state in the union.

"Andy," he said in lieu of *hello*. "Heard from Packard that everyone is accounted for."

"Yes. I'm escorting Corrigan now to headquarters."

"It's still early."

"I was thinking about what you said last night, about Glen Hamilton's childhood and everything he lost when his father went to prison. I contacted the bank that foreclosed on the house to find out exactly what happened to its contents. There could be something in the financial records, and because it was a foreclosure, it's all public information. I'm going to meet the manager before they open. He's more than happy to help."

"Great, if you learn anything about the father or kid, call." Matt glanced at his watch. "We have a debriefing at eight. Will you be there?"

"Probably late. And be careful, the roads are icy and weather is going to turn fast."

"You have a partner, correct? No one out alone."

"Yes, Officer Eric Tolliver. And I'll follow all protocols. Abigail is tracking every police vehicle in Liberty Lake so we know where everyone is at all times."

Brian was up at five in the morning, which gave Kara the opportunity to doze a bit on the couch. She didn't know how well he'd slept, but all she needed was an hour and she'd be good for a while. She was used to erratic sleep patterns, and she rarely slept more than four hours at a time, anyway. The nap she'd had yesterday at the station had sustained her, and all she needed was a little boost to get them safely downtown. Once Brian was safe at SPD, she'd crash in the break room.

Her phone beeped and she glanced down. She'd gotten a good hour and fifteen minutes, and smelled fresh coffee, bacon and eggs in the kitchen. She stretched, looked at her text message. It was from Matt.

We're on our way to escort Maddox to SPD. ETA 15 min.

She responded that they'd be ready, then walked into the kitchen.

"Eat," Brian said.

"Don't have to tell me twice." She poured fresh coffee and sat down to a plate of scrambled eggs with veggies and bacon. "Wish you were single. I'd move here in a heartbeat."

"Maybe you should learn to cook."

She wrinkled her nose at him. "I am a mean microwaver."

He rolled his eyes.

"Did you talk to Julie?"

"She sent me a text message at five this morning. Said she couldn't sleep, wanted to make sure I'm okay. I told her when we get this resolved, I'm joining them down in Scottsdale. I could use a day of spring baseball right about now, and I'm not looking forward to this storm. It's going to be nasty."

"We should be at the station before it hits, then we stay put. You promised."

"Did you hear from Corrigan?"

"All is well."

"Good."

"Costa will be here in ten or so minutes to escort us in. Another patrol is going to relieve the guys outside and sit on the house to make sure Hamilton doesn't come around here and make himself at home."

Maddox grabbed his keys off the counter and started for the door.

"Where are you going?" she said.

"It's twenty degrees outside. I'm warming up the car. This isn't Southern California, kid."

She cleared her throat and held out her hand.

Brian was about to argue with her; she could see it in his eyes, then he relented. "I really hate this." He dropped the keys in her palm.

"I know."

She called the patrol that was down the street.

"Can you both come to the house? There's hot coffee in it for you, and your relief will be here shortly. We're getting ready to leave."

"My savior," one of the cops said.

She chuckled.

"This is overkill," Maddox said.

"Yep." Babysitting cops was no fun. She'd done it once before, backing up a federal protection detail. Even the smartest of cops didn't want to follow someone else's lead on their personal security.

She met the officers at the door. She pointed to the taller cop. "You're with me. Your partner can collect coffee for the two of you. And your relief will be here by oh-eight-hundred to watch the house."

The first snowflake fell as she stepped out into the cold.

"It's going to be a mess out there pretty soon," the cop said as he flanked her.

"I sure miss Southern California about now."

Kara walked across the yard toward the garage. This setup was tactically a nightmare. The garage where Julie had her workshop was between the house and the carport where Brian parked his police truck. No direct line of sight until you passed the garage.

"Eyes open," she said.

"He'd be an idiot to take on four cops."

Glen Hamilton was no idiot; otherwise he wouldn't have gotten away with multiple homicides. But he could be desperate. They were already seven hours into his twenty-four-hour kill window; he'd killed his first two victims in Liberty Lake before dawn.

Costa could be wrong and neither Maddox or Corrigan were the targets. He thought it was one or the other. So far, no one was missing so his protective strategy was working. They had double duty on the two likely targets. Hamilton may have done surveillance and spotted the extra firepower. Otherwise why hadn't he gone for his chosen target? Everyone else was on the buddy system. Much easier to take out two cops than four—not that taking out two cops was easy.

"Where are you?" she muttered.

"Excuse me?" the uniformed officer said.

"Talking to myself." She approached Maddox's truck cautiously. Unlocked it. Started the engine. She removed the clicker from his key ring. Under normal circumstances he'd probably leave the car unlocked and running while puttering about in the house, but she didn't want to give the killer a chance to get inside. He could hide in the back seat—Maddox didn't have a cage in the back for criminals because as deputy chief he wasn't in the field other than as a commander.

She got out and locked the car with the clicker and looked down the street. A car was idling, a steady stream of hot, white exhaust drifting in the cold air. Not unusual. Not in this weather.

Except… That car wasn't parked on the street last night. She'd done a perimeter check when they got home, then had the backup patrol check at regular intervals. She made note of all the houses and cars within the sight lines of Brian's house. Most cars were garaged. A truck had been on the street all the way down. Not that dark gray, older model Camry.

Someone was sitting in the driver's seat.

She motioned to the cop who was with her to stop—she didn't want to call attention to herself and give the Camry driver any reason to think she was onto him. Then she pulled out her phone and hit Costa's number.

"Costa," Matt answered.

"It's Quinn. I think our suspect is outside Brian's house, parked down the street in a dark gray Camry."

"Plates?"

"Can't see them. The car's running. It wasn't here last night when we arrived or during any of the hourly perimeter checks. ETA?"

"Seven minutes, maybe less. Do not confront him."

"When since you've met me have you ever thought I was an idiot?"

As she watched, the Camry started moving. Then it accelerated fast down the street.

"Shit, looks like he's bolting. He was probably expecting Brian. He's not going to engage me."

"Can you get a visual?"

Though she itched to confront the driver herself, she didn't want to tip her hand if it was Hamilton. She turned partly away from the Camry as if she hadn't noticed it, and said to the backup officer, "Don't be obvious. I think our suspect is in that gray Camry down the block. I can't really make out who's in the driver's seat, but do you remember when the car arrived?"

"No. It wasn't there last night—and I don't remember seeing it when we approached the house a few minutes ago."

The cops were inside for less than five minutes. Was the car parked elsewhere? Had he just arrived? There were a few places he might have been hidden that Kara couldn't see from Brian's house—why had he pulled out now?

Because he knows Brian's routine. He knows he turns on his truck every fucking morning to warm up.

Kara ordered the officer to go back into the house and stick with Brian, then she ran back to the truck and jumped in. She immediately backed out and just missed hitting the Camry. Damn! She thought she could nail him with her bigger truck, but he was moving too fast. If she hit him and it wasn't Hamilton, she'd have apologized. That's why she had insurance, right?

She caught a glance at the driver as he rounded the corner. She was certain it was Hamilton, though he didn't look much like his license photo. But he *was* familiar. Had she seen him recently?

She put Costa on speaker as she pursued the suspect.

Costa was in the middle of a sentence. "…dammit, she's gone and…"

"I'm still here," she said. "I'm in pursuit."

She hadn't driven a squad car in years, and this truck was decked out completely differently than the LAPD black-and-whites.

"Is it him?"

"He bolted when he realized we spotted him. I've seen him before. Recently. He doesn't look like his photo—I'll get it, just give me a minute."

"Plates!"

"Washington state. Alpha Romeo Tango one niner zero niner. Dark gray Toyota Camry, tinted windows. Fuck!"

Hamilton was driving too fast for the icy roads, but he didn't care. Kara finally found the lights and sirens on the truck, flipped them on. As Hamilton turned another corner, his rear wheels skidded. He gained control and sped up. Kara made the turn smoother, the larger truck tires giving her better traction.

A group of kids started to walk across the street, and that bastard was going to hit them.

"Quinn!" Costa shouted over the phone. She could barely hear him over the sirens.

"Get out of the way!" she shouted, even though the kids couldn't possibly hear her.

The kids—six or seven of them—hesitated as they realized the cars weren't stopping, then split up and started running in different directions as the Camry barreled down the narrow street. The driver intentionally swerved into the group and clipped one of the kids, who went flying into a yard, his head slamming into the hard ground.

"Shit! He hit a kid. I can't pursue. He turned north on Liberty Lake Road."

Kara stopped the truck and turned off the sirens, then fumbled with the radio. "This is Detective Kara Quinn in Deputy Chief Maddox's vehicle. We have a 10-57 at my location, call a bus."

"Who is this?" the dispatcher asked.

"Quinn. With Maddox. Kid is injured in a hit-and-run." She couldn't just sit here and explain herself. She grabbed her phone and jumped out of the truck. "Costa, find that bastard, I have to check on the kid."

She ran over to where several kids were standing around the boy who had been hit. He was conscious, but unmoving. Stunned. In shock. Dammit, a kid!

She took off her jacket and put it around him. "An ambulance is coming," she said.

"Are you a police girl?" one of the children said.

"Yeah."

"You're not wearing a uniform."

"I'm a detective."

"Is he going to be okay?"

"What's your name, kid?" She leaned over him,

looked in his eyes. His pupils were wide. She didn't want to move him, but it was freezing out here.

"That's my brother, Joey." The little girl who spoke couldn't be more than seven. Her big brown eyes were rimmed with tears. "He's going to be okay, right?"

"Yeah, we just need to keep him warm."

Within seconds, all the kids had their jackets off and were handing them to Kara. She wrapped Joey up the best she could. Then she noticed the blood on the back of his head.

She pulled out her phone and called 911. "I need an ambulance here, now!" She gave them the corner she was on.

A moment later, the operator said that an ambulance had already been dispatched, ETA fifteen minutes.

"Make it faster." Kara would never forgive herself if her pursuit of Hamilton had caused a kid's death. She needed Joey to be okay.

People started coming out of their houses, some carrying blankets. One by one Kara returned the coats to the children who had shared them, replacing them with the blankets.

"Joey, you with me?" Kara said.

"Y-yes."

"Good. You're going to be fine. You get to ride in an ambulance, okay? And they'll take real good care of you, make sure you get fixed up."

"M-my head hurts."

"You know what? I've had a concussion before.

It hurts a lot. But it got better, and you'll get better. Just do everything the doctors tell you to do, okay?"

"I'm going to be a doctor," Joey's little sister said.

"Good," Kara said, because what else did you say to that?

"Shouldn't we bring him into the house?" one of the adults said.

"We can't move him," Kara said. "We don't know the extent of his injuries. Does anyone have a portable heater? An umbrella?" The snow was coming down lightly, but it was getting heavier with each passing minute. She was doing her best to keep the flakes off Joey's face.

Three minutes later she had an umbrella over the kid, and a minute later a portable heater was blowing lukewarm air on both of them.

"Joey, keep talking to me," she said.

"I'm sleepy."

"I know, but you need to stay awake. If you have a concussion, the doctors like it when you stay awake, so they can ask you questions."

"My arm hurts."

She figured from the odd angle that it was broken.

"I had a cast once," she said. "Broke my wrist. It hurt a lot, but everyone on my squad signed it."

"How did you break your wrist?" Joey's little sister asked.

"Catching a bad guy." She wasn't going to tell a seven-year-old that she'd finally caught up with a serial rapist at UCLA and beat him up before her partner Colton Fox pulled her off. That wasn't one of her finest hours, but damn, that bastard had ruined the lives of a dozen women, and Kara had wanted to make him hurt. It was worth the broken wrist.

"Like that man who hit Joey?"

"Yeah. Exactly."

"You'll find him, right?"

"You bet we'll find him. He's going to jail, I promise."

She finally heard the ambulance in the distance. A car pulled up on the street and Costa jumped out of the passenger seat. He squatted next to her.

Joey was closing his eyes. "Hey, Joey, stay awake, okay? Um, my name is Kara. Do you have a dog?"

"Two," he said sleepily.

"What are their names?"

"Fred and Daisy."

"I like those names. What kind of dogs?"

"Um, mutts, my dad says."

Joey's sister said, "Mom says they're lab mixes."

"Joey, do you like playing with your dogs?"

"We walk them every night."

"That's great." She glanced at Costa.

"We couldn't find him," Costa said. "But we have an APB on his car. Every cop is out looking for him now."

In a low voice, Kara said, "He deliberately ran into these kids. To stop me."

"You had to stop," Costa said. "You had to help. You didn't have a choice."

She knew it, and it still made her angry. "I want him, Costa. I want him bad."

It could have been so much worse.

42

Liberty Lake
8:10 a.m.

Glen's heart was racing. He forced his right foot to ease up on the gas.

That bitch cop had spotted him. How had she known? Nondescript car. Down the street. It made no sense!

But she did, and she followed him. He hadn't wanted to hit the kid, but he needed to buy time, to get away. He thought she was going to keep coming for him, so he detoured, went east, kept off the interstate.

He drove ten miles east, almost to the state line, before his heart slowed down. He took a deep breath. Then another.

Okay. He was okay.

He had to assume that the cop got his license plate. If she didn't, the cop cars' dashboard cameras would have, so he had to assume they *could* get his plate.

He'd hidden the car and rental house under his

shell corporations, but this was the FBI—they had more resources than local law enforcement. He'd never seen anything like this before, an entire team working practically 24-7. Why him? Why couldn't he have just made his last kill before the feds got involved? He could have been back in his house. He'd been saving up for it for years. He had a plan to get those interlopers out of his house, then he would buy it. It would be his forever.

The way it should have been.

He'd feared this day would come that he wouldn't be able to punish the man who deserved it most of all.

No. No! I will kill Brian Maddox. He will bleed.

He would get him. He had to. Then everyone else who messed with his plan.

First Maddox, then the interlopers who stole his house, and of course the feds. Especially that bitch cop who made him hit that kid. Glen didn't want to hit that kid. She *made* him do it.

His head ached as the same questions kept coming back to him. Over and over.

How had she even noticed him? How had she known?

His father's voice rang in his head. *"Because you're a weak, stupid kid. Because you are an idiot. If it weren't for you, boy, your mother wouldn't have gone out that night and got killed. You are a failure."*

"I am *not* a failure! I am *not* weak!"

It was time to draw the line in the sand.

43

Liberty Lake
8:30 a.m.

Andy Knolls met with Bernard Younger at the Liberty Lake branch of a major national bank. It was the only national bank that had an office in the small town, and everyone did their banking here. Andy knew Younger from the Chamber of Commerce, where the manager was active, and the bank sponsored the town's softball and baseball teams.

"Thank you for coming in before opening," Andy said.

"Anything to help," Younger said. "All the information is online, but it would take you hours to get information out of headquarters. I know what I can share, and if you need additional information, provide a warrant and I'll have it ready."

"Appreciate it."

Officer Tolliver waited in the bank lobby while Younger took Andy to his office. Younger logged into his computer, but it took a good fifteen minutes before he was able to retrieve the file and print it out.

"It's archived," he explained. "We don't keep print files anymore, and sometimes computers make you jump through hoops."

"No worries, Bernard. Anything leap out at you?"

"To be honest, Andy, no. I was here at the time, but it was handled out of our legal department at headquarters." He rose and walked over to his printer as the machine spat out multiple pages. "Mr. Hamilton stopped paying his mortgage after his incarceration. He'd lost his job at the high school before this, and we helped him refinance his house. There was equity, which helped. After his incarceration, he couldn't keep a job and there was no more equity to refinance. He refused to sell. We never want to foreclose on anyone, and we have several layers of help we offer, plus a counselor who can work with the homeowner in finding government programs to assist until the individual can get back on their feet. Mr. Hamilton didn't take advantage of any of these. Then came the unfortunate situation of the police having to be called in to remove him from the home."

"Did he threaten you or anyone at the bank?"

"No. We hired a realty company to prepare the house for sale." Younger pulled the papers off the printer and sorted through them. "I can't give you everything here—but this should help." He pulled a short stack of paper and handed it to Andy. It was the court order of foreclosure, the eviction, the sale report, and the police report. It had been signed by Liberty Lake Senior Officer Brian Maddox.

Andy read through the sale report. The realty

company packed up all the furnishings and personal items and stored them. It was a facility in Spokane that Andy knew had closed down several years ago, but that would have been long after the unit had been sold off. He doubted it would be easy to get those records.

"Is there anything else you need?"

"Not right now."

"Do you really believe that Hamilton is responsible for the two recent murders in town?"

"No. This isn't public information yet, but we're looking for his son. Just to talk to him for now." Andy pulled out his phone and showed the manager Glen Hamilton's DMV photo. "Have you seen him?"

Younger shook his head. "No. I hadn't even remembered that Mr. Hamilton had a son."

Andy looked at the address—369 Vine Street wasn't far. Maybe Andy should drive by, or talk to the owners. He couldn't think of a scenario where Hamilton would go there, but maybe he had driven by, been seen in the area. It might be worth talking to the neighbors and ask them to be watchful, especially before the storm hit full force.

"Thank you for your help," Andy said, and rose. "Be safe out there."

"We never like to close the bank during business hours, but I'm going to assess the weather at noon. We can get by with a bare-bones staff. Both myself and the head teller live close by."

Younger let Andy and Tolliver out, and Andy said, "I want to drive by this house on the way to Spokane." He knew where it was, but typed the address into his GPS to confirm. "It's not even ten minutes away."

"While you were in with the manager, there was a report that the suspect was spotted outside Deputy Chief Maddox's house. Detective Quinn pursued and lost him when the suspect drove into a group of children."

Andy's stomach fell. "Injuries?"

"One serious, a nine-year-old boy on his way to the hospital."

"And the suspect?"

"Driving a dark gray Toyota Camry, approximately five years old, license and description in the system."

Andy looked at the report. "They already have a statewide APB on the vehicle. Good. Where did they lose him?"

"Heading toward the interstate."

He called Matt Costa.

"Costa," Matt said.

"It's Andy Knolls. I just saw the APB on the Camry."

"Did you learn anything at the bank?"

"Nothing that'll help us find Hamilton, but I'm going to drive by the house on Vine, talk to the current owners. They may have seen Hamilton if he has been in the area for as long as we think he has."

"Debriefing has been postponed an hour."

"If it's all right with you, I'll stay here. If Hamilton was in Liberty Lake just an hour ago—I know all the places he might hide."

"Be safe, Andy. Don't confront him. He's agitated

and volatile. He was sitting in his fucking car down the street from Maddox's house when Kara spotted him. He hit a kid to get away. If you see the vehicle or Hamilton himself, call it in and wait for backup. I'm going to release his photo and a sketch Kara is working on to the media, then I'll be in the field. He's going to make a mistake, and when he does, I want to be in his fucking face."

Costa and Maddox were at the debriefing at Spokane headquarters while Kara worked with the sketch artist. As soon as the sketch was done, she knew exactly where she'd seen Glen Hamilton.

Hamilton had done something to tweak his looks for the driver's license photo. The whole shape of his face was different. In subtle but important ways. Now he appeared leaner, to the point of being gaunt. Instead of shaggy brown hair that almost hung in his eyes and over his ears, it was now short and cut conservatively. It was the same person, but he'd changed the things people would notice first—the shape of his face and his hair.

She asked for a copy of the sketch and immediately went to the debriefing. Costa was finishing up, and Packard gave everyone their modified assignments. Maddox had two cops on him; she knew he wasn't going anywhere.

Costa made a beeline to her when Packard dismissed his officers. "You have something?"

She showed the picture to Costa. "He was at the hotel bar," she said. "When I was having drinks with Brian Saturday night."

"You sure?"

Of course she was sure. "We'd been there about twenty minutes. He came into the bar and ordered a beer. I didn't think much of it, but when you work undercover, you have to know every face you see. Shit."

"What else?" said Matt.

"Brian left alone and I went up to the war room. This bastard could have gotten to him then."

"It would have broken his pattern, but I agree—that was bold, coming into the hotel where every FBI agent is staying."

"Fuck the pattern. He nearly killed a kid this morning. The kid is nine years old, just walking to the bus stop, and he gets mowed down by that psycho."

"We need to get this out far and wide, along with the DMV photo. Good work."

"Is Ryder an agent?"

"Analyst."

"Can he carry? Is he protected? Hamilton could have a room in the hotel for all we know. Ryder's at the hotel by himself most of the day."

"I told him to be alert, and he has a sidearm. He was in the military for three years. He can protect himself. But I'll call again—we need the feeds from the hotel not only on Saturday, but all week."

"Any update on the kid?" she asked.

Matt's face softened, just a bit. She didn't want to read too much into it, she didn't want to be coddled. She wanted information.

"The hospital knows to contact us, and Harris

will follow up. We know he's stable right now, and awake, and that's good."

"The bastard didn't think twice about running into those kids. He's not going to care about collateral damage, not anymore. We took his prize off the table. Does your shrink know what he's going to do next?"

"My gut? He'll do anything he has to in order to get to Maddox. And that means he'll have to engage us, because Brian Maddox is not leaving this police station until we have Glen Hamilton in custody. I'm going to make damn sure that every cop in the Spokane Valley is prepared."

44

Liberty Lake
9:30 a.m.

PJ Richmond turned five last month and he really, really wanted to go to school with his sisters. But he had to wait until August 24 to start. He had the date circled and starred on his calendar because he wasn't a baby. *Sheila* was a baby. She wasn't even one and she couldn't walk and the only words she knew were *no* and *mama* and *dada* and *cookie.*

PJ was proud of the fact that he taught his baby sister how to say *cookie.* It was a very important word. Cookies were PJ's favorite food and he loved helping his grandma bake them when she came over to babysit. It was the *only* good part of not going to school.

His sisters walked to the bus stop at seven-forty every morning. Sometimes his mom went with them and he got to push Sheila's stroller. But not today because it was cold and had started to snow.

His dad was working from home today because the roads would be crap coming home tonight. His dad said *crap*, which made PJ giggle, which made his mom frown, which made PJ laugh even more. And the best thing was that his mom said that school would probably be canceled by noon because the storm was coming in faster than the stupid weatherman predicted. His mom said stupid, and that made him giggle more, and then his dad laughed.

Noon couldn't come fast enough for PJ because his sisters would be home and play with him. Maybe even in the snow. Their mom made them play with him and they pretended to not like it. Jilly pretended—sometimes she would play with him even when Mom didn't tell her to. Ashley said she was getting too old for playing kids' games. She was almost twelve, which meant that she was almost a teenager, which meant she didn't need a little brother and sister following her around.

He was only allowed to watch one hour of cartoons in the morning and he'd already had his hour. He got to go to school three days a week for the whole morning—but not Tuesday and Thursday. And it was Tuesday; his calendar said so. He marked off each day before he went to bed, and yesterday was Monday, March 8.

He wandered through the house because he was bored. His mom was on the phone and sounded upset.

"Is he okay? Debbie must be frantic! What hospital? Good—I'll come over as soon as the girls get home. Did they catch the driver? What was he thinking? On purpose? *Really?*"

"What happened Mommy?" he asked.

She turned to him and put a finger to her lips, then pointed to the phone she held to her ear.

PJ frowned and walked back to the den, where his dad was working. He was reading his spreadsheets. His dad was an accountant, which meant that he helped people with their math. He was really, really good at math and people paid him lots of money to help them with their math so they didn't get in trouble with the IRS. PJ didn't know what the IRS was, though his dad tried to explain to him. All he knew was that if you made a math mistake you could get in real big trouble and have to pay lots of money.

PJ vowed to never make a mistake in math *ever.*

"Daddy, Mommy is on the phone and I'm bored."

His dad looked up. "It's a workday for me, buddy. And it's a busy time."

"Because it's almost April 15." That was his dad's busiest day.

"Exactly. You're so smart. Your mom's probably right and the schools will close at lunch, and by then I'll need a break. You can come with me to get the girls, okay?"

"Okay."

"Go play with Sheila."

"She's boring. She doesn't do anything but drool and laugh."

His dad smiled, then turned back to his work. PJ walked out.

His mom was still on the phone. But she was talking to someone else. "Now? They're closing the schools *now*?"

"Can I come? Mommy? Can I come with you? Please?"

His mom put up her finger. "Yes, I'll pick them up."

PJ was excited—his sisters were coming home *now.* He turned to Sheila, who was sitting—drooling—in her high chair. He tickled her and made her laugh.

"PP!" she said.

"P.*Jay.*"

Her head bounced up and down. "PP! PP!"

She was never going to say his name right.

He glanced at his mom. She wasn't paying attention. He sneaked a handful of cookies and put them in his pocket. He would teach Sheila to say his name right or he was going to change it.

"Mommy, I'm changing my name," he said. "I want to be called John. Sheila, say John!"

"PP!"

He sighed.

His mother finally got off the phone. "I need to go get your sisters."

"I wanna come."

"Honey, the roads are a mess, and this storm is really coming in fast. Your dad is working, and I need you to be a big brother and play with Sheila upstairs in the playroom. You can get your dad if there are any problems."

He frowned. *"Mommmmmy."*

"Please PJ?"

"Call me John."

"Why?"

"Because it's part of my name. Peter John. Sheila calls me PP. That's like when you pee and I don't like it."

"All right, John," his mother said, and laughed. She picked Sheila up and carried her upstairs. The playroom was babyproof. All the small toys were way up on the shelves. His mom put Sheila in her playpen. "I'll be back in thirty minutes, and then we'll all play. If you have any problem, just get your dad. You're a good big brother, PJ."

"John."

She smiled and kissed him on the head. "Love you, *John*." She kissed Sheila. "Love you. Be good for your brother." Then she left.

Sheila gurgled in her playpen and PJ moped. He didn't really mind watching his baby sister—his mom trusted him. She always told him that he was an "old soul," whatever that meant. But Dad said it was because he was responsible and he knew that he couldn't give Sheila Legos and that he couldn't carry her down the stairs and that he couldn't leave her alone even for one minute to go pee because Sheila might climb out of her playpen and fall down the stairs and hurt herself.

He talked to her about what they would do when their big sisters came home, then he read her a book with simple words that even he knew.

"Bear!" she pointed to the Brown Bear.

"Bear, that's right!" She said a new word, and PJ couldn't wait to tell his mom that he heard it first.

"Cat?" He pointed. "Say *cat*."

"Bear!"

He frowned. Did it take him this long to know the difference between a bear and a cat? He heard the front door close. It was loud, maybe because of the wind. He looked at the clock. It was digital, so he could easily read it—9:34. It couldn't be his mom. She just left at 9:21, and it hadn't been thirty minutes.

He wanted to go downstairs and see who the visitor was. Ashley would tell him that he was nosy and to mind his own business.

There was a loud crash and PJ jumped. It sounded *really* big, and he couldn't even think about what had broken. Then a *thump-thump!* and he heard his daddy's voice. It didn't sound right.

"Please! No! What do you—"

Then his daddy screamed, and tears burst into PJ's eyes and he didn't know what to do. He was so scared. He looked at Sheila. She wasn't laughing and she wasn't saying *bear* and she looked like she was going to cry.

A strange voice was yelling downstairs. PJ only sort of knew what he was saying. He was mad about something. Really, really mad and he said a lot of bad words and said this wasn't Daddy's house.

PJ wanted to help his daddy, but he was so small, and he wasn't very strong.

But he could pick up Sheila. He picked her up. A loud crash downstairs made PJ jump and he almost dropped her, but he didn't, and he held her tight and ran to Jilly and Ashley's bedroom because they had a really big closet. He went inside with Sheila and closed the door. It was really dark. Sheila started to cry.

"Shh. Shh. Sheila, no crying."

She whimpered. And PJ was very scared, though he didn't hear anything downstairs other than someone walking around.

Dad?

Sheila wailed, and PJ remembered he had cookies in his pocket. He took one out. He couldn't see anything, but he could feel Sheila's chubby hands. He put a cookie in her hands and whispered "Cookie."

"C-c-cookie."

"Eat the cookie," he whispered.

She sniffled and PJ hugged her on his lap, all the way in the far corner, behind Jilly's baseball equipment and Ashley's stuffed animals and all their dirty clothes they threw in the closet when mom said to clean up their room. Pretty soon PJ thought that he and Sheila were very well hidden and no one could see them even if they opened the door.

Someone was downstairs breaking stuff. He was so scared, what if the bad man came here? Sheila chomped on the cookie with her four teeth but she wasn't crying. He hugged her tightly and closed his eyes.

"We have to be very quiet," PJ said. "Daddy will get us when the bad man goes away."

Andy Knolls and Officer Tolliver pulled up in front of the house on Vine Street at 9:45 a.m. It was one of the older homes in town, but had been recently updated and painted and had an addition upstairs. Many of the houses in this neighborhood had done the same thing, and Andy liked what the upkeep did for their small town. He and Gracie had been looking for a house for after they got married—she lived in a duplex next to her parents, and he had a small house he'd bought his third year on the force. But that house wouldn't be great for raising kids. He'd like to be on the lake, because he liked to fish and hike, but those homes might be too pricey for them on a cop's salary. Here, though, they could bike in good weather to the lake, and the homes were more affordable. Maybe they could get an older place like this one and fix it up together.

He called in his location to Abigail. At the same time, the APB came in from Spokane PD with the DMV photo of Glen Hamilton, and a sketch that looked similar but different. Leaner face, shorter and darker hair. He'd seen this guy.

"Detective?" Tolliver prompted. His hand was on the truck door, but he didn't open it.

"Take a good look," Knolls said. "I know I've seen him, but I can't place it."

Tolliver stared. "I haven't, but I've been on traffic detail until two days ago."

It would come to him. "The residents are Peter and Denise Richmond. Records show that they've lived here nine years." He nodded toward the porch, which had several bikes stacked. Probably used them over the weekend and hadn't put them in the garage before the storm. "Looks like they have kids. Don't want to spook them, but we should convey that they need to be cautious."

They got out of the police truck and approached the house. Andy rapped on the door, then they both stepped back. He took a look up and down the snowy street. It was nice, with mature trees, looked like a good neighborhood to raise kids. Most of Liberty Lake was.

He narrowed his gaze. A dark gray sedan was parked on the T intersection, on Dover Street. Was that a Camry? He couldn't tell; snowfall was interfering with his sight.

Tolliver knocked again before Andy could tell his partner to hold off. "They could be at work," he said.

Andy spoke into the radio on his lapel. "Officer needs assistance three-six-nine Vine Street. Dark gray Camry parked at corner of Dover and Vine."

Tolliver whirled around. "Shit," he said.

The door opened.

Andy put his hand on the butt of his gun. Three thoughts went through his head simultaneously.

I don't want to scare the Richmonds.

I smell blood.

I know where I've seen Hamilton.

Tolliver was looking at the car.

Andy was pulling his gun.

"Hands where I can see them!" Andy ordered Hamilton. "Drop the knife!"

Glen Hamilton had blood on his clothes and hair, but he had clearly washed his face and hands, which were starkly white against his stained clothing. He ran out the door, right at Andy. Andy pulled his gun, but Glen pushed him down the front stairs before he could fire. His gun fell from his hand into the snow. He reached for it as the knife came down.

He tried to roll to the side for his weapon.

"Eric!" Andy shouted. "Shoot him!"

Sharp pain tore at Andy's side, a stinging sensation that had him frozen.

Fight back. Fight back or you'll die.

Hamilton screamed, pulled the knife up along Andy's side, and Andy drew in a sharp breath as waves of agony pulsed through him.

Eric Tolliver struggled to pull Glen off Andy.

"Shoot him!" Andy tried to scream again, but he couldn't catch his breath.

Hamilton didn't hesitate. He stabbed Tolliver in the chest as Andy watched, his vision fading.

Andy reached out and his fingers found his own gun in the icy snow. Shaking, he pulled his arm up and fired at the killer.

The killer ran. Andy didn't have the strength to pull the trigger again. The gun slipped from his hand as he lost consciousness.

45

Liberty Lake
10:30 a.m.

Matt stared at the bright yellow tarp that covered Andy Knolls's body. Blood had seeped out into the snow next to him. Ten feet away was more blood, but no body—the paramedics rushed Officer Eric Tolliver to the hospital before Matt arrived, though the prognosis was dismal. He'd lost a lot of blood. But Andy had been dead on the scene.

He hadn't gone inside yet, but the first responding officers had cleared the house. One deceased male, identified as the owner, Peter Richmond. His family wasn't here, a small blessing.

Michael gave Matt a moment alone and took charge of the scene, for which Matt was grateful. Two officers were putting up a tent over Andy's body to protect him from the falling snow until the coroner could arrive and transport him to the morgue. Matt moved one of the bricks that had been placed on the corners to keep the tarp secure. He held up the canvas and stared down at Andy's body.

He'd been stabbed in his side, and the knife had gone deep. The killer sliced up. From the amount of blood and the location—and how quickly he died—Matt suspected that his heart had been compromised.

Andy had gotten off a shot and based on the evidence in the street had hit the subject. There wasn't a lot of blood, but drops led to the corner, where they stopped.

Andy had reported, only minutes before the report of shots fired, that he spotted a dark gray Camry at the corner of Vine and Dover.

"I'm so sorry, buddy," Matt whispered.

What had gone wrong? How had the killer gotten the drop on them? Did they see something suspicious inside? Did the killer surprise them? Why would he approach the house at all once he saw the car? Had it already been too late?

Michael came over. "Matt, we have a huge problem."

He covered Andy back up, replaced the brick. "What?"

"Liberty PD has the victim's wife and two daughters at the roadblock. She says that her husband is in the house with her two youngest children. PJ, age five, and Sheila, ten months. Wants to know where they are."

Matt immediately shouted for the responding officers. "Who cleared the house?"

"We did." A cop approached, and gestured to his partner. "The deceased was found in the hallway. The suspect isn't inside."

"There were two children in the house."

The cop paled. "We didn't find any other bodies."

"Could they have run out?"

"A five-year-old in this weather?"

Matt was furious. He pointed to the two cops. "Talk to every single neighbor on the street. About what they saw, about the kids. Harris, with me. We're searching the house again."

"Matt, he could have taken them as hostages."

"No. Andy would never have fired at Hamilton if he had a kid as a shield. They're in that house, or they ran when Hamilton arrived." He pointed to the SPD officer who drove him and Michael here. "Grab a partner and search the garage. The father could have sent the kids there if he thought there might be trouble."

That didn't feel right, but anything could have happened.

What would he have done?

The question is, what would your father have done?

His dad had been raised during the most brutal era of Castro, and there had been times when soldiers had walked the streets, entered houses, searched for contraband. His father would share the stories on rare occasions, usually solemnly before he praised America. He had fought hard to make it to Florida, had lost half his family in the process.

If his father was a little boy and danger came to the door, he would have hidden. He would have been as quiet as possible so the soldiers or the gangs wouldn't hear him.

"We clear the downstairs first," Matt told Michael.

The living room was a mess. The television had been knocked to the floor. To the right of the doorway, a table had been shoved, all the breakables had fallen to the floor and littered the carpet with glass. Blood dotted the walls in the hall. He smelled it, saw it, tasted it in the air.

On the hardwood floor, a man wearing jeans and a button-down shirt lay half in, half out of a doorway. Blood covered his back. Spread over the wood. Matt didn't need to check for a pulse; the paramedics had been in here and declared him dead. As he looked at the body from a different angle, he realized that Peter Richmond had nearly been decapitated.

"We have to find those kids," Matt said. "If they saw this—they could have run out before the first responders arrived. You look everywhere down here—and see if there's a basement. Cabinets. Under the sink. Anywhere a little kid could hide. I'm going upstairs."

"Roger that."

Matt walked up the stairs and one thing became quickly clear: there was no blood up here. Hamilton had to have been covered in blood based on the amount around the victim. But there was none here. No footprints. No handprints. No drops falling from the knife.

Hamilton hadn't come upstairs. Did that mean the children weren't here? Or that maybe he didn't know there were children in the house?

Matt stood in the center of the playroom that was

at the top of the stairs. The downstairs couldn't be seen from here, and there was a child safety gate across the opening, which he stepped over. Two doors, both closed, went off the playroom.

"PJ," Matt called out as he opened one of the doors. It was the boy's room, which he clearly shared with his baby sister. His half was all blue and gray and airplanes. The baby's half was gray and green. He looked in the small closet. No place for two kids to hide. "PJ, I'm Matt Costa. I'm an FBI agent. Your mom is looking for you."

He went to the other room off the playroom. A girl's room, messy, with movie posters and lots of little things, trinkets and perfume bottles and lip gloss and books and baseball trophies. One of the girls pitched on a Little League team.

"PJ, are you in here? I'm an FBI agent. That's like a policeman. I'm here to help you. You can come out now."

Silence.

He opened the closet. It was a mess. He moved some things around but didn't see anyone hiding.

He was about to close the door when he heard a small cry. Where was the light switch? He found it and stared. Didn't see two kids. It could have been his imagination.

"PJ? Are you in here?"

Something moved. Just a little.

Matt moved aside clothes, an old blanket, and a baseball bag. In the far corner of the closet a little boy was holding his sleeping sister. He was half-asleep and had a bat in his hands. Relief flowed through Matt, and he spontaneously crossed himself, though he hadn't been to church in years.

Gracias a Dios.

He squatted to be closer to the child's eye level. "PJ. You're safe now. Are you okay?"

PJ opened his eyes, then rubbed them. "My daddy."

"Your mommy's outside. Do you want to see her?"

He nodded. "A bad man hurt my daddy."

Matt prayed that this little boy hadn't seen what happened. "Did you see the bad man?"

He shook his head and hugged his sister tighter. She gave out a half squeak, half cry.

"I heard them fighting. And things were breaking and I was scared so I took Sheila and hid."

"You did the right thing, PJ." Matt helped PJ and his sister out of the closet, then picked them up. He hugged them. "I'll find that bad man and put him in jail. I promise."

In jail or in the ground.

46

Spokane
11:15 a.m.

He'd fucked up. He'd *really* fucked up. And now he had a bullet in his arm and it hurt and he hadn't killed the cop who stole his house.

Glen Hamilton sat in the kitchen of his rental. He hadn't been tailed—he knew that—but he didn't know how long he would be safe here. How did they know about his car?

That bitch cop.

How long would it take for them to trace his car to this house?

How did they know about the house on Vine? Did they know his identity?

Glen didn't turn on the television, instead he went online, where he was more comfortable and news broke faster. He had all the local news sites bookmarked and he scrolled through.

His heart nearly stopped beating.

He saw his picture—his image, really—in a sketch.

The police had released his driver's license photo along with a sketch that looked exactly like him.

> Spokane Police Department issued a statement this morning. They are looking for this man, Glen Vincent Hamilton. They indicated that he is wanted for questioning as a possible witness in the two recent murders in Liberty Lake. Contact the Spokane Police Department at their 24-hour hotline.
>
> UPDATE: SPD Police Chief Packard has updated the earlier police report regarding the search for Glen Vincent Hamilton.
>
> "Hamilton should be considered armed and dangerous. He is wanted for the attack on two Liberty Lake police officers this morning, and the hit-and-run of an elementary school student. He was last seen driving a dark gray Toyota Camry, Washington State license plate ART 1909. If you see him, do not approach. Call 9-1-1. Hamilton, 31, is a former resident of Liberty Lake and currently resides in Tacoma, Washington. Spokane Police Department is working closely with the Sheriff's department and the FBI to locate Hamilton."
>
> Our news desk will keep you informed as soon as more information is available.

No. No, no, no, *NO!*

How did they have his name? He'd been so careful! He hadn't rented in Liberty Lake on the off chance someone might recognize him—even though he'd left when he was fifteen. He didn't use his own name to rent the house or the car. He hadn't talked to anyone beyond small chitchat since he arrived, he hadn't gone to the same store twice. He was so diligent! How could they know his name?

This was very bad.

He hadn't meant to go so far. All he wanted was to look inside the house. The idiot didn't want to let him in. Why? *Why?* It was *his* house. All he wanted to do was *see it*. Remember his mom. Remember when she had been there, when she had baked for him and helped him with his homework and read him bedtime stories.

Then he saw red. Peter Richmond was exactly like his father. Depriving him of his family home. Denying him his due. What he wanted. What he deserved. All he wanted to do was to look around—and everything had changed. They hadn't just added on the second story, they'd changed the entire *house*! Took out a wall, made the kitchen bigger, destroyed his mother's roses. Just pulled them out like they meant *nothing*.

The guy deserved to die. Just like the cop.

Glen took a deep breath. Now he had a hole in his arm. He didn't know how bad it was and went to the bathroom, took off his shirt and winced as the material pulled at the clotting wound.

It was really more of a graze. The bullet wasn't in there—it looked like a chunk of his flesh had been torn off. He had a first aid kit in the medicine cabinet. Taking the time to clean and bandage his wound calmed him down. It hurt like hell, but it really wasn't that bad.

You were lucky. Real lucky.

Lucky. And smart. He'd gotten out of the house fast. Stabbed the cops and fled, rather than waiting around.

He inspected his bandage. Okay, a small bit of blood seeped through, but not much, and that was good. Now he could think. He had to find a way out of this mess. He always had alternate plans, but which plan did he need now?

You need to go. Disappear. Get out of the Spokane Valley and never come back.

They had his name. They would find him, eventually.

Get a new name.

Not that easy. He had some money, but it wouldn't last forever. If they had his name, they knew where he lived. Where he worked.

And Brian Maddox was still alive.

Glen squeezed his eyes shut and pressed his fingers against his temples. He willed himself to find the answer. Disappear… But he couldn't leave. How could he leave his job unfinished?

You can come back. Come back when he least expects it. Kill Maddox and his entire family. Like your family is dead; take his. Be patient!

He knew he should wait, but he didn't know how long he could live in the shadows. He would be running, running, running… He didn't want to run. He didn't want them to know his name! That ruined *everything.*

But one thing was clear. He couldn't stay here. If they had the car, it was just a matter of time before they found his rental house.

He needed another car. Another place to stay.

He smiled as he realized fate would save him. He had checked into the hotel spontaneously Saturday night, mostly because he didn't want to seem suspicious. But now? Now it would be to his advantage. No one was at the hotel because they were all looking for him. And he had the card key, so he could slip in through the side door and no one would see him. It was risky driving out now that they were looking for his primary car, but he had a backup. He just had to get to it, and taking his Camry was a no-go. Time—it would just take a little time. Then he'd park someplace near the hotel, but not at the hotel. In case they tracked his second car. Walk in through the back and wait.

He was smarter than the police. He would have a couple days to figure out exactly how to kill Brian Maddox.

And if he got a chance to take out that blonde fed who screwed everything up, all the better.

47

Liberty Lake
11:40 a.m.

When a cop was dead, it was amazing how fast the damn warrants started coming in.

Matt stayed at the crime scene long enough to meet with Jim Esteban. He pulled him aside. "You're in charge. I want everything, I mean *everything.* Any resources, any people, you have them. I'm leaving the Seattle agents here to back you up. I already have Packard on board, and we have all the people we need."

Jim nodded solemnly. "I haven't gone through the house in detail, but I can tell you he didn't use gloves. There are bloody fucking prints all over the place. And if that blood in the street that the first responders had sense enough to cover before it was buried in this snow is the killer's blood, we'll nail him."

"I'm not concerned about identifying him. We have his image, we have Quinn's eyewitness testimony that he hit the kid, and we have Andy's last call into dispatch about the Camry spotted on this block."

"Still need a conviction, unless SPD gets itchy trigger fingers."

Matt didn't want Glen Hamilton dead. Well—he wanted him dead, but he wanted a trial first. He wanted to do this the right way. Find him, arrest him, prosecute him, execute him. The evidence was slowly but surely being collected, and they would have more than enough for a conviction.

Now they just had to find him before anyone else got hurt.

Matt glanced at his phone. "Shit. Andy's girlfriend is at the station. Dunn went to do the notification, but she'd already heard a cop was injured. I need to talk to her."

"You need to find this bastard."

"We got all the warrants we wanted, but we don't know where he is. Ryder is working with headquarters on getting his phone, bank, and credit records, which could be a huge win for us. He has to be staying somewhere in the Spokane Valley. But it's going to take a couple hours."

"Andy was a good cop. Tell her that."

"Andy was a small town cop. He wasn't supposed to be murdered."

Matt found Michael Harris putting Peter Richmond's family into a police car and sending them off. "We're taking them to her sister's house in Coeur d'Alene for now," Michael said. "I have their contact information, but they're not going to be able to get into the house for a while."

"Thanks." For the last hour the family had been at the next-door neighbor's house, but getting them out of town for a couple of days was smart. Not so much for their safety—Matt didn't think Hamilton would go after them again—but to ease the shock. "Anything from the canvass?"

"One witness. A neighbor kitty-corner," Michael gestured to a small, older brick home across the street, "said she'd seen a dark gray sedan in the neighborhood several times over the last few weeks."

"It's a common car."

"She's a Mrs. Kravitz."

It took Matt a minute to understand what Michael meant. He wasn't in the mood for pop culture references. "You mean she keeps an eye on the neighborhood and knows everything that goes on. Gotcha."

"Yeah. She didn't recognize Hamilton's picture or the sketch, but the car stood out to her because twice it parked at that corner and the driver didn't get out. She almost called the police the second time because she thought it was odd, but then he drove away. She said he was a youngish man, but couldn't identify him."

"Did she see it today?"

Michael nodded. "She came out at eight-thirty this morning to bring in her flowers because of the storm, and said the car wasn't there. But she didn't look out again until she heard the gunshot. She then saw a man—she again couldn't identify him, and he was wearing a dark jacket—running to the car. He was holding his left arm. He drove down Vine—past the house—and turned right."

"Which is toward the freeway?"

"Yes, though there's also a frontage road that goes almost all the way to Spokane. He might not have used the highway."

"And in this weather and poor visibility, we might not even notice him. But that's good—and confirms that Andy did in fact hit him. If he's hurting, he may not be rational."

"This *carnage* isn't rational," Michael said.

"To Hamilton it is. A strange family is living in *his* house. He wanted *his* house back, my guess, and was willing to kill whoever was there. No matter how irrational that might seem." He came here because he couldn't kill Maddox this morning. Maddox was alive, but Andy and an innocent man had died instead.

Matt hated this case.

They walked to the SPD truck and climbed in. Matt told the officer to take them to Liberty Lake PD. He would have to talk to Andy's girlfriend and offer condolences, but he wouldn't stay long. As soon as Ryder had the information from the warrants, they would find Glen Hamilton and lock him up for the rest of his miserable life.

Ryder Kim was a miracle worker.

Less than two hours after Ryder and FBI headquarters executed the warrants on Glen Hamilton's employer, bank, phone company, and credit companies, they found a company that Glen Hamilton owned through the registration records of the Camry. Ryder said he thought it was a company on paper only—a shell corp. But the public information on that company gave them enough information to track Hamilton down to a house in Spokane, Washington, which he had rented under the same name as the corporation that owned the Camry.

The house was a small, one-story bungalow near the university on a wide lot with a small garage. A lot of privacy, and because it was close to the college, neighbors wouldn't think twice about a new person or car in the neighborhood. Smart on Hamilton's part. He was young enough to blend in, could easily pass as a college student.

The snow continued to fall steadily. The squall was fast becoming a blizzard, and the locals who knew more about storms than Matt told him by dark it would be a mess. Already visibility was next to nothing and the roads were seriously hazardous. It wasn't the amount of snow—they only expected two feet—but it was the wind and ice that was creating the bulk of the problems. Power outages had been reported in several neighborhoods.

Matt wasn't taking any chances, so had asked for a SWAT backup. He didn't want to get in a car chase in this weather and put more civilians at risk. Andy had been dead for three hours; Hamilton could be almost anywhere by now, or he could be holed up in this house waiting for the cops to extract him. They'd alerted every airport and border officials—Canada was a hop, skip, and jump from Spokane. If Hamilton was smart, he would have an exit plan that would take him into Canada, because they wouldn't extradite on a capital offense. The US government would then negotiate on a life in prison charge, which was fine with Matt as long as Hamilton was under lock and key. But all that was above Matt's pay grade. He didn't want it to get that far; he wanted to find him now. In the US. Where he could be prosecuted for multiple homicides.

As soon as the SWAT team arrived, Matt told them to clear the house. He itched to be part of the team, but he had to let those trained do their job. He had been a SWAT team leader in Arizona, up until he received his own office in Tucson, but that had been years ago. Sometimes, he missed it. By the look on Michael's face as they waited in the tactical truck, watching the operation through a body camera attached to the team leader, he missed it, too.

It was immediately clear that Hamilton wasn't there.

A secondary team of two searched the garage. The Camry was inside; Hamilton was not.

"Where the fuck is he?" Matt asked rhetorically. He called Ryder. "I need everything on Hamilton—he's in the wind. Search far and wide under his name and the corporation for a second car. Find out if he has more than one shell corp. Also contact SPD and see if there are any cars reported stolen in this neighborhood. Do you have his credit reports? Anything pop?"

"Yes, but as we're going through them I'm certain he has more than one corporation. I've reached out to the white collar team to help navigate a series of shell corporations because we don't have all his financials yet. This guy is smart, at least on paper. The corporation that leased the Camry also leased the house. But that corporation is tied to several others through layers of paperwork. Weeding through it is going to take time, plus we have to expand the warrant to get those records because we have to name the corporations individually. Once we have them, we may need additional records. It just depends how far he extended this out."

"Faster is better," Matt said. "Good work," he added before he ended the call.

The SWAT team leader told Matt that the house was clear—Hamilton wasn't there, and there were no booby traps. "Keep a perimeter in case he's watching," Matt said, and slipped on latex gloves. "I need to find out where he's hiding. And if you can conduct the canvass, show his picture around? Someone must have seen something."

"You got it," the team leader said, and gave orders to his men.

Matt and Michael walked through the house themselves. It was an older home and had once been attractive—a lot of detail work including crown moldings, wainscoting, and hardwood floors. But the paint was dull and tinged gray, the heavy drapery so outdated it was almost in style again, and throw carpets were worn and stained. It had been a rental for a long time and had certainly seen better days.

The smaller bedroom had a double bed, where Hamilton had been sleeping. Clothes were strewn in the corner, the bed was unmade. The bathroom reeked—Hamilton had been there, taken off his bloody clothes and showered. A first aid kit was spread out on the counter. The clothes were still on the floor in a pile, blood from both his gunshot wound and his victims seeping into the bathroom rugs.

They needed someone to process the house, and Matt wasn't going to pull Jim or Miles Jordan from the crime scene in Liberty Lake. SPD would have to send another team here.

The larger bedroom in the back of the house was clearly used as Hamilton's office. Matt flipped on the light switch.

"Well, shit," Michael said.

The room was empty of furniture except for a small desk and color printer. The walls were covered with photos of his two recent victims and Brian Maddox. A large wall calendar mapped out their routines, neat and color-coded. Victoria Manners was in red, Jeffrey Ogdenburg was in green, Maddox in blue. A map of the region had been tacked up on another wall. He'd highlighted different routes. Matt stepped closer and tilted his head.

"He had an escape plan this morning. Look—he has different routes marked from Maddox's house, plus routes from the Richmond house. He has six different routes from here. This guy wasn't leaving anything to chance."

"But everything is local," Michael pointed out. "There's no route to the airport, for example, and this map doesn't even show Canada."

"Good point. He was here, left—without his car. I think he has another one. Maybe stole one, so we need to check the reports hourly. Must not have been wounded too badly. He didn't take his pictures and maps, but he took his computer." Matt put his hand on the desk where a computer most likely had been sitting until recently. "See—cords going to the printer would have hooked up to a laptop. He grabbed what he needed and bolted."

"He could be watching."

"I told SWAT to be aware, but I still think he has another hidey-hole. Maybe another lease under a different name."

"A guy like this," Michael said, "who has so many backup plans around all his targets, is going to have a second car as well as an alternative hiding spot."

"Did you reach out to the aunt?"

Michael nodded. "She doesn't believe Glen could hurt anyone, but she sounded cooperative and said she'd call if he contacted her. I also talked to the Kennewick PD and they have a patrol sitting on her house."

"Good."

Matt studied the pictures mounted on the wall, snapping his own pictures so he could study them more carefully and send them to Catherine.

Everything was attached to the wall in a neat and orderly fashion. Sticky notes gave minimal information; some were only a word that made no sense to Matt, but would to Hamilton. Pictures of the victims going about their daily routine. Notes of deviations. Of Maddox. Family. A note that indicated *wife worked from home*. The kids' schedules. A chart that indicated what time Brian left for work every day.

6:37: warm car; 6:48: leaves.

6:29: warm car; 6:38: leaves.

And a photo of Kara and Brian at the hotel, in the lobby, as Brian was leaving.

"Kara was right," Matt said.

"About?"

"Hamilton was at the hotel." He tapped the picture. "He thinks Detective Quinn is one of ours."

The note read: *Blonde with FBI*

"Because he's been here for weeks stalking Maddox and hadn't seen her until we came into town," Michael said.

"He's been watching us. Here's you—me—nothing on Ryder. The kid doesn't look like a fed—he might not tip him off. He assumed Kara was with us because she went up to the war room after having drinks with Brian. Shit—he does have Ryder." There was one picture of Ryder in the lobby talking to the clerk. A note underneath read:

Likely FBI.

He had photos of Andy, Andy and Kara, and one of Matt and Michael coming out of the hospital after they picked up the boxes of lawsuits from the administration. Matt hadn't seriously thought that Hamilton would go after his people. His target was Maddox; now that his plan had been shot to hell, he could go after anyone because he knew who everyone was.

"We have a patrol at the hotel," Michael reminded him.

"But it's a public place, and we know that this guy can disguise himself. He's nondescript as it is. It would be easy for him to make some minor changes and someone might not recognize him at first glance. And there are four entrances to the hotel. If he steals a card key—he may already have done it—he can get in through any of them, and two are open from 6:00 a.m. until 10:00 p.m. without a key."

Matt called Ryder.

"Yes, sir?"

"Do not leave the room. Do not open the door to anyone until I can send backup."

"What happened?"

"Hamilton knows everyone on the team. The only person he doesn't have a picture of is Jim Esteban, but Jim has been spending most of his time at the lab. He has you, Quinn, Michael, me. Maddox and Andy Knolls and any cop who has been with them over the last week."

"I'm good, sir."

"You're an analyst."

"I'm authorized to carry a sidearm, I won't leave it behind."

"Glad you're calm. But stay put."

Matt hung up.

"You don't think he'll go after Ryder in the hotel."

"I think that's down low on his list, but I'm not going to leave my people unprotected."

"What about Quinn?"

"As far as this case, she's one of ours because Hamilton thinks she's one of ours. She's good right now because she's at SPD with Maddox. And..." Matt narrowed his eyes at another photo. "Fuck, fuck, fuck. That's Quinn's grandmother's house. He knows where she lives."

First thing Matt did was call Maddox. "Brian, it's Costa. We have a potential situation." He told him they found Hamilton's house. He was in the wind, but they had evidence that Hamilton had stalked everyone involved in the investigation. "He followed Kara home." Or, he may have followed Matt to Kara's house on Sunday. "He has a photo of her house. I know every cop wants to be searching for Andy's killer, but we need a pair on Emily Dorsey."

"Agreed. I'll make it happen. But Kara isn't going to stay here if her grandmother could be in danger, and I'm not keeping that information from her."

"I know. Make sure she has backup. Does she know about Andy?"

"Yeah."

"And?

"She doesn't want to be here, that's for sure."

"Do not leave the station until we bring in a detail to take you to the hotel, and that isn't going to happen anytime soon."

"I'll stay here all night if I have to."

Matt ended the call. He wanted to call Kara himself, but he trusted Maddox to relay the information. Still… He should have called after he learned about Andy. There's just so much he had to do right now that he couldn't take five minutes to make sure his team was emotionally okay.

"Matt, you gotta see this."

Michael had been going through the desk. He'd found a couple knives—identical, and likely the same type that had been used to kill the first eight victims. And a box of bullets.

".45s," Michael said. "And this box is empty."

"No gun?"

"Not that I could find. But this box is also empty." He held up a box that had once held a high-end hunting knife.

"That could have been the knife he killed Andy with."

"And it's not here. It's a good tool, better than the four-inch double-sided blades he used on the other vics. It's better balanced."

Which meant he could throw it and hit his target—if he had even a little practice.

Matt stepped out into the living room and called Packard.

"Press is everywhere. Andy's name was leaked, and it wasn't my office."

"Not mine, either," Matt said, "but there were a lot of cops and civilians at the scene, not to mention paramedics, fire, and a press crew. You'd think they'd stay in when it's twenty-five fucking degrees."

"I gotta give them something, Agent Costa."

"Agreed. I need a forensics team at Hamilton's house, competent and tight-lipped. There's a lot of evidence here, and some of it is sensitive. Jordan is processing the house in Liberty Lake."

"I don't want to pull him off."

"Agreed."

"I'll put the fear of God into the rest of his crew. They'll do a good job."

"Appreciate it. I'll be there to help with the press. This is one time I think we can use them to our advantage."

"Can I announce we'll have a statement in thirty minutes?"

"Yes. I'll be there."

Matt said, "I need you here, Michael—I'll talk to the SWAT team and have them split. We don't need all six of them for backup, but I don't want anyone exposed. If Hamilton returns, no one is going to be caught in his crossfire."

"Understood."

"Search the car, every drawer, see if there's any hint of what other names he might be using, the other corporations Ryder says he may have, evidence of another car. He's not on foot, not in this weather."

Matt stepped out into the freezing cold. He had an overcoat, but it didn't do much good against the biting wind. He found the SWAT team leader, told him what he needed, and was confident it would get done. Then he had his SPD driver take him back to the station. On the way he called Catherine.

"I just got the photos," she said. "This is great stuff."

"He's in the wind. He's wounded. He knows what my people look like. He's followed several cops home and knows who their families are. I'm giving a statement to the press in—" he glanced at his watch "—twenty minutes. What do I say?"

"It's already been released that he's a suspect in the murder of a cop. He's going to be in hiding. If he hasn't left town, he has another place. Vacant house. Someplace he feels safe enough to regroup."

"I don't think he's left town."

"Why?"

"Because Brian Maddox is still alive, and he wants to kill him."

"But he has also exhibited signs of self-preservation. I talked to Jim Esteban while he was processing the double homicide in Liberty Lake. He thinks that Hamilton killed the owner, then was going through the house looking for something, or perhaps just trying to remember what it was like there when he was young and his mother was alive. Detective Knoll's arrival surprised him, forced him to act. He didn't hesitate. He could have run out the back, but he didn't—because that would give the police time to catch up with him. Instead, he chose confrontation—he came out and attacked immediately. The officers weren't prepared because they hadn't been expecting Hamilton. He's injured—not life threatening, but enough to where he should be considered a wounded animal."

"Wounded animals fight back."

"Or hide and lick their wounds."

"So he's licking his wounds waiting for an opportunity to act. He knows everyone on my team. Even the detective from LA—he thinks she's a federal agent because he hadn't seen her before the investigation began—because there was no reason for him to. He followed her to her house. Or me."

"Excuse me?"

"I drove out there on Sunday to discuss the case with her and dammit, I know how to spot a tail. Either I'm off or he's good."

"He's good, Matt—really good. And planning this killing spree for a long time. According to these pictures he followed several cops, and no one realized it. He blends in. Uses his cell phone camera because no one thinks twice about someone on their cell phone."

"I'm going to tell the press almost everything. I need everyone alert, calling in with any tip. It's a fucking blizzard here, getting worse. People are going to be staying indoors."

"I'll go over all the photos again, see if I can see something that might help."

"Ryder is going through Hamilton's finances—he has at least one shell company in addition to his regular employer and that's how he stays off the grid at times. He works remotely, so no one thinks twice if he's not around the office. He gets his work done, that's all they care about. If you need more, call Michael Harris—he's at Hamilton's house searching top to bottom. Forensics is on their way."

"Does the detective from Los Angeles have a protective detail?"

"I told everyone, even Quinn, not to go out alone. Right now she's safe at SPD, but when she learns that her grandmother may be in danger, she'll go there."

"I'm looking at the photos and also that she's the one who saw him outside of Chief Maddox's house. He's going to know that she was the witness who helped with the sketch, which is an up-to-date image."

"And?"

"He's going to be angry. Perhaps she should leave town with her grandmother, until you find him."

Matt didn't know Kara well, but he could pretty

much assure Catherine that Kara would never run away, especially now that Hamilton killed Andy.

"Did you hear about the blizzard? All flights delayed. Roads are shit. I'll put them someplace safe."

"He's angry, which makes him reckless," Catherine said, "but he still has a plan. Remember that. Be alert."

48

Liberty Lake
5:15 p.m.

Kara packed her grandmother's suitcase because Emily wouldn't do it herself.

"I'm not going anywhere," Emily said.

"You have to."

"I don't have to do anything."

"Grams, Detective Andy Knolls was murdered. We know who killed him, and the FBI found photos of your house at the killer's place. He knows where I'm staying. You're not safe here."

Emily frowned. "I just don't understand what's going on."

Kara wanted to beat Glen Hamilton to a pulp for putting fear into her grandmother's heart. "I'll stay here if you want me to," she said. She didn't want to. She wanted to find this bastard before he hurt anyone else. "If you don't want to leave, I'll stay here and protect you."

Emily frowned. "You need to work with the police and find him."

"I *am* the police, Em. He killed Andy. I don't have a lot of friends, Em. But Andy was one of them. But you're family, and I will do anything to make sure you're safe."

Kara pushed aside the competing guilt. Over what she'd said to Andy the other day, and wanting to work this case even though her grandmother needed her.

"Can you take me to Flo's house?"

"Flo Abbott? Sure. No problem. Call her, tell her you're coming for a few days."

"She has cats. I like cats. I thought of getting a cat or two to keep me company."

Leave it to her grandmother to find the bright side of a terrible situation.

While Em called her longtime friend, Kara finished packing everything her grandmother would need—clothes, medication, toiletries, even her marijuana stash. She found two books on the nightstand and put them in, too.

"Flo's excited. Said we're having a slumber party. Can you get the whiskey on the top shelf? Flo likes whiskey."

Kara brought it down and put it in the top of the suitcase, then helped Em on with her heavy coat.

"Two police cars," Em said as Kara helped her out to the street. "I've never had a police escort before." She smiled at the officer assigned to escort them to Flo's house. "You look too young to be a policeman."

"I'm thirty-two, ma'am."

"Too young," she repeated.

"I'm thirty, Grams," Kara said.

Em just looked at her with raised eyebrows. Kara didn't need this argument.

She went with Em to Flo Abbott's house. Flo lived in the country, halfway back to Spokane. Five acres in the middle of nowhere, and there was no reason that Glen Hamilton would know about this place. She'd made sure they weren't tailed, and was confident that her grandmother would be safe here. While Kara didn't think that he would go after Emily, she couldn't take the chance.

She felt comfortable, at least, letting Em stay out here, and the Sheriff's escort promised they would check on her frequently. Flo herself had a shotgun by the door, and assured Kara that she would shoot first, ask questions later. Kara didn't need to hear that. One pull on the shotgun and Flo would probably be knocked on her ass.

But in addition to at least six cats, Flo had two German shepherds who would make good protectors.

"Don't open the door to anyone," Kara reminded the two women.

"Dinner's almost ready," Flo said. "Can you stay for a bite?"

"It smells great, but I really can't."

Em walked over and put her hands on Kara's shoulders. She looked up and said, "You be careful, Kara. I know you think you have to do this, and I won't tell you that you can't. Not that you'd listen to me. But I love you, and you need to know that."

Kara wasn't good with emotions, but ever since Hamilton hit the kid, her emotions had been going up and down. Andy's death made them even rockier. "Love you, too, Grams."

She left before she did something stupid like cry.

She slipped back into the police car—the front seat this time, which made her feel more in charge.

"Your grandma's going to be okay," the officer said.

"Yes, she will. Have they had the press conference yet?"

"Over and done. Packard let the fed talk almost the entire time. It was brief and to the point. Glen Hamilton is wanted for the murder of a police officer and civilian. No connection to the Triple Killer, but when asked by the press, Costa said he's wanted for questioning in both previous Liberty Lake murders. He's considered armed and dangerous, *yada yada*. Where to? The station?"

"Head there, I'm going to call Maddox."

The phone rang twice before Brian picked up. "Em's safe with Flo Abbott. Sheriff will patrol regularly. What's happening?"

"Costa convinced me to stay at the station all night," Brian said. "I didn't argue. No way is Hamilton getting in here, not with our security. You don't need to babysit me."

"I love babysitting," she said. "But seriously, if you're staying put and I don't have to worry about your safety, I want to be in the field."

"I understand. Costa's still here—wants to talk to you."

A second later, Matt came on the line. "You're not staying with your grandmother?"

"She's safe. I'm heading back to town. What can I do?"

"Stay at the station with Maddox."

"No. I'm the only one who has seen this guy up close and personal."

"He thinks you're a federal agent."

"Because he saw me at the hotel?"

"Yes. We all have targets on our back."

"I'm not running away. This is my job." It wasn't—not this specific case—but it felt like it. "Matt, dammit, I'm not sitting on my ass when there's a cop killer out there."

"Understood. Forensics just finished processing the Richmond house and is heading to Hamilton's house near the university. Agent Harris is taking the lead there. I'm finishing up here at the station, then will head to the FBI war room. I have two officers watching the hotel for signs of Hamilton, but I would feel better if Ryder had backup, plus he's going over all Hamilton's financials."

"That I can help with. Only one person?"

"No, Ryder is working with HQ on the financials, but he's point. We think Hamilton has another car, and everything he owns seems to be under one of multiple shell corps. Ryder has now identified three different paper companies."

"Not my strength, but I can take some of the load off."

"I'll call Ryder and tell him to expect you."

"It'll be at least twenty minutes—the roads are shit."

"You're not alone."

He sounded angry.

"No, Costa, I got the memo."

"You need to be extra careful. He knows you're a cop."

"I don't have a death wish," she said, and ended the call.

49

Spokane
8:45 p.m.

Matt left SPD later than he planned. Packard, though pompous and controlling, had proved that he would do what it took to keep his men and women safe. The foul weather had created other issues—traffic accidents, power outages—but Packard partnered with the Sheriff's department to ensure that he had a full contingent of officers through the night.

Matt didn't think that Hamilton would go for Maddox at the police station though he realized the clock was ticking for the sick bastard. But it would be suicide, and like Catherine said, Hamilton had a self-preservation streak. Liberty Lake PD was dealing with their own issues, much of it grief related. Andy Knolls had been the heart and soul of that department and his death was tearing it apart. But they vowed to keep an eye on Maddox's house in case Hamilton returned for an encore. Matt had finally met the police chief, Pierce Dunn, earlier when he sat down with Andy's fiancée. That had been awkward. Dunn was every bit the doofus Andy had implied, and it was clear no one was really in charge with Andy gone.

But Matt didn't think that Hamilton would return because there was no one in Liberty Lake he could target. Still—Catherine felt that *any* cop was in potential danger if Hamilton couldn't get to Maddox, and she didn't count Andy's death as the final act.

"He killed him in a rage, in a need to escape. It wouldn't be satisfying for him in the sense of any completion of his pattern."

Matt wasn't as certain, and he feared that Hamilton had slipped away in a vehicle they didn't know about, leaving the city before the storm really hit. He'd taken his laptop and left Spokane. If that were the case, they would be stuck. No one would feel truly safe until they found him, and it would take far more time.

Where the hell did he go?

Matt hated not knowing. He wasn't as good as Catherine at getting into the criminal mind, but he was good enough. With this guy, he wasn't certain. Catherine thought he was nearby. Matt felt he had been too smart, too methodical to sacrifice himself now just because he wanted Maddox dead.

Catherine had always told him he thought too logically in situations like this.

"You have to think like your suspect. You have to recognize they'll have different priorities, and while self-preservation is usually important, it's not always the most important."

Matt arrived at the hotel at nine. His driver, a seasoned officer, was staying until midnight, meeting up with the four officers who were on duty outside the hotel. At that point he'd be on for twelve straight hours. No one wanted to take a break—not when they were now looking for a cop killer—but they had to, or someone was going to make a mistake.

He went immediately up to the war room. Ryder was there, but not Kara.

"Detective Quinn should have been here over an hour ago," Matt said.

"She was—she went to the manager's office about twenty minutes ago to review the security video."

"Why?"

"The pictures you found at Hamilton's place. Since he was here on Saturday night, she thought he might have returned."

"Why the hell would he return knowing that the FBI is here?"

"Dr. Esteban called in and said he's staying at the lab all night. They're processing the evidence from the Richmond house, and the ME is performing Detective Knolls's autopsy tonight. He said he'd sleep in the break room, and the facility is secure."

"It is. I was there."

"And Harris will be back by ten—the secondary crime team is nearly done with Hamilton's residence. They're leaving a unit behind in case he returns."

"Have we heard anything about Eric Tolliver? He was still in surgery when I left SPD."

"No change, but the boy who was hit this morning is stable. He has a hairline fracture on his skull, concussion, and a broken arm and rib. They're keeping him for a couple of days to make sure there's no swelling on the brain, but the doctors are optimistic that he'll make a full recovery."

"Glad we have some good news."

"I took the liberty of reserving Detective Quinn a room for the night."

Matt hadn't even thought of it. And he couldn't very well tell Ryder that she could stay in Matt's room.

Instead, he said, "Appreciate it." He sat down and grabbed a stack of printouts. "What am I looking for here?"

"Those are Hamilton's personal financials. The lab at Quantico flagged everything they thought potentially could help. I'm going through the corporations now."

"How many corporations are we talking about?"

"We're now up to five, and have to run each one. We're not going to have most of the information until tomorrow." He slid over another folder. "Those are phone records. We traced his cell phone. It's in Tacoma, and it's clear he hasn't used it since the end of February. We found another phone under one of the corporations, different carrier, and we'll have those records in the morning."

"And his employer knew nothing about this? How did he keep his job for so long if he was never around?" Matt asked, half to himself.

"Our agents in Seattle followed up with his employer there. They indicate he always did his work on time and several of their employees work from home. No one knew he wasn't in Tacoma, but that wouldn't matter—he's been working from here. He's a programmer and apparently very good at his job. I think that's another reason he set up these corporations—if he has the skills, he could easily move money around as needed."

"What's taking so long on the phone records?"

Ryder gave him a sly look. "Not everyone works 24-7. We put in the request this afternoon as soon as we identified the phone, and they promised within twenty-four hours. It's either off or disabled, however, because we haven't been able to trace it."

Matt rubbed his eyes. Ryder was right. There were people in the world who only worked eight hours a day. Businesses that actually closed at night.

He started looking through the files when Michael Harris called.

"We've secured Hamilton's house," Michael said, "and we found something—in the trash a receipt from a hardware store for a dozen mason jars, cotton rags, wire and a forty-five-foot portable chain ladder. Paid cash yesterday, and none of that stuff is in the house."

"What the hell for?"

"Molotov cocktails. A variation. Punch a hole in the lid, put gasoline or lighter fluid inside, soak the rag. They don't have to be thrown. He could have bought candles elsewhere if he plans a slow burn, or he could be using them as grenades if he's holed up somewhere."

"And the ladder? Planning on scaling a wall?"

"More like getting down something. He'd have to attach it to a roof or ledge to use it."

"Maybe his Plan B is to force Maddox out of the station, but I don't see these grenades doing it. That building is solid. And I can't imagine what he would do with the ladder, unless he has a completely different purpose for it."

"Considering the structure of the police department, and the fact that it's a blizzard out here, he can't do much damage. He could have intended to use them at Maddox's house if he returned—thrown through a window they would do serious damage. The initial explosion is minor in the scheme of things, but depending on the accelerant he's using, the fire can easily spread."

"Thanks—I'll get the word out."

Matt hung up, relayed the information to Ryder, and sent a message to the team leaders in the field, plus Maddox and Packard.

"Where are you?" Matt whispered as he scoured the financials looking for anything that could direct him to where Glen Hamilton was hiding.

Kara had spent the last two hours going over the security footage from the hotel. She'd started with today's tape and moved back. They were busy, and the manager said they were completely full because of the storm.

"Can you show me the footage from Saturday?" She thought back to when she and Brian had drinks in the bar. "Evening. Start at eight and we'll go forward from there."

The manager found the right video files. Kara had already figured out how to change from camera to camera, and she located the lobby feed. She watched it in triple speed until she saw Matt Costa walk in. He made a beeline for the staircase, bypassing the elevators. Glen Hamilton followed five minutes later. He was wearing a dark gray trench coat and hat, not suspicious considering that Saturday night had been cold. But it took her a minute to recognize him.

He looked around, then walked over to the bar. She found the security feed from the bar. Located where she and Brian had been sitting in the corner, both with eyes on the entrance. Hamilton clearly spotted them, hesitated, then went to the bar. Ordered a beer. Chatted with the bartender a bit.

"Is this guy on duty tonight?"

"No, he's a grad student, only works weekends."

Kara watched as she and Brian got up and left. She remembered they chatted in the lobby for another few minutes. Hamilton sat at the bar for three or four minutes, then got up.

She switched back to the lobby feed and watched Brian leave and Hamilton look after him. Her stomach twisted as she realized how easy it would have been for Hamilton to follow and kill Brian then. But he didn't. He watched as she went up in the elevator.

Then he left.

Was that it? She sped up the video, and almost missed it.

Five minutes after he left, he returned and approached the reservation desk. He now had a black backpack with him.

Leaning forward, Kara flipped through the feeds

until she found the reservation area. This camera was different in that it was behind the employees in both corners, providing a clear view of the customer's face.

Hamilton talked to the employee, then handed over a license and credit card.

"Holy shit!" She nearly jumped out of her seat. "He got a room here? Is he still here?"

The manager frowned. "I don't know."

"But you know when people check in. What name. This was…nine-thirty-four Saturday night. I need to know what room he's in and when he checked out."

"Give me a minute."

The manager left the room.

She had looked at all the footage from the entrances and hadn't seen Hamilton again, but she hadn't been able to clearly identify each patron. What if he changed his appearance again? What if he came in with a group? Pretended to be with someone?

She called Matt.

"Are you back? At the hotel?"

"I'm with Ryder," he said.

"Hamilton got a room here on Saturday night. After I saw him in the bar, he got a room. The manager is checking to see under what name and if he checked out."

"Are you certain?"

"Yes. I'm looking at the security feed now." She switched over to the entrances and ran through them triple time. "He left by the side exit an hour later."

"He got a room here...shit shit shit. Where are you?"

"Security room. Behind the reservation desk."

"I'm coming down."

Glen had made a tactical error by returning to the hotel. He watched from his window as Matt Costa, the fed, entered through the front door. There were three police cars outside, each with two officers. He was confident that he could slip out—they didn't know about this identity or his second car. He had altered his appearance a bit. It wouldn't hold up under scrutiny, but at a glance he didn't think anyone would realize it was him.

He didn't see Brian Maddox come into the hotel. The snow came down at an angle because of the steady winds, and driving in this weather would be difficult, at best. He wanted to stay the night, come up with a plan in the morning, but he was itchy. Itchy to act.

He wouldn't be able to get to Maddox before midnight. The realization irritated him, like fingernails on a chalkboard, but once he accepted that Maddox was scared and in hiding, a certain peace fell over him.

He would, eventually, get to the old cop. He wouldn't know when. Next year? Three years? He would live his life in constant fear that he would die.

And then Glen would kill him.

Glen breathed in, breathed out. Calmed and focused himself.

If he had difficulties driving, then so would the

police. They might have four-wheel-drive vehicles, but it was dark, helicopters couldn't track him, and he would have an advantage of getting out first.

You should have left this afternoon. You should never have come back to the hotel, you idiot.

His father's voice echoed in his head. Glen scowled, drowned it out by hitting the side of his head until his skull hurt.

His father was dead, long dead.

Glen had everything ready. The jars, the accelerant, the locations. He'd studied enough science to know that the top floor—since there was no basement—was the best place to start the fire. Everyone would leave. He would be waiting. In the chaos, he would take as many trophies as he could before he slipped away. And by the time anyone realized what had happened, he would be gone.

It had to be chaos. Chaos was his only chance to fix this.

Fix? Maybe he hadn't screwed up. Maybe it was always supposed to be like this. Bring all the FBI agents into one building and destroy it. Destroy them. They were the ones who caused all these problems. If the FBI hadn't arrived so quickly, Glen would have killed Brian Maddox and disappeared. No one had acted so fast in the other two cities he hit. How they had found him now—and got his name... He took a deep breath before he got angry again.

So he'd made a mistake. He hadn't made many. He'd killed for the first time fifteen years ago and he hadn't made any major mistakes after that. He'd learned from that first time—don't kill in a rage.

What happened today? You lost it with that interloper in your house. You killed him, you killed those cops, you got shot yourself—all because you were angry.

That wasn't his fault, not really. The man should have just let him in the house to look around. He didn't have to be a dick about it. And the cops—they were in the way. They would have stopped him. He had no choice.

But anger would get him in trouble. It made him stupid. Anger caused mistakes.

He was calm now. He had everything set up. Now that the head FBI agent was in the building, it was time to start the show.

And in the chaos, he would disappear.

Glen Hamilton had checked into room 460. It was in the front north corner of the hotel, next to one of three staircases. The second staircase was next to the elevator, and the third on the opposite end of the long hall. Sixty rooms each on three floors, and twenty-four rooms on the first floor. They were at full occupancy, every room reserved, with a total of 387 guests and twelve staff members on-site. They couldn't confirm that all the guests were in their rooms.

Matt called in SWAT. Their ETA was more than twenty minutes because of the weather, but they were already geared up and ready, on call at SPD. Harris was only five minutes out. They had six uniformed officers on-site, and Matt called them into a conference room, along with the manager. Kara was still going through the security feeds putting together a timeline, and Ryder was tapped into the live feeds. The hotel had cameras only at the elevators above the first floor, but the lobby, bar, and all entrances were covered. They hadn't confirmed that Hamilton was in the building, but they confirmed he had registered under the name Glen Montclair—his mother's maiden name—and the company GAM Computer Systems.

"Our number one priority at this point is to evacuate the fourth floor as quietly as possible. SWAT will be here shortly, and they will take the tactical lead, while we will assist in bringing all the guests on the fourth floor into the conference rooms. One officer will be with the guests in each room, at the door. Hamilton is armed and dangerous. May be wounded. We get the civilians out of harm's way and then we can engage the suspect."

Matt drew out on a whiteboard the rough diagram of the fourth floor. "Under no circumstances are we to use the north staircase. SWAT will position two men outside this door in case he attempts to escape. All guests need to be taken out via the southern staircase. SWAT will be there directing them."

Michael Harris walked in and Matt was relieved. It was situations like this that he had wanted Harris on his team. "Agent Harris? Comments?"

"Suggestion that we also evacuate the rooms immediately below Hamilton. If there is gunfire, they would be the most likely to take collateral. We can do that before SWAT arrives."

"Excellent. Let's do it." Matt ordered the six officers—two each—to stand guard at each of the staircases. No guests would be allowed upstairs until they cleared the building. There were some grumblings, but the hotel provided everyone with free drink coupons.

Matt and Michael went to the third floor and quietly spoke to each of the guests in the four rooms in the northern corner. Two were businessmen traveling, and another room was a young couple. The room directly below Hamilton was a family—parents and two young kids, including an infant. They had all been sleeping.

Michael said quietly to Matt, "Take those four down, I'll help the family out. This is starting to get noisy, and we don't want to alert him."

Matt agreed, left Michael with the family and escorted the other guests to the southern staircase and downstairs.

He was about to go back up to assist Michael when Kara called.

"He's here," she said.

"When?"

"He walked in with a group at two-thirty this afternoon. Blended right in. Could have been waiting outside until he found the right way to enter. I missed him the first time. He wore a brimmed hat, but the same trench coat he had on Saturday. It's the only way I noticed him. Went straight to the elevator and hasn't left."

"Excellent. Ryder is monitoring the live feeds. SWAT is here, I told them to set up in the back in case Hamilton is looking out his window. If you're done, we can use help with the evacuation and keeping everyone calm."

"I'll be right there."

Matt pocketed his phone and went back up to the third floor. Michael was still standing outside the door that housed the family. Michael held up his hand to have Matt stay where he was, then Matt got a text message from him.

These people don't know the meaning of be quiet. I'll get them out but be alert.

Matt was about to confirm when an explosion shook the hotel. He looked down the hall and saw dust falling on Michael as Michael ran into room 360.

Then another explosion sounded, and suddenly, one came after another, the lights went out, and the fire alarms wailed.

50

Spokane
11:35 p.m.

Kara froze when the lights went out, then a generator kicked in and emergency lighting engaged.

She ran back down the hall to the security office where Ryder was going through the video feeds. They were all black.

"They're gone," he told her, shouting over the piercing alarm. "Emergency power isn't going to run the cameras."

"That was six explosions," she said.

"His makeshift Molotov cocktails. He could have six more, based on the receipt."

"We have to get these people out."

They left the security room and people were coming out of the stairs in various states of dress. SWAT rushed in through the side doors.

"We have to contain this," Kara said. "He could slip out with the crowd." Which was probably his intention.

Ryder ran to the main doors and whistled loudly.

"I need your attention! I am Ryder Kim with the Federal Bureau of Investigation. We need to evacuate in a calm and orderly manner. We need to verify that everyone gets out safely. I will take your name and your room number as you exit."

"It's freezing out there!" a woman said, her arms around a young girl. They had grabbed coats, but the girl only had socks on.

Shit shit shit! Could this get any worse?

Kara said to Ryder, "They can sit in their cars. If they don't have a car, someone will share. I'll look for Hamilton. Just keep them exiting single file."

Ryder nodded, relayed the information by shouting over the alarms. There were grumblings, but Ryder was doing a great job dealing with it. SWAT headed up the stairs.

"What happened?" someone cried out.

"Is it the boiler?"

"It was on the top floor," another person said.

"I saw smoke in the staircase."

"The elevator, too."

Kara kept her attention focused on the people leaving. SWAT had the other exits covered. Glen Hamilton was not among these people.

She sent Costa a text message.

125+/-people have been evacuated, mostly from the first and second floors. Hamilton not among them.

Another group of people came running down the main staircase.

"There's fire on the top floor!" one of them said. "It's spreading, I didn't think that could happen."

Another explosion caused several people to scream. Kara itched to run upstairs and help with the evacuation, but right now she was the only one who had recently seen Hamilton.

And he wasn't among these people.

Three more explosions sounded. They sounded a lot closer.

Ryder frowned. "I think he set them on each floor, at the north end." He hooked on an earpiece. "Costa, it's Ryder Kim, you there?"

Silence.

"Dammit," Ryder mumbled. He looked at Kara. "Coms are down."

She tested hers. "No they're not," she said. "It's just Matt, isn't it?"

"And Michael. They were on the third floor."

That's where she needed to be. But Hamilton was creating a diversion so he could escape—which meant she needed to be here to spot him.

Shit. She felt helpless to help her team, but no way in hell was she letting Glen Hamilton walk out of this hotel free and clear.

Matt ran down the hall to where Michael had disappeared. The emergency lighting was on, and the hall was filling rapidly with smoke.

People were running out of their rooms and down the hall. Matt directed them to the southern staircase. They were panicked, but mostly orderly.

"Harris! Dammit, Michael! Can you hear me?"

Matt reached the door. The ceiling tiles had fallen and dust was everywhere. He couldn't tell where the smoke was coming from. The first explosions came from the top floor, but the next three sounded like they were on the second floor.

He looked in the doorway. The ceiling above had collapsed, the tiles smoking and burning, and Michael was pulling away debris to get to the family. The drapes had caught fire.

The bastard had rigged his room. Which meant he wasn't there, he was somewhere else in the hotel. Hiding. Waiting for the right moment to escape.

Matt helped Michael get to the family. The mother clutched her infant, and the father had the toddler. "We need to get you out."

"I got them," Michael said. "Find Hamilton."

Matt realized his com had disengaged. He reset it. Ryder was talking, but not to him.

"Ryder."

"You're there."

"Yes."

"We've cleared half the hotel. Hamilton has not exited."

"He rigged his room. The other explosions sounded like they were coming from below."

"The second floor—there are people trapped in their rooms next to the north stairwell. SWAT is working on getting them out. Fire is on its way, but they won't go in until we locate Hamilton."

"Keep your eyes on the door. He's betting on distracting us."

"Quinn asked if you've checked the utility closets. There's one on each floor next to the elevator."

"I'm on it."

He rigged his room, and either he went up to the roof, or he went to the second floor, where the second explosions occurred, and planned to slip out with the guests. Matt trusted Ryder and Kara to handle the main doors, but the explosions created havoc among the guests.

"Ryder," he said, "you still there?"

"Yes, sir."

"Find out where SWAT is, I'm on the third floor, heading up to four. I need a team. We'll clear from the top down and the bottom up."

"Roger. Stand by."

Matt took the center staircase up to the fourth floor, passing several guests coming down. He looked at each face. No Hamilton. Used the master key the hotel manager gave him to check the utility room. No Hamilton.

The center staircase was the only one that went to the roof. The door should be locked. It wasn't. It had been broken open, cold air rushing through the crack.

Matt said, "Tell all teams that suspect may be on the roof."

There would be ladders that could be dropped.

Plus, Hamilton had his own ladder. Dammit, he might have already slipped away!

"Where are the ladders on the roof?" he asked.

"Stand by," Ryder said.

Matt didn't want to stand by. Hamilton could have

already escaped before SWAT arrived. They could guard the hotel ladders, but Hamilton had his own. He could descend anywhere at any time.

He was about to go through the roof door when Ryder said, "Ladders on both the north and south faces, but they're locked."

"So was the damn door."

"SWAT has teams both north and south, also sending officers your way."

He wasn't going to get away. Hamilton had to see that, right? That there was no way out?

Two SWAT officers met Matt in the stairwell. "Did you see the suspect?" one asked. Matt recognized him as the team leader at the raid of Hamilton's house.

"No, but this door is busted open. My people are in the lobby looking for him among the guests, and your people have the other exits covered. He's either up here or still inside. But this could be a trap—he had enough supplies to make twelve Molotov cocktails, and I counted nine explosions."

"Six on the fourth floor and three on the second," the team leader said. "Fire suppression system launched in multiple rooms. We're still assessing injuries."

"How do you want to do this?" Matt asked.

He squatted and checked the door for wires, then peered through. "How certain are you that he's out there?"

"Eighty percent," Matt said. "He purchased a forty-five-foot chain ladder. He planned this." Though *why* was the million-dollar question. It seemed foolish for him to stay in the same hotel as the FBI—and Hamilton knew that they were here.

Unless he thought they'd bring Maddox here—which, until Andy had been killed, had been the original plan.

"There's a duct system that, if we stay low, will cover us," the team leader said. "Stay here until we clear the roof, Agent Costa."

Matt hated sitting on the sidelines, but he concurred.

"Three, two, one."

The two SWAT members pushed open the door and ran toward the closest duct. Almost immediately, Matt saw a flash of light, then an explosion right next to the duct.

"Man down! Man down!"

Matt ran over to the duct. One of the officers was bleeding in the leg. "Glass," he said through clenched teeth.

"Medic, stat," the team leader said.

"I'm fine," the officer grimaced.

He wasn't. He was immobile and losing blood, but he would live.

"Stay put," Matt said. He looked over to where the makeshift grenade had come from. Hamilton was jumping over the side. The fire was burning out quickly—the icy roof coupled with the snow and wind ensured there wouldn't be an extensive burn.

Matt ran over while talking into his com. He slid twice, caught himself. "Suspect is descending the western front of the building on a ladder! He's armed and dangerous."

Matt looked over the side. Hamilton was already halfway down, half climbing, half sliding down the ladder.

He hesitated, then Matt saw that he had another glass jar in his hand.

"Freeze!" Matt shouted. He had a shot, but right below Hamilton were dozens of guests who had been evacuated. SWAT was already trying to clear them out of the way, but Matt couldn't risk hitting a civilian.

Hamilton lit the rag, and it had already started to burn. He threw the jar into the crowd. Screams echoed in the storm. The explosion was big, but fizzled quickly. Unfortunately, it gave Hamilton enough time to descend as everyone below took cover.

SWAT would get him, and while Matt didn't think he had any more of those bombs, he could have purchased other supplies that they didn't know about.

He has one more. He detonated eleven; he has twelve.

"I'm coming down the ladder," he said. "He's almost at the bottom."

In his ear, Ryder said, "Harris and Quinn are in pursuit."

Matt scaled down and heard another explosion, followed by an earsplitting scream.

Kara was right behind Michael Harris as they exited the lobby and ran in the direction Costa said Hamilton was scaling down. SWAT and SPD officers were doing everything they could to get the panicked guests out of the way, but the Molotov cocktail

Hamilton tossed into the crowd resulted in several injuries. SWAT was protecting the medics who ran over to work on the injured.

"I see him," Harris called, and ran on the icy walk. He slipped but didn't fall.

Kara pursued, saw a skinny man drop eight feet from the bottom of a hanging ladder. He had a gun in his hand and was aiming it up.

Shit, Matt was on that ladder.

"Drop the weapon!" Kara shouted.

She didn't have a clear shot—beyond Hamilton were people, including a fire truck.

"Everyone out of the way!"

Harris had a much louder, booming voice. "Everyone down!"

People started to drop to the wet ground.

Hamilton fled instead of shooting at Matt. Hamilton had a good thirty-foot lead, but Harris was quick, even in the snow. Hamilton rounded the corner. Harris was about to follow, when Kara saw a flicker of light in the dark.

"Bomb!" she shouted.

Harris didn't hesitate. He threw himself into bushes just as Hamilton tossed a Molotov cocktail around the corner.

It exploded exactly where Harris had been.

Kara was knocked on her ass, but she scrambled up, then helped Harris up.

"Thanks," he shouted, his ears obviously still ringing from the explosion. "I owe you one."

"How many of those fucking bombs does he have?"

"We think twelve. He shouldn't have anymore. He's covered in gas—I could smell him as I pursued."

Matt caught up with them.

"Where'd he go?"

"Around the corner. SWAT is on those doors."

Matt stood at the corner of the building and looked down the side.

Glen Hamilton stood only feet away, gun in hand.

He fired as Matt jumped back. The bullet hit the corner of the building.

"Fuck that," Matt said. He leaned just around the corner and fired as soon as he caught sight of Hamilton.

He hit him once, twice—then saw a flash and he jumped back as Hamilton burst into flames. He screamed in agony, the accelerant he was coated in burning rapidly.

Harris got up and ran to Hamilton. He tackled him into a snowbank, and rolled him around, effectively putting out the flames. His body was still smoking.

"He's alive," Harris said.

Though Hamilton was seriously injured, Harris cuffed him, then searched him. Found two knives. He kicked away his gun, which Matt picked up.

"You should have let him burn," Kara said, her voice hardened. "He killed a cop."

"And he'll pay for that," Harris said.

Matt called over the paramedics. He searched Glen Hamilton one more time, determined that he couldn't hurt anyone, but had two SPD officers stay with him. "Go with him to the hospital. Do not let him out of your sight. As soon as the doctors clear him, he goes straight to the infirmary at the state prison while we wait to arraign him. Understood?"

"Yes, sir."

Hamilton moaned as the paramedics worked on him. Blood soaked into the white snow. Matt knew he'd hit him at least once, but didn't know where.

"I'll kill him," Hamilton said. "You can't keep that cop safe forever. I will kill him!"

Matt walked away. Kara and Michael followed. "He's never getting out of prison. He killed a cop and nine other people—more if we tie the homeless men and his father to his killing spree. He'll be sitting on death row until he's dead."

Kara looked upset, and so did Michael. Matt needed to fix this, but he didn't know how.

"You did the right thing, Michael."

"I know."

"I want him dead, but I want him dead the right way."

"There is no wrong way," Kara said. She took a deep breath, let it out. "Well," she said, her voice a hair lighter, "you fibbies sure know how to have fun. And here I thought you were all a bunch of pricks with sticks up your ass."

"Only the feds in LA," Matt said and caught her eye. She smiled, but it didn't reach her eyes. She had to deal with not only Andy's death, but her case in LA. He didn't say anything, but he might be able to help get Thornton off her back. Quietly.

Matt cleared his throat. "Now, paperwork."

Michael groaned, and Kara laughed.

"What's so funny?" Michael said.

"I'm on vacation. That means no paperwork. I'm ready to give my statement whenever you're ready to take it." She winked, and walked over to where Ryder Kim was helping one of the victims.

But instead of taking a break, Kara dived in and helped the medics and cops create order.

Matt had learned to expect nothing less from Detective Quinn.

51

Friday, March 12
Liberty Lake
Morning

Andy Knolls had a funeral worthy of a hero.

Every cop in the Spokane Valley, and many from other parts of the state and adjoining Idaho, came to pay respects to the fallen officer Friday morning. His fiancée took condolences, but she looked shell-shocked. Matt had tried to talk to her earlier, but she didn't want to discuss Andy or how he died.

Brian Maddox gave the eulogy, which hit Matt harder than he thought. Matt had known Andy Knolls for less than a week, but he had been a good cop and an even better man. He had a large family, and even more friends. He saw Kara's grandmother sitting in the large church with a woman even older than her, but Kara wasn't with her.

Everyone was mourning. Tears flowed freely, even on the rigid faces of law enforcement. They had caught Andy's killer, but Andy was still dead.

Matt would do anything to bring Andy back. To

erase the pain that filled the church as his friends and family grieved; to erase the sorrow in his own heart. He'd buried too many good men and women, heroes who gave their lives for others. But Andy's death hit him harder than most.

Kara stood in the back, in the far corner, away from most everyone. At first Matt hadn't seen her—she'd dressed to blend, her hair up, little makeup, dark, nondescript clothing. She had a cut on her neck that was healing from being clipped by a shard of glass at the hotel. She had a cop's face—solemn, serious, almost emotionless.

Matt had tried to talk to her yesterday, but she'd given him an excuse involving her grandmother that he just didn't buy. At first he thought he'd made her mad, but realized today that she had taken Andy's death particularly hard. She hadn't been able to deal with her grief until after Hamilton had been caught.

After the funeral, Matt didn't feel the need to go to the Knolls's house. He'd already spoken to Andy's parents and that would suffice. Instead, he followed Kara to her car on the edge of the church parking lot.

"Hey."

She looked up at him. Tears glistened in her eyes.

He rubbed her arm. She closed her eyes. "I hate what I said to him."

"Don't go there."

"I can't help it. I pushed him to be bolder. He should never have gone up to that house. He should have never been put in that position."

"He was doing his job, Kara. I knew he was checking up on the family. I didn't think twice about it. We were spread thin and trying to cover every possible scenario."

"He didn't have the right training. He didn't know how to respond to the threat." Her voice cracked as her eyes drifted back toward the church where Andy's coffin was being loaded into the hearse.

"He did everything he could have. More training is always a good thing, but he couldn't have predicted that Hamilton was in the house. Tolliver woke up yesterday, gave his statement. He blames himself as well. Says he should have shot him, didn't see the knife until Hamilton pulled it out of Andy's body. Said Hamilton was in a rage, a wild animal, and it happened so fast he could barely react."

"I'll be fine," Kara said, though she sounded forlorn. "Better than his fiancée." She shook her head. "I can't believe what I said to her, about the killer preferring knives. I hate myself. I don't think."

"Stop. You're a great cop, Kara." Matt put his hand on her forearm and squeezed. He wanted to give her peace but didn't know how when his emotions were just as raw. Yet, in that brief moment, she silently acknowledged their shared pain.

"You're not half-bad, for a fed."

"You know, we don't have any place to be," he said. "I've already wrapped up most of the paperwork. Ryder said you came and signed your statement yesterday. You may need to testify at a hearing, but it's a formality and it won't be anytime soon. You really went above and beyond. I'll make sure your boss knows that."

"You don't have to do anything for me."

"I'm not doing it *for* you—I'm doing it because you were an asset, especially since my team was so thin. By this time next month I'll be fully staffed."

"You have a good thing going here," she said. "I can see the value." She smiled at him and spontaneously kissed him. "And you've convinced me that not all feds are pricks."

"I saved the entire profession."

"I wouldn't go that far," she said.

He wanted her again. That one kiss when he thought they were done was not enough. He wanted more. "I can take a day off—we earned it. Maybe go skiing. Take a night up at Mount Spokane. I heard they have a nice resort. One night to unwind." He rubbed his palm against hers. She felt the jolt, just like he did. "What do you say? Nothing is better than fresh powder." He paused. "You ski, don't you?"

"I'm pretty good."

He suspected that was an understatement. "So? We both deserve a night off. A little skiing, good food, great sex." He kissed her, but she averted her head.

"I'm leaving tonight."

"It's not the fifteenth."

"I can't stay here. I need to fix what's broken in LA."

"Just one more day?" He hated to plead with her, but dammit, he'd earned a night with her. A night when there wasn't a killer stalking cops.

"There's a lot going on with my department, with my case. You have a job, I have a job."

Matt knew that Kara was right, and neither of them were in a position to have a relationship.

He didn't want it to end like this. "Maybe I want to go away for a night because I like morning sex."

"All men like sex in the morning. And afternoon. And evening. And—"

"Maybe it's more dependent on who we're having sex with than most women think."

"How 'bout this? Stop talking."

"Kara—"

"And I'll let you know when I can get away for a couple of days and if you can get away for those same couple of days, maybe we can spend them together. Besides, you promised to teach me to scuba dive."

"I did?"

"Not in so many words." She smiled. "Deal?"

Matt had a feeling this was as close as Kara would allow him to get. And she was right—they both needed to get back to work.

Though he really, really wanted twenty-four hours alone with her. Just the two of them. No case, no violence, no clothes.

Instead, he said, "You're right."

"I usually am."

52

Saturday, March 13
Los Angeles, California
8:00 a.m.

Kara arrived back in LA the previous night, leaving Spokane right after Andy's funeral. She did everything she could not to go into the office straight from the airport. Instead, she went home to her condo in Santa Monica, both hating and loving the traffic. Hating it because who the hell liked all the people and sitting on the freeway for hours? But loving it because it was familiar.

She was back. She never wanted to leave again.

She opened all the windows in her condo and enjoyed the cool ocean air. She paid a pretty penny for the tiny one bedroom on the beach, but she didn't need a lot of space and it had an ocean view. She had a trusted neighbor—a rarity for her, because she didn't trust many people—keep an eye on her place, but she didn't like anyone going inside when she wasn't home. So she lived sparsely—no plants to water, no pets to feed. Though it was a two-room spread, it was all hers—her sanctuary. She had mail go to a PO Box near the police station; all her bills were paid automatically through her bank; and none of her neighbors even knew she was a cop. She could be anyone she wanted, and she wanted to blend in at home so no one would look twice at her.

But even though she slept in her own bed in her own apartment, she didn't sleep well, or long. She wondered what Matt Costa was doing, and if she would ever see him again.

Does it matter?

No, she convinced herself. It didn't matter. Sure, they had fun—but he was also arrogant and judgmental, and she didn't need to account for her lifestyle or her career to anyone. She wouldn't mind sharing a vacation with him, however. There was something powerful about having sex with him. And she couldn't discount that, because she had rarely felt so intimate with anyone.

Yes, it scared her.

Maybe they could spend a week in Hawaii where they could play hard and make love harder. She had been to Hawaii once, alone, loved it. Had always wanted to return; never found the time. Never made the time. One week, then go back to their jobs. She wasn't into long-term relationships, and neither was he. That would work for her, she figured.

Still. She'd probably never see him again.

Even though she wasn't technically supposed to be back to work until Monday, Lex had left a message on her phone Friday night.

"You left Spokane? Don't screw with this case. Call me."

Instead of calling, she went down to the station at eight Saturday morning and brought Lex his favorite flavored coffee from his favorite trendy coffee shop.

"I'm back!" she announced with a smile and put the coffee down on her boss's desk.

He stared at her for a long moment, long enough that she knew he wasn't happy to see her. He was tired, looked like he hadn't slept in a week.

She slammed his door shut. "I know," she said, "I can't come back until Monday, *yada yada*. But we wrapped things up in Spokane and I couldn't stand it anymore. I had to leave. Just give me a case to research, and I promise I'll spend all my time at the computer this weekend working up a plan instead of in the field."

"The FBI called me last night. Tony Greer, an assistant director. He runs the Mobile Response Team."

"Yep. Heard of him."

"His staff submitted a report, wants to put a commendation in your file."

"That's nice of them. I didn't do anything that any other good cop wouldn't have done." He was buttering her up for something bad. Lex always did it like this—gave her something good, then pulled the rug out from under her.

Still, she waited. Watched.

Damn, he started tapping his fingers on his desk. This was really bad.

"The feds took our case."

She shook her head. She couldn't speak.

"Chen is out on bail."

"*Bail?* That's fucking bullshit. He's a flight risk! He'll go under again. It'll take us weeks to flush him out."

"And that reporter from KTAG outed you."

She opened her mouth. Closed it. Her fists clenched.

"You're burned, Kara. There's no going back, not undercover, not here."

She shook her head. She almost couldn't speak. "How?" Her voice was barely a whisper.

Lex turned around and pressed a couple buttons on the small television behind him. A tape started to play, a news broadcast. "It aired Tuesday night, prime time, after Chen made bail."

The beginning was just rehashing the sweatshop network in Chinatown that Chen and his cronies had run. How many indentured slaves they had from China, most illegal aliens brought here against their will, threatened, some citizens who were forced into work to protect their families. Chen had run six sweatshops locally and they'd shut them all down. The victims were being processed and helped—but that wasn't Kara's job. Kara's job was to stop the brutality and take down the principals. And she'd done it.

"LAPD claimed that a tip from someone inside Chen's network led them into a yearlong investigation that culminated in the arrest of thirty-two individuals and the identification of more than nine hundred forced labor workers. The oldest worker was a ninety-six-year-old woman, the youngest an eight-year-old boy who'd been told his mother would be killed if he didn't 'pull his weight.'

"But new revelations indicate that LAPD had an undercover officer deeply embedded in David Chen's criminal organization for nearly a year. Detective Kara Quinn posed as a clothing buyer in order to gain the trust of the organization—and access to their records."

Kara's LAPD graduation photo came on screen, followed by the clip of her frisking the dead Xavier Fong after he threw the knife at her.

"Questions about the ethics of such deep cover investigations have been asked by both civil and victim's rights groups—namely, what did Detective Quinn know about the working conditions of the sweatshops and when did she learn it? Could she have saved the lives of those who died from abuse and deplorable conditions over the year she was in deep cover? How far do undercover operations go—and how are they justified? Join me tonight and all this week for a deep investigative report into the dark side of LAPD undercover operations."

Kara kicked Lex's file cabinet. She left a dent. It wasn't the first. "No. No! This is bullshit, Lex! She can't get away with this. Did she out anyone else? Did she—"

By the look on Lex's face, the news was worse than she had thought.

"Colton Fox was killed Thursday night. We don't know if the gang knew he was a cop or just suspected, but it happened the night this bitch ran her exposé on how you—a white girl—infiltrated a Mexican gang."

That was years ago, when she was right out of the academy. They knew everything—everything they should never have known.

"Thornton," she spat.

"I went to bat for you, ran this up to the top, had Thornton reamed a new one. He's not getting away clean on this. But the damage has been done."

She sat down because she felt sick. "He needs to be fired. Prosecuted! He got Colton killed. That's on him. Dammit, that's on him!"

Tears burned behind her eyes. She and Colton had worked so many ops together that it was like being married. And, yeah, they'd hit the hay together a few times. Relieve stress and all that. But more, they were friends. He was one of the few people she trusted in this business. He'd always had her back… And she always had his, until now.

If she hadn't been sent away, she could have stopped this.

As if Lex read her mind, he said, "You couldn't have saved him."

"I have to work it. You can't pull this from me."

"If I let you work it, it would be from behind a desk."

"You know that won't do shit! I have to go out. I can change—dye my hair. Get new tats. Remember when I went under at the punk club? *No one* recognized me, not even you."

"No."

"I can—what? No? You can't mean that. Lex—"

"Do you think I like this? Colton is dead. He was mine, my cop, my responsibility."

She knew this was hard on Lex, but she couldn't ride a desk. "Chen—" she began.

He cut her off. "You've been burned. Your life is in danger. The feds have the Chen case, and he's out walking free. He will have you killed, Kara. I can't let you go out on the street again."

Kara stared at the face of the reporter, frozen when Lex paused the recording. "I could kill her." She meant it. The damn reporter and then Bryce Thornton. Colton was dead because of them. First Andy, then Colton. How many good cops had to die? It wasn't fucking fair! *Life isn't fair, Kara, and you damn well know it.*

"There's another option."

"I'll take it. Anything."

Damn, she sounded desperate. All she wanted was her life back the way it was. And now everything had gone to shit.

"The FBI offered you a position. I'm talking to this assistant director, um, Tony Greer, shortly to hash out the details. Then I'll bring it to you, okay?"

"I'm not working for the FBI."

"Listen to me, Kara! You are *burned.* You can't work in the field. Hell, I don't even think you would be safe if I put you in uniform and assigned you to fucking airport duty! You need to leave Los Angeles. Chen is going to put a hit out on you if he hasn't done it already. And either you leave LA without a badge, or you consider their offer."

"Offer." She said it as if it was a nasty word.

"Greer has to check a few things, but he knows that you were burned, and he has sympathy—I told him what happened between you and Thornton years ago, and that this was a personal vendetta by one of theirs to destroy one of ours. He was surprisingly contrite and receptive to my comments. You'd still be LAPD assigned to the DC-FBI, specifically their Mobile Response Team. I'll know more in a couple hours. Look—they value you and what you can contribute. Greer thinks that an undercover cop has an unusual and useful skill set. And you'd be back here when Chen goes to trial."

"If he doesn't leave the country first," she snapped.

Had Matt set this up? Had he convinced Greer to hire her? Why?

She didn't think so. That wasn't his style. Still, none of this was sitting well with her.

"Kara—go home. Relax." He laughed. "What am I saying? I know you. Go to the gun range and blow off some steam. Come back at three this afternoon, and I'll lay out the deal for you. This may be a great career opportunity."

"I'm not in this job for career advancement."

"Don't I know it," he muttered.

"There has to be something we can do."

"Kara, this is truly the only option if you want to stay alive and keep your badge. And dammit—watch your back."

53

Sunday, March 14
Stafford, Virginia
Afternoon

"Uncle Matt! You made it!"

Elizabeth ran into his arms and hugged him. Affection washed over Matt at the unconditional, innocent love of a child. Though Lizzy was hardly a child—she was a preteen. Eleven.

He handed her a small wrapped box. "Happy birthday, kid."

She smiled, looking both like her mom and dad—and her aunt Beth. The pain that shot through him was real, then it was gone.

"Mom and Dad are on the patio. I gotta go, but I'll be right back!" She ran upstairs, taking them two at a time, and disappeared down the hall.

Matt stood in the entryway. The party was out back, but he took this moment to regroup. He hadn't been in this house since Beth's funeral eight months ago. He'd come then out of duty, when all he'd wanted to do was fight back. When some cops turned to the bottle out of grief or anger, he turned to his fists. He'd learned to temper his anger by beating up dummies and punching bags instead of people, but there were times when his rage returned, and it took every ounce of his self-control to tame it.

Beth had been dead nearly nine months. A year this coming July. The guilt that came with her life and death was still with him, but it had shifted, changed. He didn't know when. He didn't know if he would be able to forgive himself for not loving Beth like she loved him. Maybe he was incapable of loving anyone. He'd let Kara leave.

You couldn't have made her stay. Her life isn't with you; her life isn't even her.

Kara would stay in Los Angeles because that's where she could disappear into her dangerous world. That's what she wanted, and Matt knew from himself and everyone around him that you couldn't change people who didn't want to change.

And he didn't want to change her. Then she wouldn't be Kara. He just wished… Hell, what did he wish? That he could spend more time with her? That he could get to know her—the real her? Even now, after he had a couple days to reflect, he wasn't sure she had ever shown him her real self.

If she knew who her real self was.

Kara would stick with him for a long, long time. She'd told him they'd find time—a couple days when they both had time off. *Right*. Because they both had jobs that enabled them to take time off.

Chris walked in from the back and seemed surprised to see Matt.

"Catherine said it was okay for me to come," Matt said.

"You're always welcome," Chris said.

"Lizzy ran upstairs, if you're looking for her."

"Her friends are up there. The adults are around back. Want a beer?"

He hesitated, then nodded. "Thanks."

"You're not blood, but you're family. That's not going to change."

Matt followed Chris to the kitchen, where he retrieved two beers from the refrigerator, but instead of taking him out back with the crowd of birthday guests, they went down the hall to Chris's office. Matt was relieved. He wasn't quite ready to socialize.

Chris tapped the neck of his bottle to Matt's and drank. "Catherine told me about the case."

"We couldn't have solved it without her. She also told you I want her on my team. I was surprised when she said you were okay with me coming here."

Chris nodded. "We both care about Catherine, but I love her, and you need to give her more time."

"It's been nearly a year, Chris."

"You need time."

Matt shook his head.

"You jumped right back into work after Beth died."

"Beth was murdered, Chris. I couldn't sit back and trust someone else to catch the bastard who killed her."

"You know it's more complicated than that."

Matt knew, but he didn't comment.

"I want Catherine home. I'm close to bringing her back, and I won't have you ruin it."

"I want her back home, too. I'm on your side, Chris. I always have been. Catherine is the best profiler the FBI has, and I need her. But I won't push it right now. Fair enough?"

Chris nodded. "I convinced Catherine to pull her resignation."

That surprised Matt. "I thought you wanted her to quit."

"No. I want Catherine to be happy. That's all I've ever wanted. But Catherine isn't someone who can let herself be happy, not like other people."

Matt thought about himself. About Kara. Was Kara happy? He didn't think so. But she was comfortable in her own skin. She had a confidence about herself that most people didn't have.

"I'm teaching a six-week seminar in England starting in April. Catherine and Lizzy are joining me. I lecture twice a week, then we're going to do things as a family. We'll be back Memorial Day weekend, and Catherine's boss has given her a sabbatical through June 1. I'm asking you to leave her alone until then. Let her make her own decision."

Matt hesitated, then he nodded. "I told her to take the sabbatical."

"I know you did, and I think that might have helped. We both want what's best for her. Just sometimes—what we think is best differs. She needs me, Matt, to keep her level. You know how she gets when she works a case. You know how dark it is inside the minds of these people. If she's going to continue going there, she has to have a secure, a safe, home base."

"That's exactly what I want her to have, too."

Chris nodded. "I'm glad you came. Come out when you're ready. Fair warning—Catherine's mother is here."

"I'll avoid her as best I can."

"Good idea."

Chris left Matt alone in his office. Chris was right—about so many things. He was a good man, and if anyone could help Catherine get through the pain and grief of losing her sister, it was her husband.

Matt pulled out his cell phone. He was both surprised and disappointed that he had no messages.

He wanted to talk to Kara. Just to make sure she got back to LA in one piece. Just to hear her voice.

He called her cell phone. Immediately, a recording sounded.

The number you have reached has been disconnected or is no longer in service. If you believe you reached this recording in error, hang up and try again.

Matt looked at his phone. The name *Kara Quinn* was on the screen. He'd been calling her at this number all week.

Had she lied to him? Told him what he wanted to hear? That they could see each other down the road? Maybe that's why she was such a good undercover cop. Because Matt didn't know what was real and what was fake.

Angry, he deleted Kara's dead number from his phone, left Chris's office, grabbed another beer and was about to join the birthday party for his god-daughter when his phone rang.

For a moment, he thought it was Kara. He glanced at the number. Tony's private line.

"Costa," he answered.

"Enjoying your weekend?"

"Trying to. I'm at Lizzy's birthday party."

"Good—you need to unwind."

"Why do I feel this call is just going to tighten me up again?"

"Hardly. It's good news, of a sort."

"I'm all for good news. Shoot."

"I just got off the phone with Sergeant Popovich with LAPD. I talked to him on Thursday when I sent him the commendation for Detective Quinn's file."

"I'm glad. She was an asset." The commendation from a high-ranking FBI director would go a long way in smoothing things over with the local FBI. Even though Matt was angry at how he and Kara had left things personally, she was an outstanding cop. He would do whatever he could to ensure she didn't have any FBI trouble in Los Angeles. He owed her that much.

"I don't know how much you know about her last assignment in LA before her administrative leave."

"A bit," Matt said. He had wondered at the time what, if anything, Kara had left out. But he also knew that she wasn't supposed to talk about her job. "She took down a human trafficking organization that ran sweatshops throughout Los Angeles."

"Correct. One of the reasons she was on administrative leave was because her boss had intel that her cover may have been compromised. He didn't tell her that—he wanted the time to investigate the situation without his detective potentially in the line of fire. The other reason was she used deadly force, and LAPD has a mandatory three days paid administrative leave. He extended it because of other circumstances. And apparently his fears were justified. The media exposed her role in the sweatshop takedown and she won't be able to go back inside—Popovich is concerned about her safety in any undercover operation, at least for the time being. In addition, they need her to testify against the organization—but the AUSA took over the case."

"We took the case from her?"

"'We' is subjective. The LA field office took the case from LAPD. I don't have a comment on that because I don't know the details."

Kara must be livid.

"Is she in protective custody?" Matt asked. She would hate that, too.

"Not at this point. When I talked to Popovich, I thought about how valuable she was to your unit. And after reading her file, I called him to offer her a position on your team."

Matt leaned against the kitchen counter. He felt hot and cold at the same time.

"Matt?"

"And?"

"I haven't talked to her yet—she's flying out to DC tomorrow to meet with me, and you should be there. But she's receptive. I promised you veto power over any placements, but you also gave me some leeway because we need this team fully staffed. We need someone like Quinn. She's a local cop—she can easily liaison with local law enforcement. She's used to working undercover, and there are many times when that skill set will come in handy. Undercover cops are particularly adept at reading people. And honestly—Popovich sent me her jacket, and while I'm only partly through her files, I'm wholly impressed. She is a bit of a hothead and a maverick, but then again, so are you. And for this team to work, we need people who can think outside of the box." Tony paused. "I read your report, Matt. Was there a problem you didn't tell me about?"

"No problem. I'm just surprised, that's all. Kara made it very clear that she loves her job."

And that *was* going to be a problem.

"We worked well together," Matt said cautiously, "and I think she'll be an asset to the team. But she's been an undercover cop practically since she got out of the academy. I don't know how she's going to adapt to taking orders."

"Point taken, and I'm sure there will be a learning curve, but Matt, you've rejected virtually everyone I've sent to you. We had a major win in Spokane, the bosses are happy. We need to fully staff your unit now while everyone remembers what a great job you did."

"Okay."

"Okay? You mean it?"

"Yes. When does she start?"

"As soon as I can get her through a two-week FBI training session."

"What? She's not going to be an agent?"

"No—she'll still be employed by LAPD and assigned to the FBI. We don't do it often, but it's not unheard of. I'm going to have the AD at Quantico customize a program for her—part physical, part tactical, but mostly legal issues. Federal warrants, rules and regs that differ from LAPD. But if she's half as good as you say she is, I'm not worried."

"She is," Matt said.

He wasn't worried. Because Kara Quinn could be anyone she wanted—or anyone she thought was needed. And that was the problem.

After eight days of working together, of talking with her, of sleeping with her, Matt didn't know if he knew the *real* Kara Quinn.

Or if Kara even remembered who she was.

* * * * *

Acknowledgments

My family puts up with a lot from me! When I'm writing (which is most of the time) I can be absent-minded. If I didn't have a calendar on my computer, I would forget the day. My kids, those still at home as well as those making their own way in the world—I would be a lesser human without you all in my life. My mom, who has supported my dreams from day one (literally!)—thank you for being both my mom and my friend. And my husband, Dan, who has picked up the slack when I slack off on day-to-day life—I couldn't do this without you.

Research is critical, especially when you write crime fiction. I rely on many people to help me get the details right. While sometimes I tweak things for the story, I try to avoid errors. But on occasion, I make mistakes—if you find one, please blame me, not the people who generously gave their time and talent to help me get the facts right.

Retired FBI Special Agent Steven Dupre is always willing to listen to a scenario and if he doesn't know the answer, he finds someone who does. I don't think I could write FBI stories with his counsel!

And thank you to Crime Scene Writers, a group of selfless professionals, retired and still working, who answer questions for writers. In particular, I want to thank Wally Lind, Steven Brown, and Dr. Judy Melinek for help on this particular book. I post some odd questions and no one bats an eye.

Writers form an amazing community for other writers, and when we need help or encouragement, writers are there. In particular, the super-talented and generous Catherine Coulter, who has been not just a mentor, but a friend, deserves a big shout-out. And always, J.T. Ellison, who I met at my first ever Thrillerfest, and has been a sounding board ever since. Thank you for all your support over the years, and in particular with this book. I'm excited that we are finally under the same umbrella!

My team at Harlequin/MIRA deserves an extra acknowledgment, especially my editor Kathy Sagan, who loves these characters as much as I do and who really helped make this book shine. The entire team works hard on my books and so many others, especially Vice President Margaret Marbury and Editorial Director Nicole Brebner, who together run an amazing group of talented editors, artists, publicists, and more. Thank you all for believing in this book and this new series.

And a very special thanks to my agent, Dan Conaway, who has stuck with me through good times and bad, who is always thoughtful and willing to listen and discuss anything. But mostly, a big thank you for believing in THIS book, and this series, and finding the best team to bring this story to life. And I certainly can't forget Dan's super-capable assistant, Lauren Carsley, who keeps Dan on track and makes both of our lives easier. Thank you, thank you, thank you.

Turn the page to begin reading Allison Brennan's
Tell No Lies, *the next book in this series.*
Available from MIRA April 2021.

PROLOGUE

Two months ago
Tucson, Arizona

Billy Nixon had been waiting his whole life to have sex with Emma Perez. Okay, not *all* his life. Two and a half years. It just felt that way since he'd fallen in love with her the day they met in Microeconomics, on his first day of classes at the University of Arizona. Love at first sight is a cliché, and until that moment in time Billy didn't believe in any of that bullshit. His parents were divorced, his older sister had been in and out of bad relationships since she was fifteen, and his friends slept around as if the apocalypse was upon them.

But in the back of his mind, he remembered the story about how his grandparents met the day before his grandfather shipped off to the Korean War, how they wrote letters every week, and how three years later his grandfather came home and they married. They were married for fifty-six years before his grandfather died; his grandmother died three months later.

That's what Billy wanted. Without having to go to war.

It took Emma two years before the same feeling clicked inside her. They'd been friends. They both dated other people (well, Billy pretended to date because he couldn't in good conscience lead another girl on when he knew that he didn't care about her like he cared about Emma). But it was three months ago, when Emma lost her ride home to Denver for the Christmas holidays and he found her crying in her dorm room, that he said, "I'll drive you there," even though he was a Tucson native and lived with his dad to save money.

From then on, she looked at him differently. Like her eyes had been opened and she saw in him what he saw in her. From that point on, they were inseparable.

The morning after they first made love, Billy knew there was no other girl, no other woman, with whom he wanted to spend the rest of his life. Call him a romantic, but Emma was it. He had started saving money for a ring. They were finishing up their third year of college, so had a year left, but that was okay. He did well in school and had a part-time job. He already had a job lined up for the summer in Phoenix that paid well, and he could live there cheaply with his sister—though the thought of spending two months with his emotional, self-absorbed sibling was a big negative. And the idea of leaving Emma for two months made him miserable. But if he did this, he'd have enough money, not only for a ring, but to get an apartment when they graduated. And—maybe—his job this summer would be a permanent thing when he was done with college next spring, which meant he'd have stability. Something he desperately wanted to provide for Emma.

Emma rolled over in bed and sighed. He loved when his dad was out of town and he had the house to himself, since they had no privacy in Emma's dorm. Billy kissed the top of her head. He thought she was still sleeping, or in that dreamy state right before you wake up. It wasn't even dawn, but how could he go back to sleep with Emma Perez naked in his bed?

"Billy?" she said.

"Hmm?"

"Can I ask you a favor?"

"Anything."

"I need to go to Mount Wrightson today. The Patagonia side of the mountain."

"Okay."

An odd request, but Emma spent a lot of time these days in the Santa Rita Mountains and surrounding areas. She was a business and environmental sciences double major who worked part-time at the Arizona Resources and Environmental Agency—AREA, as they called it—the state environmental protection agency.

"For work, school or fun?" he said.

"Last week my Geology class went out to Mount Wrightson and we hiked partway down the Arizona Trail. I noticed several dead birds off the trail. My professor didn't think it was anything, but it bothered me. So I talked to my boss, Frank, at work, and he said if my professor didn't think it was unusual, then it wasn't. But I couldn't stop thinking about it, so went back a couple days ago on my own. One of the closed trails has been used recently. And I found more dead birds, more than a dozen."

"Which means what?"

"I don't know yet, but birds are especially vulnerable to contaminated water because of their small size and metabolism. Remember when I told you my boss got an anonymous letter two years ago? Signed *A Concerned Citizen* and postmarked from Patagonia? The letter writer claimed that several local people were being made sick and that the water supply was tainted. Frank tested the water supply himself after that, but he didn't find anything abnormal. So he dismissed it. But no one has been able to explain why those people were sick."

"And remember—there was no evidence that anyone *was* sick," Billy said. "The letter was anonymous. It could have just been a disgruntled prankster. Didn't Frank talk to the health center about the complaint? Didn't he investigate the local copper refinery?"

"Yes," she said and sighed in a way that made him feel like he was missing something. "Maybe two years ago it wasn't real," she said in a way that made Billy think she really didn't believe that. "But now my gut tells me something's going on, and I want to know what."

"You told your boss about the dead birds. You said he was a good guy, right?"

"Yeah, but I think he still thinks I'm a tree hugger."

"You certainly gave that impression when you first started there and questioned their entire record-keeping process and the way Frank had conducted that original investigation."

"I've apologized a hundred times. I realize now how much goes into keeping accurate records, and that AREA uses one of the best systems in the country. I've learned so much from Frank. I really believe I can make a difference now, and be smart about it too. All I want is to give him facts, Billy. And the only way I can do that is if I go back up there."

Billy didn't have the same passion for the environment that Emma had, but he loved her commitment to nature and how she continued to learn and adapt to new and changing technologies and ideas.

"Whatever you want to do, I'm with you," he said. He'd follow her through the Amazon jungle if she asked him to.

"It's going to be a beautiful day," she said, as if he needed encouragement to do anything for her. "I just want to check out the trails near where I found the second flock of birds. We can have a picnic, make a day out of it."

"Good call, bribing me with food."

She smiled. "I can bribe you with something else too." Then she kissed him.

An hour later the sun was up and they stopped for breakfast in the tiny town of Sonoita, southeast of Tucson where Highways 82 and 83 intersected.

Emma had been quiet the entire drive, taking notes while analyzing a topo map.

As they ate, Emma showed him the map and her notes. "The dead birds I found last week with the class were Mexican jays. The ones I found after that on my own were trogons. I've been studying both of their migration patterns. The jays have a wider range. The trogons are much more localized. It seems unlikely that they just dropped dead out of the sky for no reason. I'm thinking, logically, they might have been poisoned. I don't see any large body of water near where I found them, but there's a pond here that forms during the rainy season." She pointed.

While Billy couldn't read a topo map to save his life, he trusted her thinking.

"That pond, or this stream—" she pointed again "—are right under one of their migration routes. I've also highlighted some other seasonal streams, here and here."

"That seems like a huge area. North *and* south of Eighty-Two? How can we cover all of that in one day? Where are the roads?"

"We can hike."

He frowned. Hike, sure. But this looked like a three-day deal.

"Emma, maybe you should talk to your boss again, show him the map and tell him what you suspect."

"But I haven't found anything yet—just on the map!"

Tears sprouted to her eyes, and Billy panicked.

Don't cry, don't cry, don't cry. "Okay, what are we doing, then?"

"If you don't want to help me, Billy, just say so."

"I do, Emma. I just need to know the full plan, and I don't understand your notes. I don't even know where exactly I'm going."

"This is the town of Patagonia, see?" She trailed her finger along one of the paths that went from Patagonia up the mountain. "And this is Mount Wrightson, to the north."

Billy had hiked to the peak of Mount Wrightson once. He wasn't into nature and hiking like Emma, but he liked being outdoors, so he took a conservation class that doubled as a science requirement. His idea of being outdoors was playing baseball or volleyball or riding his bike.

"Okay."

"We need to hike halfway up Wrightson. I found a service road that I think we can use to get most of the way to the trailhead. Okay?"

"If you're sure about this," he said.

She frowned and looked back down at her map. He hated that he'd made her sad.

"I'm sorry," he said. "It's fine."

"You don't want to go."

"I do. I just don't want us to get lost."

She smiled sweetly at him. "Stick with me and you won't."

That was the smile he needed. He took her hand, interlocked their fingers. "I trust you."

"Good." She gave him a quick kiss, and they left the café and got back on the road.

* * *

Several hours later, Billy wasn't as accommodating. They'd parked at the end of a dirt road near the trailhead halfway up the southeastern side of the mountain and been hiking through rough terrain ever since. The landscape was dotted with some trees and pines, but not as dense or pretty or green as on the top of the mountain. The land wasn't dry—the wet winter and snow runoff had ensured that—so the area was hard to navigate, and the paths they were on weren't maintained. Billy doubted they were trails at all.

The hiking had been fine up until lunch. At noon, they ate their picnic, which was a nice break, because then they had sex and relaxed in the middle of nature. It wasn't quiet—they heard birds and a light breeze and the rustling of critters. A family of jackrabbits crossed only feet from them as they lay on the blanket Billy had brought. Afterward, Billy suggested they head back to the truck. He was tired, and they had already walked miles, which meant as many miles back to the truck.

But Emma didn't want to leave. He was pretty sure she didn't know exactly what she was looking for, but that she had this idea that if she walked long and far enough, she'd find evidence to support her theory that something nefarious had been happening out here to kill all those birds.

So Billy kept his mouth shut and followed her.

By four that afternoon, Billy was pretty sure Emma had gotten them lost. They had seemed to zigzag across the southern face of Mount Wrightson.

He was tired, and even the birds had gone quiet, as if they were getting ready to settle in and nest for the night, even though sunset was still a few hours away.

He stopped next to a tree that was taller than most and that provided much-needed shade. It was only seventy-six degrees, but the sky was clear and the sun had been beating down on them all afternoon. He was glad he'd thought to bring sunscreen, otherwise they'd both be fried by now.

He dropped the large backpack he'd been carrying that contained their picnic stuff, blanket, water, first aid kit and emergency supplies. He knew enough about the desert not to go hiking without food and water to last at least twenty-four hours. Like if his truck didn't start when they got back, they needed to be okay. So he had extra water—but he didn't tell Emma that. It was for emergencies only.

"We're down to our last water bottles," he said. He'd paced himself so he had two left, whereas Emma had gone through all six of hers.

He handed her one of the two. "Drink."

She sipped, handed it back to him. "Thirty more minutes, honey. See this?" She pointed to the damn map that he wanted to tear into pieces now, except without it he was positive they would be lost here forever. "That's the large seasonal pond I was talking about. It'll dry up before summer, according to the topo charts."

How she could stay so cheerful when he was hot and tired and, frankly, bored, he didn't know.

"How far?"

"Down this path, not more than two hundred yards. Three hundred, maybe."

He looked at her. Implored her to let them start heading back.

"Why don't you stay here and wait," she said.

"You don't mind?"

She smiled, walked over and kissed him. "Promise."

Twenty minutes later she was back where Billy waited. She looked so sad and defeated. "I'm ready to go," she said.

"We'll come back next weekend, okay? We'll bring a tent and food and camp overnight."

She looked surprised at his suggestion, a smile on her face. "You mean that?"

"Absolutely."

She threw her arms around him. "I love you, Billy Nixon."

His heart nearly stopped. "I love you, too," he said and held her. He wanted to freeze this moment, relive it every day of his life.

"We're actually closer to your truck than you think—we made a circle. First we went north, then west, then south, now we're going east again. When we get back to the main trail at the fork back there, we go left rather than right, and the truck is about half a mile up."

He was impressed; he had underestimated her. Maybe they weren't as lost as he thought; maybe he was the only one with a shitty sense of direction. But that was okay, because Emma loved him, and they were going to be together forever. He knew it in his heart *and* his head, and she'd always be there to navigate.

They drove down the mountain, the road rough at first, then it smoothed out as they got near town. They headed west on 82, deciding to drive the scenic route back to Tucson. Emma marked her map to highlight where they'd already walked, when suddenly she looked up. "Hey, can you get off here?"

"Have to pee again?"

"Ha ha. No. There's several old roads that go south. Sonoita Creek, when it floods, cuts fast-flowing streams into the valley. We had a couple late storms this winter. I just want to check the area quickly—we'll come back next weekend. But if I see anything that tells me the streams were running a few weeks ago, I want to come back here first. Okay? Please?"

Billy was tired, but Emma loved him, so he happily turned off the highway and followed her directions. They drove about a mile along a very rough unpaved road until they reached a narrow path. His truck couldn't go down there—there were small cacti sprouting up all over the place, and the chances of him getting a flat increased exponentially.

Emma got out, and Billy reluctantly followed. She was excited. "See that grove of trees down there?"

He did. It looked more like overgrown brush, but it was greener than anything else around them.

"I'll bet there's still water. This is on the outer circle of where the birds could have flown from. I just want to check."

"The path looks kinda steep and rocky. You sure about this?"

She kissed him. "I'm sure. Stay here, okay? I won't be long."

"Ten minutes."

"Fifteen." She kissed him again, put her backpack on and headed down the path.

He sat in the back of his truck and watched Emma navigate the downward slope. He doubted this "path" had been used anytime in the last few years. From his vantage point, he saw several darker areas, plants dense and green, and suspected that Emma was right—this valley *would* get water after big storms.

Emma was beautiful *and* smart. What wasn't to love?

He watched until she disappeared from view into the brush.

He frowned. He should have gone with her. Was he just sulking because he was tired and hungry?

Predators were out here—coyotes, bobcats, javelinas. Javelinas could be downright mean even if you did nothing to provoke them. Not to mention that these mountains bordered the corridor for trafficking illegal immigrants. Billy had taken a criminal justice class his freshman year and they touched upon that topic. He didn't want to encounter a two-legged predator any more than one on four legs.

What kind of man was he if he couldn't suck it up and help the woman he loved?

So he grabbed his backpack and headed down the path Emma had taken. He was in pretty good shape, but this hike had wasted him. Emma must have been fitter than he was, because she'd barely slowed down all day. After this, they'd go to his place, shower—maybe he could convince Emma to take a shower with him—and then he'd take her out to dinner. After all, they had something to celebrate: the first time they said "*I love you*." They'd go to El Charro, maybe. It was Billy's favorite Mexican food in Tucson, not too expensive, great food. Take an Uber so they could have a couple of drinks.

He wished he were there right now. His stomach growled as he stumbled and then caught himself before he fell on his ass.

He was halfway down the hill when a scream pierced the mountainside. Billy ran the rest of the way down the narrow, rocky trail. "Emma!"

No answer.

He yelled louder for her. "Emma! Emma!"

He slipped when the trail made a sudden drop as it went steeply down to a small pond—the seasonal one that Emma must have been looking for. The beauty of the spot with its trees and boulders all around was striking in the desert, and for a split second he thought it was a mirage. Then all he could think about was that Emma had been bitten by a rattlesnake, or had fallen into the water, or had slipped and broken her leg.

But she didn't respond to his repeated calls.

"Emma!"

He stood on the edge of the pond, frantically searching for her. Looking for wild animals, a bobcat that she may have surprised. A herd of javelinas that might have attacked her. Anything.

Movement to his right startled him, and he turned around quickly.

In the shade, he saw someone. He shouted, wondering if Emma was disorientated or had gone the wrong way. But whatever he thought he saw was now gone.

Then he saw her.

Emma's body was half in, half out of the pond, a good hundred feet beyond him, obscured in part by an outcrop of large rocks on the water's edge. He ran to her and dropped to his knees. His first thought was that she had slipped and hit her head. Some blood glistened on her scalp.

"Emma, where are you hurt? Emma?"

She didn't respond. Then he saw the blood on a hand-sized rock on the edge of the pond. And he felt more blood on the back of her skull.

"No, no, no!"

He saw her chest rise and fall. She was alive, but unconscious. He pulled out his phone, but there was no signal. He had to get help, but he couldn't leave her here.

Billy picked Emma up and, as quickly as he could, carried her up the steep hillside to his truck.

As he drove back to the main road, he called 911. An ambulance met him in the closest town, Patagonia.

But by then Emma was already dead.